I Was Chosen by a Gift

Romina Betvardeh

Publisher: Inspiring Publishers,
P.O. Box 159, Calwell, ACT Australia 2905
Email: publishaspg@gmail.com
http://www.inspiringpublishers.com

A catalogue record for this book is available from the National Library of Australia

National Library of Australia The Prepublication Data Service

Author: Romina Betvardeh
Title: I Was Chosen by a Gift
Genre: Fiction Fantasy
ISBN: 978-1-925908-71-8

In life some people are kind, loving and giving they never expect to be given anything and their only joy is to give happiness to others. They are always satisfied and never fall short in assisting others. They forgive those who do wrong to them and their policy is "Everyone deserves a second chance" and they never let material or greed take over their lives.

Then there is the other type of people whose policy is "take and take and take". By breaking and destroying someone else they feel powerful. These kind of people have no feelings or emotions. Their hunger for power and money makes them the most dangerous species on earth.

These species are unaware that the **cycle of life is vicious** and it may turn the wheels against them.

Special Thanks to

Alexander Bishop for extreme help with editing

Chapter 1

s Sandy was running to work wearing a black short skirt with a beautiful Royal Blue top the heads were turning behind her, men admired her beauty and well-shaped body and females just stared wishing for that faultless body. But Sandy was very insecure and thought something was wrong with her hair or clothing. That's why everyone was staring at her.

The insecurity came from Sandy's childhood when she was put down all the time, due to her kind nature. Her family or class mates would bully her, "Look at your hair, don't you own a hair brush?" or "God you have a big nose." At school she was pushed and her food taken from her but she never said anything and always convinced herself that they must have been hungrier than me.

Although she was a professional manger in one of the leading retail stores and loved by everybody she always underestimated herself, this young beautiful girl managed the biggest store in the country but could not manage the dark side of her own life with insecurity. She lived in such a dark world that if someone complemented her on her beauty she would get disheartened thinking they've been synclastic.

That morning when she got to work Sandy found her coffee ready on her desk and her assistant Angela standing next to it. Angela had the habit of arriving at work early and wait by window. As soon as she saw Sandy crossing the road she would run and make her coffee ready.

"Angela how many times I have to tell you do not have to make my coffee", Sandy called out with a smile on her face.

"I am happy doing this because it makes me feel better."

That morning the board of directors had a meeting. Nearly half an hour after the start of the meeting, they sent for Sandy.

For a few minutes Sandy got worried as to why they should call her to the meeting? But as soon as she walked in to the meeting Paul one of the directors looked across the table and said "Here is our relief, not only she is hard working but very trust worthy" Paul continued," I honestly believe that Sandy is quite capable of running the show while we are away in Europe for the opening of the new store."

Being a shy person Sandy went all red in the face when everyone turned and looked at her.

When Paul put the motion to the other directors they all agreed by simply putting their heads down.

"How do you feel about doing our jobs for at least three months while we travel overseas?"

"Three months overseas! Holidaying?" She asked.

"No" replied Paul "Preparing for the opening of the new store"

Sandy could not believe her ears. She was covered with excitement. This was a big honour, and with a very shaky voice she said, "Sir are you sure about this offer?"

With a cold look Paul replied "Are you doubting our decision?"

"Of course not"

"Then what is it?"

"I just think that there are more worthy people than me to take this role on."

The decision is made. Paul continued "You may go back to work now."

"I will do my best sir, to make you proud."

"I am already proud because I know you can do this."

Walking out of the board room Sandy barely could fit into her skin. She made her way straight to the ladies room, after making sure there was no one there to judge her. She started crying. The happiness she was feeling at that moment was overwhelming and crying was the only way for her to settle.

Going back to her desk after a long cry Sandy managed to do some work, but she could not wait to get home and share the good news with her parents. Her eyes were glued to the clock and from inside fireworks were exploding.

Unlike any other afternoon, Sandy knocks off work at exactly five o'clock, the beautiful smile that was glowing on her tiny face made her more attractive than ever. Not one person went pass without complementing her on her beauty.

"How come you are home early?" asked her parents when she arrived home.

Tears filed her beautiful brown eyes.

Don her father quickly noticed the tears. "Is something wrong Sandy?" He cried out

"No everything is fine."

"Why the tears then"

"You don't know how excited I am. Today was the best day of my life."

"Well hurry up and share some of that excitement with us."

"Today I was asked to replace our directors for three months while they open another store overseas."

Don was a strict man who could never show his true feelings and affections to anyone. He stared at his daughter with satisfaction. Then said "I always knew you would be successful in life, God is helping you reach your goals according to your kind heart and down to earth personality, I honestly am so proud of you."

Donna her mum didn't give a chance to Sandy to reply. She shouted, "Enough of these talks. We should celebrate this promotion".

Don smiled "And I bet you want Sandy to pay for this celebration".

Donna, "well off course, She is the one getting promoted, not me."

The three of them laughed.

Come on dad. Let's go get ready. I will pay when we finish.

"Who is driving?" Don asked

"No one dad, I will call a cab because I want us to have fun."

The bar at the beach where they went was beautiful. When their first drinks arrive Don grabbed his glass and stood up "Let's drink to Sandy's achievement and all the eyes that are glued to her right now".

They all had a sip from their drinks. Sandy put her glass down. "Thanks dad", she said "You are my inspiration and I thank you for celebrating with me tonight."

Don replied, with a wink and a smile, before picking his glass for the second time.

"I am feeling a bit hungry, I'm going to see if the restaurant is open, "Donna said while getting off her chair."

"I will go mum, you sit."

Your father is right "replied Donna" There is not one person that is not looking at you. It feels safer if I go.

"Why are they staring? Is something wrong with what I am wearing?" asked Sandy.

"No Darling. They are stunned by your beauty." replied Donna

Fortunately the restaurant was open. After booking a table Donna walked back to the bar to collect the others. As soon as they finished their drinks they walked to the restaurant. A waitress greeted them and showed them to their table.

The atmosphere was so beautiful and relaxing. There were no brick walls at back of the restaurant; instead there was a massive glass wall. The beautiful moon that was shining on the sea was completely visible. It truly was a magical view.

A few young men tried to grab Sandy's attention but she wasn't in the market for a boyfriend. Eventually one of them found the guts to go to Don. "Good evening sir do you mind if I complement your daughter?"

"Not at all" Don replied while winking at Sandy

The man then turns to Sandy. "I am lost in your beauty"

Sandy went all red in the face. "Thank you."

"Thank you for talking to me"

"Now do you mind? We are having a family time."

"Oh sorry" said the young man. "Please I beg you sir. Here is my number I would love to take her out to dinner." He then put his business card in front of Don and left.

Don couldn't stop smiling to a point that Sandy got embarrassed "Dad please stop it"

"I haven't done anything. I just feel sorry for the bastards that are attracted to you.

Donna got offended. "What do you mean by that?"

"Well look at her. Even if the most beautiful man on earth went past her she wouldn't notice. Sandy I really hope that you decide to stay single because I don't think there is a man that deserves you.

Donna slowly pushed her hand under the table and pinched Don. He screamed "What was that for?"

Sandy laughed at her parents. "Listen you two my plans are never to get married."

"You see Donna." At least our daughter has a good sense of humour.

The family were enjoying the night so much that they kept on ordering drinks all night until the early hours of the morning.

The alarm went off at six am the next morning. Struggling to get out of bed Sandy was really felling the effect of last night drinks, but finally she forces herself up and runs into the shower. After a quick wash she gets dressed, grabbed her bag and quickly ran out of the house, while tucking her shirt inside the skirt.

Driving towards work Sandy is looking around, admiring the beauty of the day. Then a man on the other side of the road grabs her attention. She slows down into the slow lane. The man stops two pedestrians and says something to them. Those two pedestrians pushed him. When he fell on the floor they spat on him and walked away.

Sandy puts the breaks on and stops to see what the man will do next. He stayed on the floor and slowly pushed himself close to the wall where he could lean.

Curiosity took over Sandy. She parked the car and walked towards the man "Are you all right sir? Do you need help?"

The man puts his head up and looks at Sandy. Covered in tears he tries to fix himself. "No I am ok. Thanks mam".

For some odd reason Sandy didn't give up. "I saw how those two pedestrians pushed and spat on you"

"That is my problem mam."

"Please tell me why they did that?"

"Why are you so nosey? Mam"

"I never look at people but there must be a reason of why you grabbed my attention before I got to you."

"You mean I was put in your path?" asked the man

"I think so."

Shame and pain reflected on the man's face while tears were pouring out of his eyes. He said "I received a phone call this morning. My son is very sick and I need to go back.

"I came here in hope of finding a good job to support my family and create a better home for them, but I not only couldn't find work but all my belongings got stolen.

"How?" asked Sandy

"I thought it is safer to leave my money and belongings in the room that I was renting than carrying them with me. One day when I came back from job hunt my window was broken and everything I had was gone."

The man stops for a second then he continues "After receiving the phone call about my son, I had to find a way to hospital, and I thought asking a few pedestrians for money is the only way to pay for my ticket home. Those two were the first people that I approached but as you saw they pushed me and started cursing me. Calling me peasant". The man starts crying even harder.

Not a word came out of Sandy. She rushed to her car, grabbed a bottle of water and a few tissues. "Here clean yourself".

While the man was cleaning himself Sandy reached for her volute, pulled out all the money she had. "Here take it; I hope this is enough to take you home."

The man with an unbelievable look looked at Sandy and said. "This is too much. I can't take this."

Sandy grabbed his hand and said. "Please take it I do not need this money now. If you have a sick child you might need it".

He tried to kiss Sandy's hand but she did not let him

The man then asked "Why are you helping me? You do not even know me"?

Sandy looked at him and said "I do not think anyone deserves to be treated the way those pedestrians treated you. They could have just said no. But remember this "no pain and no wealth stays for ever." Life has a lot of ups and downs. What happened to you now could happen to me tomorrow."

Looking at the time Sandy shouted. "Oh my god I am really late". As she walked away from the man she said "God always opens a small window when all the doors close."

The man called out. "My name is Charles. Where can I find you to give your money back?"

Sandy turned and smiled at the man. "If it is meant to be, we will meet again." She then quickly jumps in her car and takes off.

Charles waited and stared at Sandy as she was driving away. He could not believe a total stranger out of nowhere came to his aid. Soon he cleaned himself and ran towards the railway station.

A few minutes later Sandy was at work, Angela quickly ran to her. "Sorry your coffee went cold and I washed the cup. I will make you a new one now."

"Please wait. I am going to make you a cup coffee today" Sandy replied

"You can't make me coffee." Angela replied

"Why not?"

"You are my boss and it is not right for you to make me coffee."

"What makes it right for you to make me coffee. I did not put that in your job description." Sandy replied

"But."

"No buts Angela. You better tell me how you take your coffee?"

Minutes later Sandy came back with two cups of coffee. "See Angela I can make my own coffee. Please from tomorrow, I do not want you to have my coffee ready. Not only does it make me feel bad but I need to move a little bit as well."

Sandy then starts walking out of her office to do the routine check. Sandy always addressed all the employees by their names and asked them how they are. She loved making people happy. When she finished cheering all the floors she made her last stop at the basement. The cleaners were so happy for the attention they were getting because Sandy believed every human has its own values and they should respect each other regardless of their jobs or living standards.

By interacting with each employee, Sandy kept them all motivated. The levels of sick leave people having dropped by ninety percent since she started working in this department and this made her peers very happy.

This beautiful young lady glowed when talking to people. Her beautiful innocent smile and comforting voice would win any heart in seconds; her goal was to let everyone know they are special.

For weeks Sandy and Paul worked together until the time came when the directors went on their trip to prepare the opening of the new store.

"Angela, unfortunately we are going to spend a lot of time here because we will be filling in for another four people until they come back."

"That is fine with me Sandy. "Replied Angela

It is now the first week that the directors are away and Sandy is already feeling the pressure but that would not stop her from the routine cheering of her employees on a daily basis.

One morning when passing one of the employees she felt so much tension going through her body, she turned "Hi Rebeca what is wrong?" she called out.

"Nothing." Everything is good. Thanks for asking."

Although the girl was in good spirit, Sandy felt that something was terribly wrong with that young girl.

That morning Sandy did not finish her routine of cheering. The tension that she felt, drained all her energy so she went straight back to her office and leaned back into her chair.

Angela runs inside "Are you ok?"

"Yes"

"Then how come you didn't finish your routine walk around?"

"I went past this girl and somehow all my energy was drained."

"Sandy, don't tell me you believe in the evil eye." Said Angela with a sneaky smile.

"What is that? Forget I asked but can you please go and page Rebecca to come to my office."

"Ok" So it was Rebeca who gave you the evil eye."

"Knock it off Angela. Just go and page her."

When Rebeca heard her name, she started panicking, thinking she is called to the office because they want to lay her off work. She was hesitating and shaky but slowly made her way to Sandy's office.

"Hi Sandy did you want to see me?"

"Yes I did. Please come in and take a seat."

"Is everything ok?" Rebeca asked with a very shaky voice.

"Sandy looks up and notices the fear on the young girl's face." I am so sorry if I scared you by paging you.

"Not at all." replied Rebeca.

"Don't worry," Sandy said with a smile." The reason I called you is because I felt something is terribly wrong with you. I know that is none of my business to push my head into your private life but I just want to let you know I am here if you need help."

Rebeca with unbelief looked at Sandy "Why are you asking me? Did someone say something about me?"

"No." Why is there something that I should know about?

"No."

"This morning although you smiled at me your eyes were very sad. It seemed as if you've been crying. I hope no one is upsetting you at work."

"No."

"If you have a problem that I can help you with, please tell me."

It is nothing to do with you or work." Rebecca replied

"That's ok." Sandy implied." You can go back to work, but remember my door is open for you if you decide to talk."

Rebeca gets up "Thank you Sandy." Then she left.

Sandy knew definitely something is hurting the young girl. So bad that she is losing control of her feelings but without Rebecca's confession, there was nothing she could do.

Days went by and Rebecca's sad face became obvious to everyone. Quite a few times she was found crying in the rest room. Things looked so bad for Rebecca, she decided to take Sandy's offer and ask for help.

She went towards the office a few times but couldn't find the courage to knock on the door and went away. Angela, who was watching her the whole time, followed her to the rest room where she heard her crying.

"Who is crying?" called out Angela

"No one" replied Rebecca

"Come on. Whoever you are you know this place has a no tear policy?"

All sudden Rebecca walked out of the rest room. "Are you serious about the policy?"

"Yes girl." replied Angela

"Oh please, don't tell anyone I was crying, I don't want to lose my job."

"Girl something is bothering you a lot. Why not ask for help?"

"From who?"

"Your boss, she already offered to help you. Take up the offer; it will make you feel better."

"I am embarrassed."

Angela laughs "Don't worry, I will hold your hand and walk you in."

When they made it back to Angela's office, Rebecca said, "Thanks Angela but I will take it from here". She knocks on the door.

"Come in" said Sandy. Then she looked up to see who was entering her office. "Oh it is you Rebecca" said Sandy, covered in excitement.

"Do you have five minutes for me?"

"I have all the time in the world for you."

"Sandy please don't hold this against me, but I have no one else to talk to."

Sandy slowly gets off her chair and goes towards Rebeca "You know that I am here all the time. I asked you to come and see me if you need anything".

At that Rebecca started crying, and Sandy said to her "It's ok to cry. What is upsetting you so much?"

"You know that I am from a very strict family, and girls are not allowed to have a boyfriend."

" Yes"

"Well I started seeing someone a few months ago and somehow things got heated between us. Not only have I lost my virginity but I am also pregnant."

Sandy smiled. "Congratulation you should be happy. Why you are crying?"

"My brother somehow found out that I have a boyfriend and dobbed me into my parents."

"My parents were going to kill me. That's how angry they were. But instead they decided to give me a second chance. But then I started having morning sickness."

"Then what happened?" asked Sandy

"They kept on asking me questions but I had no answers and that made the situation three hundred times worse. Eventually they dragged me to the doctors and made the doctor do a pregnancy test. When the doctor came back with the results my heart dropped because he went straight to my parents."

"Congratulation you are going to be grandparents."

"At that moment I wished the ground would swallow me."

"What did your parents say or do?"

My father lost it completely. He could not wait to get home so he could punish me. As soon as we arrived home he started swearing at me then he physically attacked me. He bashed me so much that I thought I lost the baby. Somehow I don't know how I was able to escape.

Where did you go to?

I had nowhere to go, so I drove my car into a park and slept there.

Have you gone home at all?

"No, I have been living in my car since. I use the public rest rooms to have a wash and my car, to rest and sleep."

What about your boyfriend. Can't you go to him?

Ever since his parents found out that I was pregnant they stopped him from talking to me. I really don't know what to do?

I am so sorry to hear you are going through so much. This is not good for the baby. Are you going to keep the baby?

It is too late to do anything now.

Ok here is what I can do for you. I will ask the bosses if I can pay you in advance of your wages so we can find you a place to live. After you settle we will slowly deduct the money from your weekly pay.

Oh thank you so much!

Once you settle you need to find a way to talk to your boyfriend and sort something out for the baby's future.

I really appreciate it

If you would have told me when I asked you, you wouldn't have suffered so much

I was so lost

"Don't worry" Sandy replied. You can go back to work now. I will call you when I need you."

Sandy straight away calls the directors and asks for their approval and they approved it straight away. She then contacts a few local real estates and finds a one bedroom unit with low rent. She makes arrangement with the real estate so that Rebeca can see the unit. If she is happy with it, they can finalise the paper work.

In the afternoon when Rebecca finished work Sandy took and showed her the unit. Rebeca was so happy that she could not back her tears.

By that evening Rebeca had a place of her own to sleep in and have some peace of mind to deal with her other problems.

Using most of her time helping others, Sandy was getting left behind in her work. She would start at five am and work right through the night. Helping all those in need gave her such satisfaction that she never felt tired and her spirit was boosted with happiness.

The amount of work Sandy had was over whelming and it did not leave her much time to meet with her friends or go out. Slowly, slowly her friends started to keep their distance believing that the promotion she got has affected her personality.

Chapter 2

Don, Sandy's dad, was a proud high ranking business man, but away from every one's eyes he spent most of his free time helping the disadvantage families by buying them the necessary homeware, furniture. At times he would do grocery shopping for them. Don, a rich man, unlike any other rich man, believed "if someone has been blessed they should share their blessings and not store it where it will never be used.

Donna, his wife was so down to earth most of the time, people would find her cleaning for elderly people, those, whose families deserted them. She would help the elderly with their showers and daily routines. No one would believe that Donna was from a very wealthy family. It seemed that Donna and Don were a perfect match from heaven.

It was a mystery that the family would do all those good deeds but never mention it to anyone even to their small family.

One evening Don and Donna were invited to the twentieth anniversary of their friends. When they got there they were seated on a table with a few other high ranking business people.

The only subject discussed between those business people was money and the tricks they used to force small and middle size businesses out of the market by squeezing them where it hurt the most. These greedy men were hungry for power and wanted to own all the market.

Don started getting very annoyed. He hated every second and every word that came out those men's mouth. The sudden sadness started showing on his face, but Donna was quick enough to notice and react. "Don would you like to dance"?

"No not now." Don replied

"What's wrong?" She asked

"I do not know!" Don replied

Donna persisted that Don get up and dance with her. When they got to the dance floor, Donna asked again, "Don what is wrong with you? You have been quite all night and have not said a word".

"Donna you know how much I hate people that drag about their riches. Look around us. They are a bunch of people who think they have class. They take pleasure in their wrong doing. What do these kind of people think? Do they think they will take all that money to the grave with themselves? If they have so much why pray on small businesses that are barely managing to pay their bills."

Donna patiently listened to Don and when he stopped talking she said, "Don I have never heard you talking like this before. What changed in you?"

"When I dropped you at the front this evening, I went to park the car. Behind me I saw Angelo and his wife getting out of the car while their driver was holding the door for them. A kid that looked like an orphan ran to them and pushed his hand towards Angelo. Instead of Angelo putting a few coins in his hand, he turned to his driver, I do not know what he said but after that the driver slapped the kid and pushed him on the floor, he pointed to him to go away. As Don was talking about this a tear dropped from his eyes so they stopped dancing and went on to the balcony on a corner.

"Then what happened?"

"Nothing. They started walking in. As I ran towards the kid to see if I can help him he got scared. While tears had covered his face, he run away."

"Don you tried. So why are you so upset now?" Donna asked

"I am upset because you heard them on the table how they cheat other people out of business to grow their own. Look at them. They are drinking wine that is over three hundred dollars a bottle. Look at Angelo. Wearing a watch that is worth thirty thousand dollars and his wife's dress as she said cost her ten thousand dollars. So how hard was it for him to give that little boy a few dollars instead of pushing and hearting him?" (At this time tears stopped Don from talking).

Donna was touched by this story and asked Don, "Do you want to leave?"

"No it's ok. If we leave Colin and Collet would be upset. It's their anniversary. We should wait until they cut the cake."

Don then excuses himself so he could go to the bathroom to clean his face. Donna went back to their table. As soon as she sat on the table, Michelle Anglo's wife looked at her. She asks "where do you buy your dresses from?" (While looking at the other women on the table).

Donna being a very smart woman noticed where the wife was going with this, she answered back, "Obviously not from the same place that you do".

Everyone on the table went quite for a few minutes; Donna smiled, knowing that she hit the right nerve.

Although Donna was wearing a simple dress with simple jewellery, she was glowing. Her beauty was amazing. The goodness of her heart was reflecting in her face and most people fall for her beauty.

It is not long before Don is back on the table. Michael another famous business man addressed Don, "You should come to our meetings sometimes. It's going to help you grow your business plus we can have a few drinks together."

Trying to be polite Don answered "Thanks I'll do that"

The tension was growing strongly on the table. Don and Donna were very pleased when the cutting of the cake was announced. As soon as the cake got cut and served, they congratulated Collet and Colin and left.

"I am so glad we are out of there, "Donna said with a relieved voice"

"Yes, me too"

The restaurant where the anniversary was held was built on ten acres of land. It was one of those dream places. The building was historic. The garden and land escapes were amazingly eye catching. It took Don a few minutes to make it out of the gate onto the main road.

After driving for nearly two kilometres, Don notices some kids on the side of the road. When he looked closer, it was the little boy he saw earlier in the night. He called out.

"Look Donna, that's the same boy." He then quickly pulls over and runs towards the boy. Donna followed him.

When Don made it to the boy, he noticed there is a girl sleeping on his lap and a younger boy next to him, deep in sleep. Don called out "Hello"

But the boy did not answer. He cuddled his sister and brother with fear.

"Please don't be scared. What are you doing here?

The little boy replied "We are on our way home."

"Where is home?" Donna asked

"At Sunshine"

Don asked. "That is a long way from here. What are you doing here and why did you walk so far away from home?"

"I did not realise how far we walked."

Donna says "Your parents are probably worried to death about you."

The tears start running from the eyes of the little boy and said "I do not think so."

"What do you mean?" asked Don

"Nothing. Thank you for stopping. Do you mind leaving us alone? I am waiting for my brother and sister to wake up so we can start walking again."

"I cannot leave you like this plus you are still very far from home." Don replied

"Why do you care? I was pushed and frightened by one of your kind this evening. So don't pretend to care."

"I saw you there. I tried to come to you, but you ran away. Get up now. We will drive you home." Don implored

The boy looked at his brother and sister. Before he says anything Donna asked "Are we allowed to touch them. Can we pick and put them in the car?"

The boy with unbelief looked at the couple and said. "Ok"

As Donna and Don placed the two younger kids in the car, the boy stood there looking inside the car.

Donna said "Get in young man"

"Look at my clothes. Your car will get dirty." the boy said

Don with a big smile on his face said, "It is only a car and you are more important than this piece of material".

The boy then jumped in the car. On the way he asked them "Why you are doing this?"

Donna with a smart voice said "Doing what?" then she smiled.

"Helping us"

Donna, "This is no help. We are only giving you a lift on our way home".

After driving for nearly four kilometres they got to a street and the boy said "You can drop us here." Then he started waking up his brother and sister.

"Tell us where exactly your home is as we can drop you there? It is late in the night."

But the boy refused. The car stops and the three young kids get out of the car. While closing the door, the boy said, "Thank you."

Don was not the type of person to leave three kids on their own in the middle of nowhere specially at that time of night, so he parked the car and slowly started following the kids. As the two younger ones were still sleepy and were hanging on to their older brother, they did not realise they were followed.

Once they got to this shed in dark pitch he can see the boy, Stops. Looks at the sky and walks in with hesitation. Don goes around and finds a small window that was at the back of the shed. When he looked inside, there was an oil lamp on the floor that brightened the room. A woman was lying on the floor. The two younger kids have made their way to the woman and have put their heads on her while, struggling she moves her arm around them.

The older boy went to a corner and sat on the floor. He brought his knees up to his face and rested his head on them and went to sleep.

There was no sign of floor covering, food or any life in that shed. Don got very emotional and started walking back towards the car. When Donna saw how tears were flowing down his face she got worried. "Don is everything ok?"

Don then told her, what he had seen through the window.

"There is nothing we can do now. At least be happy that you know where they live." Donna said

"You are right. I can't believe that there is still people who live under these conditions. We are supposed to be a country that has welfare and ninety percent of people believe that our welfare system is good enough to look after everyone."

They both went quite. Both of them didn't say a word until they got home.

Sandy has waited for her parents to get home. When she heard their car, she was so happy. She ran to the door and said. "If you had been a bit longer I was going to call the rescue team."

Don smiled and gave Sandy a big hug.

"So come on" Sandy said "You must have had an exceptional night to come home so late."

"Yes we did" Donna said. "We will tell you all about it in the morning." Don agreed and they all went to bed.

In the morning when Sandy got up, Don was already making coffee. "Would you like some coffee?" he asked

"No Dad, I am running late. I will have one when I get to work."

When Sandy arrives at work she quickly gets in to her back log and tries to do as much as she can before the rest of the team show up.

Angela gets there at eight thirty with a smile on her face. "Sandy did you sleep here last night?"

"Don't be smart. You saw me going last night. Sandy replied

It's now around nine thirty and Sandy has done her normal daily routine of saying 'hi' to everyone. When she makes it back to her desk she sees a rose siting there. She quickly calls Angela and asks her "where did this rose come from?"

"The courier just delivered it. It was addressed to you."

"With no card and no contact name?"

That is exactly how it arrived. "Angela replied"

"Well did you look at the courier truck?"

With a very shaky voice Angela replied "No I was so excited that I wasn't thinking straight."

Sandy wasn't used to getting angry. Lifting the tone of her voice, she said "Angela next time you make sure if anything like this is sent to me you find out as much information as you can. If not, refuse to receive them."

Angela who had never seen Sandy this angry replied. "Ok I am sorry" and walked away.

Chapter 3

On the other side of the city the rest of Sandy's family are busy with their own lives keeping their distance from Sandy and her parents.

Jackie, Jasmine and their brothers Jason and Joshua seemed to get along well and have forgotten that they have another sister in the same city.

Jackie and Jasmine were the type of people who had to look good in front of others, at all times. They would dress to impress and lived a very high class life style. It was important for them to be recognized for what they had and what they wear. They were both married and each had two kids.

Their complexion was completely different to their sister, even though they were not bad looking. There was something about them that would turn people off.

Joshua was a high flying CEO proud yet he still had a bit of humanity left in him. Jason had his own small business. The two boys were happily married with two boys each. Why none of them would pay any visits to their parents, was strange. They were busy with their life style and thought it is a waste to spend their time travelling to visit their parents and their sister.

"Jasmine, have you heard from mum and dad?" Jackie asks asked of her sister when they met.

"No, I had no time" Jasmine replied. "Plus I hate calling their house, in case if that loser Sandy answers the phone."

"Don't let that bother you. She is looking after our parents. We all know that she is a loser. We should be happy that she stays with them. That means she will never go anywhere."

In this instant Jason walks in. In a very high voice, he calls out. "Hi guys how are you? What were you talking about? Why did you stop when I walked in?"

"Nothing" Jasmin replied. We were talking about Sandy. The poor loser, she is unemployed. Pretending she is looking after mum and dad or at least she thinks she is." If you ask me, I think she will be homeless without them."

"That is a bit sad. We should really see if Sandy needs help." Jason proposed

Jackie was quick in replying. "There is no need; you should only look after your own family. One approach of help will put us all in risk. She will be a burden on us."

"Anyway," Jason said "I just came around to invite you for dinner. I will call Joshua as well. Let's sit around and have a bit of fun."

Every one arrived at Jason's house at around six pm. The beautiful odour of food had filled the house. Jackie couldn't help herself and said, "Oh my god something smells so good."

"That must be my cooking." Jason replied with a smile on his face.

"Did you really cook?" Jackie asked

Jason says, "No my wife did. Any way let's have a drink."

Jasmine jumped in to the conversation "Every time we gather I feel so happy."

Joshua grabs his glass, "Cheers everyone."

After having a few drinks everyone moved to dining table. Everything was set beautifully.

At dinner Jason's wife Mandy opened the conversation by saying. "We should have gatherings like this with your parents. I bet they feel neglected plus we should show them some love otherwise they might leave their entire estate to Sandy."

Cindy Joshua's wife, agreed. "We all can do with a bit of extra money plus if Sandy is left with all that money; she will spend it on the most stupid things and would go broke again."

"We should take turns to visit them, every week. One of us should go there with the grandchildren." Jason suggested.

"That is a great idea." said Jackie.

Joshua said, "How about if we start from next Sunday. Me and Cindy can take the first turn. Then you guys can arrange your time between you."

"That sounds good"

When they finished eating the boys moved into the dining room and the ladies helped the host to clear the table, then a small desert was served. After a few short games, everyone left.

On the way home Joshua was very quiet and when Cindy asked him "Josh what is the matter. You have been very quiet?"

Joshua says "I am fine. But this whole thing with Sandy is starting to annoy me. We are all treating her as if she is our enemy. Yet she hasn't done anything to deserve this."

"Well my love, your sisters are right. We all deserve to be in your father's estate but by the looks of it Sandy is hanging around them to take it all." Cindy Said.

Josh replied, "I am not in the mood for this conversation. Let's finish it here."

Jackie was complaining all the way home, "Why should we go. I hate being under the same roof with Sandy. She brings my class down."

It seemed like the greedy woman forgot that if money wasn't involved. No one could make her go.

Her kind and loving husband said, "Jackie no matter what happens, she is your sister and I really don't like the way you talk about her. Look how happy she gets when she sees you. She is an exceptional aunt. Up to this day I haven't seen her neglecting any of her nephews or nieces."

"This is none of your business anyway." Jackie Screamed.

In the morning Donna calls Jackie. "Hi darling"

"Hi mum"

"How are you? I hope that you and your family are all well."

"Yes mum we are."Jackie replied "How are you doing?"

"I am good thanks. Just called, wanted to hear your voice."

"Ok mum. Love you"

"I love you too sweetheart"

Donna then called her other three children and had the same short conversation with all of them. When she finished with the phone calls, she sat on the couch, tears were rolling down her face while thinking, I can't believe none of my four children asked about their sister or father. The weary of this occupied Donna, she flaked on the couch, and slept.

Chapter 4

It is Friday night and Sandy's friends call her to go out. Normally each weekend they would call her because she knew a lot of bars and night clubs, and knew all the roads pretty well.

It was normal for Sandy to walk into night clubs and get surrounded by guys within seconds, but she herself had other things on her mind like finishing her studies, making her bosses proud by delivering good results and high profitability, and guys were the last thing on her mind.

Sandy had this habit to talk and dance with guys and in general enjoy her night out but the minute she left the night club she would go straight to a rubbish bin and threw all the telephone numbers given to her by guys.

Her friends were not very happy about this. They always questioned her as to how come all these guys come to you. Why don't you give one of them a chance?

"Why would I need a guy in my life, when my life is full? I have great parents, good friends that I can hang with, and I have no one to dictate to me about what I can or can't do". Sandy would reply.

One day Sandy's best friend Mona said, "I wish I could be like you but at times I really feel lonely."

"Who said we can all like the same things. We are all different and Mona from the bottom of my heart, I hope one of these days you find someone really nice." Sandy Said.

That Friday Sandy did accept the invitation. They all went to a night club and had loads of fun. On Sunday Mona calls Sandy and asks her if they can have lunch? Sandy accepted but said, "It has to be somewhere close by because I made plans with my parents in the afternoon."

Mona picks Sandy up at twelve noon. On their way to restaurant Mona said, "Sandy, Friday night I did not want to say anything in front of the others but because you are the only friend that I trust and share things with. I want you to meet someone and since we were going for lunch, I asked him to join us at the restaurant."

Sandy laughed. "Oh my god finally I am going to get rid of you."

"Not now, not tomorrow and not in a hundred years, you can get rid of me." Mona laughed back.

"What is he like?"

"He is kind and caring. Since I meet him my life has changed. He fills that empty spot in my life."

"What about looks?" Sandy asked

"You should know. I only like nice looking guys."

While they were giggling about this, a very nice looking guy walked in. Sandy said "Mona check that one out. If you look at this guy I think you will change your mind about the guy you are dating."

Mona turns around and waves at the guy while telling Sandy. "Idiot that is him"

Steve was his name. He walked to the table, gave a kiss to Mona on her cheek and offers his hand to Sandy while saying, "Hi, I am Steve."

After an hour of discussion and having lunch Sandy went to the ladies to freshen up,

Mona followed her to find out what she thinks of Steve.

"Hey Sandy what do you think?" Mona called out.

"Well I got to admit, I really like the restaurant and love the food."

"Come on silly. I was not talking about that. I am asking about Steve."

He seems like a nice guy and the respect he has for you is amazing. Please do not make him run away." Sandy replied

"In your dreams, girl, you know Sandy; I hope that you find someone nice like him." Mona continued "You mean a lot to me and I want to see you happy."

"But you know I am happy the way I am. Where am I going to fit a guy in my life between my busy work, mum, dad and studying. It barely leaves me time to think."

These things might look enough for now, Mona said. But the time will come when you will feel the pain of loneliness."

"Mona are you really looking after Steve here? While we are chatting all this time, poor Steve is sitting at the table."

Mona laughed and said. "Oh yes I forgot about him"

Finally the two girls went back to the table. Steve rose from the table. As he was pulling out the chair for Mona he said, "My god girls it looks like you were having a good chat in the bathroom. You were gone for a very long time."

The girls apologized and made a few funny comments about the girl's room.

While Sandy is out with Mona, Joshua arrives at his parent's house as planned Don and Donna were surprised to see him and his wife. They were excite to see them and did not question him.

"Mum where is Sandy? I thought she is normally home." Joshua asked

Donna without any hesitation replied "Mona took her out for lunch."

"How are your sisters Josh? Have you seen your brother lately?" Don asked

"They are all well. I saw them all last week." Joshua replied

"It looks like everybody is so busy with their lives because we do not see much of anybody these days. Lucky Sandy takes us out some times and when she has free time she spends it with us and sometimes even takes us out for dinner or drinks. Donna implied.

Don agreeing with his wife said, "Yes it is true. The poor girl does know how to look after us, while attempting to finish her studies. Not to mention her demanding job.

Cindy then got involved. "Oh so Sandy is working and studying now. We thought that she stays home and looks after you."

Don with a funny look turned and looked at Cindy then he carried on by saying, "We are not helpless. We don't need anyone to stay home to look after us, plus if her brothers and sisters would have kept in touch with her they would have known how wonderful she is. None of you know of how successful she is. The promotions she has received are beyond belief."

Donna feels the situation is getting much too tense and tries to change the subject. "Is anyone hungry? I do not know why but today I cooked for over ten people. I must have known we would have visitors."

Joshua replied, "No thanks we can't stay that long"

"Josh don't tell me that you do not miss my cooking? Anyway I will not have my son walking out of here without having lunch with us."

Joshua felt his mother's pain and said. "Yes Mum I do miss your cooking. Let me make a phone call and then we can have lunch."

Cindy followed Joshua outside "Josh how long you are planning to stay? Your idiot sister will be back soon. I really don't want to talk to her."

"Please leave it there, Cindy. A part from Sandy being nice to you, what has she done to deserve this kind of hate?"Joshua asked

"If I knew you would do this I would not have agreed to come here in the first place."

Joshua for the first time stood up for himself by saying. "Well you know what? If you are not happy you can leave."

Cindy then goes back in and waits for Joshua to make his phone call, while Donna was preparing the table for lunch.

They all sit around the table. "The food smells so good Mum" Joshua said

"I hope it tastes as good." Donna replied.

Don joined the conversation by saying. "No one has ever complained because you always make the best food."

When they finished lunch they move to the tea room.

While Donna is making the tea Sandy walks in "Oh my god is that really you?" While running towards Josh she drops her bag on the floor, then she grabbed Joshua cuddled him and gave him so many kisses. She then goes towards Cindy and kisses her on cheeks.

"How was lunch Sandy?" "Don asked

"Not as good as yours. If I knew Josh and Cindy were coming I wouldn't have gone."

Cindy tries to be smart so she says "Tell us Sandy how is work?"

"You know work is work and there is nothing new."

"But for us it is new. We didn't know you are working. What do you do?"

"I get paid for something but I do not know what. All I know is that I am earning my living and that is it."

"Do not underestimate her."Don jumped into the conversation. "You know, Sandy got promoted. Right now, she is relieving the directors for three months."

Cindy and Joshua looked at each other and put their heads down. It looked like they were embarrassed because only those two knew what was going on behind Sandy.

Don felt the shame look on their faces so he kept quite.

Sandy felt the tension and said, "Come on Josh tell us about yourself and what are you up to?"

"Nothing more than what I have been doing all my life. Replied Josh

Cindy quickly jumped by saying, "Josh has always been a CEO. There is no higher position than his."

"What about you Cindy? Are you working?" Sandy asked

Cindy tried to change the subject by saying, "Josh we have to leave now. Remember you cancelled our lunch appointment. We really have to make the other one."

Sandy was smart. She did not try to get an answer for her question because she did not want to embarrass Cindy more than that.

Joshua and Cindy then got up, said good by to everyone and left.

Monday morning, Sandy went to work. This Monday was to be different from any other Monday. She gets to work before everyone else and opens the doors. She sat behind her desk and from her window, stared at the empty store thinking I have to meet the director's approval by increasing the sales. She stayed at her desk for quite a while making plans, until she noticed the first employee arriving. She ran to the door and greeted every one of them as they walked through the door. They were all shocked as to how down to earth she was.

When she let the last employee in she went outside to take a big breath. As she was admiring the fresh morning breeze she saw an old man looking in rubbish for food. Her heart stopped. She could not believe at this time and age people live in poverty.

Tears filled Sandy's eyes. She ran to the man and said, "Please stop looking through the rubbish." The then looked at her and said, "What do you know about hunger? I am hungry and need food".

"Just stop and wait a minute. I will bring you food." She quickly ran inside, grabbed her bag, bought some food and gave it to the man.

"Thank you Mam." the old man said. "I am sorry if I was rude to you. Before I was hungry and when you approached me I thought you wanted to condemn me like everyone else.

Sandy turned around and said to him. "Who am I to condemn you?" She then walked back to work.

It was around ten am when two of her senior staff knocked on her door. Sandy asked them to come in. Rebecca and Sullivan walked in with some papers in their hands and sat in the chairs

Sandy said, "What is up?"

Rebecca then handed the papers to Sandy by saying. We have given Susan a warning which will be followed by a termination."

"Susan?" Sandy called out.

"Yes, Susan. She has been late every morning and now she pretends that she is sick. Even when she is at work she is not productive." Sullivan replied

"Have you talked to her to see what her problem is?" Sandy asked

"No everyone knows the rules, but Susan is ignoring them. Rebecca replied

Sandy looks at Rebecca with anger and says. "Sometimes we have to spend time and find out what the problem is. If we fire everyone that seems funny without finding out the cause, we will be left with no employees."

Sullivan tries to back Rebecca by saying. "We are only following the rules."

Sandy grabs the papers and says. "Thanks I will look into this. Do not take any further actions against Susan before consulting me."

When Rebecca and Sullivan left her office Sandy went for her routine check. When she got to the section where Susan was working, she paused for a while watching Susan. After a few minutes she goes directly to Susan.

"Hi Susan how are?"

"Good thanks for asking" Susan Replied

"That is good" Sandy said

While walking away Sandy turns around to have a second look. That's when she sees Susan leaning on the bench in front of her, so she decides to go back and investigate.

"Is everything ok"? Sandy asked

"Yes everything is fine." Susan Replies

"Then why were you bending over the bench?" Sandy asked

Susan's tears started rushing down on her face

"Sorry, I did not mean to make you cry."

"Sandy I am so sorry to take your time. I know how busy you are."

"Do not worry about me. Tell me about yourself?"

Susan then starts telling Sandy how she left her country and followed the guy she loved. When she got here he took her home but his parents refused to let her stay there. Away from their vision he placed her in the shed and would sneak her in and out of there. Nor did she have no money to rent a place, apart from her boyfriend, she doesn't know anyone.

"I found this job to help me save enough money to rent a place but a few days ago his parents found out that I was living in their shed. They came and kicked me out. I sneak around and sleep in the store cellars. Recently some people found out and dobbed me in. I received a warning from Rebecca and Sullivan but I really don't have anywhere to go."

"Oh my god I am really homeless." said Susan before she cracks into tears.

"Does your man work?" Sandy asked.

"He was before I got here but when all these things happened to me he quit his job so he can look after me."

"Well I can offer your man a job, but you have to promise not to let anyone know about this. When he starts working here, you have to pretend that you have just met. In the meantime just stay in the cellar until you two have enough money to rent a place."

Susan pinched herself while Sandy was talking. She was asked why you did that.

She replied. "I am making sure that I am awake and this is not a dream. Sandy, I seriously am so thankful to you."

"Don't forget your promise" Sandy said while walking away

The next morning Susan got to work early. Her face was glowing out of happiness and no one knew what had happened to make her feel so good.

Sandy went to Susan slowly and said, "Well what your man thought about my offer?

"My god" Susan replied. "He was so happy and said when we rent a place and settle down we should get married."

The next day Susan's boyfriend (Martin) meet with Sandy she was pleased to hire him straight away due to an open position in the store room.

Chapter 5

Don and Donna, although were very busy people none of them could take their mind off those kids whom they dropped at that shed on the night of Collet and Colin's anniversary, Donna couldn't help herself when she was serving dinner on Sunday night "Don do you think those kids we picked up from the side of the road have something to eat tonight?"

"You read my mind" Don replied. "I really don't know I can't stop thinking about them."

"Well if you can spare a few hours tomorrow, we can go and check on them and see if they need any help" Donna Implied

"That sounds good." Don replied

On Monday morning, the husband and wife left the house early and made their way to the shed. They waited to see if any of those kids would come out to go to school, but the school time passed and no one came out.

Don leaves the car parked as it was and walked to the shed. From the window he looks inside the shed and sees all the family sleeping next to each other all looking cold, very weak and paled. He pulls himself away from the window and starts crying. Donna rans to him "What is wrong?" he pointed to the window. When she looked inside her heart was broken.

Donna quickly turned to Don and said "Why are you crying? We have the opportunity to help them. So clean yourself up and let's knock on the door."

Don said "I have a better idea. Let's go back to the car."

When they got into the car, Don drove straight to a big shopping mall close by. They walked in to children's shop. They bought a few pairs of clothes for the two boys and the little girl. Then they went and bought some blankets so the family could put them on the floor and keep warm. On the way back they see a hardware store so they stop and buy a gas stove. They then went bought enough groceries to last the family at least two weeks.

When they went back Don drove all the way to the shed and parked the car right at the front. They walked to the shed and knocked on the door. A beautiful but ill looking woman opens the door and asks "Can I help you?" Before Donna or Don could answer a boy screamed. "Mum those are the people that gave us a lift the other night".

The woman gets very embarrassed and quietly says. "Thank you for bringing my kids home." She then carries on by saying, "I would invite you in but we have no chairs for you to sit on. The way you are dressed I would be ashamed if you sat on the floor."

Don quickly says, "That's no problem we love sitting on the floor. But before coming in we would ask you to accept a gift from us?"

The woman replied, "Why would you give me a gift?"

"The gift is actually for all of you, and we need to know that you will not be offended."

The little boy said, "Mum can we see what their gift is? You shouldn't worry mum they are not like the others."

The woman puts her head down as a sign of acceptance, and Don with a very happy and in loud voice says, "Well kids what you are waiting for. Come and help me."

Paul the oldest brother was the first one to jump up to give a hand, followed by his younger sister Pam and Brother Peter. When

Don opened the boot of the car, the three little kids went, "wow is that all for us?"

Don with a very excited voice replied, "Yes off course."

The four of them together carried nearly forty five bags

Nancy the mother kept on looking at all the bags and finally she said, "Excuse me sir, what are you doing? There is no way we can repay you for all of these. Please take them back."

"No one has to pay me back," Don replied,

"What do you mean? No one gives this much free stuff to anyone unless there is a catch to it." Nancy said.

Don, "You better believe there are still good people out there that would do the same thing. I cannot sleep at night if I know these kids don't have proper bedding or clothing. None of us can eat, since that night, wondering if these kids have eaten. Don continued. Please let me give some stuff to the kids then we can talk and I beg of you not to spoil their happiness."

"Ok" Nancy replied"

Don then sat next to Donna on the floor and grabbed some of the bags that contained clothing. He calls the youngest one first, and Peter runs to Don.

While pulling a jacket out of the bag, Don asked, "Peter do you like this?"

"Yes it's nice"

"Well why don't you try it on?" Don asked

The jacket fitted Peter perfectly. He was so happy he started jumping up and down. Donna said, "Peter look there is more stuff here for you to try."

Peter, the beautiful four year old boy was so excited he went and sat on Don's lap and asked, "Is this all for me?"

"Yes off course"

All of a sudden Peter gets very sad and says, "Thank you but I cannot accept them because I don't want to be different to my brother and sister."

Donna with tears in her eyes replied, "You don't need to worry because they have as much as you do." She calls Paul and Pam to come and collect their bags of clothes.

All the kids are now happy opening their gifts. They have never had so much clothing. Nancy looked at them thinking, my God where did these angels come from? She then moved and went through the bags of groceries, tears running down her face, knowing for the first time in months, she can make homemade food for her children.

"I think we better leave you for now. We can talk another day," Don Said

Nancy quickly jumped in by saying, "Thanks to you I am going to cook for my kids. They have not eaten in days and I would be so happy if you could stay and eat with us."

Don looked at Donna for approval, She replied "We would love to, but don't want to be a burden."

Paul grabs Don's hand and says, "Please stay."

While Nancy got busy cooking, Don and Donna started showing some of the toys to the children and in some cases even taught them how to play the game.

It didn't take long before the smell of the beautiful food fills the shed up. Pam leaves the toys and goes next to her mum, waiting impatiently to eat, when Don witnessed Pam's movement, tears filled his eyes.

Nancy spreads a peace of material on the floor and starts setting it with plates and drinks.

When the food was ready she asked everyone to find a spot around the material. The kids were so hungry, that they kept on eating and eating until they went to sleep in their spot. Don thanked Nancy and told her that he would be back the next day to make some arrangements with her. Donna grabbed Nancy's hand.

"It was so nice to meet you." she said. They then made their way to the car.

After leaving the shed Don drops Donna at home and makes his way to work. So much work is awaiting him as he had fallen behind. For some reason he was very dissatisfied with himself.

After sorting a few things at work Don asked his secretary to re-schedule his next morning appointments. He then goes home for dinner.

The next morning after a few discussions with Donna, Don goes to the bank and makes a withdrawal. He then makes his way back to the shed as he promised.

When he got there, the kids were playing with their toys. He asked Nancy if they can have a talk outside. Nancy agreed, by following Don outside.

Don for a minute felt really uncomfortable but for his own sake he asked, "I am sorry to ask, but how did you and the kids get into a situation like this?"

Nancy looked at Don and replied, "We had a big house and a good life me and my husband were both working. We created such a beautiful life for our kids, we even had a nanny looking after them that way they never felt alone or neglected. About two years ago my husband started feeling very tired. Then the weight loss started and finally one day he collapsed at work. He was taken to hospital and was diagnosed with a very rare disease. Things were getting very bad and he worsened by day."

"Months went by. He was still in hospital then I lost my job. When that happened I couldn't afford the Nanny anymore, so I let her go. The whole world started collapsing around me. We were under so much pressure with no income coming in. We had to use our savings for food and mortgage. Then my husband's medical bills started to purr in. It got to a point that I sold all our belongings, including the house to cover the debt."

Nancy stopped for a minute then carried on. "I tried the welfare to get some assistance but they drove me mad. We wasted all our money to find a cure for my husband but nothing worked until finally one day his body gave in."

"When he died, the funeral costs added to the debt. The welfare system had not paid me a penny yet. So I had to use the rent money for the funeral costs. This caused our rent to fall behind. A few times I went to social services and begged them to help me by paying what rightfully, was my entitlement. They made me wait and wait. That is how the rent arrear kept on building and building until we were thrown out. Not having any money or anyone to go to. We ended up living in the streets."

One day this kind man who was watching us for a few days came to me, and said, I am so sorry to bother you, but if you and your kids need a place to stay in, I have an empty shed that never gets used. You can live there as long as you want for free. I cannot bare seeing these kids sleeping on cold floors in the streets.

I tried to kiss the man's hand but he did not allow it. I agreed to move in to his shed because of my kids. At least that way they would have a roof on their heads.

The man then put all of us in his car and drove us to this shed. All those blankets that you see on the floor were given to us by him.

I never even had time to mourn the death of my husband. All that stress and cold sleepless nights finally caught up with me, I got so sick, I almost lost my life.

Not being able to move, naturally, I couldn't feed my children or myself. When I was unconscious, the kids took the matter in to their own hands by going out and begging for food. If anyone gave them food they brought it home and shared it with everyone. Sometimes for days no one would give them anything. On those starving days they would go to bed early in hope that the following day someone would give them food."

Nancy stopped for a second as tears were pouring out of her eyes, then she continued. You have no idea what it is like to see your kids starving in front of your eyes. They are not upset that we lost everything, they always tell me, Mum we should be thankful for all those good times we had.

Well this is our story. Sorry to bother you with it but you asked and since you were so nice to us I thought you have the right to know everything."

Don was still in shock when Nancy finished. He could not believe how the system has failed this mother and her kids. Who would have believe in this time and age, genuine honest people would live on the street and in poverty.

Nancy noticed the blank look on Don's face so she calls out, "Sir are you alright?"

Don looked at her and said, "oh yes I am ok" He stops again for a few seconds and says "I am sorry to push my head in your business, while putting his hand in his pocket, "I would like you to get you a place close to the city and once you settle in there put the kids back to school once all these things are taken care of come and see me." He then pulls his hand out of his pocket and points to Nancy, Please take this money I believe it's enough to pay the rent and some living costs until you settle in.

Nancy looked at him with disbelieve then said, "Why are you doing this? Thank you but I don't take donations."

"Who said its donation, Don replied, "I am only given it to you as a loan. I know that in a months' time a clerical position will be available in my company. You will be offered that position and if you do accept it, then you can work and pay me back."

"Are you serious" Nancy replied?

"Off course I am serious." Don replied

"I do not know how to thank you." Nancy said

With a smile on his face Don said, "Don't thank me yet until you get your old life back."

By now the kids got bored and run outside asking Don and Nancy what took them so long, Don excused himself and went back to work.

Nancy took the kids back into the shed and showed them the money. Tears were pouring off her face when she said. "And people don't believe in miracles. What just happened to us is a miracle. How this kind man followed Paul, lost him and then found you all together again after a few hours. God surely works in mysteries ways."

Paul went and hugged his mum quietly. Nancy gave him a kiss on the cheek and said, "Thanks to you none of us will ever again be hungry or cold."

That night Nancy asked the kids to go to bed early so they could get up in the morning because they had a long day ahead of them.

In the morning the kids woke up earlier than usual. They were so excited to find out what their mum had planned for them. By the time Nancy woke up the three little people got dressed in their new clothes, had their breakfast and quietly waited.

Nancy who had not seen her kids clean and in proper clothing for some time opened her eyes when she saw the kids. Tears filled her eyes and she said "My little angels you all look so beautiful." She then got up and placed a kiss on all their heads.

By nine am they left the house and caught the bus to the city. They were all very quiet over the years. They had such a hard life they went through hunger, cold, pain and agony of losing their father, and worst of all they begged for food. Now they are clean with their stomachs full and they are not ashamed to be among people on the bus because they have new garments.

Once the bus stopped in the city, Nancy asked a few people and found two real estate's that had units for lease, but the rent was so high that Nancy started losing her confidence.

After so many hours of walking and searching they were all so tired, and decided to go back home.

On the way back Nancy couldn't remember the way to the bus station. While they all were trying to find their way back they got to a very small street. Nancy notices a real estate office in that street. Not having any confidence left Nancy went straight past the real estate, without even looking at it. She didn't want to torture her kids any more.

All the sudden Paul screamed "Mum, Mum check this out," Nancy turned around and asked what?

"Paul replied, please come on. At least have a look."

Nancy loving her kids did not want to disappoint Paul so she went back and looked at the picture that Paul was pointing at. It looked so beautiful, a three bedroom unit, fairly new relaxing colours on the walls and the description included, close to shops and school.

Nancy opened the door and went in. She inquired about the rent with hesitation because the other units that they saw were a lot smaller than this one. To her surprise the rent on this one was a lot less.

Being so excited about the price, Nancy quickly says "When can we inspect it?"

The real estate guy said, "If you like I can take you right now?"

With so much excitement Nancy replied, "That would be great"

They all went and inspected the unit. It was beautiful and they all seemed so excited, especially when they saw the school was only a few minutes away.

The real estate guy then asks Nancy, "Do you like it?"

"Oh yes" Nancy replied. When can we move in?"

"Tomorrow, if you want." The guy replied.

On the way back to the real estate the kids kept on pressuring Nancy. "Mum can we really move in tomorrow?"

When the real estate guy saw how excited the kids were he asked Nancy if she wants to sign the contract when they went back to the office. Nancy agreed.

While Nancy was signing the contract the real estate guy couldn't help himself. He was so amazed at these kids excitement that he told Nancy, "Your two weeks rent is free."

When Nancy and the kids got home that night they all were dreaming of their new home although they did not have any beds or furniture to move but this was a happy new beginning for them.

The following morning Nancy hires a Ute to transport their belongings. Once they moved in Nancy straight away went to the school to see if she could enrol her kids.

When the principal heard Nancy's story she was very touched and agreed to enrol all of them.

When Nancy took the kids to buy their school necessities it was like a dream coming true Pam looked at Paul and said. "You always said fairy tales exist but I never believed you until now."

Paul grabbed her hand and kissed it, then said, "Next time believe your older brother."

Monday arrived. The kids could not sleep all night due to excitement. Nancy walked them to school at eight thirty and went shopping. At three o'clock she went to the school and picked up the kids. On the way back the three of them had so many stories to tell her. Tears of happiness were rolling down her face to see her kids so happy and dressed well.

After making sure that everything is ok, Nancy decided to call Don and tell him she is now ready to work, Don was so happy that he asked her to go in the next day.

In the morning after dropping the kids at school Nancy made her way to Don's work. The receptionist announced her arrival. When Don came, he looked around and asked the receptionist where Nancy was because he did not recognize her. She was wearing a navy blue suite with a yellowish coloured shirt under neat. Her beautiful long hair was down and she completely looked different to when Don met her first.

"Oh my god, Nancy, I did not recognize you." Don implied "you look stunning."

Nancy went all red in the face and said, "Thanks to you I had a shower and was able to buy some clothes for myself."

Don smiled and said, "You did the hard work not me." He then took Nancy in and introduced her to the other employees and showed her new office to her.

Nancy settled in to her office quickly and started going through the work on her desk. After studying the work of the previous person it was easy for her to pick up and continue the work.

Before leaving work Don managed to check on what Nancy was doing and he was very pleased that he said, "My god where were you hiding all these years? The amount of work you did today is equal to one weeks work."

That afternoon Nancy picked the kids up with a big smile on her face. At dinner time Paul said, "Mum I forgot how beautiful you really are. This morning when I saw you all dressed I wanted to compliment you but I couldn't find the words."

"Oh thank you Paul."Nancy said. You, your brother and sister also looked so beautiful and charming this morning."

They all giggled and continued with their dinner.

Chapter 6

Sandy is so busy with her work that she did not even know what her parents were up to, Susan and Rebeca have become her best friends. They wait at work until she finishes.

Life is really looking good for the three girls. The stores profit is up by thirty percent in such a short time.

The directors have taken longer than planned, but knowing that Sandy has pushed their profits up made it easier for them to spend more time in the new store.

To avoid her brothers and sisters who were now visiting more often, Sandy decided to work on Sundays. This action of hers not only helped her to avoid their stupid comments but made them happy as well.

One Friday night Rebeca and Susan were forcing Sandy to go with them to a night club

"I can't go anywhere like this. Look at my clothes." Sandy Said

But the girls would not take no for an answer. Rebeca then goes to Angela's desk and picks up a dress that was in a plastic hanging on the chair. She then says, "Here is what you can wear. Angela picked up your dress at lunch time but forgot to tell you"

Sandy smiled and grabbed the dress. They went to a beautiful night club. As soon as the girls walked in, all the heads turned towards Sandy. She felt so uncomfortable that she asked, "Is something wrong with my dress, or makeup?"

"Oh yes." Rebecca replied. "Your dress is crying on you and your make up is not visible at all."

Susan laughed so loud when she saw Sandy panicking. "What is your problem Sandy? Why can't you for once be proud of your beauty? They are not staring because something is wrong with you. It's because your beauty is heavenly."

"Heavenly" said Sandy. "Are you blind or crazy? What beauty?" When it came to her personal life she had very low self-esteem because her sisters always called her ugly and unworthy.

To ease the tension Susan quickly goes and grabs drinks for all of them. "Here Sandy this should cheer you up." She said

That night the three girls had so much fun, Sandy's hand was full of telephone numbers that guys pushed at her. When she walked out she took a quick look at them, then threw them in the first rubbish bin that she saw.

When Sandy was driving home a small blue light, the size of a pearl crossed her face for a second. She followed the light with her eyes but it disappeared very quickly. She got scared thinking oh "God what was that," She quickly put herself together.

"Maybe all those drinks I had got to me." Then she laughed.

Saturday morning Sandy couldn't get off her bed. Her mum kept on calling her for breakfast but she pretended to be sleeping. An hour later she heard the door closing so she knew her parents have left the house.

At lunch time when Sandy's parents got home they found her in her bed sleeping peacefully. She stayed in bed until late in the afternoon then got up and had afternoon tea with her parents.

"Oh my" Sandy said "this was the best sleep I had in years."

"Must have been, Don replied. " I have never seen you stay in bed for so many hours, but then maybe your body needed it.

"Not only my body my brain too. I had so much fun last night and did not realise how much alcohol I consumed."

"That's my girl" Don said. "At least you had fun. I almost forgot are you home tomorrow? All your brothers and sisters are coming here for lunch."

Sandy's face dropped. "I am so sorry Dad but I am working, unless you need my help."

"No don't worry. We already arranged for the food. It will be delivered to us at lunch time." Don carried on. However there is something that has been bothering me. I noticed that you and the rest of our children don't get along well. We were hoping that this gathering would help you come closer to each other."

"Dad I never enjoy their company." said Sandy. "There is something about them. They are like strangers to me, I cannot even finish two words with any of them. They always cut me off and interrupt when I talk. I have to sit there and listen to their crap all the time."

"It's ok, don't worry about it." Don replied

Sandy then got up and kissed Don on the forehead while saying, "Dad I love you so much for being understanding."

On Sunday morning Sandy leaves the house very early. She goes to a small café and has breakfast before going to work. During that time she could not forget the look on her father's face and was hoping that she did not offend him.

While having her coffee she wrote on a serviette.

The heart is weak and the eyes weaker. Sealed lips are witness to the pain in the chest.

Oh Lord forgive me for not wanting to be with those who break my heart, and bring tears to my eyes. Oh lord my lips are sealed because I cannot be as bitter as them.

When Sandy got to work that morning, she did her routine walk around but when she went back to her office she stayed there until closing time, as if she lost interest in everything.

That evening when Sandy went home her parents had sad faces. She asked them, if everything was ok. They both said yes.

No matter how much she begged them to tell her if something was wrong, none of them would barge.

Don could see his daughter's concerned face so he said, "We are just tired darling. It was a big day for us. They all came with their families and left a few minutes before you got home."

Sandy offers them a cup of tea before she heads off to bed and they gladly accepted the offer.

When Sandy was walking towards the kitchen, Don called out, "What is that?"

After looking around Sandy and Donna called out "What is what?"

"A small blue light just flashed inside the room." said Don

"It's probably reflection of something." Donna told him

Remembering what Sandy saw in the car the other night she quickly said, "Dad was it shaped like a very small ball, in blue and glowing?"

"Yes" he replied. "So you saw it too."

"Am I the only one that missed it?" Donna asked

After the cup of tea Sandy kissed her parents "good night." When she went to bed she kept on thinking what that blue light was all about, but then she easily gave up thinking. Oh well, whatever it is one day I will find out.

The following morning on her way to work, Sandy stopped at a red light when she heard someone calling her name. She turned and found Charlie the man that she helped at her window. He was out of breath as if had been running.

"Oh Charlie what are you doing here?" Sandy asked

"Well I have been looking for you." Charlie replied

"Ok now that you found me, quickly get in the car so we can talk." When Charlie got in the car Sandy was so relieved she asked him, "Charlie how is your son? Did you make it home on time?"

"Oh thanks to you Sandy, not only I made it on time but I was able to seek treatment for him with the money that you gave me. My son was saved by a miracle called Sandy."

Sandy laughed loudly and said "Me a miracle? I think you got the wrong miracle. But I am so happy that your son is ok now." Sandy continued, "So what are you doing now. Did you find work?"

"Not yet" Charlie replied, "I came a few days ago and wanted to find you. First to say thank you and give you something."

"You don't have to thank me or give me anything. Please don't even try I will be very sad if you try to pay me back."

Charlie looked at her with unbelief and put his head down. "When I find work and settle, I will bring my family here. They are so keen to meet you."

A few minutes later they arrived at the store. Charlie did not want to take more of Sandy's time so he tried to say good bye, but she asked him to go upstairs to her office for a cup of coffee and he accepted.

When they got to her office she saw a note on her desk from the maintenance supervisor asking if he can advertise for two more employees. That note brightened Sandy's face. She quickly picked up the phone and told him it's ok. "I have a person here in my office right now looking for work. Do you want to interview him and see if he has the skills you require for the position?"

The supervisor agreed to interview Charlie, Sandy turned and looked at Charlie with a smile on her face. "In about an hour you might have a job Charlie."

It wasn't long before the supervisor knocked on the door. After introducing the two, they walked out of the office. A second later Charlie came back and said, "Sandy I almost forgot why I came looking for you." He then pulls out a very old and decorated item from his bag. It looked like a knife cover but it couldn't have been because this one was round like, a tube or just a bit wider than a hose?

What is that Sandy asked? "It has funny writing on it and it looks creepy in a way."

"That day when you gave me the money, I went straight to the train station to go back home. When I got on the train there was this very strange looking woman staring at me. Not in a bad way. She then came and gave me this with these words, "You have to give this to someone you think deserves it more than anybody else." I had no chance to think and grabbed it as I was asking her what it is? She disappeared but for some reason you came straight in to my mind; I hope it is some sort of luck."

"Thank you Charlie. I accept it with all my heart, Sandy said "You better not keep the supervisor waiting. He might hold it against you."

Sandy played with that item for a while to see if she can figure out what it was. After trying and giving up she put it in her bag to show to her parents and see if they knew what it was.

Around lunch time that afternoon the supervisor went to see Sandy. "Charlie has a lot of experience in different fields' even mechanical engineering. I think he will be an asset for the store. If you don't mind I will not advertise the other position until I try and see how Charlie will fit in." Sandy agreed with him. It was planned for Charlie to start work immediately if it was convenient for him.

That afternoon Sandy left work early to show her gift to her parents. When she got home, Don and Donna were having coffee. She walks in quickly, drops her bag in her bedroom and rushes back to where her parents were. "Look guys" She said "Someone gave me this as a gift today it looks like an antique but I don't know what it is?"

"Give us a look," Donna said while grabbing the item. "This is such a strange item. Why would someone give you this as a gift?"

"Oh well I helped somebody not long ago. This was given to him on condition that he passes it to someone that he thought deserves it. The woman who gave him this disappeared before he could ask what it was."

"Well we will find out soon, Don said, "I am glad you came home early today Sandy, I miss having drinks with you.

With a satisfied look Sandy said, "Let us drink now. Would you like that?"

"I sure do." Don replied

The atmosphere was relaxing and happy that Donna said, "I think I will join you."

"Ok you guys just stay where you are," Sandy said "and I will prepare a few things to munch on."

She then goes into the kitchen and prepares a few finger foods and decorates the coffee table in the guest room with crystal glasses, drinks and food. When she got ready she called her parents "I am now ready for you."

"Remember how many of these nights we use to have together?"Don continued "I don't know what happened. Things are very different now. Even people are different, but I am so happy about tonight and hope that from now on we can do this more often."

Sandy grabbed Don's head. Kissed it and said, "We will have plenty more of these times."

Although her parents seemed happy and even mentioned how happy they were, Sandy has been seeing certain sadness in their eyes. After a few drinks and laughs she asked, "If I ask you a question would you promise to tell me the truth?"

"If it is a hard question and one we will not like, please don't ask it now. Let us enjoy the rest of the night." Donna replied

Seeing how concerned his daughter was Don said, "It is nothing important. We are old now and your wellbeing and future matter more than ever. We were hoping that you and your brothers and sisters would get closer to each other for our peace of mind."

"You were right mum; Sandy said "let's worry about this later."

The small family spent a few happy hours together before retiring to bed.

Chapter 7

As Don walked in to his office on Wednesday morning, his secretary handed him some messages. He looked through them then asked his secretary if she knew what Angelo wanted.

"No Sir. He just left his number but he mentioned that he would like to come and see you ASAP."

Don got concerned, it is not like Angelo to waste time and visit his friends. He was the type of man that only went to places where he could make more money. Finally Don decides to ring Angelo.

"Hi Don." Angelo called out. "How are you?"

"I am doing well. How are you Angelo? I was surprised to see a message from you today."

"Called to see if you can meet with me today? To discuss a few things." Angelo replied.

"Do you want to come to my office? Don replied "I am in the office all day today."

"That will be great. I will be there around 1pm."

"Alright. See you then

After the phone call Don, got busy with his work. It was around one that his secretary interrupted him to announce Angelo's arrival.

Angelo walks in the office and after a few minutes of greetings, he said Don I have a request to make you know the company that we all bought our materials from? Well I and a few of the others thought it will be cheaper for us if we bought the company.

But that company has been trading for a long time and I don't think they will sell "Don replied"

Don't worry about that "Said Angelo" they are feeling the pressure at the moment and if we can get your help, we can either push them out of the market or squeeze them so much until they have no choice but to sell.

And how do you intend to do that? Asked Don

We already stopped buying from them, so far they lost sixty percent of their gross profits due to losing our business. You are now their sole customer if you withdraw your orders and stop trading with them they will have no choice but to sell.

"I can't believe you Angelo," Don said. "When and how much is enough for you? We have been business partners with this company for over forty years. Remember when we first started. They stood by us and helped us until our companies grew and now you want me to destroy them. Where is your loyalty or humanity?"

"I didn't come here to get insulted. I am asking you as a friend, Angelo cried out. "With or without your help, I will own that company soon."

While opening the door, Don said, "Good for you Angelo, I hope that you get richer than now. I want to see when will you stop destroying other people's lives for your own gain?"

"You will be sorry for this." Angelo said while rushing out of the office.

Don closed the door and went into deep thoughts. Only days before Max the owner of the other company told him "I can't express my sadness and worries because soon, I will have no option but to close the door of the company that my great grandfather funded."

After a few hours of juggling his thoughts Don decided to go home and discuss his concerns with Donna. After telling her about

Angelo's visit and how sad the young Max was when he saw him last, he held his head in his hand and said, "Donna I really don't know what to do?"

"Go with your heart and conscious, Donna replied. Whatever you decide I am with you a hundred percent. Before she finished her sentence Donna cried out, oh Don did you see that?"

"See what?" He replied.

"The blue light that just passed between us."

"What blue light?"

"It was like a small glowing blue ball."

All of sudden Don put his head up and looked at Donna. It was the same as what I saw the other day and you couldn't see it?"

"Exactly" Donna replied. I think something is trying to put us in the right direction."

Don gets up and kisses Donna's forehead. "Thank you. I know exactly what I will do." He then grabs the phone and calls Max.

"Max I have something urgent to discuss with you. It can't wait until tomorrow. Can you please come to my house right now?"

"If it is so urgent I will be there soon." Max replied.

An hour later, Max rang the bell. He was fixing his hair when he heard a voice saying, "Don't worry you hair looks fine." Before he gets a chance to turn towards the voice the door opens and he is greeted by Don.

"Oh Sandy you are here too." Don cried out.

"Yes dad I will be with you in a few minutes."

Don directs Max to his home office and offers him a drink. He then starts asking Max how bad his business was doing. And what would it take to save the business?

"Well you know Don nearly all of our big customers cancelled their orders within days from each other. That's where our losses started coming in. It was very sad because I had no choice but to lay off almost half of my employees. Some of them had devoted their lives to our company and spent all their young lives working for my father then me."

Max was a tall dark and handsome young man yet very kind and polite that he would not even hurt a bird. His blue eyes just like sea open and honest. The stories could be read from his eyes easily. At this time talking about his business, the tears were so obvious in them.

Don notices the tears and says "Tell me what you can do to save it?"

"In order to survive this fall, I need to produce new products in market so I can attract new customers but I don't have the funding. All my assets, including my house have been used so far to keep a small part of the company going."

"When you say funds, how much are you talking about?" Don asked

"At least 1.8 mil to cover wages and production of new products."

"Are you sure your idea is going to work?"

"I am sure it will that is if I do not have any more obstacles in my way."

"What do you mean by obstacles?"

"You know Don, a few months ago some of those customers ganged up and asked me to sell the company to them, but when I refused they told me I will be sorry. It didn't take long before the orders started to be cancelled, I believe they are trying to close the doors on me."

"It looks like you've done your homework Max because you are not wrong there. These bastards have survived by breathing on small business. One of them visited me today and told me exactly what they've done to you and asked me to withdraw all the orders I had with you. Our meeting didn't finish on good terms as he said I offended him."

"They all know that this business was handed from my great grandfather to my grandfather, then my father and after my father's sudden death I took over. Why would they want to destroy something with so much history? Plus they were so called friends of my father."

"Well son times of friendship are over. The big guys only have one god and that is money. Your father was always aware of them and he made me promise that if something happened to him that I would look after you. I gave him my word."

It didn't take long before Sandy calls out, "Dad mum said dinner is ready and if you are not at the dining table in a few seconds she will be very angry."

Don laughed and said, "Coming." He then turned to young Max and said lets continue the discussions at the table.

"O La La" said Sandy as soon as her dad and Max walked in. I didn't know you had such nice looking friend's dad."

"Max please meet my cheeky daughter Sandy. You already meet Donna."

"Oh yes, Hi Donna I hope you don't mind me staying for dinner."

"Why would you say that? Donna asked. Your parents were our best friends and we always looked at you as a son."

Max then turned to Sandy. "It is so nice meeting you." Their looks got locked in each other for a few minutes.

Don called out. Come on son sit here."

When Max sat on the table he said. "I hope I am not imposing on your quite dinner time."

"Well what can we say? Off course you are but since you are a guest, we cannot ask you to leave just because it is dinner time." Sandy replied. Then she laughed it off.

"Max you will get use to Sandy's sense of humour when you get to know her. Don continued. Let's eat."

The dining table looked like it was set for royalty, Max found it amazing. How, this small family spend their evenings together. They joke, discuss funny things that happened to them during the day and there was no mention of any disappointing moments in their lives.

After they finished their meal Max offered Donna his help to clean the table and wash the dishes. Although she refused, he insisted and was allowed to help washing up.

When they went back to the guest room for a cup of coffee, Don said "Max I will have some discussions with my finance manager tomorrow morning. As soon as he gives me some figures I will call you, but remember you promised to keep this between us.

"I appreciate your help Don, Max replied. I hope to god that one day I will be able to repay your honesty and goodness towards me." He then gets off and says goodnight to everyone.

"I could date Max anytime. He can wash dishes. He is so handsome and his body is like O LA LA. Sandy commented.

"He is a great guy I always looked at him as one of my sons. His dad and I were the best friends. He made me promise that I could look after Max when he was dying. Any other time I would have loved to see you and him dating but not right now because if they see you together they will think that we are working together and would cause both of us a lot of problems."

"Don't worry dad I will behave." Sandy replied

The next morning Don called in to see his finance manager. After a few hours of discussions and cruising through Don's finance they both left the office.

The finance manager disappeared while Don was calling Max. "Can you please meet me at that mountain restaurant that we always go to in one and half hours?"

"Sure I can." Max replied

Don then makes another call to his finance manager before he heads towards the restaurant. That was a beautiful drive. The view while driving was magical and Don felt so happy with his eyes and heart. Everything seemed to be working perfectly just like a beautiful melody.

Max had already arrived. He greeted Don on his arrival. They chat over a few drinks, and then the finance manager arrives and is introduced to Max.

"This is my finance manager and after long discussions I believe he has something to give you." Don implied

"Why would he want to give me something?"

The finance manager then pulls an envelope out of his pocket and says to Max "I am handing it to you but in fact it's from Don."

"Come on Son take it." Don said

Hesitating of what to do, finally Max collects the envelope and when he opens it he screams, "Oh my god, who on earth would do something like this for someone else. I cannot accept this much generosity."

"It is time for me to fulfil the promise I made to your father by looking after you now that you need it."

"Thank you so much but are you sure? This cheque is for 1.95 Mil."

"That's all we could give you at the moment but I am sure that you will double this amount in no time. And now before anyone sees us together we should all leave."

Max gets off his chair and grabs Don in his arms and said, "You are really like my father, Thank you so much."

"Go in peace" Don replied "I know you will be very busy for a while. The Max that I know will build the business back up in no time."

They all then said their farewells and left.

Chapter 8

On Monday morning when Sandy got to her office she found a big bunch of red roses on her desk. She called Angela. "Do you know where these flowers came from?"

"No." Angela replied. "But they do have an envelope on them, I did not want to open it without your permission."

"Oh my" said Sandy. "Max sent them. That is so nice of him."

A few minutes later Sandy's phone rings. "Hi Sandy hope you liked the flowers?"

"They are beautiful but I can't understand why would you send me flowers?"

"To say thank you." Max replied.

"Thank you for what?"

"For not embarrassing me in front of your parents that night. All night I was worried that you might say something. How I was fixing my hair before ringing the bell."

"Oh Max" Sandy replied. You shouldn't have reminded me. Now every time I see you I will laugh."

"If my presence makes you laugh, then I won't have any complaints because you have the most beautiful laugh."

"Ok Max please stop with the formality, I have to go back to work. Thank you for the flowers." Sandy then hung up the phone.

"Wow you have a boyfriend now." Angela said

"Not a boyfriend. He is one of my dad's colleagues. He is bribing me not to embarrass him in front of my parents. Any way I better go for my morning walk."

While Sandy was walking she got to Charlie and found him deep in thought. He did not even hear her when she said. "Good morning Charlie." She goes up to him and physically shakes him. "Where are you Charlie?"

"Oh hi Sandy, Charlie replied I am right here."

"How come you did not reply to my good morning?"

"So sorry did not hear you."

Sandy was stubborn and would not go away without finding out what Charlie was up to, "Come on Charlie, I am not a child. Don't you like your job?"

"It is not that I love the job, Charlie continued, it is that present I gave you."

"Do you want it back? Sandy asked

"No" Not at all."

"Then what?"

"That day after I left here I saw a little blue light in front of me. It was so small but glowing. When I made it to the metro it disappeared but once I sat in the train. Out of nowhere the woman that gave it to me in the first place appeared next to me. She said, "Thank you for handing it to the rightful owner." As soon as I turned to ask her who she is, she had disappeared."

"That's eerie." Sandy said

"Ever since, my mind has been pre occupied. What is all this about? How did that woman know who I gave the present to?"

"Don't think about it. When the right time comes, we will all find out. But it's funny about the blue light because me and my dad have seen it too and we have no idea what it is."

"Do you think that some sort of power has been given to you?" Charlie asked

"Me and power, Sandy replied. Why would I be given powers? I am only a normal simple person."

Charlie then apologises for taking so much of Sandy's time and goes back to work.

At ten o'clock Max calls Sandy again? "I am sorry, but you hang up on me so quickly I didn't get a chance to ask you out for dinner. When I meet you that night I could not take my eyes off you and haven't stopped thinking about you since."

Sandy remembered what her father told her and said, "Max, I don't think it is a good idea."

"Are you rejecting my invitation?"

"No" Sandy replied. "All I am saying is that is not a good idea, because we shouldn't be seen together."

"But why?" Max asked

"My father told us everything the other day. He said I would love to see you and Max get together but it will be dangerous for all of us, if we are seen together. They will know that my father helped you with the business. They will definitely damage both of you."

"What if I promise to take you somewhere where no one would see us?" Max asked

"Let me call you tomorrow." replied Sandy.

That afternoon, the store closed a bit earlier than usual due to some overdue maintenance. Sandy went straight home, had a shower and waited in her bedroom until she heard her father's voice. She then ran to him. "Hi dad" she said

"You are home early." Don implied

"Oh yes, they are doing some maintenance work so we had to close early."

"Let's have a drink then." Don said

Sandy quickly ran and poured a drink for Don and herself. While handing the drink to Don she said, "Dad do you know Max called me today?"

"How is the young man?"

"He sounded good. He asked me out for dinner and I told him it is not possible. But he persisted so I told him I will reply tomorrow."

"Have you decided what your answer is yet?"

"No dad. That is why I thought I will consult with you first. After what you told me the other day, I am worried I don't want the others to turn on you."

"Well we both know that we will definitely suffer in their hands if they find out that I helped Max. But if you like each other I will not stand in your way."

"I will call him tomorrow and tell him I can't go out with him."

"That is purely your decision darling, Don replied. "I am sure a smart man like Max will find a way to convince you."

"But I don't want to cause any problems for anyone."

"You know Max is well aware of all the consequences but he is brave and genuine. I have known him since he was a child. When he likes something he fights for it and never gives up."

"Thanks for the warning, Dad."

"I did not mean it that way Sandy. Max is just like a son to me, I will support you through all your decisions."

"You are the best dad." Sandy replied

They then got interrupted by Donna's voice calling out. "Are you two going to eat or should I start without you." Father and daughter giggled quietly then made their way to the dining table.

The father and daughter made their way to the beautifully prepared dinner table, holding hands and laughing. With a warm smile Donna looked at them and said "Should I feel left out?" They both walked towards her and after a family hug Sandy said. "No Never."

The following morning, more flowers were delivered to Sandy's office. It did not take long after her arrival for the phone to ring, Angela called out. "It's Max do you want to take the call?"

"Sure put him through." replied Sandy.

"Hi Max. Thanks for the flowers. If you send me more flowers I am going to drown in them. There is no more room in my office or the hall way." Sandy said

"Don't worry, I will stop sending you flowers when you agree to have dinner with me."

"That is so unfair Max. Are you black mailing me?"

"Seriously I am not. Just think about it what do you have to lose if you have dinner with me?"

"I actually give up." Sandy replied

"Oh great. I will pick you up around seven tonight."

A beautiful smile was left on Sandy's face when she finished talking to Max thinking oh I have the most beautiful life and now I am going for dinner with a very hot guy.

At the end of her daily routine walk around the store, Sandy told Angela she is going out to get a cup of coffee from the shop across the road. When she made it outside she went straight into her favourite boutique. She bought a pair of white pans, a beautiful royal blue top and classy royal blue shoes. She quickly grabbed the coffee from the coffee shop and dropped her shopping in her car before making her way to the office.

There were a few messages left on her desk. One of them was from Paul the director, requesting a call back.

"Hi, Paul." said Sandy

"Hello Sandy. Thanks for calling back. We wanted to let you know that we will be back there in four weeks' time. So far we are not happy with the opening of the new store but we want to measure the performance of it while we are not here. Can you arrange for all the reports to be ready in the boardroom upon our arrival?"

"Sure, I will do that. Is there anything else?" Sandy asked

"No." We'll see you in four weeks, Sandy."

Sandy puts the phone down and relaxes in her chair. For a second she got worried about the reports but her mind quickly turned to her dinner date.

That afternoon Sandy got home just in time to put her new clothes on and wait for seven o'clock. Her parents were out with some friends. She kept on going in front of the mirror and checking herself, making sure that nothing was out of place.

Finally knock on the door. Sandy's heart started beating. She felt like a teenager that had fallen in love for the first time. She grabs her back but then all these strange feelings attacked her that she was unfamiliar with. As she opened the door, Max just stared at her. "Oh my god. You look amazing." he said. Then he offered his arm to her. With no hesitation Sandy puts her hand on his arm and they walked towards the car. When they arrived at the car, Max opened the door for Sandy and helped her in.

After driving for a little while, Max pulled over and said to Sandy, "Now it is time for you to wear this blindfold and you are not allowed to take it off until I tell you?"

"Why should I wear a blindfold?" Sandy asked

"So you won't ruin my surprise."

Sandy then followed the instruction given to her. Max starts driving again and after twenty minutes the car stopped.

Sandy called out, "Can I take it off now?"

"Not yet? Give me a few more minutes please." He then goes to Sandy's side of the car and says to her I have to carry you from here. Then he grabs her and walks off. After a few minutes he says, "Sandy now I am going to put you on a chair. Please don't look until I say so." Sandy agreed. Max then does something and then he goes to Sandy and removes the blindfold from her eyes.

"Oh my god," Sandy continued, "this is beautiful. How did you find a place like this?"

"I come here often and when you told me that we shouldn't be seen together I thought this will be a great place to have dinner and no one would bother us."

A small table was set in front of a cave under a massive tree, metres away you could hear the sound of the waves reaching the shore. The table was decorated with blue and white table cloth, flowers and so many beautiful candles that lit the entry of the cave.

There was a very small BBQ next to the table ready to be used.

Max grabs the bottle of Champagne and pours two glasses. He hands one to Sandy and says, "Thank you for finally accepting my invitation."

"It is my pleasure," Sandy replied. "But tell me when did you prepare all this?"

"I came prepared, the table and started the BBQ. Then I picked you up. The only thing I had to do when we got here was to light the candles."

Sandy looked at Max, "Thank you for going through all this trouble to have dinner with me. I feel like I am in a story and none of this is true."

While Max was placing the steak on BBQ, Sandy grabbed her glass and started wondering down the hill. The beautiful moon and the sky full of stars had lit the walk way. What a magical view, Sandy said to herself. Luckily she left her shoes behind and was walking bare foot because it did not take long before she arrives at the sandy area of the beach. As she looked across the ocean she could not separate the sea from the sky. They were both dark blue as if they were joined towards the end. She looked up in the sky and every now and then saw a blinking star. She smiled and said, "Even the stars are happy tonight."

Sandy could not believe the magic land she was in; quite yet full of mysterious beauty. She was lost in her own world when she heard, "don't forget the gift as the little ball of blue light went past her." She got scared for a second and ran back towards Max.

"Dinner is served my dear." Max called out when he saw Sandy coming. Sandy made her way back to the table and found her beautifully decorated meal waiting for her.

"I hope you like steak?" Max asked

"I don't mind it every now and then."

Max refilled the glasses of champion. "I am so grateful to your father for bailing me out. He and my father were such good friends, that I always thought your dad was my uncle. Max continued. "I hope he does not mind me taking you out. I just could not help myself since I meet you at your house, I can't get you off my mind."

Sandy went all red in the face. She felt the same from the moment that their eyes locked, but she did not want to say anything that she would regret later, so she decided to change the subject by saying, "thank you for arranging dinner at this heavenly place."

A pleasing smile covered Max's face. "I owned all this before my business went down I am not sure if your dad told you how all my father's business partners turned against me. They pressed so hard so I would sell my business to them at a very low price. This company was run by my grandfather and my father then me. This isn't just a business. This is my memories of my great grandpa, my dad, my grandpa. The family built this and as centuries went by it grew and then the greed took over. All those so called business partners they tried to destroy it, but I was not going to give up so I started selling my assets to carry the losses the company was making and eventually I was running out of money. The night that I meet you was the night that your dad told me how they are trying to push me out of market. Not only didn't your dad accept to help them but he leant me money to try and get my business back.

This land was bought by my childhood friend. This was our hiding spot when we were kids. When he heard that I put it for sale he offered me money to take it off the market but I wasn't about to accept charity from anybody so he purchased it. He knew how much this place meant to me and told me one day I will sell it back to you."

"Wow you don't find friends like that anymore, Sandy said. Then she asked "Can we go to the beach part. I really want to have a better look at it."

When they went to the beach, Sandy looked at the stars and said "I can spend the rest of my life here, counting all these stars.

What a magical place I have never been happier in my life like this moment."

"I felt like that when I first had dinner at your place. I felt like I belonged to something again. You know that I am the only child and since my parents passed away I always have dinner by myself and that night when your father asked me to stay for dinner, I felt so happy but then I saw you. Oh my god, my heart stopped and my eyes betrayed me. They would not look anywhere else apart from your beautiful eyes.

"Well I think we better head back. My parents are probably worried about me. Sandy implied.

"Ok let's go." Max replied

Sandy helped Max pack the table and carried the stuff to his car. When they arrived back to Sandy's house, she said if it wasn't so late, I would have invited you in for coffee but I have an early start tomorrow."

"That's fine." Max said. You can invite me in for coffee next time."

When Sandy opened the door and walked in she saw her dad sitting on the couch. He called out. "Sandy I made hot chocolate would you like to share some?"

"I will sit with you for a minute dad but I had such a big meal that I can't fit anything else in there."

"Anyway Dad how was your night?"

"It was great," Don replied. "How was your night?"

"Max took me to this magical place. Oh dad you should see this place. Never in my life have I thought that you can have heaven on earth."

"Did you see Max?" Don asked

"Oh sorry. He rang me this morning and I could not get out of it and when I came home to tell you, you and mum had already left."

"That's fine, Don said. Max is a very good man; just like his father I am actually glad that you have become friends. But please don't make it public yet because they will destroy both of us."

"Don't worry Dad, Sandy continues "I already explained to Max that we cannot be seen in public together and he fully agrees with you."

"Hope fully when he builds back his business, things will change and you can freely see each other." Don replied.

"Thanks Dad," said Sandy. Then she got up kissed Don's forehead, said goodnight and went to her room. Preparing to go to bed, she remembered the voice. "Don't forget the gift." So she looked for the gift that Charles gave to her and when she found it she placed it next to her back.

The next morning when Sandy arrived at work, she saw a lot of people gathered at the corner of the block next to her building. She walked towards the crowed and asked, "What is happening her?" She then heard someone saying, "I think he is dead" Sandy pushed her way in the crowed and it was the man that day she bought lunch. He looked so pale on the floor. Everyone was standing there without trying to help saying, "he is dead", "he is dead" Sandy quickly checks his pulse. "He is not dead she screamed, please call an ambulance."

Somebody from the crowd screamed. Who is going to pay for ambulance? Sandy screams, "I will but for god sakes call an ambulance. He is a human not a PC for your amusement."

After a few minutes an ambulance arrives. After checking the man everything, seemed okay with him. One of the ambulance crew said. "Maybe he is dehydrated would you grab a drink from that café?"

Sandy didn't wait for others to move she quickly ran to the shop and bought a drink. The ambulance officers grabbed the man and put him in a sitting position. Then they forced some of the drink into his mouth. A few minutes later he opened his eyes and was amazed with everything that was around him.

The ambulance officers asked the man are you feeling better. He said "Yes I am fine."

They then looked at Sandy, "Would you buy him some food?" By the looks of it he has collapsed from hunger. He should be ok after a good feed."

Sandy thanked the ambulance officers and quickly goes back to the cafe and orders some food for the old man. She then went back and kneeled in front of the man, "How long is that you haven't eaten?"

"Four days." The man replied

"But why?" Sandy asked. "Couldn't any one give you any food or money?"

"Don't think everyone thinks and feels like you? I've been kicked, spat at and most disgusting of all was I could hear people saying he is a burden in the community. They should let him die."

Finally the food that Sandy ordered was delivered by a waitress. Sandy collected the food and gave it to the old man "Here eat and don't move from here until I come back." She then turned to the people gathered around and screamed. "How was the movie? Now move away and let the poor man breath. Come on move it. The move is finished.

When she made all those people leave, she ran to her office and checked with Angela to see if she had anything important to do and when she was assured it was her free day, she told Angela, "Call me on my cell if you need me. I have something important to attend to."

The old man had finished his food and was waiting for Sandy, when she got back to him. She said. "I am going to get my car. You should move closer to the road, so you can jump in when I come back."

Sandy picked up her car then the old man. She drove to a very quiet park and stopped. "Please forgive me," she said" but I have to ask. Don't you have anybody?"

"Oh I do but they live in another state, and I lost contact with them. They probably think I am dead or gone for good. I was forced out of my unit when I lost my job. After that I did not have money to rent a house so I threw out all my belongings, apart from the clothes that I am wearing and started living on the street. I was too embarrassed to beg for money so I can call my family."

"Can we call them now?" Sandy asked

"I don't know, although I miss them so much. Maybe they have moved on and now after all these years; I might be a burden on them."

"But you will never know, if you don't give them a chance to know that you are all right."

"But look at me. How can I face them like this, I am dead broke. Just look at me."

"Don't you think if you go back to your family, you can have a new start?"

"Ok. You are right miss."

"I will call them and give them the news of your appearance. That way if there is any rejection, you will not get upset."

"Here is the last number I had from my wife and two daughters and son."

Sandy quickly grabs the number. "Oh I forgot to ask you what your name is."

"Frank, Frank Met."

While laughing Sandy said, "Frank met who?" Then she dialled the number. A woman picks up the phone. "Hi my name is Sandy. You don't know me but I have someone with me that knows you."

The woman asks. "Who is that person?"

"His name is Frank" Sandy replied

The woman screams. "Frank, are you sure? What does he look like?"

"He is a handsome middle aged man." Sandy replied

"You are not planking me are you?" The woman asked.

"No. Seriously if you are ready to hear his voice, I will put him on." She then puts the speaker on and asks Frank to say hello.

"Hello" said Frank

The woman on the other side of the phone started screaming. "Girls come here your dad is on the phone.""Oh hi Frank"

"Hi Kate How are you?"

"Oh Frank it is really you. We listed you on the missing person's bulletin. Every day and night I pray to God that you would come back to us in one piece."

"I am so sorry if I caused you all that pain." Frank replied

"Don't worry. Are you coming home?"

Before Frank could answer the question he heard the girls. "Is that really Dad? Where has he been?"

"It does not matter where he was until now. It matters that he is coming home alive." Kate replied.

Tears were pouring out of Frank and Sandy. Frank then says. "Yes I am coming home if you would still accept me."

"What kind of question is that, Kate asked. This is our home."

"I will come back in the next few days. There are a few things I have to do first."Frank continued. "Thanks to this young lady that helped me find you again."

"Bring her with you so we can repay her for her good deed."Kate said.

When the phone call was finished Frank turned to Sandy. "I don't know how to thank you."

"I haven't done anything yet." How old are your daughters." Thirteen and fifteen

Sandy then drives to a motel. She books a room for Frank and says to him. Have a shower and shave that beard which makes you look really old, and give me all the clothes you have on before you go in shower."

Frank pushes the clothes out of the bathroom; Sandy grabs them and goes back to work. That day she never did her routine walk. Instead she checked all her mail and replied to all emails and phone messages.

She then calls Angela and gives her some money. "Can you please find a few sets of clothes that are the size of these clothes?"

Angela takes the money and walks off. After an hour she comes back with a suite and a few sets of pants and shirts, socks and underwear. Sandy checked them and complemented Angela on her good taste. She then books a flight for Frank on the internet and then goes out for lunch. Instead of eating lunch she went and bought a brief case, perfumes ladies bags and put them in her car.

When Sandy finished work that afternoon she went straight to the hotel. She gave all the clothes to Frank and showed him the gifts for his daughters and wife. He was startled for a moment then he said, "Why are you doing all this? I don't know when I can pay you back?"

"I didn't ask you to pay me back. My reward is getting, a family back together and see them happy again."

"I will pay you back and if anything happens that I can't, then I hope God rewards you for all your good deeds."

Sandy looked at Frank and started laughing. "My god all that beautiful body and face were hidden behind that long beard and dirty clothes. Look at you, you look so handsome."

"I really don't know how to thank you." Frank said

"There is something you can do for me." Sandy replied

"Whatever, you want."

Sandy then reaches to her wallet and says. "Here take this money. It should last you a while until you find yourself a job. Go pick-up where you left with your family and be happy." She then grabs her bag and says good bye.

The next morning Sandy wanted to make sure that Frank, was going home. She waited outside the hotel. She saw a cab picking Frank up. She followed the cab to the airport and waited around until the plane flew away.

With a smile on her face Sandy went back home to have breakfast with her parents.

Chapter 9

It did not take long for Michael to notice the change in Max's business. He called a meeting with, Angelo, Colin and a few other high ranking businessmen that were their friends.

When the meeting opened, Michael addressed Angelo, "I thought you had taken care of Max."

"We all did" Angelo replied. Apart from Don, I went to see him and explained our plan but he didn't welcome me and the meeting ended up in a disaster."

"So what is happening?" Colin asked

"You know how we tried to push Max's business down so we could buy it at lower price? Well we did a good job. He sold all his assets in order to keep the business going. When he ran out of money we were all ready to take over but in some mysterious way his business has picked-up." Michael replied

"I wonder if Don had anything to do with it." Michael implied

"It doesn't matter. We have to come up with another idea to own Max's business. Can you imagine the profits we would make from it? We can sell to ourselves at lower price and call back all those who we stopped dealing with Max." Said another

"Why can't we just leave him alone? He always supplied us with the best products at the lower prices. So I cannot see a reason to force him out of business."Colin said

"Our costs will go down by eighty percent and our profits will be more than you can imagine, if we could just force him to sell." Angelo implied

Colin was not very impressed about what he was hearing. Just like Don, he was scared that all those so called good friends would turn against him and that meant they would kill his business in no time.

"How about if we try to find out what Max's secret is first?" Michael said

Angelo quickly replied, "I will try to pay one of his closest production managers in return for some information."

"I will go and have coffee with Don to find out if he knows anything, Michael continued. We will meet the same time next week to see what information we all have gathered."

Next morning Michael rang Don. "Where have you been?" he asked Don.

"I am where I always am," Don replied

"Do you think we can get together to have a cup of coffee?" Michael asked

"Of course" Don replied. Unless if you want to come to my office?"

"Yes, I think we will have the coffee in your office. I want to see if you made any changes there." Michael replied

When Michael arrived at Don's work he noticed a beautiful woman. Men like him always thought that they can buy anything they want.

Don welcomed Michael to his office. He had already asked his staff to prepare coffee and snacks in the conference room.

"So tell me Don how have you been?"

"Great Michael. How about you?"

"I have been good." Michael continued, "What was that young man's name, the one that his dad was your friend?"

"I am not sure who you are referring to." Don replied

"His name was Max I believe." Michael said

"Oh Max. I haven't seen him for a while. Hope he is doing well."

The last I heard he was about to sell his business, but yesterday I was told he is not selling anymore." Michael implied

"Never heard of such a thing. That business has been running for over a hundred years. I hope he never sells because the business was built by his father and grandfather. It means more than just a business."

Michael went quite for a minute knowing that Don will not spill any information. He said. "Me too." The wheels might have turned around for him." Who is that beautiful woman that directed me to your office?" Michael asked

"That is Nancy one of my staff. She only is covering for my PA while she is recovering from an operation."

"Oh my god. I have never seen such a beauty." Michael said

"Let's go and have lunch." Don continued. We can catch up on other things while we eat."

Michael agreed. They went to a restaurant close to Don's work. There they met Colin. Michael invited him to have lunch with them but he made an excuse and walked away.

During lunch there was no more mention of Max and his business, Michael was scared that if he asks more questions, Don will be suspicious.

After a few drinks and a beautiful lunch Michael and Don departed, Don never trusted any of those high raking business men, but he was wondering about Colin and how he made the excuse to get away from them.

Angelo had gone and waited behind Max's business right at the back where the workers use to get out. He saw a sick looking person walking out. He quickly recognized him. He was the top operations manager of Max's manufacturing company.

He runs towards him "Hi Daniel. How are you doing?"

"I was fine before you showed your face." Daniel replied

"Come on. What is wrong with you? I saw you from my car and just wanted to say hi." Angelo said

"That is very strange, Daniel continued, what are you after Angelo? If you didn't want something you wouldn't hang around here. How funny you are pretending to be a friend of mine."

"I thought we were friends. Angelo said. I want to make you an offer which I don't think you will reject. I will make you so rich if you tell me what Max is up to and where he got the extra money from to rebuild his business."

"You are pathetic. Daniel retorted. Why can't you just leave us alone? Are you not the guy that stopped all our orders and almost send this company into bankruptcy? It was you and your partners that almost put all of us out of jobs. Now you can take your money with you and get lost."

Angelo did not like to be treated like this and said, "Daniel I will make you sorry for talking to me like this." Then he walked away.

Going straight to Max, Daniel told him about his encounter with Angelo. Max got worried for a second then he said "Don't worry Daniel, as long as we all stick together they cannot conquer us."

The week went by pretty slowly for the greedy directors as none of them had any good news to share apart from Colin. He was like Don. Minded his own business and never tried to ruin someone for his own gains.

Angelo was furious when the meeting opened. "Do you all know how I got treated by that operations manager? He called me pathetic."

"Well I can't blame him. He almost lost his job because of the pressure we put on Max." Colin implied

Michael with anger looked at Colin. "Don't tell me you have a change of heart."

"I never agreed to this in the first place, Colin stated. "I mean what else do we want? We are all so wealthy and the profits that we are making should be enough for three hundred years. Why do we need to keep on forcing our friends out of business so we can own their shares of market?"

The other directors went quiet and changed the subject. It got around lunch time Colin went to arrange for lunch. While he was away the others decided that Colin should not know about everything that they do. As one of those directors said, "By the looks of it Colin has got the cold feet. We should not tell him of our plans as he might use them against us."

When Colin came back to board room he found that everyone's attitude has changed. They are telling jokes and laughing. He knew straight away that he has been placed on the firing line as well, but he went along with them and laughed with them at the so not funny jokes they were telling.

When Colin got home that afternoon he seemed so depressed, Collette his wife asked him what was wrong with him, but he was too ashamed to say anything. Instead he asked "Have you seen or talked to Donna at all?"

"Not since our anniversary. Collette replied. "I meant to call her because not only did they not seem happy that night but they left very early."

"How about paying them a visit?" Colin continued. "Why don't you call them and see if they are free for us to pay them a visit."

After agreeing with her husband Collet makes the phone call. Donna was so excited to hear from her that she said if you haven't had dinner please come and eat with us. Collet agreed to have dinner with them.

An hour later Colin and Collet arrived for dinner, Don and Donna were so pleased to see their friends plus every time someone came over to have dinner with them made them so happy.

At dining table Don notices the sad look at Colin's face and asks him if everything is ok? Colin was not sure if Don was like Michael and Angelo so he hesitated to say anything. Then he asked. "How come you were not at the meetings past two weeks?"

"I was not told about any meetings." Don replied

"I thought that you were very close to Michael and Angelo." Colin implied

"God forbid. I don't want to be a part of their evil blood sucking schemes." Don responded

"What happened?" Colin asked

"How much wealth dose a human wants to gain? These people are never going to have enough. I have been witness to all their evil doings." Don replied

"Did you have a visit from Michael?" Colin enquires

"How did you know?" Don asked

"Well last week's meeting they made all this arrangements to find out why Max is not ready to sell his business, Michael was to come to you and find out whatever you knew about Max. Angelo went and tried to bribe Max's production manager. Colin replied

"When will these people stop? I am surprised that there was a mention of me because when Angelo came and ask me to withdraw all my orders from Max, it turned really nasty between us. I even got warned by him."

"Sorry Don. I didn't know they didn't say anything to me, plus now that I refused to be a part of their scheme towards Max. They don't discuss anything in front of me."

"Don't worry Colin. Every dog has his day. Just watch yourself because we will never know when they will turn on us."

"I just don't want to be a part of their scheming; Colin added. I worked hard. Now want to enjoy my family and friends without worrying who has what or who does what. Don you were always different from them. That's why me and Collet always like being around you and Donna."

With a pleasing smile Donna Said, "About time you two mentioned me and Collette."

They all had a good laugh. After dinner the guys offered to clean the table and make coffee. Donna and Collet went to the guest room where they sat on the couch. Collette said. "This is so nice. It feels like home. You know a few times Angelo and Mitchell invited us for dinner I hated every moment of it. They have all these servants who constantly got told off in front of us."

"I know "Donna said. "I made it clear to Don that if he ever accepts a dinner invitation from them he has to go alone, because I refuse to be anywhere near them. Thank God finally Don stood up to Angelo and got rid of him from our lives. We have more time to attend to activities that gives us joy."

"What kind of activities?" Collette asked.

"I am involved in a few groups. We help those less fortunate than us." Donna replied

"That sounds so satisfying; I always wanted to be involved in something like that. Me and Colin often go to poor areas with food blankets and drinks and give them to those homeless people that we find sleeping on the streets."

"We didn't know you guys would do something like that." Donna said

"You know how judgmental everyone in our group was. We would have been crucified if the others found out."

"Well Collette, I and Don do similar things. We never mentioned anything because our policy is to do good but never mention it. Sometimes we don't even tell each other who we are helping, unless if we get to situations where we require each other's help."

"Somehow I knew you are the type." Collette continued. "I even saw your daughter Sandy having lunch with a homeless man. That was the best view I ever had."

"Here you go ladies. Coffee and sweets." Don and Colin walked in.

While Colin was carrying the tray with coffee cups, his eyes wondered. When the others followed his look, they noticed the little blue gluing bowl disappearing.

"What was that?" Colin asked

"Some sort of spirit."Collette replied.

"It's probably reflection of something. "Donna implied. But both Donna and Don knew that there is a secret to that blue light. It would only appear when certain people are around.

"Collette and Colin you should do this more often. It is so nice to have friends like you around." Don Said

"Now that we decided to live comfortably and cut off all those who stressed us out of our lives. We would love to spend more time with you." Colin said

The two couples then shared some funny memories and laughed. They had so much fun that none of them wanted to depart, but eventually Collette said. "Colin we better start moving".

After saying good night they departed. Colin and Collette went to their car.

Don and Donna went straight to bed.

Chapter 10

Jasmine and Jackie are still up to their evil plans. After lengthy discussions between the two of them they call their brothers and tell them, "We should surprise Dad and Mum." When asked how? They replied by saying, "All of us showing up at their front door on Sunday."

When all the brothers and sisters agreed to meet on Sunday, Jasmine's evil personality showed in her evil smile.

She said "You know Jackie, the last time me and my husband went to Mum's place, I noticed something antic in Sandy's room. It looked like a dagger but I doubt that it was. I tried to get my hands on it, but Mum showed up in front of me and quickly closed the door. I asked her what it was and she said it is a special gift that was given to Sandy. I begged her to let me see it. She refused to go in the room. She said when your sister gets home you can ask her to show it to you. But you know I would never ask Sandy for anything."

"What does that have to do with anything?" Jackie implied

"Well I am sure that gift is of some value. On Sunday when everyone is busy, I will try to take it from her room. Jasmine replied

"I still think that is not right." Jackie said

On Sunday all brothers and sisters arrive at the same time as planned. When they rang the bell, a strange voice said, "I will get it." When the door opened they all gazed in. Jasmine called out "Who are you?"

"I am Max. Everybody was busy in the back yard. That is why I offered to open the door. Please come in." He said.

The smell of BBQ filled the entire house when they walked in. The kids quickly ran into the backyard and cuddled their grandparents. They were followed by their parents.

Joshua seemed so disappointed and said. "You guys were having a party without us?"

Looking straight at his son, Don replied. "It wasn't planned. Max came to drop something urgent for me. While me and him were discussing something, your mum and sister started the BBQ because they were bored. I asked Max to stay and have lunch with us."

"We better leave and let you have fun. Sorry we arrived at a bad time." Jason Said.

"Everyone you know, your mother well. She still thinks you are all kids. Just come and have a look at all the food, Don continued. Did she know you were coming?"

"No Dad. We thought we would surprise you." Jackie said

"That's great. Grab your drinks and come back out. It is such a blessing that you all came." Don Said

Donna and Sandy quickly brought more meat out. They were so excited that their quiet Sunday turned to such a big gathering.

"Oh mum this is so pleasant." Sandy called out to Donna.

While everybody was drinking and munching, Jasmine sneaked in and went straight to Sandy's bedroom. The gift was still in the same place. She tries to pick it up but can't do so. It is as if it was glued to the dressing table. Jasmine tries so hard. She even goes and picks a knife to loosen it but the gift is not moving and somehow Jasmin gets pushed on the floor. The nasty fall hurts her foot. It is not long before she hears her husband Adam, calling her. She quickly goes out and says. "Sorry I had to go to bathroom."

Adam notices that his wife is limping and asks what happened?

"Nothing" Jasmine replied. "I slipped in the bathroom."

Jason tries to have a conversation with Max, by saying "Max I heard your business is doing really badly."

Don overhears the question and starts panicking. He looked at Max with a question mark.

But Max being a very smart and madly in love man he replies. "I don't know where you heard that because my new products are running out of the door. We are so busy that we even ran production on Sundays."

Jason did not like what he heard. He had an odd smile on.

Max excused himself and went to Sandy "MY GOD YOU LOOK SO STUNNING."

"Cut the crap." Sandy replied

"I am serious." Max said

Jason and Joshua were staring at Sandy and Max and did not like what they were seeing. Jackie noticed the unhappy faces of their brothers and said, "How funny. The stranger feels more at home than the children of the house."

"Being so offended by what he heard" Don said, "There are no strangers here. You are all my children."

Sandy tried to ease the situation by saying, "Come everyone. Let's drink to mum and dad for having such a great family."

But no one picked their glasses. Max who was the only one with his glass up waiting to cheer the parents, felt so uncomfortable, that he put his glass down and said. "I better leave."

Don noticed how offended Max was and said. "Son please don't go yet."

"You promised you would play the water game with us." Sandy implied.

"Ok I will stay and play the game." Said Max

It wasn't long before they finished eating. They started playing a few games but Max during all that time, felt the tension.

When the water game started, Sandy and Don had hidden water balloons everywhere, under chairs, tables, garden and surrounding areas. When they saw the tension, they winked at each other. Sandy grabs the first water balloon and throws it at Donna, then Don at her and so on. It got to a point when everyone was looking for water balloons and throwing them without prejudice.

At some stage without any pre meditation Sandy, threw a water balloon at Jasmine. She got so angry and said. "You idiot. Why did you do that? Having your presents glued to your dressing table shows how smart you are."

Max and Sandy stopped and just stared at Jasmine; Max then said," I really have to leave." and excused himself and left.

Sandy came back to Jasmin after seeing Max off. "Jasmin what was all that about?"

"You should know. Jasmine continued. Which idiot would glue things to their dressing table?"

"What glue?" What are you talking about?" Sandy asked

Then the gift was mentioned and Sandy said "Why would I glue it? Come with me. You will see that nothing in my room is glued to anything," She then invited everyone to witness her incense.

When all the family got to Sandy's bedroom, Jasmine again tried to pick up the gift and this time she was able to do so. As soon as she picked up the gift it went black and dark stuff started to flow out of it, Jasmine screamed, "See I knew you are a freak."

Surprised by the event Sandy grabs the gift but in her hand it turns in to a glowing blue light. Don looks at his daughter with unbelief and says, "Oh Sandy that looks like that ball of light that has been appearing."

"Are you kidding me?" Jackie implied

"Is this something to impress us?" Cindy said. "Because it really isn't funny."

Sandy looked at her parents and said. "I really don't know what happened there."

It didn't take long before Donna answered her back. "Remember darling special gift for special person."

Jasmin got offended and said. "What do you mean by that? It's only a dagger."

"Are you sure?" Asked Sandy, "We don't know what it is."

"Don't pretend to be an angle." Jasmine implied.

"I am not pretending," sandy replied. "Honestly when it was given to me, I brought it to Mum and Dad to see if they know what it is. None of us knew what it is."

"It's some sort of black magic." Cindy suggested.

Don who was getting frustrated with all the comments said. "Ok that's enough. Let's go and have a coffee. None of you were asked to walk in someone's room without their permission and touch their stuff."

At hearing what her father said Jasmine started crying. "I will never come here again. It seems that we are not welcomed." She then grabbed her bag and asked Adam to grab the kids.

"What is wrong with you Jasmine? We were all having a good time." Donna continued. None of us know what that thing is."

"If you didn't go searching in the bedrooms none of this would have happened."

"I am leaving anyway. So you can blame me as much as you want." Jasmine replied.

It did not take long for the others to excuse themselves and follow Jasmin. Adam was driving the car going home. Jasmin was still in shock and trying to make sense of what just happened. Her emotions were so unclear. Sad? Confused? Scared? Yet her evil side was still trying to come up with a story to make everyone feel sorry for her.

Adam pulls over into their drive way and takes the kids inside. It is not long before the other cars pulled over at their drive way.

Adam invited all of them in and offered them drinks but it seemed that they also were still in shock.

The silent got broken when Jasmine said. "I always told everyone how freaky Sandy is but no one believed me that she is into black magic? If she is, who is she using it on?"

"I think that was just to scare us off. She is making sure we keep our distance from our parents. It is all about their estate. Jason continued. "Can't you see what she is up to? Jasmine, the reaction you showed, made Sandy feel more powerful because it created tension between you and dad."

"But you all saw how scary everything was. I can't believe that Dad did not question Sandy." Jasmine cried out.

"Seriously people" Adam said. "It was you guys that have been going there with evil intentions. Think twice before you carry on like this. You all should know evil brings evil. Jasmine, why can't you admit for once to your wrong doing? Why would you even go to someone's bedroom and touch their stuff without their permission."

"Shut up" Screamed Jasmine. "No one was talking to you Adam. Evil intentions are you serious? We are only trying to protect what rightfully is ours."

Adam quietly left the room and tension took his place. Jasmine quickly said, "Don't worry. We have an understanding. Never to get involved in each other's family matters. "

"Now that we are all here today there is something that has been annoying me." Jason continued after a small pause. "A few days ago, I was at a business lunch when I met with Angelo. He sounded very concerned and asked me if I knew how Max was able to protect his business when it was already in the gutter. I told him that none of us has much to do with Max but Angelo reckons that Dad might have helped him financially."

"Why does any of that concern us? Why can't Angelo ask dad?" Joshua asked.

"Because last time they met, things got really ugly between them. Dad forced Angelo out of his office and Angelo frightened dad."

"Somehow we have to find out." Cindy implied

Being very quiet listening to everything that was said, Jackie called out. "Did you see the way Max and Sandy were looking at each other? I am definite something is going on between them."

"Dad and Max's dad were very close friends and dad always treated Max like his own son." Joshua said.

"Angelo is a very powerful man. He takes what he wants and destroys anything that stands in his way. He has been after that business long before Max's dad died. If Dad really helped Max, he will be Angelo's next target and that means we all lose." Jason implied.

"It is not an easy issue to start a conversation with Dad. He will be suspicious, and how are we going to find out?" Joshua asked.

Remember that it was us that didn't want to be involved in Dad's business, although many times he told us we should be working for the family business but for some reason we all rejected his pleads?" Jason responded.

"Well it is not too late. Maybe one of you two brothers should work with Dad. That way you can gain as much information as you can. Said Jackie

"I diffidently can't, because if I go Mandy can't run our business by herself, and I don't want to lose my business because that is my joy. Said Jason. "What about you girls. One of you can go for a PA job with dad."

"Well I am never in his good books." Jasmine said "Maybe Jackie can."

"No you know what? I will do it myself." Joshua cried out.

"Angelo gave me his card and asked me to call him and let him know what we do." Said Jason.

"Call him and tell him we are trying to find out, but don't tell him of our plan. Ask him to give us a few weeks." Jasmine implied.

Based on their discussion Joshua decided to take three months off his work to fulfil their evil plan.

It was around eleven pm when everybody left Jasmine's house. She was surprised when she found Adam sleeping in boys room, Adam was a very nice man. Polite, quiet in general just an average family man. He let Jasmine wear the pants from the beginning of their marriage but at this very moment Jasmine felt the heat. Her husband for the first time is not sleeping in their bed.

The next morning Adam wakes the kids up and prepares them for school, Jasmin was as usual still in bed but that very morning she decided to go and say good morning to everyone before they left the house. She gets down with a smile.

"Good morning everyone" she said while trying to place a kiss on Adam's face, but Adam pulled himself away while saying. "Come on kids lets go."

Jasmin looked at him with disbelieve. "Is something wrong?" She asked

"You should know better." Adam replied.

"Don't you dare walk away from me, Adam?"

"What are you going to do? Call your family."

"Talk to me. What is wrong?"

"I do not know you anymore. I married that sweet young lady that wouldn't even harm an ant and now she has become a greedy evil and selfish person."

"How dare you talk to me that way?"

"We are late" Adam said as he slams the door on his way out.

Jasmine opened the door to scream at him but was dysfunctional after seeing the same blue light around Adam and his car. What is that? Then she walked back in and went back to bed hoping that by the time Adam comes back home everything will be back to normal.

<h1 style="text-align:center">Chapter 11</h1>

Don and Donna were heartbroken. What started like a beautiful Sunday end up in a disaster?

That night when Don went to bed he said. "You know Donna may be that is really a special gift. Did you see how scary it looked in Jasmin's hand? I think it was reflecting the true Jasmine. When Sandy grabbed it, it looked so beautiful just like her."

"Now we know that blue light has to do with that gift." Donna said

"I wish we could somehow find out more about it." Don Said

In the meantime Sandy was crying in her bedroom. Finally she thought she is going to have a break with her brothers and sisters. As usual it turned to be just another nasty gathering."

In the morning at breakfast table Don noticed Sandy's puffed eyes. He said. "Have you been crying?"

"No Dad" Sandy replied. " I was thinking to give the gift back to Charlie. Maybe he can give it to someone else."

"That is entirely your choice." Don replied. "But your mum was saying, there is a man that knows a lot about this ancient stuff. If you like, me and her can show it to him before you give it back."

"I don't mind Dad. Do that."

"Ok darling. You will be late for work. We will have some answers by tonight." Don said.

When Sandy left, Don said. "Come on Donna. Hurry up. Let's take it to the man.

When they got there, the shop was full of old books and old ancient stuff everywhere. An old man walked towards them and asked, "Can I help you?"

"Oh hello" Donna said. "We have something that was given to our daughter as a gift. We have no idea what it is but it looks ancient."

"Let me have a look" the old man said. When he laid eyes on the gift he was amazed. He quickly went to the back of the shop looking for something. A few minutes later he came back with a book that looked hundreds of years old. He opened the book and looked for a page. Then he said to Don and Donna. "Look this gift is thousands of years old I can't tell you what it is but it definitely is a gift. There was a legend that there were only three of these and every few centuries, somehow they reappear. And when they do appear, they have to be given to the rightful owners in that particular century. Only those who receive it know what the gift is. They are never allowed to reveal the secret of any of those three gifts."

"But my daughter doesn't know what it is." Don called out.

"I know" the old man, replied. "But who gave it to your daughter?"

"A man that she helped one day. He came and gave her the gift. It was given to him by another woman that told him, to make sure you give it to the right person." Donna said.

"So your daughter is rightful owner." The old man continued. She is being watched at the moment and when it is time, the gift will reveal its secret."

"Can she give the present back to the man that gave it to her in the first place?" Don asked.

"Unfortunately from what this book says only those who are chosen will receive it. Even if she gives it back, the gift will find its way back to your daughter."

"Why then it turned black in my other daughters hand and black stuff started coming out of it?" Donna asked.

"It is said that the gift destroys its physical body in the hands of evil, then it appears again in the hands of the right full owner." Old man replied.

"Is there anything more you can tell us?" Don asked

"I do not want to scare you but, those who receive this gifts go through so much heart ache and suffering until they are made strong enough to handle the gift."

"What do you mean by suffering?" Donna asked

"There is nothing more I can tell you." the old man said. "But your daughter must be a special person to receive this gift."

The couple thanked the old man and walked out of the shop quietly. There was a café across the road. They sat there and tried to make some sense of what they just heard but couldn't do so. Instead they decided to take the gift to Sandy's office, so she can return it to Charlie.

Once the parents brought the gift back, Sandy quickly grabbed it and ran to Charlie.

Don was very worried about his daughter. He said. "Donna, when we are gone what will happen to Sandy? Look at her brothers and sisters. It feels like they think she is their step sister and now this gift. What if she is the rightful owner?"

"You saw with your own eyes that Sandy gave it back to Charlie. He was a bit offended. He took it anyway." Donna replied.

"I know. But something is bothering me and I don't know what it is." Don said

"Would it make you happy if we pay a visit to our sons and daughters to make sure everything is ok? If you like, we can start from tomorrow."

"I think we should do that." Don replied

The couple got back home just a bit after lunch. None of them were in a mood to discuss anything anymore as if they each got lost in a different space. Donna broke the silence by saying. "I think I will have a nap before I start preparing dinner." Don agreed and they each went to a different room and laid down.

The house that was always full of love and blessings was so different. Everything seemed dull and sad.

At around five, Pm, Donna forced herself out of bed knowing that Don went to bed without having lunch. When she got to the kitchen she saw Don in deep thought sitting on a chair so deep in thoughts that he did not hear Donna coming in.

"How long you've been up Don?"

"Not long."

"Are you hungry?"

"Not hungry but I think I will have a drink. Would you join me for a drink?"

"Certainly sir. Thanks for the offer." All Donna was doing was trying to cheer her husband up and if it made him feel better she would have the drink with him while preparing dinner.

It was around six thirty when Sandy got home. Don called out. "Do you want to join us for a drink?"

"I will join you as soon as I get changed." Sandy replied.

Sandy got changed quickly. When she was about to leave her room she screamed, "Guys this is really not funny. Why would you do this to me?"

"We only asked you to join us for a drink and we haven't done anything to upset you." Don replied.

When he heard Sandy crying, he rushed to her room and found her sitting on the floor with the gift in her hands. She asked. "When did you take it back from Charlie dad?"

Instead of answering the question he called out, "Donna for god's sake come here for a second."

Knowing her husband never screams, Donna rushed to Sandy's room but even she froze when she saw the gift. She shouted. "Sandy why did you take it back from Charlie."

"But I didn't." Sandy cried out.

"If you didn't take it from Charlie how in the hell it got back here again?" Don asked. However he remembered what the old man said. "Even if she gives it away it will find its way back to your daughter."

Sandy grabs her phone and rings Charlie. "How did you put the gift back in my room?"

"It is still in my back pack. Maybe that's another one."

Sandy cried out." That is the very same one."

Charlie while grabbing his bag, said. I put it straight in my bag as soon as you returned it. If you want I will show it to you tomorrow. When he opened the bag the gift was not there. He went so quite not knowing what to say.

"What happened to you?" Sandy asked

"I swear from the time I put the gift in my bag, no one has opened it. Now that I did the gift is not there."

Sandy started crying even harder thinking that everybody was in on this. All of a sudden the blue light appeared again for a few seconds then it disappeared.

Everyone was quite for a few seconds, and then Don said. "Come on Sandy. Clean yourself up and have a drink with me."

"Ok Dad."

While Sandy was washing up, Don consulted with Donna to see if he should tell Sandy about their visit to the old man and it was agreed to tell her.

Don put a double shot of Scotch with ice in a crystal glass for Sandy and waited for her. When she arrived Donna came and joined them.

"Dad how do you think the gift was back in my room?"

"Well sweetheart me and your mum did take the gift to that old man. He told us if you are the rightful owner of the gift, even if you give it away it will find its way back to you."

"How can I be rightful owner of something, that none of us knows what it is?"

"Apparently they reappear every few centuries and no one knows their secrets apart from the people that are rightful owners."

"But what is it?"

"We were told it is a gift and it will reveal itself to the rightful owner after some trial times."

"What trials?"

"He could not answer those questions for us but me and your mum think that the light is blue. When it is close to pure people like yourself. Yesterdays you yourself saw how it turned black and ugly in Jasmine's hand and all that black stuff started coming out of it. The man told us that happens when someone evil touches the gift.

"So I can never get rid of it?"

"Unfortunately, no"

"Mum, is Dad playing with my mind or is he serious?"

"He is telling you exactly what the old man told us. He also showed us the book which looked hundreds of years old which contained the picture of the three gifts. They all look exactly the same but over centuries no one has been able to find out what each gift represents."

"I shouldn't have accepted it in the first place."

"That wouldn't have made any difference. The light we have been seeing is connected to the gift. No matter what it would have found its way to you."

"What am I going to do?"

"Nothing" Don replied. "Just wait and don't think about it until it reveals itself to you."

"Ok Dad. I think I need another shot of what you poured earlier."

"Me too." Don said, "Donna isn't it your turn to pour the drinks?"

"Off course darling, but don't complain if the dinner is not nice because I am getting drunk."

The three of them relaxed with another round of alcohol.

At dinner Don asked Sandy. "Have you heard from Max today? I felt so bad when they treated him so badly yesterday."

"Oh yes. I called and apologized on behalf of my brothers and sisters."

"You are one smart cookie." Don said, with a smile on his face.

The next morning Donna and Don went their own way but they were both looking for the same answers. They were investigating more through library sources. Finding out more about the gift was their mission.

At around lunch time Nancy came into Don's office and told him that Joshua was looking for him as soon as she left the office someone knocked on the door. "Come in" said Don.

Carlos the operations manager opens the door and enters. "Take a sit Carlos my friend" Don continued, "It's been a long time since me and you had a drink together." Don then grabs the bottle of brandy and pours two glasses, handing one to Carlos before he sits back in his chair. "Is everything ok?" He asked

Unusually sad looking Carlos looked at Don. "Everything is fine." he said

"Why the sad face then?"

Carlos sculls the brandy without saying anything.

"Oh boy" said Don. "By the looks of it something is bothering you. He then poured another drink for Carlos.

After a small pause Carlos said. "I am really sorry." while handing an envelope to Don.

"What is this?"

"Maybe you should open it when I leave your office."

"No. Please you have me worried. Wait."

"I really would appreciate it if you would excuse me."

"I can't let you go like this. I can see that something is terribly wrong with you today." He then opens the envelope and to his surprise it was Carlos's resignation.

Don got very sad. It was his turn to scull his brandy and go for another one. Then he sits back in his chair.

"Why?" he asked. "We have been close friends all our lives. I never question your work or dealings because I have put all my trust in you, Is it money?"

"No, Not at all" Carlos replied.

"What is it then? Has anyone done something to hurt you so much that you want to resign?"

"Please don't ask me any more questions. My reasons are personal, and have nothing to do with you or my job."

"I refuse to accept you resignation."

"Well old friend I will leave with or without your acceptance. Please Don, don't make this hard on me, like you just said we have been friends for a long time. Let's at least keep our friendship."

"It is going to be so hard to let go of you. You alone know all the things we went through to keep this company, and you are the only one I trust."

"I know and again I am very sorry. May be in due time you will find someone better than me."

"I can see that you want to finish by next week. That only gives me a few days to find someone."

"I will do my best to stay until you find someone."

"That will be appreciated"

"Ok I better go back to work." Carlos said

"Don't worry about work. Let's have another drink and go out for lunch."

After the drinks Don and Carlos went out for lunch. Don was very sad but didn't want o put Carlos in an acquitted situation. They spent a few hours together sharing old memories. Although at times they might have been sad at that moment they seemed so funny.

When they got back to the office, Nancy again told Don. "Joshua was here looking for you."

"I will call him when I get home." replied Don

That afternoon when Don arrived home he called Donna. "You know Joshua has called the office. In the afternoon when I was out with Carlos, he went to the office. Do you know what that is all about?"

"No" You better call him in case if something is wrong. It is not like Joshua to call and drop in unannounced." Donna replied

"What a day I had. After twenty years Carlos came and put his resignation in today. He looked so down as if he was forced to do it, I asked him for a reason but he told me to just accept the resignation."

"I am so sorry." Donna said. "What will happen now?"

"Just have to hire someone else." But these days who can you trust with the business secrets."

"Go get changed, I think we both can do with a drink."

While Don was changing the phone rang "Hi mum."

"Hi Josh is everything ok? Your dad said you were looking for him."

"Oh yes. Everything is fine. I just need to talk to him. If he is in now I will drop in."

"Yes. He is home" Donna said

An hour after the phone call Joshua arrives. Don opens the door and invites him in. "Is everything Ok?" Don asked

"Yes Dad"

"Something must be very urgent that you couldn't wait for my return phone call."

"Well Dad you know how you always wanted your children to be involved in the business and learn all the aspects of it, well I've been thinking maybe it is time for me to do that. Not only I will be able to spend more time with you but if anything goes wrong we can run the business for you."

"What? Give up your CEO position to work for me?" Don implied.

"I want to work for the family business."

"You know we can't afford to pay you as much?"

"I have already built my life and got so many assets, so will be happy to get whatever you pay me."

"How did this come about? I tried for so many years to get you and your brother involved but you two always rejected my proposition."

"Back then we were young and thoughtless. We needed to make our own achievements."

"Have you already resigned from your job?" Don asked

"No" I wanted to talk to you first. What do you say?"

"Well we don't have any positions open yet and we don't want to fire anyone. Give me a few weeks to see what comes up."

"Ok Dad" Said Josh.

Suddenly black smoke came through the room. "Is something burning?" Josh asked

"No" Donna replied

"Then where did this ball of smoke come from?"

Donna and Don looked at each other before saying. "What smoke? What are you talking about?"

To ease the situation Donna gets up and says. "Me and your dad were about to have a drink. Would you like to join us?"

"No mum. Thanks. I better go home before they send the search party."

"Josh left and Don got buried in thoughts. He felt something was very wrong but didn't know what. He called out, "Donna don't you find it strange that Carlos resigns on the same day that Josh asks for a job? And did you see that ball of black smoke? Every time someone evil is around that appears."

"Why is everything suspicious for you? We both know how much you wanted our kids to be involved in running the business."

But these days everything is different. Look at the way they treat their sister apart from Sandy. It has always been about money. Josh talked about achievement. We bought their houses. We looked after their finances until they were financially secured. Look at Sandy. We never did anything for her. She even worked and paid for her own school and uni."

"I know, but maybe finally these kids have some sense about themselves."

"I truly hope that is the case and not the influence of the outsiders."

"Didn't you just say Carlos resigned? Why don't you give that position to Josh?"

"I wish it was that easy. An operation manager is the heart of company. If he leaks any information out we will be in deep trouble."

"For God's sake Don, finish your drink and stop being so negative."

The next morning Don calls Carlos to his office and tells him how Josh wants to work there. "Please Carlos, if you know anything that I don't please tell me."

"Know what? I don't know anything." said Carlos. However from his eyes Don could see his concerns and how for the first time in their lives he knew that Carlos is hiding something from him. The bubbly man, Carlos, was so broken that his sadness became obvious for all those around him.

"Don promise me something." Carlos said

"I promise. What is it?"

"Promise me not to even trust your own shadows. Give the job to whomever you want. Never walk around with your eyes closed."

"How can I do that? When my heart and instincts don't agree?"

"You are a wise man, I am sure soon you will find the right answers."

When the discussions with Carlo's finished, Don rang Joshua and told him about the position that was opened.

Joshua got excited and told his father he would put his resignation in that afternoon and should be able to start there in a week's time.

Don then calls Nancy in and asks her to arrange for something really good for Carlos's farewell.

Don has once again gone into deep thoughts. Did I just dig my own grave? Or am I just paranoid for nothing? Why am I having these evil thoughts surrounding my children? Oh. Well what is done it is done. All I have to do is wait and see how Joshua performs.

Chapter 12

Sandy and Max are seeing each other more often. They have become very close friends. Max couldn't survive a day without being in contact with Sandy. However the directors were back and she had to go through all her reports with them. Her demanding position left little time for her to go out but Max would go to her parent's place and wait for her to come home.

After a few days going through all the reports and analysing the activities of the store, the directors were amazed with the increase in profits since they went away so they decided to send Sandy to their new store which was doing so badly. They had to pull money out of this store to keep it going.

Paul called Sandy into his office and told her about the decision they made. She was so excited and sad at the same time. She never had been to another country and this was truly a good opportunity for her. On the other hand she had to live away from her parents.

That afternoon when she got home, she found Max waiting for her. His face lit up when he laid eyes on her.

"Oh sorry I didn't return your call. Had a hectic day." she said

"Not to worry."

"You will not believe it, the directors decided to send me to the new store, they reckon I can bring it back to life."

"You didn't accept did you?" Max asked

"Not yet but this sounds so exciting for me."

"Sandy you know how good my business is doing now" Max continued. The new products are selling so good we have orders for the next ten years."

"Good for you" Sandy replied

"I mean, don't go. We can work together here in my business."

"Look I didn't even work in my dad's business, purely because at nights we can talk about our day adventures. If we work together we won't have anything to share with each other."

"So how long do they want you to go there for?"

"Not sure, I suppose as soon as the store's profits increase, I can come back."

"That might take a long time I don't think I will make it without seeing you."

"Don't underestimate yourself. You can handle it plus if you really miss me you can fly to me."

"Donna can you please talk your daughter out of going?" Max said

"Sorry Max but I will not get involved. You are on your own on this one." Donna responded.

"I think it is going to be a good experience for you." Don called out

"Thanks Dad. You are my hero. I actually am very excited and don't think I should miss this opportunity."

"So you are going?" Max said

"Yes I am"

"Ok. Then can we at least have a few days away from everything. Out of the city before you go?" Max asked

"That will be so nice. Is that ok with you, Dad?"

"Off course, darling."

"I will look for a nice place tomorrow. I will call you before I book anything." Max said

"Ok. Then it is all settled. Let's have a drink now."

When Sandy went to get the drinks Don called out. "Max I have to thank you. Before you came in Sandy's life, she was very isolated. Now I can see her eyes glow."

"You should say I am lucky to have found someone like her." Max replied

Sandy walks in with the drinks and everybody went quite. "What is the matter? Why is everyone so quite?"

"Nothing" replied Don. "We were gossiping behind your back."

"Is that true" she said, while handing the drinks to everyone.

That night was a magical night for Sandy. She was so excited that she is going to see another country. At the same time she had the best looking guy that was madly in love with her.

Next morning as promised, Max started looking for holiday places and found an isolated island that was ideal for two. He emails all the details to Sandy to get her approval, before booking.

Sandy's reply to his email was. "Where do you find all these magical places?"

"Is that a yes?" Max wrote

"100%" replied Sandy."

The flights were booked for a week before Sandy was to leave. Don and Donna drove the two young people to the airport and said goodbye to them.

The plane lifted around 7pm. The young friends were bursting with happiness. Twenty minutes into the flight there was a big bang and everything was gone.

Donna and Don had the radio on with relaxing music. All of a sudden a news flash was broadcasted about the crash of the flight their daughter was on. Danna's tears started. "Oh god please let my baby be alright."

Don quickly makes a U turn and decides to go back to the airport. Their cries and screams attracted a lot of attention. It wasn't long before the management came and took them to the office and told them they were not sure how bad the crash is until the rescue team gets to the area of crash.

"Can we go with them?" Asked Don

"Unfortunately no" said one of the officers. There is nothing you can do here. You better go home and rest. We will contact you as soon as we have some news."

"I can't rest" Don said. "Until I know our daughter is alright."

"Please sir," the officer said, "don't make it harder than it is. Please go home."

"We will go and wait outside. Here is my number. You can call me." Don said

As the two worried parents were sitting around quietly, images of the crash started emerging on the TV. Don with unbelief, tried to distract Donna so she wouldn't make a scene, hugging her and saying. "Why don't we go home?"

Easy going Donna, looked at her husband and nodded in agreement.

When they got home, Don said. "Go to bed darling if there is any news. I will wake you."

"I can't sleep. Not until we hear something from them." She then turns the TV on and in the news flash; she could see that there was no hope for survivors. She kept her spirit up and said. "Don Do you believe in miracles?"

"Is this the time to ask this kind of questions?" Don responded

"Yes because from the bottom of my heart, I know my daughter is not dead."

"I know that" Don replied

The couple had a few drinks quietly to force themselves to sleep.

"Don, Don Come here." called out Donna, the next morning.

"What is it?" He asked

"Look how many have survived. Although they have been hurt, that is a good sign. That means Sandy could be one of them."

It was asked of the families of the passengers, not to make it hard on the staff at the Airport. Instead they should wait for the news of their loved ones at their own home.

Twenty four hours after the accident they were able to release the names of all those found dead or the ones transported to hospital. Max's name was on the list of the survivors but there was no mention of Sandy among the dead or injured.

"Let's go" Don said

"Where to?"

"The Hospital. Where Max was transported to."

"Are you sure?"

"I need to find out how my daughter is."

Neither of them bothered changing. They grabbed a few necessary items along with spare clothes and left the house.

After two long hours of driving the couple make it to the hospital. When they went to reception and asked where Max was. They said he was still undergoing a major surgery.

"Why? What is wrong with him?" Don asked

"I am sorry" said the nurse, "almost every bone in his right hand and leg have been crushed."

"Oh my god, is he going to be alright?" Donna asked

"I don't know. It doesn't look good. Wait and see what doctors can do for him." the nurse said.

Again the two of them went to the waiting room and waited patiently. Three hours later the nurse came and said. "The doctor can see you now."

The doctor told them that they have done their best to save Max's life but his chances of survival are very tiny. Don asked him if they could see him. The doctor replied. "You can but he cannot hear you or speak to you."

After seeing Max's condition, Don walked outside and cried like a baby. He then went to the nurse and asked her if they could stay the night next to Max's bed and she of approved their stay.

After waiting all night hoping that Max would wake up so he could tell them about Sandy, the doctor walked in and said. "I am sorry. If he is not awake that means he is in comma and god knows if he will come out it."

It was even more heart breaking for Don and Donna when they found out that a lot of those who were taken to hospital lost their lives. So far Max was one of the lucky ones.

After leaving the hospital Don drives straight to the airport and goes straight to the office asking if they had any news on his daughter.

"The search is still on sir." There are one hundred and fifty passengers still missing. By the looks of it your daughter is one of them." The officer continued. "The second shift of the rescue team will leave in half an hour to relieve the others. If you wish you can go with them. I truly hope you don't."

"Don please let's go with them," Donna cried out.

"Ok. We will."

Half an hour later the officer called them and introduced them to the head of the rescuers.

They were flown by a helicopter to the crush site.

The site was shocking; half of the plane was hanging right over the cliff of a tall mountain. What was left of the other half was all the pieces that were scattered everywhere for hundreds of metres? The couple were given some safety clothing and shoes and were asked to join the wide search.

Time went so fast and it started getting dark so the search was called off until the next morning.

On the way Donna's tears were pouring like a black cloud on a stormy night. The only difference was all the storm lighting was from inside her. Although deep inside, she could feel that her daughter was ok. The thought that she is hurt, hungry and all alone in that isolated place was filling her heart with fear.

On the way back home Don first made the trip to the hospital to see if there was any improvement with Max, but he still hadn't woken up.

"You know Donna; I never knew what pain meant. Right now, every inch of my body is aching and I can see that the same thing is happening to you." Don said

After having a few strong drinks Don and Donna fell asleep. On the couch they were so lifeless. A massive chunk of their life was missing and there was no one to make them feel better.

After not seeing or hearing from Don for two days, Nancy called him to see if everything is ok.

Don Asked. "How is my son doing?"

Nancy replied. "Well he is working? I asked him today if he has heard from you and he said no."

"Did he even care?" Don asked. Then he quickly apologized to Nancy. "Sorry I did not mean to upset you but here you are calling me to see if everything thing is ok but my own son doesn't even notice my presence."

"I am sorry Don." Nancy said

"Nothing to be sorry about. Nancy. I am going to tell you something but don't mention any of it to Joshua. Please this is very important." Don then tells Nancy about Sandy missing.

"Oh my god. Is there anything I can do?"

"No thanks Nancy. You just keep your eyes open at work and if you see anything suspicious please let me know. I won't be back at work until I find my daughter.

"I can understand. You saved me and my children from poverty. I will never forget that and the least I can do, is look after your work."

"Thanks Nancy. Good bye for now."

It is now time again to join the search group. The search started early in the morning and the couple were asked to leave when the relive team arrived. They refused and decided to keep on going. When the relive team arrived they laid their eyes on a very familiar face.

"Oh Charlie. What are you doing here?" Don asked

"As soon as I left work, a blue light like a ball appeared and I started following it. At one stage I felt stupid and tried to go on my own way but the light came back for me as if it was taking me somewhere and I ended up here."

Charlie then asks. "What you two are doing here? Are you volunteering?"

"Sandy was aboard of this flight and she is missing." Donna cried out.

"Oh no, not Sandy." Charlie said

"What happened to the blue light? It is not here?" Don asked

"Oh yes it came into my hand when I got here, and no matter what I did I couldn't get rid of it." Charlie then opens his hand and the light starts moving.

"Oh well we better follow the others. The team left a few minutes ago." Don said

But when they tried to follow the others the light came on and made a circle around the three of them and then went to the front and stopped, Donna screamed. "Oh my god, it's asking us to follow."

When the team leader saw the three breaking away from the others he called out. "You better stick to the team. It is easy to get lost around here and we all know there are still a lot missing."

All of a sudden, a blue light appeared in the middle of the mountain where no one was even thinking off searching. The light turned in to a massive slide from where it started to where the team was. From where Don and the rest were standing it looked like something was placed on the slide and hundreds of other little lights were surrendering to it.

The closer everything was getting to the team, the clearer everything was. It was Sandy who was on the slide with hundreds and hundreds of little bluish coloured angels protecting her. What an amazing sight, no one could believe that this was all happening in front of them.

Donna rushed to her child crying. "Oh my god. This is a miracle."

"I wish this miracle would find some more of the missing passengers." cried out the team leader.

To every one's surprise all of a sudden, Sandy opens her eyes. She moves her hand in a very gentle way while talking in a very low voice. Minutes later Sandy screams, "where ever you see one of these angels stopping go. They will not rest until you find all of the missing passengers.

Before they could ask her any questions Sandy went into a very deep sleep, but the angels started their work and located all the missing people.

The massive slide slowly shred until it turned to the original gift that was given to Sandy by Charlie.

The news of this miracle travelled so fast, that the media started pouring into the site. It was unfortunate for them, they missed the most spectacular sight.

The search groups were so happy for finding so many of the missing passengers in such short time that they did not want to call it a night. Tomorrow could be different because whatever these things are could go away. Most of those found, although badly hurt were still alive and those who had not even a scratch on them, were found in isolated places, starved, thirsty and scared. Without these little angels there was no way these people would be found.

The search was called off at 11.30 the next morning as all the passengers and crews were accounted for.

Don and Donna went straight to the hospital that Sandy was taken to. Although Sandy was still unconscious it was a relief for them to know their daughter was alive.

<h1 style="text-align:center">Chapter 13</h1>

Angelo still has his spies out there and it does not take him long to find out that Josh is running his father's business. The opportunity seeker, Angelo dose not waste any time and calls Josh and congratulates him on his achievement.

Although Don warned his sons about Angelo on many occasion. Josh never took his dad serious. Hungry for success, Josh decides to meet with Angelo.

Josh was looking at every opportunity to convince his dad to hand down the business to them, with no considerations for all the hard work that Don put in to building the business. A business that eventually is going to be his children's. Greed has over taken them and they have forgotten about family values.

Meeting with Angelo was another one of Josh's tactics. What he did not know was that Angelo will not take any steps unless they are beneficial for him.

At the meeting Angelo picked up on the greed that blinded Josh, and he knew exactly how to earn Josh's trust. "Josh I am having a dinner party at my house on Saturday. I would love to see you, Jason, and your sisters there."

"I will consult with them and let you know." responded Josh"

The fact was that there was no dinner party prior to Angelo seeing an opportunity. In seconds he decided to have the dinner party so he could study Don's family before he makes his move.

Angelo in matter of minutes invited over a hundred people to the party so it could look legitimate to Josh and his family.

The following morning Josh told Angelo. "The family has accepted the invitation."

Ungrateful children of a great man got so excited to be invited to such an elegant evening, unaware that their host one day will tear their lives away.

Joshua his brother and sisters arrived at the function around 7.30 pm and were welcomed by their host Angelo and his wife. After complementing the sisters on their appearance they were escorted to the bar for drinks and refreshments.

Jackie and Jasmine felt like princesses, although their father was as rich as Angelo, but he preferred simple things in life. In place of all the unused luxuries he preferred to share his fortune by helping others less fortunate. His wife Donna and his daughter Sandy were exactly like him, but these four sisters and brothers were completely opposite. They were greedy and liked to drag about everything.

Although Angelo was greeting the other guests he never took his eyes off Don's family. At one stage he went up to Michael, "Look at them. Greed is my prey. It won't be long before I teach Don a lesson."

The room went quite for a few seconds. When Nancy walked in she was wearing a simple blue dress but her long black hair and natural beauty caught the eyes of all guests. Jasmine complained as to what was she doing here? "Doesn't she work for dad? I am really disappointed to be under the same roof as her."

Don't worry Joshua replied. "I will get rid of her." He then starts walking towards Nancy. Very quietly with a smile on his face he whispered in to Nancy's ear, "What are you doing here?"

"Angelo invited me, Nancy continued. Plus I am your dad's PA. That's why since he has been away. I get invited in his place."

"Well now I am your boss, I am telling you to leave my family alone. They feel uncomfortable with you around." Josh implied.

"I was going to leave any way; I wouldn't want to be under same roof as people that dig their father's grave for money." Nancy retaliated

"How dare you talk to me like that?" Joshua shouted

Nancy then walks towards Jackie and Jasmine gives them a funny look and says "I am glad that you have found your match." she walks out.

Angelo follows Nancy out and asks her, "where are you going?"

"Oh sorry, an emergency just came up." Nancy replied

Angelo was not happy that Nancy left. He wanted Nancy to collect information, as Don's PA. He thought she can give him a lot of personal information. His idea was to get close and then offer her a lump sum of money that she won't resist.

Michael calls Jason. "Where is your dad these days, I haven't seen him for a while."

"I really don't know." said Jason"

"Don't you keep in touch with him?"

"Yes. But you know I've been busy with my own business and I don't have much time, even for my own family.

With a sneaky smile Michael then said, "I am glad that you found the time to come here tonight." He walked away.

Two maids walked in and told everyone, "The dinner is served." Each grabbed one side of a big door and opened it, Jackie was speechless she just stared at the dining table. It looked as if it was prepared for the Queen. As they walked in there was a maid behind each chair to help the guests sit.

Angelo had already directed his staff to make sure that Josh was seated on the first chair on his right hand. This would be a good opportunity for him to ask Josh a few important questions.

"Well tell me Josh, how is the old Don doing?"

"He is good. Thanks for asking." Josh said

"I heard that he hasn't been to work for a while. Is he sick?"

"Oh no. I think he and mum were going on holidays." Josh replied

"You think?" Angelo said while laughing. "You think they are on holidays?"

Feeling really embarrassed Joshua responded. "I haven't seen him since I started working there. May be he is at peace now that I am running the place and he can relax.

"That's really good" Angelo said

"What about Max?" Angelo asked

"I don't like him. Don't know what he is doing and hope that I never face him again.

"I heard his business is doing really well." Angelo continued. Up to this day I still don't know who helped him financially because without help, his business would have been closed by now."

"Don't know anything about that." Josh said

"I am definite your dad had something to do with that." Angelo implied.

"I really hope not". Josh responded

All of a sudden a golden light flashed in the room. All guests got into panic. Angelo called his butler to go and investigate. He addressed his guests. "I am sure it was an electrical fault somewhere. Please enjoy your dinner."

But Jason got really uncomfortable. He remembered the day at his parents' house with the blue light. He felt that they were doing something wrong. That is why the flashing happened while Angelo and Joshua were talking.

Jason was in such deep thought that caught every body's attention. Angelo called out. "What is the matter Jason? Don't you like the food?"

"It is not that. I just don't feel well, I am so sorry but I need to leave." Jason replied.

"But we all came in one car and if you want to leave, we all have to leave." Jackie uttered

"There is no need for that." while pointing to the maid behind him. "Would you be kind enough to call me a cab?"

Jasmine had never seen her brother like that and said to the mate. "There is no need for that. If Jason is not well, we would like to accompany him." She then, with the shake of her eyes asked Jackie and Joshua to get up.

"Leaving so soon?" Angelo said.

"We apologies but an unexpected thing has happened." Jason stated.

The two brothers and sisters then said goodbye to their host and got on their way.

In the car Joshua was very unhappy. What was all that about Jason?" he asked.

"What do you mean? Didn't you see the light that flashed in the room every time we did something wrong. That light appears.

"What are you talking about?" Jackie said. "Didn't you hear Angelo he said it was an electrical fault."

"Electrical fault, and my arse." Jason lost his temper. "Here we have a businessman that sucking the life out of other business is his greatest hobby. He invites us for dinner but our father who is his long term friend and business partner is not invited. Come on guys what is wrong with you? Joshua I heard that you haven't seen Dad since you started there. Did you even bother to call and check on him? Or has the power that he has given you blinded you."

Angrily Joshua replied. "If you are so concerned, why don't you call them?"

"I still can't understand Jason. What do you mean by the light?" Jasmine asked.

"Do you remember that day at Dad's house? That is what I am talking about."

For the rest of the trip home they all went quiet. It seemed that Jason had hit the right nerve. They all went into deep thoughts.

However Angelo seemed very happy with his achievement. He could see that the family is easily fooled. He looks at Michael and says. "This is going to be a lot easier than I thought."

While putting his glass up Michael said. "Let's drink to that"

The other guests did not know what all that was about but they put their glasses up and said cheers.

Chapter 14

At hospital when Don found that his daughter was still unconscious, he found the opportunity to ask the rescue group and the authorities not to release Sandy's name due to a fear for her life. He then went back to Sandy's room and sat next to Donna. "I better call Nancy and see how everything at work is?" He then walks out side and makes the call.

Shocked, Nancy did not know how to react. The first thing she asked. "How are you and Donna doing? Any news on Sandy?"

"Thanks god we found Sandy. She is in hospital unconscious."

"Oh that is so good. At least you found her and let's hope she gains consciousness soon."

"Thanks Nancy." Don replied

Nancy was full of fear and sadness. she knew she eventually had to tell Don about the dinner party the night before. Suddenly Don asks. "How is everything at work? I hope that managing everything is not too much pressure on you?"

"Not at all" Nancy said

After a second of silence Nancy continued. "Don I am so sorry. Although I know, you have too much on your plate; I have to tell you something very important."

Don knowing Nancy would not bother him unless something was really important got worried and asked. "What is it? Come on tell me."

Nancy then tells him all about the night before, and how Joshua told her he is her boss and she should obey him.

Saddened Don asked himself, how can these be my children, whom all their lives I thought to be caring and loving. I provided everything to them. Right at this moment, I feel that they are strangers.

"Are you alright?" Nancy asked to break the silence.

"I am fine" Don replied. "I want you to find Carlos then meet me tomorrow at the Rocks. Bring the chq books with you. Please don't let anyone know where you are going.

If you notice anyone following you, go back."

Nancy with a worried voice said. "Don there is something else I have to tell you. This morning when Josh came in he called me to his office and asked me for the books. Of course, that was after he told me off for showing up at Angelo's party. He made it clear to me that he is the boss, but I told him that Don hired me and until such day that he fires me no one has the authority to tell me what to do."

"Well done." replied Don

"Oh no. He is coming to my office right now." Nancy called out.

"Ok go. Don't let anyone tell you what to do and don't forget about tomorrow." Make sure you tell Carlos everything on the way." Don uttered

Donna saw the pain on Don's face when he walked back in the room and asked what was wrong? "Did the doctors tell you something that you don't want to tell me?"

"No news can be worse than the news that my own kids are ganging up against me."

"What do you mean?" Donna asked

He then told her about the conversation he just had with Nancy.

"Oh, my god, Are you serious?"

"Yes, I asked Nancy to find Carlos and meet me tomorrow. I have a plan, I know Angelo. He will use my own kids against me to get his hand on my companies."

Donna sank." How could the children of such a loving mother turn against their own father? He has done nothing to them but loving and supporting them in everything."

The next morning Don arrives at the meeting place and finds Nancy and Carlos waiting for him. After greeting each other and checking on Sandy's conditions, Don said, "Let's get to business."

"Here is the plan. Carlos is the only one that my financial advisor would trust and talk to in my absence. I want you to go and see him and tell him about the situation. He will ask for a password. Just to make sure that your instructions came from me. It is "beautiful green box." "He will then call me to confirm."

"Tell him I want to buy three properties which you two will find for me outside the city. Two of them will be in Nancy's name and one in your name Carlos. Here are three blank cheques to use. He will sign the other side of the chq on settlement of the properties. You two should not be seen together in public. Try to travel individually. Here are another two. When you buy the properties make sure you fully furnish them."

Nancy was starting to get scared and said, "Don what are you doing? What is all the fuss about? As soon as Sandy recovers, you will be back to work and everything will be alright."

Carlos replied. "Nancy you have no idea who Angelo is and how he can send the biggest companies broke overnight."

"He is right, I have to be cautious." Don implied.

"Carlos you better keep the cheques with you, because I have to go back to the office. The way things are I can't trust anyone there." Nancy said

"No worries."

Don again apologized to his loyal aid and is sorry to put them through this.

"Right now we cannot let anyone know about Sandy or Max. That is why I will not show my face at work or home. If anybody asks where I am Nancy, you should tell them that we are holidays. Right now all that matters is Sandy's recovery. Her brothers and sisters always had something against her. If they find out she is in this condition they will make sure Angelo gets rid of her."

The three of them say goodbye. Don goes back to hospital and tells Dona all about his plan and how he got his two most trusted people to carry out his plan.

The next day the financial advisor calls Don and confirms everything. He then assures Don that he will do everything in his power to help Carlos and Nancy to buy the properties quickly.

Don thanks him and asks him to transfer a certain amount of money to his account just in case if things went wrong. "I don't want you to be left out."

Four weeks went by. Max has gained his conscious but his movement is very limited. The doctors told Don that he will require a lot of care and treatment and that he might never walk again. Although Don was saddened by the news he was happy that finally Max was awake. As for Sandy she would wake up every few hours for only a few seconds and then back into deep sleep. Doctors were not sure what was happening to her. They did every possible test to find out the cause but they came up with nothing.

Don and Donna were at hospital day and night. The only time that they went to their hotel was to have a shower and change clothes. One day when they arrived back at the hospital, as they were walking in, they heard a familiar voice calling, "Donna." When they turned around they saw Michelle Angelo's wife.

"Hi Michelle" Said Donna

"What are you two doing here? Angelo told me you went on a lengthy holiday. I wasn't expecting to see you here."

Don quickly replied. "We are visiting an old friend. We visited some friends in the area and they told us about him."

"What a coincident." Michelle said

"Anyway what are you doing here?" Donna asked

"Oh I was on a road trip with my grandchildren and one of them got food poisoning. This was the closest hospital. Michelle continued. "You know, I heard there are people here for over a month from that plane crash."

"What plane crash?" Donna asked

"Apparently it happened five to six weeks ago. I personally didn't know about it but this morning when I went to buy coffee I met some of their relatives who told me the story."

"I hope your grand child is feeling better now." Donna said

"Thanks."

"We better keep on moving." Don said

They said goodbye departed from Michelle. They kept on looking behind themselves, making sure that she was not following them.

"How long do you reckon they will keep the child in the hospital?" Don asked

"I really hope they release him in a few hours" Dona replied

They went into Sandy's private room and closed the curtains so that no one passing would see them there. They also made the nurses aware of the situation in case any one comes asking for them.

The financial advisor called Don and told him. "Joshua was here asking for company books."

"What did you do?" Don asked

"Nothing" I told him apart from you being my client only Don can release any information about the company. Don, I don't mean to upset you but Nancy is going through a very hard time. She told me that Joshua's sisters been going to the company more often and harassing her. Apparently last pay day they went in there and asked her to give them the passwords for the banking and when she refused they kicked her out of her own office. The pays didn't go in on time and all employees were complaining."

"What are my kids up to?" Don asked. "They did not even call us once to ask how we were since the crash."

"Don you need to show yourself at the company and straighten out the situation." said the financial advisor.

"Ok no worries. Leave it with me." Don replied

After a discussing with Donna, Don decided to pay the company a visit. He went mid-morning. When he was walking in the hall way towards Nancy's office he realized something was wrong because everybody seemed panicky.

When he got closer he could hear Joshua screaming. "Who do you think you are? This is my dad's company and I can fire you anytime."

Don quickly opens the door and asks, "What is going on? Why are you screaming?"

Joshua looked at his dad with unbelief. Nothing Dad I don't know why you hired this woman. She is so incompetent. Doesn't do her work on time and employees have been complaining about their pays."

"You couldn't even bring yourself to say. Hi dad. How are you? Before you start telling me how incompetent my PA is."

"I am sorry Dad" How are you?

"Alright Josh. Can you now leave me alone with Nancy? There are a few things we need to discuss."

While opening the door to leave, Josh said. "Dad I meant what I said about her."

Don then sat on the chair and asked Nancy to bring him a cup of coffee. When she came back with coffee, he had a piece of paper on his lap with big letters written on "Don't say anything. We need to talk elsewhere."

Nancy shook her head in agreement then said. We missed you here Don, nothing was the same."

"I just dropped in to see how everything is. I left Donna alone in the hotel."

"Everything is good. You don't need to worry." Nancy said

Handing the cup back to Nancy, he passed her a note too, telling when and where to meet him. Don then said. "If everything is ok, I will be leaving." He then went to Joshua and told him not to scream at Nancy in his absence.

A few hours later Nancy met Don at a deserted place, and told him that all three houses have been bought and once they get them cleaned they can furnish them.

"Thank you for everything. Don Continued. "I am so sorry if my children are giving you a hard time. Right now I cannot concentrate on work knowing my best daughter is fighting for her life."

"Nothing can be compared to what you did for me and my kids" Nancy responded.

"Has Angelo been here again?" Don asked

"Yes, a few times." Nancy replied. "From what I heard he even has people watching Max's company. He knows Max hasn't been going to work. He has been knocking on all doors to find out where he is and what he is doing."

"How can a human being be so greedy? He has everything. I don't know what he wants from Max?"

"Angelo seems so satisfied." Nancy said

"That man can never be satisfied. He wants to own the world." Don implied

After a few business discussions, Don and Nancy departed. Don went straight back to hospital. When he got to Sandy's room he found Donna crying. When he asked her why, she replied. "There were some private investigators here and somehow the conditions of Sandy and Max have been leaked."

"But how?" Don asked

Probably Michelle told her husband that she saw us here yesterday. Knowing Angelo he did not lose anytime to investigate.

"Don't worry, I will see if we can transfer them somewhere else." Don said.

All of a sudden Don's phone rings. It was his financial advisor. He looked at Dona and said this is unusual. "I better answer it. Something must be wrong."

Walking out of the room Don answered the phone. "What is wrong?"

"We closed for lunch today. I took my partner and staff to a restaurant but when we came back all the glass doors were broken. All my client documents were ripped and thrown on floor. They left a note on the wall." "You are next".

"Who would do such a thing?" Don asked

"I believe it could be Joshua and Angelo."

"Joshua doesn't have that in him. He might be a money lover, but would not damage anyone's property."

"Don seriously I didn't want to worry you but, Joshua has been here a few more times after the first time. He keeps on asking about company files. Two days before this incident, I had a warning either to give up your client Don, or put up with the consequences."

"That is so funny. All my life I worked and gained my wealth with honesty. Who would be this interested in my life and my financials?" Don implied

"I don't know," answered the financial advisor. Don we have been friends for a very long time. I am telling you, I can't risk my family or staff. I need you to find another advisor.

"If you think you are at risk because of me, then I will find someone else." Don said with a very sad voice.

"Trust me Don, behind the walls I will do everything for you, but right now I will let everyone think that we no longer have any business dealings."

"Thanks, I will come and collect all my stuff tomorrow."

The next day as promised Don went and collected his belongings from the office of his financial advisor. This time things were different. They didn't sit and talk, nor did they have a few laughs over coffee. The staff were amazed but not sure why the two old friends were so cruel to each other. Unaware that the two men were putting on a show in public and pretended that they were no longer friends.

Don now was a hundred percent sure that Angelo and others have ganged up against him, not because he has done something to them but because they saw a light of success to overtake his business.

Before going back to hospital Don rang Nancy to see how everything was, but there was no answer. He rang the office and asked for her. They told him following, an argument between Joshua, Angelo and Nancy, she left and never came back.

Concerns and regrets started filling Don's heart. The very woman that he helped to have a new start, and a normal life for her kids had been bullied by his own son.

When he arrived at the hospital Donna noticed the sadness on his face and asked him. "Is everything ok?"

Don replied, "Off course not." After telling her about Nancy he cried. "I really hope she is safe."

It didn't take long before Don's phone rang. "Hi Don its Nancy"

"Where are you? I got really worried. I heard about what happened?"

"I am well, they started frightening me and when I ignored them, they went to my children's school. Lucky I got there on time. They were trying to make them sit in the car. I started screaming. My kids ran and people gathered. Although they took off I knew me and my kids were not safe. I went back to the office Angelo was there with Josh I screamed and carried on when I went back to my office I collected all the necessary documents then went to a hotel."

"Oh I am so sorry." Don responded

"I don't know what is going on but it does not look good at all." Nancy said"

With a broken heart and tears in the eyes Don said. "I want you and your kids to move into one of those houses that you bought until things quieten down."

"Ok I better go. Oh don't forget this is my new number. I had to get rid of the one you gave me."

"Not to worry. Don said. I will call and check on you every day."

As Donna ran outside to give some good news to Don, she saw him with his head down and tears pouring from of his eyes. "Don" she said. Forget about everything Sandy is awake."

Don ran inside with unbelief. He looked at his daughter. "Thanks God." He said before grabbing her hand and kissing her.

"How is max?" Was the first thing that Sandy asked of her father?

"He is fine. We will look after him. Don continued. "What took you so long? You scared us."

"You won't believe me even if I try explaining it to you."

"Why don't you try us?" Donna replied

"Help me up mum. Let me sit." After Sandy sat in her bed grabbed her parent's hands and told them. "You have to promise me that you will be the only two people on earth to keep this secret and not leak any of this out to anyone."

"We promise"

"When the plane crashed I was close to the door and before the plane hit the mountain rocks, somehow the door opened and I was thrown out. While flying down between two massive rocks, a blue light from the bottom of the mountains started opening up. Just like a massive flower until it reached me and made sure I rested there without any harm. The flower, then slowly started shrinking until I found myself underground. There it all shrank and became the gift that Charlie gave me."

"I was screaming and asking." Where am I?" There was no sound I picked up the gift and started crying from fear. Then I thought maybe I am dead. Out of fear I threw the gift and said. "Keep away from me. Ever since you showed up in my life I had nothing but bad luck."

The gift again opened. Blue like the sky, Shiny just like gold. Assuring like a mother's promise.

I sat on the floor amazed by its beauty. All of a sudden, I found myself in the same colour dress. Then the gift turned into royal stall back into my hands, glowing with light blue colures. It opened its mouth and said behold the queen of karma. "I panicked and, said where is she?"

All of a sudden I saw little creatures coming out from everywhere and bowing to me. Shocked and confused, I said. "I am no queen."

I started running everywhere. As I was trying to hide, more and more creatures were coming out and bowing to me.

The story of Sandy was put on hold when Jackie, Joshua, Jason and Jasmin walked in, Don and Donna were shocked. They looked at each other with unbelief. Don put his head down as a sign of disappointment, but Donna like many mothers doesn't lose hope in her children, asked. "What are you doing here?"

"We heard you were here. We got worried and thought we should check on you two." Jackie explained.

Jasmine followed. "Now we can see that you are ok. By the looks of it your daughter Sandy, was too precious. That is why you left your home and business unattended."

Don walked out. Donna screamed. "What kind of talking is that? Your sister was unconscious all this time and just came back to life about an hour ago."

"That makes sense. Another perfect act by our dear sister to win, the hearts of our parents." Jasmine added

"Don't Judge me if you have not walked in my path. Watch what you are doing." Sandy quoted.

"Now you are frightening me?" Jasmin asked

"How dare you come in here and act like this. I want you all to leave right now." Donna screamed.

"We are your children too?" Joshua implied.

"I don't recall giving birth to such heartless people?" Dona cried out.

Donna then opens the door and shouts. "Get out, get out."

Hearing Donna screaming, Don ran towards the room. Jasmine said. "Look dad. She is kicking us out. "Don put his head down. Without saying anything, he walked back in the room and sat next to Sandy.

Donna was holding back her tears when the others left. She could not recognize her own kids.

"Don't worry mum." Sandy said. "I think you two should go and get some rest. I don't want to see you until tomorrow morning."

"Oh no, we knew this would happen. We are hoping to move you and Max out of here before anybody comes to visit you." Don said.

"Is everything ok?" asked Sandy

"Let's put it this way. Your brothers and sisters have become very greedy." Donna replied.

After talking to the doctors and explaining the situation, the doctors agreed to release the two patients into Don and Danna's care on the condition that they will constantly have two qualified nurses, present taking care of them. Everything happened so quickly. Don arranged for two cars to drive them to Nancy's house. When they got there he asked Nancy if she could give the keys to the other house she bought.

Nancy with no hesitation gave the address and the keys to Don. Then she said. "Why don't you stay the night here, so you can rest? Tomorrow morning we will take you there.

Don agreed.

Paul, his brother and sister were so excited to hear Don's voice so they ran and grabbed his leg. Kissing them on the head Don said. "Let me get the others in first."

Nancy quickly started preparing some refreshment for them. Max was taken to one of the bedrooms. The rest stayed in the lunch room.

While sitting there Donna said. "Nancy I like the way you decorated the house. You have a great taste."

"You should see the other one." Nancy said

"I am sure I will like it." Donna replied.

After a few minutes of rest and small conversations Don said, "I think Sandy should get some rest now." They all went to their rooms.

Next morning after breakfast Nancy handed the keys to Don. "I have already been last night and made sure everything was ok. Also did some shopping."

"Thank you Nancy. You have been a good friend." Don said

They were all so excited when they got to the other house. It was situated on top of a beautiful hill facing the river. It was even more beautiful when they got inside. The walls were painted in black and white with matching furniture. The bedrooms all decorated with each person's favourite colour. A spare room next to the balcony was turned into an office complete with desk, computer phone and all the necessary stationery.

"How beautiful, look she even created a sitting spot on the balcony." Sandy said.

"Indeed, she has done a good job." Don replied.

After settling Max in his new room, Don said. "Sandy since the night of the crash me and your mum haven't had a drink. I think we both need one to celebrate this very special day."

"I can have a small one with you." Sandy uttered.

While they were drinking Donna asked. "Sandy are you in the mood to finish your story? You were up to where you run away but more creatures were coming out."

Don handed everybody's drinks and rested in the couch waiting for the rest of the story.

"I kept on throwing the gift away and it kept on showing back in my hand. I settled for a few minutes not knowing what to do, so I asked what do I have to do as a queen? A voice came and said "watch." All of a sudden this big screen appeared. There were a lot of activities then. It all started. It showed what was happening to people who lied and destroyed lives of other people. It showed those who stole from the poor for their own gain and how they end up losing everything they.

Sandy stopped and had a sip from her drink then continued. "There was so much more that was shown to me. I was very sad from what I was watching and my tears started. I screamed why are you showing me all this? What have I done?"

"The answer was. You are the queen of Karma. You were chosen because of your kindness and wisdom and you need to try and educate people about karma. Every time they do something wrong you will see the consequences they have to deal with. Every time you wake someone up and direct them towards the right path more glowing little angels come to life."

"I replied. This was not my choice and I don't want to be the queen. I cannot see people suffer in front of my eyes even if they've done wrong. This is a burden on me."

"All of a sudden everything disappeared and I found myself hanging between two massive rocks in the middle of mountain. It didn't take long before it got dark and I was terrified. Every now and then there would be a small sand and rock slide. I barely could hold on."

"At one stage I even went unconscious but somehow I made it to the morning. Hungry with little to hang on to. I was crying and saying. "What happened to my choices?" After swallowing so much dust from the sand and rock slides I became unconscious once more and don't know how I ended up in hospital."

Don with a smile on his face explained, to her how she was brought down from the mountain unconscious and how she demanded the little angels to glow wherever they see a passenger and not to rest until everyone was found.

Sandy unaware of what she just heard went quite for a few seconds.

"In the hospital you kept on coming back then going back into comma. Was something happening to you?"

"It must have been the time where they took me in to this massive ballroom where there were tables and chairs facing the centre of the room. They were all glowing, so I could only hear their voices but wasn't able to see who was sitting on those chairs behind the tables."

"A group was saying she is refusing her destiny. The others were saying she is human and scared. We should give her a chance. I was being picked up. Before I could make it out the other group would say no she has to stay here until we sort this out and that kept on happening a few times."

"Finally I screamed please let me go. I cannot bear to be the queen of karma; you should have chosen someone that had the heart to deal with it."

"Do you believe in punishment?" one of them asked I replied. "I do but just a slap on the hand and nothing major."

"How about those who torture and kill people? Do you have any feelings for them?" Again I replied. They need proper punishment but again I don't have the heart."

"After asking a few similar questions like that they got off their chairs and went right to the back of the room. They all made a circle. I couldn't hear what was said but I was so scared that they were deciding a sentence for me."

"Finally after a few hours they came back and said you will stay here until a decision is made."

"Day after day what I just told you got repeated, and finally after their last gathering at the back of room, they all went back to their chairs. Another gift got placed in front of me by a little creature. I got horrified. The creature placed my original gift back into my hand."

"This is the first time since the creation of the world that this is going to be done. We decided to give you another gift of judgment."

"I screamed oh no please."

But one of them said. "With this gift you will be able to save those who you think their judgment is too harsh."

"I cried but they said. "You have been chosen and you have to fulfil your destiny. As the queen you also are given the knowledge of Karma and how it works. With your kindness you will give them a chance to change their way and with your wisdom you will decide who to save from harsh judgment."

"So where is the other gift?" Donna asked

Sandy opened her hand and said. "Here it is."

"I think I need another drink." Don said

Sandy smiled. "You know Dad. This is a big burden on me."

"I know darling." replied Don.

The rest of the afternoon and night everybody was so quite. Each in a deep thought until the blue light glowed in front of them then moved towards Max's room.

Sandy and her parents thought something was wrong so they ran towards the room and found Max with his eyes open looking around not knowing where he was.

Chapter 15

On the other side of town Angelo is a very busy man. He knew the owners of two great businesses are missing together. Now he is sure that it was Don that didn't let Max's business fall into his hands.

Michelle told him about her accidental meeting with Don and Donna at hospital. He didn't waste any time to send some private investigators to the hospital. It was obvious that they saw Sandy and her parents there but did not have enough time to find Max.

Angelo is now at Don's office every day. He has become so close to Joshua and his sisters. He was the one that told them about Sandy being in hospital. He also has frightened the operations manager of Max's company. The poor guy was beaten and left outside his house because he would not let Angelo and his team inside. He was hospitalized and the business was left with no leadership.

On the following Monday Angelo and his body guards walked in and changed all the locks to the factory and offices of Max's company. They told the staff that Max had died and they were the new owners. Tears were shed and fear over took them all.

When Angelo's private detectives told him that Don has moved Sandy and Max out of the hospital, and that there were no tracks of them, he told them he wanted them found and imprison them if necessary until he talked to them.

The detectives also told Angelo that the nurses told them Max was not fully conscious when he was released.

Everything seemed to be happening in favour of Angelo. By now he has involved his other business partners and they are all working together. They all wanted a piece of someone else's fortune. They too hired people to watch everything in case Angelo tries to cheat them. The chain of crooked business men was so strong that nothing could break it; a chain made out of the cruellest of men.

The chain of business men found out who Max and Don's solicitors were and sent their men to pay them a visit. After breaking through the safes, terrifying the solicitors and their staff they picked up every document they could get their hand on. They warned the staff that if they did not tell them where Don's Estate is kept, they would burn everything.

Finally at gun point one of the solicitors hands two wills to them. He was then made to re write everything as if Don had already passed all his estate to his children prior to his disappearance. This would cover any suspicions.

Max's was re-written as if Max used all his assets to join in with the chain of business men. That meant that in his absence the chain could take control of the company, house and everything that belonged to Max.

Angelo then arranged a meeting with Joshua, his brother Jason and his sisters to tell them to quickly act and transfer everything into their names. At the same time the board of the chain had a meeting and it was discussed that Max's assets should be transferred to their names.

A lame man was passing the building where Angelo was rushing out. The lame fell on the floor following a hard encounter with Angelo. Angelo then screams. "Your mud dirtied my clothes."

All of a sudden a little light came and helped the lame man up. It then stopped as if it was looking at Angelo. It opened up and said "You will draw what you plant."

Angelo got into the cap while looking strangely at the light. "Idiots" he said. They want to play games with me."

Michael was waiting for him when Angelo got there. They celebrated with a glass of expensive champion. "To our accomplishment"

When leaving, Angelo said to Michael. "I am going away for a few days. Keep your eyes open. Hopefully by the time I come back we can completely finish Don's business." He then went straight home and picked up his wife and their luggage and went straight to the airport.

A few days went by. Everything seemed to be working out. Joshua and his sisters had transferred everything into their names.

When Angelo made sure that everything was transferred he arranged another meeting with Joshua and his sisters. This time Angelo said. There is a business that we think is suitable for you all."

"We don't want another business. We now have to look after this one and that is plenty of work for all of us." Jackie responded.

Angelo did not like the reply and said, "Think about it."

"We can't even run this one without your help." Joshua implied

"Sure I am here to help."

"We just moved into a new house and soon I will have a dinner party." Jasmine said

"Is that because you received a great deal of money?" Angelo asked

"I can't believe with all the money my dad had, we never lived like rich people. He always told us to be happy with what we have, but I always wanted expensive cars massive mansions and branded clothing." Jasmine explained

Angelo knew exactly how much money Don had because it was them that got the solicitor to change the wills. If Don wanted in time he could send everyone in the chain broke but he never showed interest in other people's property.

"Have you seen or heard from your dad?" Angelo asked

They all replied. "No"

"Do you even ask about his wellbeing?" Angelo asked

"What for? They kicked us out of hospital because of that looser. Why should we even bother?" Jasmine responded

"Did your sister get a share of the estate?"

"No. Why should she?" Joshua said

"She is your sister. If your parents die she will have nowhere to live." Anglo implied

The room filled with silence for a few seconds. It was broken by Jasmine. "Here have a glass of Champaign. Let's celebrate."

They all sat around having a few drinks. An hour later, Angelo's hired private detectives. They called him. "I am sorry sir but they are nowhere to be found. We went to the hotels and motels and asked if they had checked in, but they hadn't. We also checked all the hospitals in the country. They are nowhere to be found."

"I hired you to find them. I don't care how you do it. Find them and don't call me without a positive result." Angelo said sternly.

"Have you lost something?" Joshua asked

"No" replied Angelo

From that day on Angelo kept a track on all the brothers and sisters. He knew exactly where they were what they are doing, who they were with. He would discuss everything with his close friend Michael. He even asked Michael if he had any news on Colin and Collet but the answer was no. They don't mix with anyone anymore.

Angelo was a tall build man with brown eyes and light brown eyes. His looks were so deceiving. People would fall for his charm and women for his looks but no one knew what he really was like. The only thing he would teach his children was if you don't cheat you will not survive. You have to do everything in your power to gain what you want and never let anyone stand in your way. In the case of Don's children he was doing the opposite. He had his war armour on and no one could take it off him.

Angelo's younger son turned to be like his father greedy and spoiled. However his older son Jo, was an angel born from the devil himself. Jo was kind hearted at school he would buy food for all those disadvantage kids. If one was struggling with their studies he would donate his time to tutor them. Jo found out of what his father was doing to Don's family. One night he waited up until his father got home.

"Is it true that you are destroying Don's family?" Jo asked

"Who said that?" Angelo continued. Not that it is any of your business."

"Come on Dad, Don was the only true man that you ever became friends with. I cannot forget all those time me and Sandy use to play around while you two would have a drink and a few laughs. Do you want to tell me what happened?"

"How dare you talk to me like this? I will kick you out of the house if you ever talk to me like this. You now can get lost and mind your own business." Angelo shouted.

Weeks later, the control of Don's business had fallen into Angelo's hands. Through the connections he had with Joshua and his sisters, Angelo fired all the loyal employees and replaced them with his own people.

By now Angelo was ready to take over but he still had a fear. Jason hadn't been seen since the will change. It was Angelo's fear that Jason might be up to something and until such time when he finds out what Jason was up to, he could not rest.

Weeks went by and Angelo started to get frustrated. He told the accounts department to do doggie purchases and pay for them. This off course was his new plan to drain the company.

Chapter 16

It's been weeks and weeks Jason hasn't heard from his brother or sisters. During these times he went to his parents' house and found that the place was sold.

He even went to the hospital where they last saw their parents and kept on asking questions of his family. Their whereabouts or any leads to follow. For a time he felt so bad, thinking, what have we done?

Following his disappointments in search for his parents, he called Joshua and his sisters asking them if they heard anything and as usual the answer was no. He tried to arrange a family time with them. Just like the times when they use to gather and have dinner. None of them seemed to have time.

By now Jason was really in a panic. He remembered how good their father was to them and now he could see that the brother and sisters that once he knew had turned in to greedy evil souls.

Mandy notices her husband's sad face and decided to throw him a surprise dinner party at one of the local restaurants. Naturally Jason had no idea. He thought it was just a simple night out with his wife and children. When they got to the restaurant he was surprised. He kept on looking around to see if he could see his brother or sisters but didn't and asked his wife. "Did you invite my brother and sisters?"

With a broken heart Mandy looked at her husband and said. "I am so sorry, I did my best to convince them to come but they were busy."

"Don't worry hon. said Jason. "I am sure you did your best."

There was an empty table right at the back of the restaurant and for some reason Jason could not take his eyes off it. He turned to Mandy and said, "I swear I saw a blue light around that table."

"I am sure you did." Mandy replied

It was around seven thirty pm when Carlos and his wife walked in, they were seated on that empty table.

Jason's eyes opened wide. "Look Mandy whose been seated on that table."

"Oh, isn't he Carlos your dad's right hand?"

"Yes it is him." Jason gets up and makes his way to Carlo's table. with a lot of fear on his face, Carlos looks around and when he made sure no one was watching he called out, "Hi Jason, how are you?"

Tears filed Jason's eyes. "Please tell me you have some news of my parents."

Again Carlos looked around. "He is your dad. You should know better"

"Oh how I wish I knew. Been door knocking, everywhere. My sisters and brother have lost contact with me and I am the only one concerned about them."

The restaurant's door opened and two men walked in. Carlos said "Quick Jason go back to your table. There is no time to ask questions now."

Jason walked back to his table. While the two men were walking past their table Jason grabbed his wife's lips and kissed her passionately. The two men smiled at each other when they went past. The good thing was they did not see their faces and did not recognize Jason or his wife.

After walking all around the restaurant, the two men finally go to Carlo's table and ask him to go with them. He refused and told them he was having dinner with his wife and was not open to any discussions until the next morning.

One of the men made a phone call then looks at Carlos. "We will be in front of your house first thing in the morning." They then left the restaurant.

Jason was staring at the situation the whole time, his eyes and heart were field with questions and he was not about to walk away from Carlos without answers.

Carlos excused himself from his table to go to wash room. On his way he passed Jason's chair. He pretended to trip over the chair.

"Sorry sir" he said.

While Jason bent to help him up, Carlos slid a piece of paper in his pocket and slowly said. "Go and read that." He then quickly made his way to the wash room.

"I am going outside for a smoke." said Jason to his wife

When he walked out he lit his cigarette and pretended he was wiping his mouth with the piece of paper. He looked at the paper as if something was wrong. When he wiped his mouth but he was reading the note it said. "Don't be shocked with this but you cannot show your face in public with me. This will put me and my wife's lives in danger. Right now I don't trust anyone and expect you to be the same. Not even your wife. So many lives are in danger. Those two men wanted to take me away tonight but I told them I can't go until tomorrow morning. I will have to take off tonight but here is a number. Make sure you remember it, and then destroy this."

Jason then walked back to the washroom of the restaurant. His mind and heart troubled. When he got back he looked at the table but Carlos and his wife were gone. He then looked out of the window and saw the same two men grabbing Carlo's hand and trying to drag him. As luck would have it a cop walked past and asked Carlos if he was ok? The man took his hand off Carlos, so as not to raise suspicion.

Having over thirty of their friends there for dinner Jason called out." I need your help." "There is a man outside that is about to be Snatched off the road, I need all of you to move out now and disturb those two men while another one of you stops and picks up that couple and brings them to the mountain view."

As soon as the car arrived at the Mountain View, Carlos and his wife were moved to Jason's car. He drove straight out of the city, all the time making sure that he was not followed.

Minutes later Mandy calls Jason. "We just let those two men go. I hope that couple have made it somewhere safe." Jason thanks his wife and says. "I am sure by now they have".

"O hon, I had a lot to drink, I am getting a cab home because I can't wait for you I am going straight to bed. I will see you in the morning."

Jason knew that his wife would go to sleep straight away because of all the alcohol she had. Knowing that, Mandy was a heavy sleeper. She won't notice if he stayed up all night.

Jason then turned to Carlos. "Do you have somewhere to stay? Or should we all stay in a hotel?"

"I need to make an urgent phone call, and then we will decide." Carlos replied. He then walked away from the car.

When he came back to the car he said. "We have a place to go to, but on one condition, you put a blindfold on your eyes and I will drive us there."

Out of desperation Jason agreed but that was not the only reason. He again saw the blue light circling around Carlos and for some reason he thought that was a good sign.

Driving for about another two hours, the car stops Carlos first grabs his wife's hand and walks her to a front door and knocks on the door. He then takes the blindfold off her eyes and goes back to get Jason. He does the same with him.

But it was different when the blindfold was removed from Jason's eyes, because as he opened his eyes. Tears started rolling down like a fountain. He kneeled down and said. "Oh, how happy I am to see you."

A soft hand went through his beautiful and thick brown hair and the voice said. "I am even happier."

It wasn't long before Donna screamed, "oh my god I can't believe it's you Jason."

While moving his hand away from Jason's hair Don said. "It's really Jason."

"How did you two get together tonight?" Don asked

"Well Angelo's men came to the restaurant. They must have followed me and my wife there. They didn't see Jason because he outsmarted them and then he got his friends to surround Angelo's men, while one of his friends brought the car and picked us up and then he delivered us to Jason."

"I am so sorry Carlos." Don said

"Sorry about what?" Carlos asked

"For everything. If you were not such a good friend they would not annoy you like this."

"What's happening Dad? Why did you disappear all the sudden? Do you know how worried I was? I went everywhere looking for you."

"Don't worry about me. How is your brother and sisters?" Don asked

"Oh they are fine for now, because they are swimming in money and have no recollection of where they came from and who they are."

"What money?" Don asked. "Did they win money?"

"The money that you transferred in to their names"

"I did no such thing." Don replied

"What do you mean? My will is with my solicitor and it will be in place, only if I die."

"Dad you went and changed your will and gave our shares to us a few months ago."

"Is Joshua still running our business?" Don asked

Jason got very sad and quite

"Come on answer me." Don shouted.

"Looking for you all this time. Without any results I turned to my brother and sisters but they did not have time for me, so I decided to go to the company to see if I could catch Joshua. I noticed Angelo sitting behind your desk; I quickly took off so he wouldn't see." me.

"And where was your brother?" Don asked

"I was told he barely goes there. He is always busy dining, travelling."

"What about your sisters?"

"I have not seen them since we left the hospital that day, because we all had a big argument."

"Did they get shares as well?"

"Well we all did. I kept all your money and haven't touched anything because I want you and not your money."

"What happened to you Jason?" Don asked

I always listened to my sisters, brother and everyone else just because I didn't want to be left out. However when you went missing I realized how much I loved you all and what a big mistake I made. From the bottom of my heart I am really sorry and hope to make it up to you."

"Donna can you please let Jason, Carlos and his wife know where they can sleep." Don called out

Everybody is shown to their rooms and provided with pyjamas, Don and Donna decided to spend the night in Sandy's room so their guests could have proper rest. It seemed as if they all had a long day ahead of them.

Sandy never left her room. She quietly checked on Max and closed his door so the guests wouldn't see him.

Five o'clock in the morning Don got out of the bedroom quietly. He didn't want to wake anyone. To his surprise Jason was in the balcony staring beyond.

"You couldn't sleep too." Don uttered

Jason didn't turn his face he replied. "Yes I couldn't sleep so I came out to enjoy this beauty."

From his voice Don realized that Jason has been crying. He went and put his hand on his shoulder from the back and said. "Son don't worry too much. Everything will be all right."

A few minutes later Sandy walked in. She and Jason grabbed each other and cried their eyes out. "I am so sorry." Jason said

"Sorry for what? We all have our ups and downs. I am glad you are here now." replied Sandy.

One by one the others got up. Don and Donna prepared a big breakfast for everybody. They were so happy to wake up to a full house.

At breakfast table Carlos said. "I don't know what we are going to do."

"About what?" Don asked

"We can't go back home. Our lives will be in danger."

"I am so sorry for bringing this on you. I will take care of everything." Don replied.

"I don't want you to do anything yet. Luckily all the important documents including the deed of my house and the one that you asked me to buy are in the bank and no one will ever get close to them."

"I always knew you were a smart man, always thinking ahead." Don continued. Well I think you and your wife should stay here for a few days until we come up with a plan. But Jason should go back otherwise they might get suspicious. This is a very critical situation and we can't trust anyone out of this circle."

"To be on the safe side I will drive Jason back blindfolded, just in case they pressure him to give out details of our hideaway."

"I totally agree." Don replied. "Jason you should know my number by heart and don't call from your cell phone. Find a phone booth, or public places to call."

After breakfast Carlos drove Jason back to where they met and took a cab back home to Don's house.

"What do you think about Jason? Should we trust him?" Don asked

Jason is a man that gives his emotions away through his eyes, and from what I saw he is deeply hurt and doesn't know how to get his relationship back with you." Carlos replied.

"We should contact my solicitor, and start gathering evidence against everyone." Don implied.

"Haven't you heard? Carlos uttered. "He went missing straight after the will was changed. He's been among missing people and police don't have any leads on him. These people don't leave any tracks behind."

Sinking in his seat Don said. "Oh my god, how many people are getting destroyed just because they worked with me."

Things went quite for a while but the silence was broken by Carlos screaming. "Don" Don." It took seconds for Donna and Sandy to run to the room.

"What is wrong?" Screamed Donna

"Dad what is wrong? Please wake up." Sandy screamed before she dialled emergency.

Don was not responsive to anything. It took only about ten minutes for the ambulance to arrive, and even they could not do much and called for backup.

Finally Don was taken to emergency. Although they made him stable the doctors were not sure if he would survive long.

While her tears were pouring down like a black cloud, Sandy looked at Carlos. "I think you should go home and help your wife. We will keep you notified."

"Is there anything you want me to do before I go?" Asked Carlos

"No, looking after Max at home is the biggest favour."

Chapter 17

Sunday afternoon Jasmin, Jackie and Joshua with their families had dinner at one of the best restaurants in town. Mandy, Jason's wife was invited to the gathering because she fitted well in with the new life style they had.

When Mandy was asked about Jason, she replied. "He's been acting a bit weird. I am sure he is hiding something from me."

"Like what?" Joshua asked

"He might be cheating on me." She replied

"That's not like Jason." Jackie said.

But then Mandy went into a deep recess. "You are right Jackie. I just remembered he's been acting strangely since that night that I threw the surprise party." Mandy then went ahead and told them everything about Carlos coming to restaurant and how Jason saved him from some men that wanted to take him away.

"Where is Carlos now?" Asked Jackie

"Don't know. No one has seen him since that night and every time I ask Jason about Carlos he says." "How do I know what happened to him. Probably those people caught up with him."

"Do you think Jason and Carlos are working together?" Jackie asked

"I don't know?" replied Mandy

"Any other news guys?" Jackie asked excitedly

"Thanks to Angelo, who offered to take care of our business? Cindy and I could go on a life time holiday with the boys." Joshua said

"It was like a dream coming true." Cindy said

"That is so good. Me and Jackie have been working on a dinner party and hopefully we can set the date for four weeks from now. It is going to be just like queens dinner party. We have hired three of the best chefs in town, butlers, an orchestra made up of twenty people."

Jasmine was stopped by Joshua. "So where are you going to fit all these people?"

"Oh I forgot, none of you have seen our new house yet. You can fit an army in it." Jasmine responded.

"Joshua" called out Mandy. "Don't you think you should go back to your dad's company soon and see if everything is ok?"

"What can be wrong? Mandy, we have the best business man looking after it for us." Jackie responded

"I am serious guys. Your father always said how dangerous Angelo is. Maybe you should not trust him like this?"

"The company is ours, and it makes millions of dollars. Nothing can happen to it." Jasmine said.

"I am going to go back to work tomorrow any way, to relive Angelo." Joshua said.

Jackie and Jasmine both at the same time said. "We will meet you there so we can give Angelo's invitation."

Mandy went into deeper thoughts. Finally she realized why her husband was acting so strange. Looking at his brother and sisters putting their trust, in the biggest crook of the century, with not even a word of their sister or parents.

The following morning the sisters and Joshua meet at the company. There was a lot of new faces they could not recognize anyone. When they approach the HR they asked what happened. It seems everyone is new?

Go to the accountant. He will explain everything to you. All those people were trained prior to this visit by Angelo. When they went to the accountant they asked him for reports. Before they got a chance to see the reports, Joshua was called on the phone.

"Your father just had a massive heart attack. The doctors don't know if he is going to survive. I rang you in case if he doesn't make it. I don't want you to feel sorry for the rest of your life. You might as well let your sisters and brother knows."

That was Donna trying to do the right thing by her children, as they say a mother never gives up on her children. She gave them the location of hospital.

Joshua grabbed his sisters and drove straight to the hospital. When they walked in they saw Don lying in bed almost lifeless. Sandy was resting her head on her dad's bed, and crying quietly when Jasmine called out. "Don't worry he has nothing to leave you!"

"Are you serious?" Sandy asked. "This is my dad, the man that gave all of us a life. Who cares about what he has or he hasn't."

"It is all your fault Sandy." Jasmine continued. "You and your bloody black magic."

"You know what? I don't care what you say. Just leave me alone with him. I am not asking for money or anything. Just go away."

"Look at the loser she is talking to us as if we were her mates." Jasmine screamed. "You are a liar, opportunist and money hungry person."

"Get out. Let us spend some time with the old man." Jackie ordered.

"I think you all should get out." Dona screamed. "This is not a place to fight and argue for god's sake. That is your father. It is your fault that he is in this condition. You are his own children, stealing his home and money. Get out I don't want to see your faces ever again."

"Let's go" Jasmine said. "Dad and mum always back up this loser. Didn't you hear mum? Let's go we don't need to be here."

When she heard the news, Mandy straight away went to the company to check on Joshua and the girls. She was told to wait in the waiting room. While waiting for the return of others she notified Jason.

After a long wait, Joshua and his sisters finally came back to the office. They seemed angry. There were no signs of compassion on their faces. They asked Mandy what she was doing there and she told them. "Just making sure you are all right."

It didn't take long before Angelo showed up, to give them bad news. "The company is doing so bad that no staff or creditors have been paid for a long while and it is only matter of days before the doors are closed."

Mandy asked. "What can we do to save it?"

"The only way to save it for a bit longer is to inject money into it." Angelo replied

"I don't care." Jasmine replied. "I have enough money but I am not spending a penny to save this business."

Joshua felt so bad for not paying attention to the business that was handed to them. He said. "When I went away we had millions. What happened to all?"

Little did they know that this was Angelo's plan; to drain their company and then get them to inject more money until he drained them dry? Angelo replies. "A lot of orders were returned by customers due to a default in the products."

"How could there be a default if the same products and quality assurance were in place?" Mandy asked

"No one is talking to you. You and your husband haven't been around for any of the meetings." Was Angelo's reply to her question?

As Mandy got up to leave she said. "I warned you didn't I?"

"What are our other options?" Joshua asked.

"You can either inject money into it or, or hand it to the chain of companies. That way they will pay all the debts and you will have a small share in it."

Jasmine quickly said. "I will sign and give it away but I am not prepared to waste my money."

Followed by Jackie with the same reply.

Two days later Joshua and the sisters signed the company up to the chain but again out of their stupidity did not check on what kind of shares they would get. The chain took the company over and no shares were given to any of Don's children they were even kicked out of the office and were not allowed to go anywhere near the company.

Joshua was so down; he called Jason and told him what had happened. Jason told him. "I didn't sign my share, so I still would have something to say. But I won't' because we all let our dad down and look how Angelo tore Dad's life apart."

"But you did sign." Joshua said. "Angelo said you already signed and he showed us the signature."

"Why call me now Josh?" Jason asked. "Where were you when I tried to talk to you and tell you my concerns? Why didn't any of you stand up for Mandy when he told her she could not talk? Wasn't she a shareholder? Plus do you know that Angelo found out where my dad was and he tried to finish him off."

"What are you saying?" Asked Joshua

"While you and yours sisters were having the time of your lives, Angelo was chasing everybody that had anything to do with Dad, not because he was worried about his health but because he wanted to kill him."

"But why?"

"Because that is who Angelo is. He steals from people. He ruins the companies that he knows he can make money out of. Dad could take him on any time. He still could if he was not in coma.

"Do you know Josh? Dad never signed anything to us. I saw the original will that he was holding. We were to get equal shares after he was gone. That included Sandy. Do you know since Angelo got the will Dad's solicitor has gone missing. Angelo forced him to re write the will. I bet you he has killed him."

"Where is dad now?" Asked Joshua

Well when Angelo's people were found snooping around, Sandy did not want to take any risks. With the help of some friends they were able to take Dad out of the hospital without anyone noticing."

"Where are they now?"

"I have no idea; I heard what Jackie and Jasmin did at the hospital. That wasn't right at all. You have no idea what our sister and parents have gone through the past few months."

"How am I going to fix all of this?" Joshua cried out

"Right now none of us can do anything. Just pray that Dad pulls through. He is the only one that can deal with such a monster."

When Josh got home that night Cindy was waiting for him. "Where have you been?" She asked. "Your sisters called they are coming over."

"Why do they want to come I am tired."

"They are blaming us for the loss of the company."

"I don't really need this. However in a way they are not wrong. You wanted to go on trips; you wanted to go shopping and never had enough of dinning out. Every time I tried to say enough is enough you started crying."

"So now I am to blame?" Asked Cindy

"No. All I am saying is that we should have spent more time running the company."

It did not take long for the two sisters to arrive. They seemed worried and on edge. What worried Joshua was that he saw a black smoke looking thing it was moving around his sisters. When he asked what it was that they replied. "What?"

"Never mind" Joshua said.

"I had random people coming to my house for the most stupid things. I also noticed a car parked there constantly. I think they were watching my house." Jackie uttered.

"Now why anyone would be watching your house?" Cindy asked

"Well the same thing is happening to me." Jasmine continued. "Joshua since it is your fault we lost the company you should compensate us for it."

"Is that a joke? Why should we pay?" screamed Cindy. "You were the ones that were telling me I should stop living like a housewife, I should be in branded clothes or where I should dine so if people saw us you won't get embarrassed."

"I can't do this right now. I am very tired. There is no use for us to become enemies. Angelo is turning us against each other. Only God knows what plans he has." Joshua cried out.

"Girls, have you heard anything about dad?" Josh asked.

Jasmine turns around. With a very psychotic voice says. "Now remember they don't want to see us again."She then walks out.

As the girls walked out, the phone rang. After picking it up Cindy screamed. "Josh turn the TV on."

"Why. Who is on the phone?"

"It's Jason. Turn the TV on. Quickly."

In the breaking news it was said that the police were hunting for two fugitives that stole money from the company. The two fugitives mentioned were Nancy and Carlos. It was mentioned that they stole millions of dollars from the company that the chain took over.

"So they stole our money?" Joshua asked Jason

"No. It is a long story but they helped Dad when Sandy was in hospital. Angelo probably found out of what dad did and now he wants to get his hand on that money as well."

Chapter 18

Sandy heard the news and started panicking, although she moved her father to a private hospital, bribed all the doctors and nurses not to let anyone know he was there but fear took over.

The day that her sisters and brother came to the hospital and created that drama it effected Donna so much, that she had a stroke.

Now Sandy has a disabled mother, a father in coma and a friend that needs a lot of therapy to be able to walk again. Carlos and Nancy were the only two people that were helping her. However those two-kind people are now wanted as fugitives. Somehow Sandy said to herself, who can I trust?

Out of options and desperate, Sandy called a meeting with Nancy and Carlos. "These houses are no longer safe for any of us. By the looks of it they have found out that you helped Dad by buying these properties. Now they want to get their hands on them." Sandy continued. "I am so sorry but until my father wakes up there is nothing I can do I spoke to Charlie. He will help you and your family to pass through the borders. I really think you should leave the country while I try to come up with a solution."

"We cannot leave you by yourself." Carlos implied.

Nancy cried and said. "Don saved me and my children I will not leave."

But Sandy cried and carried on. "It is better for me to know you are safe, than see any harm coming to you."

She then went to a room and came back with a small safe. There was over a million dollars in notes. she said. "This money will be shared between the three of us. Take it and leave. I will keep you informed all the time."

Nancy and Carlos then went pack their stuff. When Nancy tried to leave with her kids and bags she noticed a car coming towards the house. They ran through the bushes from the back yard.

When they safely made it to the top of the hill she called Sandy "From where we are standing on top of the hill I can see three four wheel drives pulling in front of the house and there are people walking all around the house."

"Don't worry, Charlie should be there any minute, I will tell him where you are." Minutes later the truck became visible and an eye blinding light shone on the people who surrendered Nancy's house. The light was so strong that everyone went for cover and that gave Nancy and the kids a chance to ran towards the truck.

The truck went to Sandy's house and picked up Carlos and his wife. Nancy screamed. "If they found the other house they must know where the other two are and they will be coming here next."

"Don't worry." said Sandy. "Just help me put Max and mum in the van I am going to take off as well."

The truck left and Sandy packed all the necessary stuff into the van then drove off. After driving for a little while, she stopped not knowing where to go. She called her sisters. They both had the same answer for her. "You can't come here. Deal with your own problems." she then called Jason and told him what had happened and that he could still contact her on the same number that their parents made him learn from heart.

Jason offered his help and house to Sandy but she refused and said. "They shouldn't know we are in contact."

Finally while driving around Sandy found this remote motel. She went in and asked if they had rooms available for a month. She then drove in front of the room and opened the van. "How the hell am I going to take these two out now?" As tears started gathering in her eyes, a drop fell on the gift that was in her mum's hand. All of a sudden little blue lights started flying out. The key was grabbed by some of the flying little angels and the door was opened. Others created a big slippery slip and slide, both Donna and Max inside.

Once she placed Donna and Max on their beds, she asked the little lights to look after them while she goes and buys some food.

The room was so big it had four beds, a dining area, small kitchen and a decent size bathroom. The little lights spread themselves all over the room. That was the sign of acceptance.

While Sandy was driving to find some food stores Charlie rang her and said. "We are close to the border but there was a big hold up. When I got out and went closer to see what the delay was, I saw Carlos and Nancy's photos in the hands of guards. They were stopping every car and showing the photos to everyone."

She told Charlie. "Don't turn around. Just call my name when you only have two cars in front of you."

Charlie shocked at what he just heard. "Calling her name and appearance in seconds!" Yet something inside assured him and he said. "Ok Sandy"

Shopping for the necessary stuff didn't take more than a few minutes. She flew back to the room without taking the shopping out. She sat on the chair while holding the two gifts in her hand. "If I am really the queen of Karma I will get them through the border."

Minutes later her blue dress was worn by her again. The two gifts turned into blue glassy thorns in her hand. Suddenly she heard Charlie's voice saying. "Sandy."

As soon as her name was called she found herself at the border, not as a normal size human but a giant of blue light. No one could see her because of the strong light. Everyone was covering their eyes, not knowing what was happening. Then she slowly said. "Charlie pass"

Charlie drove through the light and passed the border. When he was out of sight Sandy found herself back on her seat in the motel room in her old clothes.

Making food feeding her mother and Max and then helping Max to stand up and try to take a few steps became her daily routine. She couldn't find time to visit her dad but was constantly on the phone to hospital.

Weeks went by and Sandy extended her room hire. One day she received a phone call and was asked to rush to the hospital. Not knowing what to do, she said. "Max I know you can't move but keep your eyes on Mum so she doesn't leave the room. I will be back as soon as I can."

When she got there the nurse said. "He is awake but hasn't got much time."

Sandy rushed in to her dad's room, fell on his bed and cried. "Oh thanks god you are awake."

Don moved his shaky fingers through her beautiful hair. "I am so sorry I wasn't there to protect you."

"I don't need protection. I am doing perfectly all right. All I need is to take you home."

"Where is your mother?"

Not wanting her father to know that she had a stroke, and that she doesn't recognize any one she came up with a lie. "Someone had to stay with Max."

"Oh, your brother Jason has been visiting me. He really has changed. Just before I die I saw how much love he has for his family".

"You are not going anywhere. We have a lot of work to do." Sandy said while kissing Don's hand.

"I hope I left enough behind for you and your mum to have a good life. Take care of each other and trust Jason."

Before Sandy could open her mouth, Don closed his eyes and his hand fell on the bed. Sandy started screaming and crying. The mountain that had given her courage and love, had finally collapsed.

The alarm went off. Doctors and nurses rushed in. They tried to revive him but the kind loving giant was gone forever. Minutes later Jason rushed in and grabbed his sister. They cried for over an hour. There was nowhere else they wanted to be. The man that gave them life, hope and a loving home had gone forever.

The hospital bill had grown markedly since the last time Sandy visited her father. It proved to be unfortunate that in order to get her father's body released to her, she had to pay the entire bill.

The body was released to the funeral directors. Before meeting with them Jason called Joshua and his sisters to come for a meeting.

At the meeting the costs of the hospital and funeral were mentioned by Jason he also suggested that they should help Sandy.

When the costs were discussed Jasmin said. "Sandy should pay for it since god knows, what dad has left her."

Jason and Mandy both turned to Jasmin and told her. "Not to worry. We will pay for his funeral with his own money."

"What money?" Asked Jasmin

"The money that was stolen from him, and given to us." replied Jason

Jackie got offended and said. "Are you calling us thieves now?"

"Whatever you call it, now is not the time." Jason replied

Sandy screamed her head off when Jasmin and Jackie didn't want to give up the argument. "What is the matter with you? Your father is dead and yet you have not shed a tear. The only thing you are worried about is who will pay for funeral."

"Keep your voice down loser. You have been living for free all these years with Mum and Dad. They felt sorry for you because they knew you are nothing but a loser. I bet you Dad had his fortune hidden which he probably gave to you out of com passion." Jasmin shouted.

Sandy replied.

"If you haven't walked in my path
When pain was the only companion
When loneliness was the only painting on the walls
When the cries of the wounded wolf were the only music
    to the ears
When skies were always grey and eyes never stopped
    shedding tears
When comfort laid behind the stars and peace was
    beyond reach
Judge me not Jasmin
Careful so that all these blessings don't become yours."

Sandy walked out of the room. Jasmin with a shaky voice said. "The poet now is telling us. I will show you."

Joshua was quiet the whole time. He could not make sense of anything. Jason was hurt more than ever and said. "Which one of you did anything for Dad and Mum, apart from helping a crook to steal all their money and home?" He then rushed after Sandy.

"Don't worry Jason, with the little that I have left, I will pay for funeral." Sandy said.

"No. I told you, me and Mandy will take care of everything. You go on where ever you are living. I will call you with the funeral date."

All the way home Sandy was crying. She has no job. Her money was almost gone and now she had two sick people on her hand.

The Funeral took place a few days later. Joshua, Jason and Sandy were the only ones that showed up at funeral to say good bye to their father for the last time. Angelo and his men showed up. He tried to talk to Sandy but she kept her head down and did not answer any of his questions.

After the funeral Sandy realized that she has been followed. As soon as she got to this isolated restaurant, that was placed there for travellers, she pulled over and went inside. She ordered food, while watching Angelo's men who thought they would have a bit to eat, while she eat her food. They had arrived shortly after her.

Sandy quickly touched the gifts and said now is the time to help me. However she knew that she should not do any favours for herself with the power given to her so she quickly moved her hand away from the gifts and called the waiters with a loud voice "Call me an ambulance. I think I have food poisoning." She made herself vomit. The waiters called the ambulance. Sandy was taken to hospital and the men went back to Angelo and told him she was in hospital.

Before going back to Angelo the two men followed the ambulance to the hospital, waited around for a few minutes then left.

Sandy noticed the two men are missing she ran out of the hospital and got a lift straight to her van. Knowing they probably have her plate number and they can easily locate her. She decide to get rid of the van and purchase another vehicle.

Sandy found a car yard that was paying cash for cars and she sold her van to them the next thing she did was going to another car yard and bought another van although this one was not as good and equipped as the first one, but she had no choice. She needed a van to carry her mum and Max.

When she got to the motel, Max was sitting up looking at the door and her mum was deep sleep. Max called out. "Sandy this is too much for you. Why don't you take us to a nursing home? That way you can go back to work and won't have this much stress."

"Not in a million year." she replied. "You and mum are the only thing I have left in this world and I will not do such a thing."

"You have been a great friend. No other human would have done what you did." Max said.

"If you are so worried about me Max, try harder because when you are able to stand back on your feet, we can fight the devil together."

"I am doing my best." Max replied. If you want we can increase my exercise hours."

"Hectic." Sandy replied.

A few hours later it got dark. Max and Sandy were watching TV when they heard screams. Sandy rushed out to see what was happening but all she could see was a massive blue light in shape of a giant. No one could look at it straight and those who were caught with this light, while driving had to stop because they were blinded by it.

Going back in the room Sandy said. "Quickly we have to leave."

"Why?" Max asked

"We must be in danger. That is why the light has appeared."

"Then help me in my chair and I will carry some of the stuff with me, while you bring your mum out."

"Ok Max." said Sandy. Before she did that, the room was filled again with little blue lights. Max was dragged into his chair. Her mum was flying toward the van and all their belongings were getting pack.

Max and Sandy were looking at all that was happening in that room with unbelief. We better move. I don't know how long the light is going to hold.

When they all were finally in the van driving off, Sandy could see that the blue light turned into hundreds of lightening arrows. "My god I think a storm is on the way." She started speeding. "I hope the storm doesn't catch up with us because it looks horrifying."

Driving on the road for hours, not knowing where to go Sandy started shedding tears quietly. Max and her mum had gone to sleep. This drive was so different to any other drives she ever had, because there was no destination, no plans and paying the hospital bill was the last bit of money she had. She pulled over in middle of nowhere and got out of the car. "Oh god what am I going to do?"

A few minutes later a Ute stopped in front of her and asked her if she needed help. She looked at the elderly couple in the Ute and said. "Oh yes I need help."

"Is your van drivable?" The couple asked

"Yes it is."

"Then follow us. It is late and the roads are not safe for you."

Sandy started following the Ute until they got in front of this very small house on an isolated farm. She got out of the car as the couple waited for her and said "I am not alone."

A worried look covered the faces of the two old people. They thought they had brought trouble to their house, Sandy quickly picked up on the worried look and said. "Please don't worry." She then opened the van and showed Max and her mum to the elderly couple. "See none of them can move. You have nothing to worry about."

The couple helped Sandy with carrying the two sick people from the van to the house. The old woman quickly made some coffee and brought in some homemade cheese and bread. "I hope this satisfies your hunger because it is too late in the night to cook."

Max looked at the couple and said. "Thank you. Even with what you are serving us, is too much as we are total strangers to you."

After everyone had their cup of coffee and something to eat, the woman directed Sandy to a spare bedroom, "Although this is not much, it should do for tonight."

Sandy thanked the lady and helped her mum and Max to bed before going outside. While sitting on the rocking chair for a few minutes she forgot about all her problems, admiring the beauty of hills and surroundings in the moonlight. Minutes later the elderly couple came out with three glasses and a bottle of brandy. The old man said "I hope you like brandy."

"Oh yes, thanks. I have not had a drink for a long time. This reminds me of all the times that my dad would say come on I think we both deserve a drink."

The elderly woman asked. "We don't mean to poke our heads into your business but it seems that you are from a wealthy family. What are you doing here?"

"It is a very long story." Sandy replied.

"We barely get any visitors here. If you want to tell us anything while we are drinking, we are all ears."

"Max is my friend and the woman is my mum. My father just died. Yes you are right. I was from a very wealthy family, wealthy with love and money. Sandy then went deep into the story of how she got to where she had being found by them. Towards the end her tears were flowing, especially when she told them that she hasn't got much money and nowhere to go and that there are people out there who want them dead."

The elderly woman then got off her seat and hugged Sandy. "Don't worry darling, as you can see we are old and don't have anyone close by. My son is in another state and only visits us during the holidays. We would be grateful if you stayed with us. We don't want any money from you. Just the company."

"Why would you do such a big favour to a total stranger?" Sandy asked

The woman replied. "You probably did the same thing to someone else at some stage in your life and now God sent us your way."

"Thank you." Said Sandy

They all then went to bed. Sandy was given an air mattress to sleep on. She placed it on the floor in the spare bedroom. For once in several months, she went straight to sleep and in the morning when she woke up she didn't see her mum or Max. She rushed to the sitting room and found them sitting on the couch.

"Thanks to these beautiful people, they showered us both and made us a beautiful country breakfast." Max said.

"Come on darling." said the elderly woman "I will bring your breakfast in for you. She then walked to the kitchen and came back with a freshly made coffee and a plate of bacon and eggs with homemade bread.

"Thank you but you don't need to do this. I don't want you to go out of your comfort zone for us."

Max quickly jumped in on the conversation and said. "Sandy, Brook and Brian were telling me that we can stay with them for a while. Have you decided of where we are going?"

"Not yet, but for now I take these nice people's offer and we can stay here. I can help them with the farm."

The couple were so happy when Sandy accepted their offer. They both got up from their seats and hugged her.

In the mornings, Sandy would help with gathering eggs, making breakfast and at night the three of them would sit outside and have a drink together.

Max started getting in his chair by himself and slowly going outside. Brian made a rail with wood on the four sides of the rail. On each wooden rail on both sides he put robe and tightened them up with nails and glue, leaving enough space for one to put their hands through to grab the robe for support.

When he finished this little therapy project, he took Max there and said to him. This is where you will be exercising your legs. I will bring you out here for an hour a day until we find out if it is working or not."

The first day was really hard. With Brian's help Max stood up and took a few steps but even those few steps took him around an hour.

Donna was completely out of this world. Not talking or remembering, one night she started crying and complaining of pain. Sandy took her to the hospital and after running some tests they found that she had cancer and hadn't got long to live. From the hospital Sandy rang Jason but could not get through. She then tried her sisters. As soon as they heard her voice they hung up on her.

The old couple became Sandy's second parents, supporting her emotionally was the only thing they could do. Finally a month later Donna died. By now Sandy has lost her phones and had no contact with anyone. The money she had left paid for her mum's funeral and now she was back to square one.

After her mum's death and not being able to reach her brothers or sisters Sandy became very sick. She would not come out of the bedroom or eat or drink. Max and the couple would take turns going into her room talking to her but she had given up and nothing they were saying was getting through to her tired brain.

The elderly couple Brook and Brian were so beautiful. They did not give up trying. They would sit for hours and read her stories with a happy ending. Brian continued helping Max with his exercise.

One night the couple received a phone call from their son. "I can't handle living like this anymore. I wish the house was bigger so I could grab my children and come and live there. I really need your help." he said.

Brook and Brian became troubled and told him he could still go to them. They could work something out. He refused.

No matter how much the old parents asked him what was wrong, he would not tell them anything. He just said. "I am tired and depressed right now. I will talk to you later."

The couple were so saddened lost their spirit very quickly. Knowing their son would not talk like this, unless something was really wrong, they went quite for days. Even Max had to exercise by himself.

One night the blue lights filled Sandy's room. This time they joined and became like a big mirror. In that mirror Sandy could see a young man with no hand. He was sitting around the table with three children. All there was on the table is the bread that everyone was feeding on. The mirror then showed Brian and Brook's bedroom and how every night after they went to their bedroom they would cry for their son.

That morning Sandy got up before everyone else and made fresh coffee and breakfast for everybody. When the others got up they were shocked to see Sandy in such good spirit.

The breakfast table was prepared. As soon as she served the coffee they all started with their breakfast. Sandy was looking at the couple and asked. "When was the last time you contacted your son?"

"He called us a few days ago when you were sick."

"Is he in trouble?"

Brook answered. "Not trouble but we believe he is in some sort of difficulty because we have never heard or seen him so low."

"If there was one wish that you could have what would it be?" Asked Sandy

The couple looked at each other and Brian asked. "What is it with all these questions?"

"Trust me. I am just asking to see if there is anything I can do. My wish is to go back to the happy times. Everyone has a wish that They believe will neve come true." Sandy replied.

"Our wish is to have a big house to be able to give our son and each grandchild their own bedroom enough cattle so our son doesn't have to go anywhere to work. Our cattle can produce enough milk and meat for all the locals." Brian said

Sandy said. "I think you should call him and tell him you know about his accident. Tell him you have a bigger house now and you can house him and his family.

"What is wrong with you Sandy?" Brook asked. "Do you think this is a joke?"

"There is nothing wrong with me. See when you make the phone call."

Hearing about the accident the couple rang their son straight away. "Son we heard you were in an accident. Are you doing ok?"

The son replied. "How did you hear? It was not on news or anywhere else for that matter."

"It doesn't matter how we heard. We just called to let you know that we have enough rooms for all of you to come and live with us."

"What do you mean you have enough room?"

The couple looked straight at Sandy wondering what to reply to their son. Sandy grabbed the phone and said. "They mean they have built a new two story house with five bedrooms and swimming pool."

"But how?" Asked the son

"Through the love they have for you." replied Sandy

The son agreed to come. The couple turned to Sandy. "Why would you do that? How are we to build a new two story house in matter of days?"

"Have a bit of faith." said Sandy

The couple then went to their bedroom worried about the reaction their son will present when he arrives and finds out that there is no big house. "Oh my god what have we done." shuttled Brian

When Sandy made sure that everyone was sleeping she grabbed her two gifts and went outside. She held both gifts up towards the sky and said. "I am the Queen of Karma and I humbly ask for Brian and Brook's wish to be granted." All the sudden Sandy was a giant in her glowing blue dress. Lighting touched both gifts and then everything went back to normal. With so much faith Sandy then walked back to the house and went to sleep.

In the morning Brook went to Sandy's room. "Wake up, Wake up" she called out and when Sandy asked her what was wrong she said. "You have to come and see."

When Sandy got out she could see herds of cows everywhere.

"Oh my god Brook, you have a lot of milking to do." sandy replied

"But how did they all get here? Look at that house. It's massive I looked all around it. It even has a swimming pool. How did it all happen overnight?"

It didn't take long before Max and Brian rushed out. Brian screamed. "Is this a dream?"

Brian called out. "Brook, this is the exact description that Sandy gave to our son last night. Don't you want to know how it all got here?"

"Regardless of how it happened, I am happy that our son won't be disappointed in us."

"Just tell me one thing Sandy. Brook implied. "Is it all going to disappear overnight?"

"I told you to have a bit of faith. Maybe your wish was granted because of all the good things you did for us and probably for other people. If a wish gets granted it will never reverse." Sandy replied

"Can we go inside and take a look?" Said Max

"Let's go" said Sandy. They all went in the house. It had two massive dining rooms, a kitchen the size of the couple's old house.

All the walls and the kitchen were decorated in different colours of blue. This was the sign of purity. Upstairs all the bedrooms were fully fitted with their own bathrooms and walk in wardrobes.

"Oh my." Said Brook. "I have never seen anything so beautiful."

"I am starving." Sandy said. "Maybe we should go and eat something then go furniture shopping for the new house."

On breakfast table Brian and Brook kept on grabbing each other's hand, looking each other in the eye. Those moments were so magical.

Before they left the house, Brook grabbed Sandy's hand and said. "I don't know who you are but I want to say thank you, because I know you had something to do with all this."

"Oh pardon me." Sandy Uttered. "I didn't ask if you had money to buy furniture. Forgive me for being so rude."

"Every year we save money for the holidays because we always love to give the best gifts to our grandchildren and son. Now that they are coming for good we can spend that money on furniture."

"Cool" said Sandy

The four of them spent the whole day shopping until all the shops were closed. Then they went to a local restaurant and had dinner.

The next morning trucks arrived with the new furniture. The truck drivers were directed as to what goes where. Within hours the house was furnished and ready to be used.

When they went back to the old house to have lunch. Brian said. "Sandy and Max, now that we have the other house, you can stay in this one by yourselves. We can be neighbours."

"Thank you." they said.

The following day, Brook seemed very impatient and kept on calling Brian to see if the family arrived? "What is happening? Why are they so late?"

"Instead of going mad on me, why don't you concentrate on making a miracle meal with a dream desert in our new kitchen?" Brian replied

They all laughed. Before Sandy calls out. "He is right I will come and help you."

While the women went to prepare the meal, Brian and Max were sitting outside chatting...

"Sandy is a very special girl." Brian remarked

"I know." Max replied. Even her parents were so special they would go out of their way to help people. When my enemies tried to take my father's factory away. Don stood by me and helped me get back on my feet. Never in my life have I seen people like them, until that night that we met you and your wife."

All of a sudden Brian got off his chair, looked outside. There was a car visible in distance. He ran towards the new house and called. "I think they are here." In seconds Brook and Sandy could be seen rushing out.

The kids ran out of the car. "Grandpa, grandma" they called out.

The son appeared trying to hide his arm so it wouldn't come as a shock to his parents.

"You really did build a big house as you said".

"Well it is a long story." Brian said. "Never mind. Let's get inside. You must be exhausted." Although the elderly couple noticed their son's arm they didn't say anything. They did not want to make him feel uncomfortable at his arrival.

"Son," Said Brian. "Do you still drink Brandy?"

"You know dad, I always enjoyed my brandy with you."

Brian then introduced Sandy and Max to his son saying. "These nice people have been my partners for a few shouts of brandy at night."

The kids were so excited that they would be living with their grandparents. They hadn't had a fine meal in months but the excitement of seeing their bedroom was more important at that very moment. "Grandma, can you tell us which bedroom belongs to who?"

Brook smiled with tears in her eyes. "Why don't you check the doors I am sure your names are on there?"

The kids ran towards the bedrooms and each found its own bedroom. Minutes later Brook shouted. Ok everyone. Let's eat."

At the dining table the son said. "I know you all want to know what happened to my arm. And are scared to ask me. Well one day on my way home from work I saw an accident it looked really bad I stopped and went towards the car and saw a young girl stuck in the car. Worried that the car could blow up, I tried to get the girl out and when I pushed her out with one hand. I then pulled her with my other hand.

All of a sudden there was a big bang and all I felt was pain. When I looked a piece of metal had gone right through my arm. It's chopped off but I still did not give up. I dragged the young girl to safety then collapsed. The next thing I knew was waking up in hospital. The doctors told me they were sorry for not being able to save my arm. I wasn't disappointed because I saved a young life and my arm was not comparable to that."

"Soon after, I lost my job and my wife left me. She didn't want to be part of a poor family."

"The bills started catching up with me and I couldn't afford to make the repayments on the house. As a last resort I took refuge at the only safe and warm place that I knew and that warm place was with you. When I called you I remembered that you didn't know about my arm and I didn't want to upset you, plus we would have been a burden living with you in that small house with only two bedrooms. When you called me, I had only two days left to leave the house with nowhere to go. That is why I say, cheers to the best parents ever."

They all picked up their glasses and said cheers to the happy ending. After lunch Sandy helped with cleaning the table and washing the dishes then she excused herself and Max. "I am sure you people have so much catching up to do. Me and Max will see you later."

<h1 style="text-align:center">Chapter 19</h1>

Claiming that Nancy and Carlos stole all those millions of dollars from the company, Angelo was able to find the three houses that they bought and he auctioned them to recover the supposedly stolen money. The sales were so successful that the total amount of the sale for the three properties reached just over eight million.

The monster was so pleased for making such a big profit with so little effort.

Joshua, Jasmin and Jackie were at the auction and approached Angelo for their shares but they were surrounded by Angelo's men who escorted them out of the area with a warning.

The dirty giant never had enough. Don's children were still a threat to him and he was going to do everything in his power to break them down. However right now he was dealing with a bigger problem. That being Max was alive and had been seen with Sandy. That could be the sign of his collapse. He engaged all his powers into finding and finishing Max.

"I want you to go back to where Donna's funeral took place and drive to all the places that you were following Sandy. I want you to stop at every house, coffee shop, and hospital and present Sandy's photo until you find someone who can establish of their whereabouts." "Angelo expected of his men.

Among Angelo's men were croaked cops and detectives who were just like Angelo. They would do any dirty work for big amounts of money.

Luckily one off the detectives had an honest partner, detective Brad who overheard Angelo's conversation with his men. It was a total accident that he could see the photo that Angelo was showing to his men. He quickly went and acquitted the identification of the person in the photo. When he saw her name he remembered he had a best friend years ago that had a sister called Sandy. When he got home after work he went through his albums and found a photo of himself, Jason and Sandy. The photo was taken years ago.

He quickly grabbed the photo and went to a public phone and called Jason. "Hey Brad." said Jason. "What a surprise what made you call me after all these years?"

"I think we should meet face to face." Brad replied. "Remember where we use to hide when we were kids? Meet me there."

An hour later Jason shows up at the Randhawa with a bottle of champion and two glasses. Brad smiled and said. You haven't changed. Always something to celebrate with."

"Off course it is not every day that I find one of my best friends." they grabbed and hugged each other "Oh remember, Max use to hide in this place as well."

"Oh yeah. I heard that he died."

Jason didn't want to give the secret away, so he said "I heard the same. Anyway what was so urgent?"

Brad then told Jason of how he accidently overheard Angelo, and that he thinks Sandy is in danger.

"How do I know you are not one of them?"

"We were friends for a long time. You should know better than that."

"I thought I knew my brother and sisters as well but look what they did to my family."

"What happened?" Asked Brad but then quickly said. "Never mind. You can tell me at another time. I am telling you because I saw my partner among Angelo's men. Whatever you do Jason don't even trust the cops. If you know where your sister is warn her."

"We lost contact a few months ago. I've been worried to death all these months and have no way of finding where she could be."

"That is a good sign. Said Brad. "That means you are off the hook for now. I hope you don't mind that I did some digging and found that your father bought properties in different names. One was called Nancy and the man, I think his name was Carlos. From what I found out Angelo accused those two of stealing money from the company and buying properties. The fact is that happened long before your dad's will was enforced and those two people whoever they were, were the true owners of four properties. Angelo got his hands on them and sold them for just a bit over eight million."

Jason's blood was boiling. "Eight million could have helped his younger sister so as she did not have to struggle. Should I take legal action against him? he asked.

"It is too late and not a good time because your dumb ass brother and sisters never confronted Angelo. The only time that they apparently went to him was when the properties were sold and they wanted shares. Which unfortunately Angelo does not leak money, even to his own son."

"My banker told me that there was a lot of enquires going into the accounts I am holding."

"What are you sitting on right now?" Brad asked

"Easily over a few billions."

"No wonder, Angelo probably started the enquiry because he must know how much you are worth. Any way let's forget about everything right now and concentrate on your sister."

"What do you want me to do? I didn't even know my mum was dead. How can I find my sister?"

"Don't worry. Please do not contact me at all. I will call you as soon as I get any news, and if I need to contact you urgently I will call you from public phone. In the meantime protect your cell phone as if it's your life, so as no one can put a bug in it."

"Ok" Said Jason

Angelo has now directed all the creditors to Joshua and his sisters. Things are so bad that their kids cannot go to school and they cannot leave the house without being confronted, threatened. Most importantly they are holding to their money like glue.

It doesn't take long for Angelo to set another trap for the two sisters and Joshua, by sending his men in, pretending they are creditors and breaking all the windows of Jasmin's house. "Why Jasmine one would ask? The answer would be she took more shares more than anyone else. She is worth over ten to eleven billion dollars.

While Angelo is busy destroying lives, his son Jo accidently meet Colin and Collet at a restaurant. He is so disgusted with his father's actions that he would spend most of his time alone in bars and restaurants trying to come up with a solution of how to help Sandy. Their childhood kept on repeating itself in front of his eyes. On that one night, when he saw the two familiar faces he was so happy. Jo always knew that Colin and Don were different to the others.

At the beginning Colin got worried when he saw Jo, but Jo assured him "I am not my father."

They joined each other for dinner and talked about old times, Colin asked, "Have you heard from Don and his family?"

"No" Said Jo, "Haven't you heard? Don and Donna are both dead."

"Oh my" Said Collet. "How? We had dinner at their place a few months ago. It was the best night we had for a long time."

"Thanks to my beautiful and loving father. He did not leave them much space to breath."

"But Don himself was a very power full man. How could he let this happen?"

"Well that is a mystery for me as well. I hope to find the truth one day."

"Where is their daughter Sandy now?" Asked Collet

"She disappeared a few months ago. For my sake and hers, I hope to find her before my dad does. I overheard him one day screaming at one of his men. "Find her" Find her do you hear me?"

"What does he want from her?"

"Sad to say, but I think my father is after her life."

"We had some problems a few months ago so we sold our business and went away. This is our first night back in town." Colin said

"Probably my dad had something to do with you selling your business."

"Whatever. It is past now." Collet replied

"Are you working with your dad right now?"

"No. I walked out of the house after we argued over Don's family. I don't think I know my father any more. He has become so evil and won't stop even for me. When I found out what he had done with Don's family I was disgusted and I told him that."

"Sorry to hear tha.t" Collet replied

"So what you do?" Colin asked

"At the moment all I care about is to find Sandy. I am truly worried that my dad's men will kill her when they find her."

"That sounds like your dad." Collet said

"We had to sell everything and run away because we didn't want to be a part of his evil tricks and greed."

"Oh well, let's hope that one day everything goes back to normal." Jo replied

For some reason Colet and Colin could see the concerns on Jo's face and tried to cheer him up. Colet asks. "Where is your girlfriend tonight?"

"Girlfriend! I don't have one. Right now I need a lot of space so I can decide what I want to do."

After spending a few hours with Colet and Colin, Jo made his way to the hotel where he was staying. As soon as he got out of the car, two men grabbed him and took him to Angelo.

"I told you to keep your head out of my business." Angelo screamed. "But what you do? Get drunk every night then walk around questioning my private detectives re their findings?"

"Why did you bring me here?" Jo asked. "Oh I forgot. You can't be a father. You can't even act like one because if you were really my father you would come and talk to me and not make your men to snatch me from the streets. Shame on you Angelo."

Angelo slaps Jo in the face and says "You are no son of mine. If you were, you would worship me."

"You are not God. Why should I worship you? Plus don't you know, none of this can be taken to your grave when you die."

Angelo slaps him harder this time. "Take him back to where ever you brought him from." His men came and grabbed Jo and took him back to his hotel.

Jo had a shower when he went to his room, then cried all night. On the other hand his father was laughing and carrying on about how he destroyed Don's empire.

When Michelle heard her husband slapped Jo, she was not very happy. "Why would you do such thing?" She screamed at Angelo

"He made me do it." said Angelo

"He is your son. If you don't respect him he won't respect you." Michelle then went running to her bedroom.

Angelo followed her to the bedroom and said. "Don't ever talk to me like that in front of my staff."

"What have I done?" Asked Michelle

"You enjoyed the best life a life that every woman prays for, that is what you have done." Cried Angelo.

Chapter 20

Breaking the windows scared Adam, Jasmin's husband. He told her you either pay the creditors and get rid of them or I will take my kids and move out. "I do not want any harm to come to my children"

"Take them." Jasmin replied. "If you have a job to look after their daily needs"

"You call this daily? This is blood money. Give it away before your sin catches up with all of us." Adam screamed.

"Are you seriously this jealous? Because I have money and you don't?"

"Go to hell Jasmin. That is your dad's blood money because you, your sister and brother went along with a crook and murderer to gain your dad's fortune."

"Oh well, if you want to go, the door is open." said Jasmine"

Adam then disappeared and a short while later reappeared with his kids to say good bye to Jasmine. "Please don't go. I am scared. What if any of the creditors find their way inside the house?"

"That obviously is not our problem." Adam replied. "Plus if you pay them they will leave you alone."

Adam and the children then walked out of the house and went to a hotel in the local area. Although Jasmin hurt his feelings but. Adam didn't want any harm to come to her.

Being so scared Jasmine called Joshua and Jackie. "I really think we should look at the creditors list and see what we can do."

"When they all agreed she called Angelo and asked him for the creditors list. Angelo already had prepared a list which he had created. There were no hard copies to prove that anything on that list was legitimate.

The total amount showing on the creditors list was just over seven billion. If they decided to pay them, a big chunk of their assets would be lost.

Joshua suggested to get a solicitor and investigate the actual creditors, Angelo was not a person to leave any foot prints behind. He actually mentioned in the sale contract that the brothers and sisters would pay the creditors. However they were so blinded by what was taking place that they did not read the contract properly. The solicitor later studied the contract. When he told Joshua and his sisters that they should have read the contract before signing it t there was nothing that he could do for them now. The solicitor also told them. "If you want to press charges you are going to need a very big firm that can handle big cases like this."

Without telling anyone, Joshua went on his own and hired a few private detectives to follow up on the creditors and their business. A few weeks later they came back to Joshua. "We checked all those businesses. None of them seem to have ever dealt with your company. The reason being, half of them belong to Angelo and the other half by the chain."

Joshua was furious. He didn't know what to do for once in his life. He felt sorry for listening to his sisters. If Angelo is behind all this there is nothing he can do because he hasn't got the sources nor the experience to deal with crooks like Angelo.

Depressed, not knowing what to do, Joshua went to his father's grave. He sat there talking to the grave and crying.

Joshua was a tall man his grey hair just started showing in his light brown hair an attractive man. Eyes would follow him anywhere that he walked. Although he listened to his wife and sisters and destroyed his father's dynasty. He was a family man and would always put his family before anything. The beautiful women would chase him everywhere. Marriage was sacred for him that's why he always disappointed those women that chased him.

Spending hours on his own at the grave Joshua finally made his way home. His son and daughter ran to him and hugged him. He hugged them then rested on the couch.

Cindy walked in and asked him where he had been. He didn't reply. For the second time she said. "I asked you where you were all this time."

"I am not in the mood to say, just leave me alone pleas." Joshua replied.

"Not until you tell me where you were. Are you cheating on me?"

"If you had half of a brain you wouldn't be asking questions like this." he replied

"Your sister rang. Her husband and the kids have left the house. She is horrified."

"What do you want me to do? Let her hire body guards."

"What is wrong with you Joshua?"

"Everything is wrong with me. I lost my parents, my father's dynasty. I don't know where my younger sister is or what she is doing. I the eldest son, ruined the life for everyone because of your and my sister's greed."

"What makes you worry about that dumb arse sister?"

"Watch your mouth." Cindy

"What are you going to do? Ha."

Joshua got off the couch and tried to walk away from Cindy. The evil woman grabbed his arm and screams. "Where do you think you are going?"

The only reaction that Joshua showed was to turn and slap Cindy in the face and walk away.

This was the first time in his whole life that he laid a hand on another human. He did not know what was happening to him. All he could feel was pain. He got into the shower and turned the water on so nobody could hear him cry. A few minutes later someone knocked on the door and a man's voice said. "Sir you better hurry and come ou.t"

When he got out of the shower there were two cops waiting for him who directed him to get dressed. They then arrested him for assault.

Cindy who was handed some photos by Angelo's men was furious and had Joshua arrested.

In the morning news it was said. "The son of the giant business man Don was arrested last night for assault after his wife called the cops fearing for her life. When the cops arrived the woman had a bruised face. His wife told the cops that it was not the first time he laid a hand on her. However she was too scared to report him."

Jasmine and Jackie heard the news and were shocked. Joshua would not even hurt an ant. How Cindy could tell all these lies about him. Unable to contact Cindy, the sisters made it to the police station to check on their brother. They told him about what Cindy said to the reports. That came as a shock to Joshua.

"What happened to Cindy? We have been married over twenty years. Why would she lie like this?" Joshua questioned

Jackie didn't have the answer. "We will try to talk to Cindy."

On the day of his appearance in court the judge didn't accept any bail. He said. "I will make an example of this man for the rest of the rich people to know when it comes to justice their money means nothing."

His sisters told him not to worry. They would hire the best lawyers for him, but as soon as they walked out of the court they forgot about him.

About three months later Joshua, was released from jail. He went home his key did not work in the door so he knocked on the door. This strange woman opened the door and asked him if she could help him.

"Who are you?" Asked Joshua

"This is my house. replied the woman. "Who are you?"

"What do you mean it is your house? It is mine I only went away for a few months."

"I bought the house about a month ago and for a good price because the people who owned it were in a hurry to sell and move to Europe."

The woman then closed the door and Joshua was left at the front. Shocked and disappointed. Where could he go? He had no ide no money and no home to go to. Once a CEO. At that very moment he felt homeless.

Joshua then went to his sister's house but the same thing happened to him. All their houses were sold and there was nowhere else for Joshua to go to. He made it to a public phone and called his sisters cell phones but they too were disconnected. The mixed emotion that Joshua was going through were not normal. One second he was smiling and thinking this is just a big joke. Then his face was going into a serious mode "What if something happened to them."

Out of desperation and out of options, Joshua made his way to the park. After a few minutes he went to sleep. A homeless man that was passing through took his only blanket out of his trolley and put it on Joshua. With the gentle touch of the blanket Joshua woke up and saw the man walking away. He called. "Why would you give me the only thing that warms you up?"

The man turned smiled and said. "What I give to you today will be given back to me in double when I need it."

"What do you mean? You will get two blankets back?"

Again the man smiled and said. "Only those who believe in Karma would understand this."

"You seem like a wise man? Would you please explain it to me?"

The homeless man walked back to Joshua and sat next to him. "In the old days they use to say what you plant you will draw from. The grave that you dig for others, will become yours."

Joshua went into deep thought. The man then asked. "You look like a wealthy man why you are in the park?"

"Because I dug a grave for someone now I am getting buried in it."

"You don't have to tell me anything if you don't want to?"

"I made a deal with the devil himself. Not only have I lost everything I caused my parents death and my sister to disappear."

"You played a game and you lost it doesn't mean that you should give up so easily and become homeless like me. You are young and have lots of opportunities ahead of you. Go find your family and if you are sincere in your regrets, you will gain everything back."

"Where do I start?" Asked Joshua

"It doesn't matter where" the man replied, As long as you start."

The man then pulled a bottle of brandy from his jacket and says. "Let's drink to your success."

After having a few drinks the man departed, Joshua seemed like a different man, I will find all my family and I will bring all of them together again.

In the morning Joshua cleaned himself up and went to the kid's school but was told that they had left the school.

Desperate and full of tears Joshua went back to the park hungry and thirsty with no money at all. He rested his tired body on a seat. Tears poured out on his face. Quietly he closed his eyes for a second when he heard a voice.

"Excuse me sir mind if I join you?"

"Not at all." said Joshua

It was the same man from the night before. He pulled out a bottle of water and handed it to Joshua. "Here it looks like you need this."

Joshua was thirsty as a plant that hadn't been watered for days. He sculled the bottle of water. He then thanked the man.

"Did you try hard enough today?" The man asked

"Not really. I went to my kid's school only to find out that they have been moved from there. I really don't know what to do. I went to all their houses. Called all their cells but haven't been able to find any of them."

"What about your brother?"

"I even tried him and went to his business but even that has been sold and all his numbers have changed."

"Don't worry son when all the doors close, a slightly small light comes through. Just be patient and everything will fall into place at the right time." The old man then got up and moved away. A few minutes later he came back with two sandwiches and handed them to Joshua.

Starring at the man, Joshua asked. "Why are you helping me?"

"I told you." said the old man. "Good or bad Karma follows us all. We should be prepared at all time. Wash your face and clean your heart so you may see the little light that will show you the way."

When the man tried to leave Joshua noticed that the man dropped a fifty dollar note on the ground he called out. "Sir you dropped your money."

The man smiled and said. "My work is done here." He disappeared"

Josh sat there for a few minutes trying to make sense as to what just happened but then he got off the seat and started running out of the park with a smile on his face.

<h1 style="text-align:center">Chapter 21</h1>

Brian and Brook are so pleased with their lives. Their son is working with them. The cattle was so big that they started selling meat and milk to local shops. The grandchildren are going to a local school and have made so many friends. It felt like they had lived there all their lives. This small and beautiful family still have their three meals with Sandy and Max.

Sandy saw everything that was happening to her family nightmare after nightmare however she could not use her powers to favour them. She would hide in her room for hours and cry. Max who was getting better by day, would kneel in front of her and ask her what he could do to make the pain better.

During this hard time Max hated his life but he never stopped trying to get better to repay Sandy for all her help.

Brian and Brook felt like they had gained another daughter and son. They never wanted these beautiful moments to end and when Brook one day asked Brian. "Do you think we will eventually loose Max and Sandy?"

"Don't even think about it because you might bring it undone. Let everything to go the way it is. Why worry about one day that might never come." Brian replied

One morning when Brian's son was dropping his kids off at school, he saw some strangers going around asking people questions. When he got closer, he noticed they were showing photographs of Max and Sandy's and asking the locals if anyone has seen them. He told his kids not to talk to anyone and if the photos are shown to them, that they should deny knowing Sandy and Max. He then kisses his kids while they walked towards the school.

That morning he was supposed to buy a few things for the farm but instead he went home. "Dad" he said, there are people looking for Max and Sandy in town. They looked really mean."

Brian's eyes filled with tears knowing the day had come for his new son and daughter to leave them. He told his son. "Hurry go and call them."

When Sandy walked in she could see that both Brian and Brook had been crying. She ran and hugged them. Those things might look bad right now but everything will be fine.

The son asked. "Why are these people looking for you?"

"Your dad will tell you everything when we are gone." Sandy replied

"How long do you think it will be, that they find out we are here?" Max asked

"No one has seen you or know you are here. You don't have to leave." Brook cried out.

"They must know that we are close by. It won't be long before they come knocking on all the doors. For your sake we cannot take the risk. We should leave straight away." Sandy said.

Brian then hands an envelope to Sandy. "Take this please. You will need it."

"Oh we cannot accept this." Sandy replied "You have done enough for us already."

"But not as much as you did. I still believe all these things that we have are your doings. There is something so special about you. Sometimes I even think you are an angel sent by God." Brian said, while crying.

"Please don't cry." Sandy said. "It breaks my heart to see you like this. We promise to come back when we sort everything out.

Thank you for the money. That will be big help for us. We will not forget your kindness."

The son then handed his keys to Sandy. "Here take my jeep because I feel you will be safe if you drive a reliable car."

Sandy and Max thanked everyone and packed only their clothes and a few small things and quickly took off.

"Where to now?" Max asked

"Wherever the destiny takes us."

Sandy drove for hours until it started to get dark. She pulled up in front of this café to get something to eat. However as soon as she got close to the glass window, she saw two of Angelo's men sitting inside. She quickly ran back to the car and waited for over two hours until the two men left. She watched the way they went so that she of course would go the opposite way. She put on a pair of glasses a hat and went into the café to order food.

When she came back to the car she told Max. "I think we should find a place to rest and have our dinner. We shouldn't show our faces in public."

About twenty minutes later while driving past this farm they saw a shed. Max said, I will check it out but Sandy said. "No I will go because if anything goes wrong I can run."

Sandy walked in to the shed with a torch. Walking around she find's a tap a bed and a few living necessities in the shed. She ran back to the car and told him it was safe. However, by the looks of it someone might have been living in there." She added

They turned on the torch and placed it in the middle of shed. It gave them enough light to sit and eat their meal. The light of the moon appeared through the old roof and lit the whole shed.

In the morning they got out of the shed to have a look around. Everything they needed to survive for a few weeks was in that shed but outside they could not see a house.

"Max do you think someone is living here?"

"By the looks of it."

"Should we leave then?"

"Maybe no one lives here. Perhaps they use it as a resting point. I think we should stay for a while and if anyone shows up we will tell them we were lost and had to rest for a little while."

"Ok let's do that." Said Sandy"

The two of them then went for a drive to see if they could see anyone, they drove on and could not see any houses or a living soul. That proved to be of comfort to them. They picked up a few things from the road side shops and went back to the shed.

While Max made himself busy, preparing something to eat Sandy went to sleep. In her sleep she kept on talking and struggling with her hands and legs. Max woke her up and asked. "What is the matter?"

Tears were rushing on her face. "I wish I could tell you."

Max then hugged her for a few seconds to comfort her then went back to finish his food preparation.

Sandy again started to talk to someone. She seemed so restless. Not being sleep at this point she was seeing everything that was taking place.

While they were eating Sandy said. "Max I have to go back."

"Back where?" exclaimed Max

"Home." she replied

"What home? Have you forgotten we have nothing to go back to, until I am fit enough to put up the fight to regain all my assets."

"You don't have to come. I will take you back to Brian and I will go alone. Someone desperately needs my help."

"I am not staying anywhere without you. I'll go where ever you go." Max replied. "When do you want to leave?"

"First thing in the morning." Sandy said

At five am the next morning Sandy and Max prepare some water and food for the road. Finally they hit the road. At around lunch time they saw massive black clouds gathering, so they turned the radio on to see if there was a broadcast about any storms coming their way. Their fears were turned to reality when the broadcast announced a massive tornado was on the way.

Sandy got into panic but Max said. "Are we not close to Brian's farm? May be we should go there until the storm passes?"

Sandy agreed. They drove straight to the big house of Brian's. When they knock on the door, Brook opened the door and screamed. "Oh my god, get inside. There is a storm on the way."

Brian ran towards the door when he heard Brook screaming. There were the two people that had changed his life forever. After hugging and kissing each other they all went to the lunch room. "You couldn't have found a better time to arrive." Brian said, "I was just telling Brook, I wish my drinking partner was her."

Sandy smiled and said. "I can really do with your nice brandy."

Minutes later the son and his kids arrived. They all gathered in the lunch room waiting for the storm to pass. An hour later the lightening and the cowling of the wind started. The house was shaking and the kids were crying.

"This is not safe, said Brook." We should have made ourselves a shelter under the ground."

"I believe we are safe and nothing will move this house from its roots." Brian continued. "That is because she who granted this house was directed back to it before the storm."

To stop the awkward situation, Max picked up his glass. "Cheers to the best people I have ever known."

Everyone put their glasses up and drank to that.

"Are you here to stay?" Asked the son

"No" Replied Max. "We heard the storm was coming and being close by we thought we would drop in."

"Won't you at least stay the night?" Asked Brook

Max and Sandy looked at each other and smiled. "Off course we will." Max stated.

That night was full of laughs and happiness. Brian and Sandy did not stop drinking until they were knocked out. It didn't take long for the morning to arrive and for the two to depart again. There was a mysterious bond with this beautiful family. Every time they had to depart things seemed really sad.

After driving for few hours, Sandy pulled in front of a park and looked around, as if she was expecting to see someone there. It did not take long before this man came to her and said. "Don't worry I looked after him."

"Before Sandy could ask any questions, the man disappeared. Of course Max asked. "What was all that about?"

"We will find out soon. Night arrived and Sandy was still waiting in the car as was Max. Max did not want to make her uncomfortable so he did not question her actions.

Suddenly a familiar face, a man with his face covered in blood and clothes torn apart appeared in the park. He walked toward a seat and rests his painful and smashed body in the seat.

"Is that not your brother?"

"Yes, it is"

"What happened to him? Do you want me to go get him?"

"No. Let me just stare at him for a few moments. Look at my beautiful brother what has happened to him."

Max slowly brushed his fingers through her beautiful black hair and said. "Everything will be alright."

The man appears before Joshua. "Here take this water wash your face. Soon you will have a visitor. As Joshua grabbed the bottle and washed his face the man disappeared again.

Joshua screamed. "If you keep on disappearing on me like this how can I ever thank you?"

A voice drafted back. "You already repaid me by turning your back on your past and becoming a new man, a good man.

Joshua puts his head down in his hand when a familiar voice called his name. "Josh"

"Josh!" He recognized the voice but said. "It cannot be."

Sandy approaches and grabs his hand. She says. "Josh it is me Sandy, what happened to you?"

He looked up at his sister and started crying. "How did you find me?"

"It is a long story I will tell you in due time. For now we all have to get out of this park."

"Well" said Joshua "Who else is with you?"

She then pointed to the car "Only him."

Joshua gets up from the chair and hugs Sandy. "You don't know how happy I am to see you."

They then walked back to the car. Joshua was greeted by Max and welcomed into the car.

"Where are we going?" Josh asked

"We don't know but we will find a place." replied Sandy

"We have enough food and drinks. Why don't we go to that secret place we had when we were kids?" Max replied

"That sounds great." said Joshua

Sandy was happy to go there. She spent one of her best nights there. When they arrived there while were unpacking the car. They heard two men talking. Fearful Sandy and Max made their way back to the car. Sandy had turned the car lights on to drive off,

When two men became visible.

As Sandy was reversing Joshua screamed. "It's Jason"

Sandy stopped the car and froze in her seat as the man was getting closer to them she too screamed. "It is Jason."

When Jason made it to the car he was so shocked that he kneeled on the floor. "Oh my god I thought you were all dead."

Sandy and Joshua rushed out of the car, Max followed them. "What are you doing here at a time like this?" She asked.

Long story "Jason replied" What are you all doing here?

"Long story."

"Who was the other man with you and where did he go?" Max asked

"That was Brad. I am sure you will all recognize him when you see him. When we saw the car lights, Brad panicked thinking Angelo's men have found us. I told him he shouldn't panic like that until I check and see who was in the car." Jason then calls Brad. He comes and greets everyone.

"We brought food to eat there you two, should join us because we are starving." Sandy said

They then helped each other and took the food out of the car. Jason had already started a fire in their hiding spot. The fire gave them enough light to see each other's faces.

When Brad found out who Max and Sandy were he screamed. "What are you two doing back here?" Don't you know Angelo has a price on your head?

"We just came back because Sandy kept on having visions. She had to return." Max replied.

"What kind of visions?" Brad asked

"I don't know. She never told me anything but when we came back she went straight to this park and that's where we found Joshua. So I think her visions were about him."

"Is that true?" Asked Jason

"What happened to me past few weeks is out of ordinary. I came out and couldn't find any of you so I ended up sleeping in this park. However there was a man that kept on appearing with food and water, and today when he gave me water he said. "Here wash your face. You are about to have a visitor."

"And then what happened?" Asked Brad

"Then Sandy showed up next to me."

"How did you know where to find Joshua?" Jason asked

"I kept on having dreams about Joshua and this park and when the dreams didn't stop I knew he was in danger and I should do something."

"I always knew you had a gift Sandy." Jason said

"Thanks Jason, but Joshua hasn't told us what happened to him and why he was covered in blood."

"Well I kept on going to all the houses even my own but they were all sold, and when I tried the cell phones they were all disconnected. With no money and nowhere to go I went to this park and fell sleep there. But then a total stranger a homeless man, came and gave me his blanket. For some strange reason he kept on asking me if I am ready."

"That's the same man that came to me and said, don't worry I looked after him." Sandy said.

"What a mystery this is, any way I am happy the three of us have found each other. Now we should work together." Said Jason

"Yes but I still would want to know what happened to your clothes and why you were bleeding." Sandy asked

"Well somehow when I was trying to locate all of my family members, Angelo's people saw me. They followed me and as soon as they found an opportunity they attacked me. There were too many of them and only one of me. It was lucky that this thing appeared and scared them off because if it didn't they could have finished me off."

Brad then got involved. "Ok now that you know what happened to him, tell me what your plans are because this could happen to any of you."

"Should we find Jasmine and Jackie?" Asked Jason

"Not right now" replied Brad. "I need to know if you have a plan first."

Max who was sitting quietly all the time said. How do we trust you Brad? I know that we were childhood friends but anytime that information leaked out, Angelo's men located us easily."

"I am not telling you to trust me. All I am saying there is a price on your heads, especially you and Sandy. You need to come up with a plan."

"It's been a rough road for me and Sandy especially her. When I was unconscious all those months she looked after me and her parents at the same time. In time the doctors told Don that I would never be able to walk again but thanks to Sandy and Brian who helped me, it gave me a reason to push myself with exercises. Now as you can see I still have some work to do on my right hand side of the body. However the day that I avenge myself and Sandy's family is not that far away."

While grabbing Sandy's hand, Jason with tears in his eyes said. "Oh poor Sandy. What have you gone through by yourself?"

"There is no time to sit and think about what happened. We are lucky that so far we are all alright and should start making plans for tomorrow and the day after tomorrow. What has past us cannot be changed."

Sandy was feeling so happy. She could see the massive change in her brothers and that meant a lot to her because she would have the power to ask for their forgiveness before Karma attacks.

"Won't you all come and stay at my house?" Asked Jason

"That is a very bad idea." Brad called out. "They need to do what they have been doing all this time. It would be harder for anyone to trace them if they keep on moving. Staying with you means suicide for all of you."

"He is right." Said Joshua

"At least meet with me tomorrow night so I can bring you some money for hotels." Pleaded Jason

"Don't worry Jason." Said Sandy. "What we have will last us for a while."

"How do we contact each other?" Asked Max

"You should all get yourselves some cell phones. Here is my number. You can send your numbers to me and I will pass them on to all of you."

They all agreed to Brad's idea. The sister and two brothers hugged for the first time in their lives. They gave hope to each other.

After saying goodbye, Joshua went with Max and Sandy and became a fugitive like them. While driving out of town they saw a man walking on a deserted road. They stopped and asked him if he needed a lift. To their amusement he was the same man that gave his blanket to Joshua.

Joshua quickly jumped out of the car and grabbed the man's hand. "Please let us give you a lift. What you did for me showed me how good humanity is."

The man looked at Joshua and said. "I don't need a lift. I am here to make sure you make it out of the city without any problems."

"But why?" Joshua asked

The man looked at Sandy and smiled. She knows and if you truly have changed you will understand why." The man then disappeared again.

"Sandy what did the man mean, when he said "she knows?"

"Not now" she replied. "In due time everything will work out."

That night Sandy drove into the woods and they spent the night in the car. In the morning they again hit the road. By lunch time they came up to this sign in front of a ranch. Have a feed; have a rest, the sign said.

They drove into the ranch and were greeted by the owners. "Are you here for a feed or to stay?" asked the owner

"Both" replied Sandy. We would like to have rooms for a few days, if that is possible."

"You are the one that is paying, so it is up to you how long you want to stay" Said the man. He then took them inside a massive house to show them the bedrooms. You can freshen up." he said. Before he left he said. "Lunch will be served in half an hour. If you don't make it on time you will starve until dinner."

After putting their bags away, and refreshing themselves, they came down to where there was a wooden table. In the middle of a massive kitchen all the food and refreshments were decorated and placed on the table. The owner's wife said "Welcome to our humbled ranch." She asked them to help themselves with the food and move to dining room.

When they walked into the dining room, they found a man sitting at the end of the table. "Today you seem very tired." he said, but tomorrow if you are up to it we can give you a tour of ranch."

Max and Sandy got so excited. For a second it reminded them of Brian and Brook. They truly were missing those kind faces that took them in, for all those months.

"We will be delighted." Max replied.

Joshua who had never seen a ranch or a farm, kept on asking questions. Are there dogs? Is there any animals that might attack us?"

But all those silly questions made everybody laugh. "Don't worry Joshua nothing in this ranch eats people?"

"That is good to know"

After lunch they all went to their rooms. They were so tired from driving in the car for hours. An hour later Sandy goes to Joshua's room and asked. "What happened to you Josh?"

Josh told her all the story of how his wife got him arrested. Falsely accused him and how his sisters went and visited him and promised him that they will take him out in no time but they disappeared and never came back.

"So you have no Idea where your wife and children are?"

"Not at all"

"How about Jasmine and Jackie?"

"No Idea"

"Do you think they are safe?"

"I don't know and I don't care to be honest after leaving me in that whole."

Firstly we should find out if they are ok. May be something happened to them. That could be why they never came back to revisit you."

"You know Sandy, I cannot believe that after all the things they did to you, and you still have feelings for them."

"Don't forget we are family plus I don't really care about the past as long as we become the family that Dad wanted us to be."

"From what Max was saying you have been through a lot. I am so sorry that I was a jerk and never came around to help you out."

"Like I said, what has passed cannot be changed but what is to come can be changed. We must forgive our enemies and try to show them the right path. We cannot give up on anybody without trying."

"I never realized how wise you are."

"Wisdom comes from experience. Hardship that you don't wish on anyone. Wisdom comes when your body is broken and you can barely move, yet you have to force yourself because others are depending on you. Trust me wisdom does not come cheap."

"So ashamed am I. Looking at my younger sister with so much wisdom, yet I as an older brother, I am empty like a jar. Not only I did not gain any wisdom but I betrayed my family, my father, mother and you."

"If you can't let go of yesterday, your life will keep on repeating yesterday. Think of tomorrow. A brand new day full of life and opportunities."

"I wish I had hung around you more."

"Come, on let's see what Max is doing?"

The brother and sister then went and checked on Max. He was getting ready to go downstairs so they joined him. When they got downstairs in to the lunch room they found the TV on and the owner sitting in the chair looking at some photos.

"Oh sorry to disturb you." Max said

"Not at all please do come in."

The man then got off his chair and went into the kitchen a few minutes. Later he came back with a bottle of brandy and a few small glasses. You care to join me for a drink before dinner?"

"We shouldn't." Sandy replied

"And why not? I thought you liked your brandy."

"I do but how do you know that?"

"When I first saw you it was as if I knew you. Trying to remember, how I knew you I couldn't work it out. But this afternoon when I came in here, my wife was looking at some old photos. She showed me something that I think you all should see."

The man then goes and grabs the album. There were a lot of photos of the man and Don in the album, fishing, driving, dinner tables and so much more. Photos taken from different occasions. During all this time the man was holding something in his hand.

Sandy started to panic. She looked at Max and Joshua with a very worried look. The ranch owner realized how scared Sandy was and said. "Why are you so worried?"

"Why would you show us this photos? And what are you hiding in your hand?"

The owner smiled and opened his hand. It was a photo of Sandy and Don with a bottle of Brandy in front of them and cheering each other.

"How did you get this?" Asked Sandy

"Relax for a moment. See those two little girls in the photos. It is you and my daughter. We use to do everything together. Picnics, holidays you name it until one day my daughter got sick. We had to sell everything we had trying to find a cure for her.

Selling and having to travel all the time. With no income coming in.

In time we realized we were bankrupt and had no more money to spend on our daughter.

My whole world was a sick daughter, a loyal wife and a friend, a friend that I didn't want to bother but he did not give up on me and found me in the most desperate situation. At that time Don had his own family to look after but he did not neglect me. He kept on sending us money on a weekly basis. When I say money, I don't mean a little. He would send enough to pay our bills and continue with my daughter's treatment and have a place to live."

"One day Don rang me, he was so happy and said "since I don't have you around anymore, I found a new drinking partner just like you." When I asked who? He sent me this photo of you and him. He always told me how you two have a drink together at nights.

But that was not the only reason that Don had rang. He called me because he found the only doctor in the world that could cure the disease that my daughter had.

He made an appointment and arranged our flights. This was the miracle that we needed. That doctor did cure my daughter and now she is one of the best lawyers in the country."

"Everything that me my wife and daughter have we owe to Don."

"I have no idea how destiny brought you here but I am so thankful for this moment for being able to serve Don's daughter in my house."

Sandy's tears were dripping. She remembered some of those times. Her playing with another little girl.

"Don't cry" the man said. "Let's have a drink in Don's memory. I bet he brought you here."

Sandy grabbed the glass and held it up to you dad for leaving so many beautiful memories behind and to this beautiful family that took us in for your sake.

They all cheered and pulled their glasses up. They all stayed up late that night. The host had so many stories to tell about him and Don. The atmosphere was so calm and loving that none of them wanted the evening to come to an end.

The following morning Sandy went to Joshua's room and told him how she was worried about her sisters and that she was planning to see if Brad could get her some info about them.

Joshua told her. "I don't believe you after everything they did to you. Why would you bother?

Although there was some rough times between the brothers and sisters, Sandy couldn't give up on any of them. As soon as she walked out of Joshua's room she called Brad to see if he could find their whereabouts.

Brad cautiously looked at the police records in the hope of finding some information on the two sisters. With no success.

Sandy asked Jason to provide Brad with photos of Jackie and Jasmine, as the hope of finding them was slowly starting to fade. He arranged a meeting with Brad in a hotel. They were supposed to pretend they saw each other accidently. However when Jason walked in he saw a familiar face his eyes kept on following the familiar face until finally he restrained his feelings and called out "Adam" Adam turned around and was pleased to see Jason.

"Hi, I have been thinking about your family. What happened to you all?"

"It is a long story" Said Jason, "I am sure glad to see you. Are Jasmine and the kids with you?"

"The kids are but I have no idea about Jasmine."

"How come you are her husband?"

"By the looks of it you haven't heard? We are divorced. The kids live with me but she never tries to see them."

"Sorry to hear that I didn't know. Actually none of us knew. So you don't know where I can find her?"

"I really don't know where she is. By the looks of it she has changed her name."

"So how are the kids?"

"They are ok I suppose. But surely they miss their mother. I miss her too but my children's safety is more important than anything."

"What about the house?"

"We sold it at the time of our separation and each got half of the shares. Although she wanted it all. However the Judge was kind enough to grant me half because I look after the kids."

"So where do you live now?"

"I bought a house on the North Shore because it is a safe area for the kids."

"Is there anything I can do for you?"

"No Jason. Thank you. We are doing alright. The only thing that worries me is the kids don't see any of you anymore. I really hope that we could keep the family gatherings for the sake of our children."

"That I agree with. Right now there is a lot happening that we are trying to sort out. Once everything goes back to normal we can start once more."

"That will be so good. How are Sandy and Joshua? Do you see them?"

"They are not bad but live in a very difficult situation."

"What do you mean?"

"In time we will tell you everything."

"Here is my number," said Adam. "Call me if you want to visit the kids. Please pass it on to others as well."

Now Jason saw Brad walking through the doors. He quickly got up and said goodbye to Adam and pretended he was on the phone and accidently walked into Brad, "Oh I am sorry sir" Jason said while dropping an envelope on the floor.

Brad bent down, picked the envelope and says "No worries sir" then they both walk away.

One night when Jason was really down, the whole situation was getting tiring. He called Sandy and cried. "Where did we all go wrong? We had everything and look at us now. Broken into pieces."

"Don't worry" Said Sandy. Did you hand the photos to Brad?"

"Yes, but what is the use?"

"I cannot give up on them before trying."

"What do you mean you can't give up on them? They gave you up a long time ago."

"Knowing what is in their path, I have to try this last time to save them."

"What do you mean?"

It is a long story but I cannot tell you yet. Why don't you call Brad and ask him if he had any success in locating them."

"Ok, by." said Jason. Then he called Brad, and asked him if he had any news for him. Brad didn't reply to the question and said "Meet me at eight at our usual hiding spot."

That evening at around eight thirty pm, Jason and Brad met after shaking hands and greeting each other Brad said. "I found your sisters."

"Where?"

"They both live in the same mansion on the south of the city. The reason that none of us could locate them was because they changed their names. I purposely drove all the way there to make sure it was them. After spending hours waiting in the car, I finally got a visual and was able to do a video for you."

"Where is the video?"

"I am scared to show it to you. You have to promise me that you are not going to do something stupid first."

"I promise."

Tears started pouring from Jason's eyes when he was watching the video. These were not tears of joy, they were tears of disappointment and breaking. He slowly cried out. "How could they?'

Brad put his hand on his friends shoulder and said. "I am so sorry"

"Why are you sorry? How can they go hand in hand with the men that destroyed our lives? Look at Jasmine hugging that fat pig. He ruined my family."

No matter how hard Brad tried to calm him down it was of no use. Only God knew what kind of pain Jason was going through at that very moment. He screamed "Oh god how am I going to break this news to Sandy and Joshua?"

"If you want, I will meet with them and tell them?" Brad asked

"Thanks Brad. As it is you are doing too much for us plus it is better if it comes from me."

The two friends then departed. However Jason was still very upset, so he pulls to the side of the road and called Adam.

"Did you know about this Adam?"

"I did Jason. But didn't want you to hear it from me."

"How did you even survive with these people?"

"Well I have police protection for me and my children. Angelo and Jasmine wanted all the money. They made an attempt on my life."

"Oh my god. What kind of creatures are these people?"

"Jason you sound very upset. Why don't you come here? I will come and pick you up. Where are you?"

"No thanks, I need to be alone. I need to find a way to tell the others. I am so sorry for bothering you Adam."

"That is fine my friend. We are all in it as a family."

So confused and hurt was Jason, he began driving around like a mad man for hours. When he got home he found his worried wife waiting for him.

"What is wrong?" Asked Mandy

"Not in the mood right now. I am sorry will talk in the morning." he replied.

In the morning Jason said, "I have to call Sandy and Joshua and give them the bad news of how our sisters are sleeping with our enemies."

"What do you mean?" Mandy asked

He quietly passed her the little video player. Watch this while loading the video.

Mandy screamed. "Oh my god you poor man."

After sitting there for a few minutes not knowing what to do, Mandy broke the silence. "Jason do you want me to invite Joshua and Sandy here for dinner so you can show them this?"

"No, thanks. That would be very risky for them. Remember they still have a price on their heads. I will make other arrangements with them."

Jason then called Sandy, "Hi sis I need to meet with you and Joshua."

"Is everything ok?"

"I don't know. I will let you be the judge when you come."

"Ok. Where do you want to meet at?" Asked Sandy

"Same secret place." replied Jason

Sandy quickly grabbed Joshua and drove to the meeting. When they got there, they found Jason deep in thoughts. His eyes were shedding tears. Sandy called out. "Are you Ok Jason? What is wrong?"

"I am fine thanks, I brought coffee and some cakes for us."

"Yum" said Joshua

They poured their coffee and sat in a circle, Jason took his small video player out and said. "I hope this is not too disturbing for you. "He then showed them the video that Brad took.

Joshua was clearly upset. "How could they do this?"

"Well there must be a reason for it. We don't know all the facts." replied Sandy.

"Whatever the reason." Jason screamed, "There is no excuse for them to sleep with the enemy."

"Do you have their address Jason?" Asked Sandy

"Brad gave it to me. But why did you ask?"

"I have to give them one last chance. I owe it to the bond of sisterhood."

"And how are you planning to do that?" Asked Joshua

"Well I will do what Brad did. I will go and wait in the car until I get the opportunity to talk to them."

"You are crazy. Screamed Jason, What if they trap you?"

"No matter what you say, I have to try. It is my duty."

"What duty?" Joshua said in a very loud voice. "They always hated and treated you so badly."

"When the day comes you will know why?" replied Sandy

"Then I will go with you." Joshua said

"So will I." Jason followed.

"None of you can come. I have to do this alone. Remember nothing can happen to me." Sandy implied

"What makes you think nothing will happen to you. We are coming and that is the end of the discussions?" Josh screamed.

"Ok. We will met tomorrow morning. I will arrange for a road work van, so that no one gets suspicious." Said Jason

"That is fine." replied Sandy. "We should met here."

When she got home she found Max waiting for her anxiously. "Where were you? I was worried to death."

Sandy then explains everything to Max. "I can't believe it. You sound like the others. You have seen my powers. So what is there to worry about?"

"OK" said Max. "I still get worried."

The next morning the two brothers and young sister met and went on their journey as promised. Jason had a council van and some clothing for them to be able to hang out of the car. When they got close to the mansion they parked on the side of the road and waited. It seemed like a very long wait because there was no movement what so ever around the mansion.

Around seven pm they had to move so people wouldn't be suspicious. They spent the night in a motel but in one room.

As soon as they got up in the morning they grabbed some take away food and coffee and went straight to their spying zone.

This went on for nearly three days and nights until the fourth day when a car came and picked up what looked like Jackie and Jasmine. They followed the car into the city and into a public parking area. They waited where the car was parking to see who was driving and to their surprise Jasmine emerges followed by Jackie. Finally the driver their own sister in law Cindy, Joshua's wife.

Joshua's blood was boiling. He tried to open the door but Jason grabbed him quickly "You have to wait. Rushing like this will ruin everything."

"What do we do then?" Stammered Josh

"First let's see where they are going. Then we can decide." replied Jason

"I will go first. I will send you message when I know where they are going." Said sandy. She started following them from a distance. Finally they went into a restaurant. Sandy waited until they were seated then she sneakily looked through the window to make sure they were on their own. She messaged the boys.

When her brothers caught up with her she cried out. "They won't let us in dressed like this".

I actually think we all need new clothes and now is the best time to do it."

"Jason we can't" Said Sandy

"Why not?"

Josh and Sandy looked at each other. They were both dead broke. They couldn't spend their emergency money on clothes.

"What was that look?" asked Jason

"What look?" Joshua replied.

"The way you and Sandy looked at each other. You talk with your eyes. Anyway I am treating all of us to new clothes."

Ten minutes later they were all dressed in beautiful clothes. Joshua in a navy blue suite with a white shirt, Jason in white suite with blue shirt and Sandy in a beautiful white body fitted dress. The two brothers and Sandy looked like models when they walked into the restaurant. All the eyes turned towards them. The owner quickly walked towards them and welcomed them. He asked them where they prefer to be seated, after taking a quick look from behind her dark glasses, Sandy said. "There."

She choose a table that it was easy for them to see her sisters but that they had no way of seeing them.

All the waiters in the house offered service to Sandy and her brothers. They ordered their drinks and food and enjoyed a nice meal together, waiting for the right moment to make their move.

Sandy waited patiently for her sisters to leave the restaurant. As soon as they did she called out their names "Jackie, Jasmine." They turned around and were shocked to see their sister.

"What the hell are you doing here loser?" Jackie screamed

"Money hasn't been able to buy you manners, I see." Sandy replied

"Ignore her girls." Cindy called out

"You keep out of it. I will deal with you later Cindy." Sandy responded.

"What do you want from us, I made it clear to you that we want nothing to do with you." Jackie screamed yet again.

Jasmine was still looking at her sisters beauty and feeling intimidated. She took a note of a hundred dollars out of her purse and threw it at Sandy "I hope this pays for one week's food for you." Then she poured the drink that she had in her hand at Sandy's white dress.

At this point Jason rushed to the scene and said, "Why in the hell would you do something like that?"

"Oh look the losers have found each other." Jasmine laughed.

"Losers. Who are the losers?" asked Jason. "You are the ones that are losers. You are the ones that sold your family to the enemies and you are the ones that are sleeping with the enemy. Have you no shame? The whole world knows what these men did to our family and now our sisters are the whores of my father's killers."

"Go to hell Jason" said Jasmin, "We have everything we ever wanted and really don't have to listen to two losers move or I call the cops."

By this time Joshua had lost his patient and came out of hiding. "How about you Cindy? Are you sleeping with one of them?"

"That is not your business."

"What did you do to my home and money?"

"Go and beg elsewhere you beggar." Cindy screamed.

"No matter how much money you three have, you will never have class." Joshua responded.

All of a sudden the stains on Sandy's white dress disappeared. She kneeled in front of her sisters. "I beg of you again, please come to your senses."

With a kick from Cindy, Sandy was pushed to the floor. "You heard me. Go and beg somewhere else."

As Cindy, Jackie and Jasmine were about to walk away, a strong wind surrounded them. None of them could take a step further. Joshua and Jason looked with unbelief as Sandy stood back up and opened her hands. "I truly feel sorry for you, although I lost the battle with you today. I still feel sorry for you."

As soon as Cindy and the two sisters were able to move, they started walking towards the parking area. As they did a homeless man approached them, he had a little child in his hand and said.

"Please give me some money to feed this child."

"Jasmin pushed him away, "If you knew you can't feed him, why did you give him life?"

The kid fell out of the homeless man's arms on the floor. He too dropped on the floor picked the child up and said "I am so sorry."

Looking at this Sandy's blood started boiling. She checked her wallet. There was still a few thousand dollars in there, which she saved for emergency. She pulled all the money and went to the man. "Here take this and go and help your child."

"I will only take enough for tonight's meal. Here, please take the rest back."

"Take it" Sandy replied. "Feed your child as many times as you want and find a roof over your heads."

"God bless you." The man said. He then disappeared, while curious Jason followed him to see what he will do.

Jason was surprised when he saw the man buying all this food and then going in to this alleyway. When he got to the middle there was a deserted building. The man walked inside. Jason hid himself in the door way. When the homeless man called out, "come out everybody" for one second Jason thought that was addressed to him. But soon enough before he did anything stupid, all these children, women and men started coming to the middle of the hall, where the homeless man was standing.

The homeless man put all the food on the floor and said "I think we have enough food for a while and we should all share it together.

Jason's tears started. He could not believe what he was seeing. He ran inside and said to the man.

"Don't you think the money was enough to just save you?"

The man smiled and said. "Maybe if it wasn't for them God wouldn't have advised that lady to give me so much." The man then continued. We are now going to cook for ourselves. You are more than welcome to stay and join us for this blessing."

Jason rushed back to where he left Joshua and Sandy.

"Where the hell were you?" asked Joshua

"How did you know that man would put the money to good use?" Jason asked

"I just know." Sandy replied. She then started walking toward the isolated building and said to Jason. "This is where the man came?"

"Yes. How do you know these things?"

She then stood in the middle of the hall and opened her hands. Within seconds hundreds of little lights appeared. They each were carrying something and it was not long before the hall turned into a most beautiful and expensive restaurant. The homeless man came back to get something from the hallway. When he saw himself in such place, he quickly rubbed his eyes, then he looked at Sandy. "Are you an Angel?"

"For the sacrifice you made today, you will get back double of what you sacrificed for others." She then grabbed her brothers and ran out.

Jason was full of questions "What are you? Are you an Angle?"

"In due time you will know, but for now we have to go back."

By the time Jason got to his house and the others to theirs, the news flash showed their photos. "The two brothers and their younger sister, the children of Don's empire are fugitives tonight as the police and the entire country is looking for them. It is said they are armed and dangerous. If anyone sight them, they should call the federal police on...............

Joshua cried "What happened my own wife, she sold me to my enemy. They caused me to do time in prison and took away everything that I worked hard for. I wonder how my kids are. All the time that we watched the mansion there was no sign of them."

Listening to her brother and watching the news saying that they were fugitives. Sandy slowly started to get frustrated. The doors and windows started shaking. She ran to her room and started crying quietly. Why didn't they listen to my pleads. Oh how can I watch them paying back for all they have done? Then she remembered Jason. She closed her eyes and saw how Jason's house was surrounded. Jason had a hidden tunnel under his house and escaped from there with his wife and kids.

Chapter 22

Cindy who was dating another partner of Angelo's Alberto went home and told him what happened after they went to the restaurant.

"Does Angelo know?" He asked

"I don't know if Jasmine has said anything to him. At the end of the day that's her family."

Alberto quickly got on the phone with Angelo, who was dating Jasmine and Michael who was dating Jackie and asked them if the girls have said anything to them about their encounter with Sandy and her brothers.

Angelo and Michael both replied "Yes they did"

The three men then arrange to have an urgent meeting with the chain. Once the meeting was concluded the three men call the police and told them that Sandy and her two brothers held the three women at gun point. They asked for money, it did not stop there. They had paid some low lives to come and give evidence that they witnessed the rubbery by Sandy and her two brothers.

The following day the media was following Angelo and asked him. "Their father owned Don's empire which is worth billions and billions of dollars, why do they need to rob?"

"Well they started using the money. For pleasure and never attended to their father's businesses until they all collapsed." Angelo stated.

The next question was "You were a close friend of Don's. Shouldn't you have helped his children?"

"We were already helping. Two of them. May be if the others come and accept our help, we can help them. Angelo said

"Which two are getting help?"

"Two of the sisters"

By lunch time that day, more witnesses started rushing to the police stations reporting that they were rubbed at gun point by three brothers and sisters.

Angelo, Alberto and Michael talked between themselves and said. "Maybe we should tell the girls to keep their distance, until they find their brothers and sister.

That didn't go down well with the girls. They asked to meet the three men at some stage to discuss some business.

When the six of them sat at the table in an isolated restaurant, Jasmine said. "Angelo, so you think you are helping us?"

"I had to come up with something." he responded.

"Well why not? I am dating one of the sisters?"

"Are you crazy? That will blow the whole thing in our face?"

"What about you Alberto?" asked Cindy

"Listen to Angelo. He knows what he is saying."

"Oh so now, I should listen to him."

"Don't get so power hungry." screamed Angelo. "Remember Cindy, when you were dating Alberto and you needed help I was the one that kept your ex-husband in jail. I was the one that sent my men to frighten him in the park so he would not come and ask for his share of money."

"What about you Jasmine? When your husband left you I was the one that took all the legal action against him. I was able to convince the judge to at least divide your assets in half. You very well know that Adam was going to end up with at least eighty percent because you left your kids."

"And you Jackie, didn't you ask Michael to get rid of Phil your husband? But when Michael found you had kids, he paid Phil off to disappear with the kids?"

"So don't play games with any of us. We will have to be calm during these times while the search is on for Sandy and her brothers."

There was no reply. To Angelo these women were so evil. What they had was never enough. They wanted to hook up with these three powerful men for more. Their hearts only sought money and not love or family.

Finally Jasmine the greediest of all said. "Why are you getting so upset? You know how much I love you?"

After she said that, the other two slowly started to get closer to their men and hug them and pretend they were so madly in love with them.

"I am starving." said Cindy.

"I too." followed Jackie.

They all decided to order their dinner. Before their dinner arrived, the restaurant's door opened Joe and this woman walk in. As the waiters took their coats, he ordered a table for two.

Walking behind the waitress to be seated at their table Jo noticed the three women, his father and his friends. Angelo's face dropped when he saw his son he reached and grabbed his hand. "What are you doing here Jo? Are you spying on me?"

"There is no need for spying Dad. Everyone knows what kind of an Arse hole you are."

"Shut up and tell me what are you doing here?" Angelo asked once more.

"Look, I always go to isolated places with my girlfriend. I am being cautious because I don't want you or any of your colleagues to know who I am dating."

"What does your dating have to do with me or my friends?"

"Come on. You or one of your colleagues has paid enough money to all of my ex-girlfriends to sleep with them."

"Well. That means they were whores."

"Dad, the only whore I know is you. Look at those bitches. You destroyed their family and brought Don's empire to its knees and now you are using his daughters as sex slaves until you get sick of them and rid them of their assets."

All Jo could feel after saying those words was a slap on his face. It was so hard that it made his body shake. Jo then grabbed his girlfriend's hand, and tells her of the decision to find another restaurant. .

"Who was that?" asked the girls

"No one important." answered Angelo

"Well what did he mean, when he said you paid his girlfriends to sleep with colleagues?" asked Jackie

"I am not really in mood to answer questions. It has been a long day. Can't we just enjoy our meal and drinks?" replied Angelo

However the evil man had already made plans for his son's girlfriend. He excused himself to go to toilet. In fact he just went out to call his men and put a tail on both his son and his girlfriend.

When they got out of the restaurant Kate, Jo's girlfriend said. "Was that Angelo?"

"Yes,"

"How come you never told me he was your father?"

"Because I am ashamed."

"Don's empire. What did you mean by that?"

Jo said. "It is a long story; I don't really want to get in to it now."

"Come on please. Tell me."

"Well my dad and Don were best friends for so many years. At some stage my dad started getting involved in other businesses that Don wasn't so keen on and slowly, slowly Don started breaking away from all the partners. Because he was a good man, he did not agree with the way things were being done."

"Oh look how good is that restaurant? You can finish the story while we eat." Kate said excitedly.

After they got into the restaurant and ordered their food Kate said. "Continue"

"As the years went by, the chain of the business men got bigger and more powerful. They were all controlled by my dad because he held the most shares in everything. However, all those shares came at a price of other people's loses.

Don was a man of honour.

He was blessed. Everything he touched turned to gold, but that gold was used to help people that were desperate, homeless and less fortunate. The more Don helped, the more his assets built."

For a second Jo stopped and cried. "I wish I could find my old friends and help them."

"My father is not a nice person that is why I don't want to be a part of his life. I believe that everyone, one day will pay for their sins."

"And who were those women with him?"

"Two of them were Don's daughters, the other one was his ex-daughter in law."

"Aren't you scared that he might cut you from his will?"

"Why should I be? I rather eat a five dollar burger than a meal worth thousands. All made out of sucking blood from less powerful people and businesses. Plus how can one spend thousands of dollars on a stupid meal then go past a homeless person and not give them a coin? I truly believe that is pure evil."

"I have never been rich. It makes me wonder how it feels to be rich like them."

"I will tell you how it feels. It makes you like a piece of stone. The more you have, the more you are going to want. Your life becomes competition, a competition in clothing, business, food, mansions and the list keeps on going."

"How come your needs are so different to your fathers?"

"Because I saw how he ruined my friend's families and robbed them of everything they had. Now can we stop talking about this?"

Jo at that moment was unaware that his evil father has already put a tail on them. While driving home he noticed a car following him. He asked his girlfriend if he could get a cab for her because he was feeling so tired. She agreed. Jo pulled into a service station, where cabs were located. He hired one of those cabs and paid the driver in cash. He then waited to see if the car was going to follow the cab. When they did he drove behind the vehicle that had followed them. His aim was to distract and stop them from following the cab.

Jo looked for an opportunity to pull in front of the car that was following the cab. When he scorched his plan worked. Because the other car was damaged so badly that it wasn't drivable and they couldn't follow the cab anymore.

Jo then quickly got out of his car and went to the smashed car; he pulled his father's two employees out of the car. Both men were speech less.

He continued driving while cursing his father, at the same time. Hours later he felt tired, and hungry. He pulled into this small café and ordered breakfast, while eating he nodded off at the table.

The waiters tried to wake him. In doing so they were concerned about the distance he may have travelled without a break. After providing him with a top up with coffee, he was questioned.

"It must have been a long trip." Said the waitress

"I think so." said Jo

She then said. "You look familiar. Are you a famous person?"

"No, I am not. You probably have mistaken me for someone else."

While they were talking the news again showed the photos of Sandy, Max and the two brothers again. Jo screamed, "Oh my god what does he want from them?"

The waiters got scared and moved back a little. The waitress said. "I know. Aren't you the son of the billionaire Angelo?"

"I am no billionaire. I am just a middle class person looking for his friends. But now I can see that I will never find them."

"We will leave you alone sir." Said the waitress she and other staff walked away.

Jo finished his breakfast and walked out of the café. Before he sat in his car he saw a familiar face. "Jason he called out."

Jason got the hold of his children and wife and tried to run, possibly back to his car but Jo screamed. "Please don't. Wait a minute please, I beg you."

"Why so you can let them know we are here?"

"I will do no such thing."

"Why not? You carry your father's bloodline."

"That might be so but please Jason for the sake of our childhood friendship, give me a chance.

"Let me buy you breakfast and we can talk."

Mandy screamed "Jason please don't trust him" but some good child hood memories came to Jason and he agreed to Jo's offer.

After they sat and ordered their breakfast Jo said. "You all look so tired."

"Thanks to your father we had to flee in the middle of night"

"I only saw the news this morning. How ashamed am I that I have a father like that."

"What are you doing in this deserted place so far from your mansions?" Asked Jason

Jo then went ahead and told Jason everything that happened the night before.

"Oh. Sorry to hear. That man doesn't even show mercy to his son."

"I have been looking for Sandy and Max for a while but haven't be able to locate them. Thanks to my father they keep on moving from one place to another."

"And why is that?" Asked Jason

"Because I want to help them to take their revenge on my father."

"Why would you help someone to destroy your father? What is in it for you?"

"Satisfaction and with the hope of having my old friends back in my life. If it wasn't for Don, my father would have never made it."

Jo then started mentioning a few memories they had together. "Do you remember when we were hiding in the garden and we saw my dad making it with another woman?" At that time we were laughing and everything seemed funny but later it was not funny for my mother."

"Also do you remember when there were dinner parties, and Don used to come out and play with us. He never enjoyed their company and loved having us kids all together."

"That was my dad." Jason said. "Nothing but a good man."

"If you escaped from your house, how then were you able to get your car?"

"I think it was a miracle, because we were surrounded. We were led out of the house by a little blue light and when we reached the outside, a blinding blue light appeared. Everyone was covering their eyes but then somehow our car came towards us without anyone being able to see that."

"Are you joking? Because there is no time for jokes."

"No" said Mandy. That is exactly what happened."

"My god, may be Don is still looking after his children."

They were halfway through their breakfast when a blue light appeared and started going around them in a circle. Jason looked around and saw the waiter waiting. He quietly packed everything in one plate. "Let's go."

Mandy started quickly packing the rest of the food, while Jo was sitting there stunned.

"What happened? Why do we have to leave?"

"Look at waiters she is waiting for someone. She must have recognised us and notified the authority."

"How do you know that?"

"The blue light was the sign of danger. When it appeared I looked around and saw the waitress checking the road."

"But how do you know its sign of danger?" Asked Jo

"Never mind." replied Jason. Let's go. He then threw the money on the table and one by one they left the café pretending they are going to the bathroom. They ran to their cars and took off. A few trucks were pulling into the café car park which made it impossible for the waitress to see the cars leaving.

While driving Jason put the radio on. A news flash came on which said one of the fugitives with his family was seen in an isolated café and that the police were on their way there.

Driving for a while Jason stopped the car, gets out and goes to Jo's car.

"Why are you following us?"

"What do you want me to do then?"

"Go home."

"I can't go home not until I make everything right for you."

Jason then contacted Sandy. "Can you meet us in this park?"

Sandy quickly, asked Joshua, if he wanted to go with her. They both leave and meet up with Jason.

"What are you doing here?" Asked Joshua

"I am here to help." replied Jo.

"I think your dad helped enough."

"Please do not mistake me in the same light." He then ran to Sandy and hugged her "Oh my friend. How happy I am to see you are ok."

"I know you are." Sandy said this because she had the power to see everything as the day unfolded. Sandy's powers were getting more and more to a point that she herself was so surprised by them.

"What do we do now?" Asked Jason. "Where can we go?"

"I think for now we all have to stick to each other and stay in one place. We should find a shed or a location out of the way. That way we don't put anyone in danger."

"They all agreed. Sandy called Brian as soon as she was in her car and told him about the situation. Brian was so happy to hear from Sandy that told her. "I will be very disappointed if you don't come here and stay in the old house." Although Sandy said "But there are too many of us plus we can't put you in danger."

"What is danger where there is love and unity? We will unite and conquer everything that comes our way."

Sandy then agreed and told the boys of her decision. They then went and picked up Max and said good bye to the nice couple that housed them for a time.

Jo was so amazed with everything that was taking place. For a second he stopped and looked in the sky. Look how my father is stealing from others but look how God looks after all those affected by such an act.

When they arrived Brook and Brian had all the lights on waiting for them. Brian ran to the car and hugged Sandy. "My beautiful friend. We are very pleased that you came back." He then rushed to Max. "How are you doing my friend? By the looks of it, you are moving better."

Max smiled and said. "Wouldn't be here without your help."

Brook then called out. "Come in, we turned the lights on for you. I think this house is too small for all of you. Sandy why don't you and Max come and stay in the big house with us?"

"Thank you." Sandy replied. "Don't worry. We will all fit here. Once more you are kind enough to let us stay here."

"Ok. We will leave you to refresh. When you are ready come to the house for some refreshment. I have missed all those nights where we use to sit on balcony for a drink." said Brian.

Mandy followed Sandy into the shower. "If I ever have done anything to upset you I apologise. I never had a chance to get to know you. As you know your sisters have always surrounded me and it was only a few month ago that I started seeing the true you and now I am so ashamed to have missed all those years of friendship."

"Can you bring yesterday back?" Sandy asked

"What kind of question is that? Of course no one can do that."

"Then stop apologizing for what happened. Yesterday cannot be changed but tomorrow is a new day and you can do whatever you want."

"I always knew you are a wise person." Mandy replied.

When sandy got dressed she sat on the couch waiting for others to have their shower. As she was drifting away she heard Jason's kids. "We missed you aunty."

"Come sit on my lap." said Sandy. "I missed you too."

Everyone had their showers and a change of clothing. They then went to the big house. Brook, Brian, their son and grand children were all excited to have visitors. The grand children were happy to have two new friends to play with.

Brian as usual had his brandy sitting in the middle of coffee table. This time there were more glasses. "I hope you guys are like your sister love a good drink."

"Oh sure." Joshua replied. "We all remember those good times having brandy with our dad."

"Then let's drink to his memory." Then he sculled his drink.

When Brian told Brook that Sandy and her family were coming to stay, she was so happy that she started cooking for two reasons one for her hungry guests, secondly she was so excited that she couldn't sit still.

"As usual something smells so good in here." Sandy said.

"Well, why don't we go to dining table and find out how it all tastes?" Brook replied.

"I am not going to say no. I missed your food and now the smell has made me so hungry." Sandy said.

Everyone laughed. They all walked to the table. As usual the dining table was decorated to perfection.

"Sorry for putting you through so much trouble." Mandy called out.

"It's no trouble. We are always alone, so it is nice to have an excuse to cook." Brook responded.

"How is everything going Sandy?" asked Brian

"Not too good at the moment. However while we are here we will work on a plan."

"I think we should be ready to head back to our lives within a few weeks." said Max. "Then it will be your turn to come and stay with us on holidays."

"I can't wait to see you getting your lives back." said Brian.

Towards the end of dinner Jason's phone rang. He excused himself from the table to answer the phone.

"I found Joshua's kids." Brad the caller said.

"Where did you find them?"

"Well Sandy told me how concerned Joshua was about his kids so I used the police tracking system and I found them in a boarding school. I enquired about them. Apparently no one has been to see them since they started there. They don't get any phone calls or have anywhere to go to on holidays. But their school fees have been paid for years in advance. Their principal was saying how sorry she feels for them for not being a part of a family. They are really good at their studies."

"Can we go and visit them?"

"I don't think that is a good idea at the moment. Just let Joshua know that they are safe and healthy."

"Ok, thanks Brad. Hope one day I can pay you back."

"Putting these basters behind bar is going to be my payback."

Jason then went back and told Joshua, that Brad was on the phone and gave him the good news.

Joshua's tears appeared once more. "I hope they don't think that I isolated them."

"Don't worry." Jason responded. "When everything is over you can spoil them as much as you want."

Chapter 23

Back in the restaurant the night of Angelo and Jo's argument, after they had dinner Angelo was in a hurry to get home thinking that his men have found the girlfriend's address. He was very disappointed when they told him what had happened.

He then shouted at his wife. "Call your son and ask him to come home right now?"

"First you tell me where you were?"

"That is none of your business. Do as I say."

"If you want him home, call him yourself." The wife then walked away and called Jo from her bedroom. "Where are you son?"

"Mum I can't tell you and please don't let dad get his hand on this number because he can locate me."

"Did you see him?"

"I will tell you when I see you."

"He was with those bitches again, wasn't he?"

"Mum don't upset yourself. I will call you and arrange a meeting time with you alone."

Door opens and Angelo walks in. "Did you call your son?"

"I told you call him yourself."

Angelo walked out and took his security with him. The giant business man began to feel frightened. He knew if he does not get to Sandy and Max, on time they can ruin him. He called Michael and asked him to meet shortly.

"Well Angelo in that case the whole chain could be wiped out and we could all go to gaol." said Michael.

"It seems that they are always a step ahead of us."

"What about the cops? Do they have any leads?"

"Not as far as I know."

"Can't you get Jackie and Jasmine to get close to their sister and brothers pretending that you ripped them off of their wealth?"

"I don't think they will buy it, because those two never had a good relationship with their sister and it was only a few days ago when she came and approached them plus they gave reports to the police that they were held at gun point."

"Let's hope that our men find them first. They must be up to something. That is why they are keeping a low profile. From what I heard, Sandy is a very smart person. Only God knows what her next move is going to be."

"I will go in the morning again and give the media attention. May be by increasing the reward, more people will come forward with information."

"That is not such a bad idea. Where did they see them last?"

"Well the last time anyone reported seeing them was by that waitress. I don't know how they got away that time. It was as if someone tipped them off."

"What do you mean? I bet the waitress panicked and that made them suspicious. Everyone else was getting paid and I don't think they would risk their jobs to double cross us. I will put some more men out there."

"I think I will do the same."

The next morning Angelo took Jackie and Jasmine, with him to media because he personally could not show too much interest in finding Sandy, Max and her two brothers.

The two sisters told the media that they wanted to increase the reward to anyone coming forth with information as to the whereabouts of the four fugitives.

By the afternoon the news was broadcast and quite a few hotlines were put in for people to call.

To keep the sisters happy, Angelo and his two friends rang the girls and told them they would bring dinner and drinks to celebrate.

When they got there they each had a massive bunch of flowers in their hands. One for each for Cindy, Jackie and Jasmine.

"Have you heard anything from your brothers?" Angelo asked

"No" Jackie replied

"I am a bit concerned. The first time the boarding school called me about my kids, was when they asked me if they were coming home for Christmas. I said no. Then yesterday again they called me telling me I have to do something about them because they are so isolated and could be going through depression, from not seeing their parents." Cindy said

Angelo asked. "And what did you say?"

"I told them that me and my husband were away and as soon as we come back we will pay them a visit."

"Tomorrow just go in there and pay the school more money and tell them that they have to take care of the boys."

"Ok."

"We will worry about these things tomorrow. For now let's have fun." Jasmine said while turning the music on.

That night the six of them had so much fun, got drunk and all went to sleep on the couches.

The next morning around eight am when Angelo and his friends woke up, he screamed, "We are late for the meeting. Move it."

When they got to the meeting Brad's partner was there as well but again he told Brad to go for a walk or get something to eat. This meeting is private and it shouldn't take that long.

"Ok I will go and get a cup of coffee. Brad bought the coffee from the machine in the hallway so he could hear what they were saying.

"You useless scum bags, what is the matter? Can't you do your jobs properly? It is almost a year that I have been paying you for nothing. I personally will give an award of a quarter of a million dollar to any of you scumbags that comes back to me with those three fugitives."

Angelo was off course addressing the detectives that were working for him.

The detectives responded "Every time we get close to them, they move."

"Well if you move fast enough you can catch them next time. We made your jobs easier by placing call centres for people to report and doubled the reward amount."

As they were talking one of the detectives received a message. "We have to leave Joshua and Sandy have been located in a shopping centre about two hours away from here."

"You heard him, Angelo screamed. "Move it."

Brad quickly took off and went downstairs. He leaned on the car and pretended that he was playing a game on his phone. His partner on approach said. "Let's go."

Angelo and his partners ordered lunch in the office while waiting anxiously for the men to come back with the brother and sister.

On the other hand Cindy sent one of the security guards to her children's school with an envelope.

"Go there, she said. Once you have the right person get them to call me. Do not hand the envelope to them without calling."

An hour later the security called. He had the president and vice president of the school on speaker. "MS Cindy. You can talk now." he said.

Cindy addressed the two men, "I am paying you enough to keep those two kids there. I don't care how you do it but don't call and bother me with stupid things like that."

Cindy then addressed the security guard. "Give them the envelope."

She addressed the two men again. "That is a lot of extra money for you to do your job. Do not bother me anymore".

One of the men said. "What about your kid's happiness? Don't you miss them? These kids would have to be only kids that I know that are not taken during the school holidays nor have any contact with the outside world."

Cindy screamed. "That is good. It should be kept that way." She then hung up.

The security guard's eyes were full of tears. He had kids of his own and would not survive if he did not spent every night with them.

The men noticed the security guards emotional state. "What is wrong?" One of them asked.

The security guard got scared and said nothing.

The man again said. "Don't worry. What you tell us will stay within these four walls, plus you heard her we are not allowed to call her and we are not sure where their father is."

"I have two kids myself." replied the security guard. "They are my world. Every night when I get home they get so cheerful. It is as if they haven't seen me for ages. I can't imagine how desperate these two kids must be and how could that woman do this to her own children?" For a time he continued to weep until he seemingly stopped.

"What about their father?" asked the man?

"His wife had a boyfriend. They framed him about a year ago and put him in jail. While he was in jail they forged all the signatures and overtook all his business, houses and any assets he had."

"Is he still in jail?"

"From what I heard they accused him of armed robbery and is a fugitive now."

"Is there anything we can do to help?"

"It is the best if I and you don't get involved because these people have no hearts."

The security guard added. "There is one favour you could do for me."

"What it is son?"

"For the next school holidays will you put the two kids in my care so I can take them out with my children and show them a bit of the outside world?"

We will be happy to do that but we need to make sure these two kids are safe and can't just be handed to a stranger."

"What about if I bring my kids and wife to take them out one day, or even have a picnic with them in the park?"

"We will think about it." Before the man could finish the consideration, a few blue lights started floating around. The two men looked at each other and excused themselves. In private they said. "What was that?" When they looked back, the security guard had his head tilted down crying and those little lights were just floating around him.

The two men then decided that was a sign, to show them how sincere the security guard was so they went back and one of them said. "Son we will grant your wish. You can take them out for a few hours and once we feel confident you can have them for more time.

That evening the poor security guard was so down. However he felt lusted when he remembered he could do something about the situation regarding the kids.

In the morning the security guard went to his superior and asked him if he could be moved to another area of work because, he felt down in that environment. The superior agreed and gave him a job in the middle of the city close to his home.

Chapter 24

Brian enjoyed his evening drinks with his newly found friends. Sandy and Joshua felt bad for drinking all his alcohol so they decided to go and buy some liquor. As they were walking around, the little lights started showing up.

Joshua screamed. "Look Sandy Look" but before she could answer, her phone rang.

"Sandy grab Joshua and go home."

"What is the matter Brad?" she asked.

Angelo's men are on their way. Someone from that shop rang the cops. There are numerous crook detectives that are involved. Just ran please."

Joshua and Sandy then quickly paid for their drinks and walked out.

A customer at the liquor shop screamed at the shop keeper, "Why did you serve them?"

"Well what did you want me to do? It is my job to serve customers."

"No. I mean you should have delayed them."

"I think you are crazy."

"No I am not. They are fugitives and there is a reward for whoever locates them."

"They seemed like nice people. Even if I knew they were fugitives I would have served them. You are a sneaky person. You rang the cops. That is why you hung around here all this time."

"Well the reward is really going to help me."

"Come on get out of my shop."

While the shop keeper and the customer were arguing, Sandy's car left the parking lot the informer was not able to take their plate number.

Hundreds and hundreds of little blue lights gathered and became one giant light globe and blocked the view from the helicopters that were flying overhead.

While the light globe blocked the possibility of anyone locating the car, Sandy and Joshua made it safely to the farm.

"Look what we have." screamed Sandy, when they got there. Brian came out smiling.

"You had to do that didn't you?"

"Oh Brian it felt so good, to go to shops." Sandy replied

"I am glad you enjoyed it."

When they sat down for their afternoon drinks the news came on. The shocked journalist was talking about a blub of light. No one knew where it came from although they recorded it for the news. When they came back to their office to process the film it was all blank and none of the crew knew how that lengthy video just wiped itself out.

"I have never seen anything like it." another detective said.

The helicopter crew said. "We were forced to go down because we couldn't see anything."

Brian looked at Sandy "How come you didn't tell us you were located?"

"How do you know that was about us?"

Then the channel showed the video from the shop which clearly showed Joshua and Sandy's faces paying for the drinks.

Jason and Mandy got into a panic. "It won't be long before they locate us."

"Don't worry." Brian said while you are with Sandy nothing can come near you."

"Anyway" said Joshua. "Let's drink to my children and Brad who located them. And they are safe and sound."

Sandy was the first one to grab her glass "I will drink to that."

Brook added "I am drinking to that too."

That night was so magical for all of them. They talked, laughed told jokes but towards the end Sandy excused herself. As soon as she entered her bedroom, she disappeared and found herself in the middle of a yard. She could see the lights of a window and lots of cars with their lights on. When she got closer she could see Nancy from the window. Two men were holding her children, while another was physically abusing her.

Nancy was screaming. "Leave my children alone. I swear we don't know where Sandy is."

As the man lifted his hand to strike Nancy, the light filled the room. A giant figure appeared and stopped the man's hand from touching Nancy. The men were so scared they did not know what was happening. What followed was Sandy's voice. "That is not the way to treat an innocent woman."

The man quickly grabbed Nancy by the neck and tried to hide behind her. "Let go" the voice said. "I am giving you a chance to leave in peace."

The men dropped the kids and Nancy, and ran towards the door. Everything again returned to normal. Nancy was shocked and asked her kids "Was that an angel that saved us."

Peter the older son answered. "It sounded like Sandy."

"But how?" Asked Nancy. She noticed a note on the table. She picked up. It said. "Times like this just call my name and I will be here. Sandy."

Tears flooded Nancy's face. She could not believe that the daughter of the man that one day saved her and her children, was still looking after them.

While Sandy was away, Joshua went to check on her but couldn't find her. He asked the others "Do you know where Sandy went?"

They said she had gone to her room.

"I just came from there but she wasn't there."

Suddenly Sandy appeared and said "Josh remember when we were kids and we use to play hide and seek. I was always the first one that you found. Look at you now you couldn't find me in my room tonight."

Everyone laughed, but Joshua wasn't convinced. He was sure Sandy wasn't in her room.

When everyone went to bed that night, Sandy paid Joshua's children an invisible visit. When she got there they couldn't see her, so she sat at the corner of the room watching them. The younger one called out to the older one "Do you think if we are good dad and mum will come for us?"

"I don't know. We never did anything wrong."

"But we must have otherwise, why don't they visit us?"

"Go to sleep."

"I can't. Do you remember dad use to say he cannot live without us? What happened?"

"Dad would never leave us. One day we will find out the truth. I just hope that he is ok."

"I wish we could at least receive a sign that he is ok."

Sandy was dying to make herself visible and hug them. That was too risky. Instead she circled her finger where she was sitting on a glass photo frame. A happy picture of Joshua and his two kids appeared in the frame.

In the morning the two kids noticed the picture and believed there was the sign they were hoping for.

Sandy however went back to the house and stayed up all night. The beautiful kind girl was thinking how humans can be so cruel. We are all made out of the same flesh and blood. We all want to have a happy and loving life. How can anyone make another person's life miserable? Oh Mum and Dad, how I miss you. There is a big burden on me. Even if people are wrong, I don't want to see them hurt. What about my sisters and Cindy. I tried so hard to save them and now I am so sad for what is coming their way. There is nothing I can do to stop it. Especially tonight, after I saw those two little angels. How they have been neglected and brought up by a bunch of nuns.

Early in the morning when Brian and his son came out to gather some eggs for breakfast he noticed Sandy sleeping on the front veranda. He ran to her "Sandy are you alright?"

"Oh I am fine, I came out for some fresh air but I must have gone straight back to sleep."

"Do you want to go back to bed? Or do you want to come and have coffee and fresh eggs with me?"

"Brian, I think I will have the eggs and the coffee with you."

When they got inside the smell of fresh bread had filled the house. "Oh Brook" said Sandy. "You are the best."

"Thank you Sandy, I enjoy homemade bread. Hope you do too."

"I haven't smelled fresh bread like this for years. I just love it." replied Sandy.

When they made their coffee and eggs, they sat around the table, Brian could see how troubled Sandy was so he asked, "Sandy, something is bothering you but you are hiding it from all of us."

"I am very tired and you are right Brian, I am troubled."

"But why my child?"

"People amaze me."

"Well I have seen your powers. Why can't you do something?"

"I can't abuse my powers and use them for myself. I have to help those who are kind and generous and fulfil their dreams.

Those who are lost like my sisters, I am supposed to win and bring them back to reality before karma knocks on their doors. Oh Brian, I am so sad. I am failing badly."

"Who said you are failing? Look at what you did for us."

"But I have not been able to take away the badness of people and bring them back into doing well."

"I can see that you are trying so hard and it is not your fault that your sisters and others like them, don't want to give up their evil doings."

"I am supposed to save them and I have failed."

Brook got off her chair went and hugged Sandy. "We know you have a big burden on your back, but you are gifted for a reason. You have to use your judgment and not your beautiful kind heart. If someone does evil to someone else then they should expect that someday they will wear the same shoes."

"I don't know what I would have done without you and Brian. You have filled the empty spot of my parents in my life and for that I am forever in debt to you and I promise that no harm will ever come to you or your family."

"What a beautiful smell," said Joshua upon his entry. "I could smell it all the way from the bedroom. I tried to resist it but couldn't. So here I am."

Brook quickly jumped off her seat and baked fresh eggs for Josh, while Brian made Josh's coffee. "Here son enjoy." he said

"We are going to check on the cattle Sandy. Would you like to come with us?" Brian added.

"I would love to. I will get changed."

While driving in Brian's little open four wheel Sandy was amazed at the beauty of the surroundings, "You know Brian I could live here forever this is so beautiful."

Brian with a smile said. "I would be happy if you stayed forever."

"I feel like time is getting closer even though I don't know what will happen. Max will be fully mobile within a week or two and we have to start planning of how we are going to do this."

When they came back to the house everyone was up waiting for them. Max called out "Sandy can we have a talk?"

"Yes sure" she replied

"I am fully functional now and I think it is time to put a plan together of how we are going to do this."

"In that case, let's gather everyone, I will ask Brian's son to look after the kids so they will not hear any of our discussions."

"Max you started. Do you want to continue?" Sandy asked

"Well I was thinking may be Brad can give us some names that we can trust to contact in the meantime. One of you Joshua or Jason can call the media and asked them to have a conference. But you have to make it clear to the media that no information can be leaked out due to the sensibility of the case. Once everything is secured we will show up at the police station where the media is going to be waiting. That way if any one tries to take any of us by force the media will cover it."

"What are we going to do after that? What if we all get arrested?" Joshua asked.

"Well I will go in first, with all my paper work. Birth certificate, driver's licenses and the ownership of my house and company documents. Of course I have to thank Don for preparing all these documents for me when I was in coma."

"What next?" asked Jason?

"I will prove that all the accusations against you are wrong then I will take the media to my company and from there we will see who is in control."

"What if they kill you first?" Sandy asked.

"That is why we need Brad to be our ears and eyes and give us the names of those who can be trusted."

"I still think that is risky." Joshua called out

"But not as risky as the way we are living right now."

"That is true." Brian said

"And Josh I am sure you are dying to see your kids. This will hopefully put an end to all our problems."

"Oh that is so true." replied Josh

"Today is the fifth of the month. Everything should be arranged for the fifteenth. The media should be told that we will be there at ten thirty am. We will arrive at eleven am. I will grab my documents and walk in while Josh, you will cover the right hand side of the entry and Jason, you and Mandy can cover the back. You should be prepared to escape in the cars." Max added

"What do you want us to do?" Brian asked

"You will go in first before any of us because no one knows you. Then if you see anything that is suspicious, you will let us know not to go in. It would be good if Brook went in with you, that way no one will be suspicious about you."

"That is fine with us." replied Brook

"Jason, do you think Brad will help us in this?" Asked Max

"I will talk to him tomorrow and let you know." Jason responded.

"Let's talk again tomorrow as soon as Jason has a reply from Brad." Max said.

The next day when Jason called Brad and explained to him what they want to do, Brad was very happy. "I have been waiting for this moment for a very long time."

That afternoon Brad gathered a few loyal friends whose lives had been affected by the crook cops and detectives. Those, who just like Brad, were in those jobs because they believed in justice and peace. A few of them offered their help to capture the bad guys. Brad told them, have patience day of justice was near.

Brad called Jason. He gave him the names of a few detectives that he trusted with his life and told Jason. "Please make sure Max asks to see them."

Jason assured Brad, and then rushed to give the good news to the group. That night over drinks they started making the plans.

Brian and Brook were supportive at all-times but they looked very worried. Sandy uttered. "Why so worried?"

Brook said. "As much as we want you to have your lives back, we are going to miss you."

"We won't let you to miss us because we will visit all the time plus you will have an excuse to come to the city." Sandy replied.

Brian if you see the smallest thing that is out of place you call me straight away, otherwise I will come into the police station straight on time." Max called out.

"And Jason you should make sure that the car is on and ready to get away. I just hope that no one from media is paid by Angelo to be an informer otherwise, it will be like a nightmare and things could really go wrong."

"Don't worry" Sandy replied. "After what we have been through we can handle anything. Let's hope that it doesn't get to that."

"I think we should contact Adam and tell him what we are up to. I met him a while ago. He is still under police protection. Jason added.

"I agree" said Sandy. "We should contact all those involved who lost lives and were affected through all this massive disaster."

"Like who?" asked Joshua

"Like Daniel, Julio, Nancy, Adam Jasmin's husband, Michael Jackie's husband and Max's loyal employee."

"And tell them?" Asked Jason

"No, ask them and tell them what we are doing and if they are prepared to give evidence in court once the case hits the courts?"

"That is right" Max called out. "We should know who will stand by us although we might not need them because of all the evidence in my hands. By the way dose anyone know where Jo has disappeared to?"

"No. He left one night and never came back. He was truly concerned about his mother." replied Joshua.

"He seems like a good kid. We should not leave him behind." said Max.

Chapter 25

On the other side of city Angelo and his partners were waiting anxiously but when the news came on. He started screaming. "What kind of disaster is this? Every time we think we have them, something out of ordinary happens and they get away."

When Angelo's men came back he was furious. "Can't you do anything right? Should I, myself, go where there is a lead to catch these people?"

Angelo then turned around and asked Brad's partner. "What kind of detectives you have put to work. None of them have any idea what to do? Are these really your best men? I want you to pay all your men today and get rid of them and bring me a new batch that can do the job."

Alex, Brad's partner knew he hasn't been given an easy task to do. When he went back to his shift with Brad, he was very down and unhappy. Brad asked. "What is it partner? You seem very down?"

Alex wasn't sure if he should say anything. He was scared of Angelo and had to do something before he destroyed his life. "Do you remember those private meetings I use to go to?"

"Sort off" replied Brad

"Well that is to do with Angelo and the chain. I was approached a few years ago but when I refused they took my family as ransom.

To save them I had to do whatever Angelo told me. My kids and wife were horrified from the abduction and stupid me did not have anywhere to escape to. When I joined them they asked for more detectives to be hired by me. At time that was easy because everyone needed extra money. So they joined me. But now he wants me to fire them and hire a new batch of detectives.

I am horrified both ways. It is not going to work for me.

If I don't do what Angelo wants? Again he might attempt to do something to my family and I cannot bear that.

Secondly with all those detectives that I have to get rid of I know they will not be happy. They will seek revenge, because letting them go from Angelo's gang's means less money for them."

"Oh my god. What did you get yourself in?" Brad asked

"I am so lost and don't know what to do?"

"Are you prepared to get rid of Angelo and chain for good?" Asked Brad

"I will give my life as long as I know my wife and children are going to live safely."

"Then would you accept if me and some other detectives became your new batch. That way it will be easier for us help you."

"Like I said. I am stuck in hell right now and I am prepared to do anything to get out of this mud. You know during all those times that I have been with them, I never hurt anyone or did anything against my belief as a detective. So many times I got into trouble with Angelo for helping the people escape death."

"If you are really genuine, we should go to our superior and tell him the story. I have already spoken to him about arranging a group of honest detectives to overcome these crimes of the chain."

"But won't he take my job away and charge me with misleading info and other crimes?"

"No we will tell him that you were working undercover and couldn't trust anyone because of your family. Plus if you genuinely care about your family you won't need to live in fear all the time."

"Oh how I wish I would have talked to you earlier. You can see how scared I am."

"That is fine. There is a saying that anytime you catch a fish in the water it will be fresh."

"Thanks mate, so when do we go?"

"I will arrange a meeting with him."

In the meantime Angelo was telling Michael. "Make sure you and Alberto are nice to the girls. We have to be so careful that they don't turn on us and that the day that we capture and get rid of Sandy, Max, Jason then we will make the girls disappear too."

"But I really like Cindy and I wouldn't want any harm to come to her." uttered Alberto

"We will discuss these things in due time." Angelo Screamed.

Michael nearby called out. "Guys now it is not the time to fall on each other. If we go down we all go together."

They then leave the office. Angelo always thought that he could buy and sell everything including people with his money. When he got to Jasmin's house he was all stressed and asked her. "How much do you really love me?"

"What kind of question is that? You should know how I feel after all the things I have done for you."

"I know but I am wondering what you would do if your family eventually goes to court along with me. Would you help them or me?"

"Off course I will help you. I never had feelings of belonging towards that family now that I have you and everything I always wanted in life."

"That is good to hear." Said Angelo

"Where is everybody tonight?" asked Jasmine. It is so quiet and boring I am going to ask Alberto, Cindy and Michael to come and have a drink with us. Jackie should be home soon."

Tell the kitchen to make the tea and ask everyone to come for dinner."

"That is a good idea" Jasmin replied. She departed to the kitchen to give the orders for dinner.

When everyone arrived Angelo asked. "Cindy how did you go with the school?"

"Good I made it clear to them what I want. However, one thing that upset me. The company that my security guard was working for, moved him to another area and replaced him with a new security guard. I was used to the old one."

"Did the security guard ever tell you that he wanted to be relocated?" Asked Michael

"No" replied Cindy. "I have not seen him since he went and handed the money to school."

"So he never came back here?" asked Angelo

"No. He didn't."

"I will make an enquiry tomorrow morning. You know Angelo, this doesn't sound right." said Alberto.

"You are right," replied Angelo. "Go and talk to the company tomorrow morning. If Cindy was happy with that security guard they should send him back. Cindy did you call the school to see if anything happened when he delivered the money to them? May be something happened there? Up to when he went to school he seemed happy acting as your security guard."

The next morning Cindy called the school the principal was shocked when she asked him if there was anything unusual about the security guard when he delivered the money.

The principal, remembering the security guard said. "Why did something happen to him?"

"I don't know. I haven't seen him since he came to school. He was supposed to come back here. Because there was still a few hours left for his shift to finish."

Knowing what went on that day the principal said. "He seemed unwell. Maybe he is sick. He didn't spend much time here. As soon as he handed the money to me he left.

The principal did not mention anything of what happened that day, but somehow in his heart he was very happy that the security guard had followed his inner guidance and left the job.

At the same time Alberto paid the security company a visit and asked for the security guard but the owner told him that he wasn't feeling well and asked for some time off. "I tried to check on him but was told that he and his family are gone on a trip."

"Do all your employees walk out of jobs without warning your clients?"

The owner said. "Sir, people simply do get sick and there is nothing we can do."

"Sick or not sick, you either bring him back to apologise to Cindy or you will fire him straight away."

"Sir, the law won't allow me to fire someone while they are on sick leave. Why is it, that you are making a big deal out of this? I have already replaced him with another trusty security guard."

"You can't talk to me like that. I am the law. Fire him did you hear me or you will put up with the consequences."

The company owner was not very happy with the way he was spoken to, so that afternoon he told all his employees to resign from their jobs at four sites. Alberto's, Angelo's, Jackie and Jasmin's, Michael's and Cindy's.

Angelo was furious and called the company. "Is this a joke? Are all your employees resigning?"

"I am sorry sir, I have no control over them. If I lose all my employees, there is nothing I can do. May be you would be better off going to another security company or hire them directly."

"I will deal with you later." said Angelo. "For now I have to go."

That night Angelo and his partners were so unhappy about everything. This was the first time that they lost control. He then called Alex. "I want you to plant something in that company and have their doors shut."

"What happened?"

"They all quit at the same time and the owner doesn't want to replaced or fire them."

"Ok" Alex replied. "Leave it with me."

"Have you gathered your new team yet?"

"I should bring them around in a day or two."

The next day, Alex called Brad and told him it was an emergency. Brad told him not to worry. "I will talk to our superior."

However Angelo called his partners and warned them that they were getting really loose with their dealings with others. "We have concentrated on finding those brothers and sister so much that everything else around us is falling apart."

Michael suggested to hire their own security guards directly. However after a few advertisements through radio, papers and TV, no one was applying. Day by day the partners were becoming more and more aggressive.

The men that run the companies now can't even hire security. When other security companies fund out that one company had pulled out all their security guards from the four sits they were cautious that something must be wrong or dangerous at those sites and would not supply security guards to Angelo and his partners.

From then on, every time the chain had a meeting everything was so tense. All the people involved in the chain, started losing their security guards followed by some long term employees especially, in those companies that the chain took over by force. The chain is slowly rusting and falling apart. The powerful men tried everything to put fear back in people's lives but it didn't work because somehow the news came out that Max was among the fugitives and he wasn't dead. This came about when Max and Sandy were sited at a petrol station.

Chapter 26

Sandy is more at peace and hears that people are retaliating to the force of the chain. She calls Brad and briefs him of their plan to take place in a few days.

"Sandy, my partner is now with us as well." Brad uttered.

"How do you know Angelo hasn't paid him?"

"He has spoken to me and I've been to his house, met his son and wife. The mark of torture is still on his wife's face from the time that they got abducted by Angelo's men to force Alex to become one of them."

"Did you see anything unusual around you when he was telling you his story?"

"Yes, now that you mentioned it, there was a blue light making circles around his head but I though it was just a reflection of cars."

"In that case you can trust him. The plan is in two days. Make sure you guys are in the surrounding areas."

"Why did you say in that case you can trust him? Is it to do with that light?"

"You will know in due time."

The night before the plan takes place Brian went to the lunchroom and found everybody sitting on the couches, quietly and all in deep thoughts. He walks out, goes to his room, and then comes back with a bottle of real expensive brandy that was nearly a hundred years old.

"Why are you all sitting there like a broken army? We have to celebrate tonight when you make your plans and be happy. Everything will be all right because happiness brings happiness but if you make your plans with a broken faith then the outcome will be sad like your feelings."

Sandy jumped from her seat and said. "Always, wise words Brian."

"Ok now that you are happy with me Sandy, you might as well get some glasses and ask Brook to bring some munchies."

As Sandy was walking to the kitchen the doorbell rang. Everyone stayed still for a second. Brook said. "Don't worry I will get it." When she opened the door she screamed "I am going to kill you Jo. Where did you disappear to without saying anything to anyone?"

"Brook these are really heavy. Can you kill me when I put them down?"

When he made it to the lunchroom and put the stuff that he was carrying on a couch everybody yelled at him. "Where have you been?"

"Well I went to do something. You guys are soon going to face the media and I didn't want you to look like crap when you do."

Joshua had a little ball in his hand. He threw it at Jo "Now we look like crap?"

"Sorry. Didn't, want it to sound like that. Jo then started opening the boxes and bags. Here you go Sandy. This suit is for you with matching shoes and bag. Max, my friend this suit with matching colour shirt, belt and tie is for you."

"Thanks Jo. But how long did it take you to buy these? One or two hours? You were gone for days."

"No. I also found an excuse to go to the police station and install a few cameras so we can watch you every second that you are in there."

"In the police station, didn't they ask you what you were doing?"

"Thanks to our friend Brad and his superior, they arranged it for me and no one got suspicious."

"After all the hard ship and heart aches, the time has finally arrived. Max stayed up most of the night thinking about the morning and how everything will take place. He wasn't alone. All the others, each in their bedrooms were praying for things to go according to plan.

Finally the morning arrived. Everyone is up early. In fact not one had any sleep. They all got in to their suits and business like clothing. At the breakfast table everyone was quiet. No one had anything to add to what was previously discoursed.

Once they cleared the table and washed the breakfast plates they were ready to leave Brian held the door and said. "Good luck everyone. Don't worry I am sure everything will go according to the plan."

Jo was the first person to take off and make it to the police station to look around in case there were some unusual activates. After searching all the surrounding areas he rang Max and assured him that the meeting spot was clear and safe.

Jo then stayed around to observe. It wasn't long before the media cars started pulling. They were all early in order to grab a key spot to cover the situation.

Although Max and Sandy were not expected until ten thirty am, the crowed of journalists started moving in from eight am. When Jo saw the crowd he started worrying again. He called Max and told him about the situation. Max told him not to worry. He added that the more people around, would prove safer for them to escape if necessary.

People were going past the area not knowing what is going on. Even Angelo's men called him and told him how busy certain police station was but Angelo told them. "If you are worried just stick around and find out what it is all about."

Angelo's men went around asking what was going on but no one knew and they were told. "We are not sure but whoever called media media has first class news."

Jo kept on looking at the activities from the cameras that he installed in the police station earlier. He couldn't see anything out of normal.

It was nearly eleven am. Everyone was already tired and frustrated. All of a sudden four cars pulled over near the police station. Brian and Brook climbed out of the first car and made their way inside the police station, while the other cars drove away.

The media ran to Brook and Brian but noticed nothing special about them. They retreated. The couple walked in and asked for the senior officer. When he came they asked. "Is it a safe time for the others to enter?"

The senior officer said to them to wait a moment and called a few of his loyal detectives, which included Brad and his partner Alex. He then addressed everyone. "The minute you get suspicious that Max is in danger, take him to the car and make sure he gets away."

After Brian called Max again three cars pulled up in front of police station. This time Sandy and Max got out of the car. The media started whistling and taking photos. "Max we were told you are dead."

Max with a smile looked but didn't say anything. They quickly entered the police station and went to the counter.

Brian and Brook left to have their car ready for get away.

The senior officer asked Max if he was ready to start. Max replied. "I want a few camera men and women including a few journalists to witness this. If you don't mind could you choose a few that can come in?"

The senior officer agreed. He told Brad to let three of the major media representatives in. Brad was not to let those journalists from the smaller outlets to slip in.

Brad then walked outside and with his hand pointed to the ones that he wanted to take into the police station.

Once inside the conference room, the senior officer, asked Max again if he was ready.

"Yes thank you. Hello everyone I am Max from Max's enterprises. That created a storm amongst the media. They all looked at each other. "Didn't Max die last year?"

The senior officer then said. "Max died last year and we have the death certificate and everything to prove you are not him."

"And I Max have everything you need to prove that I am Max the owner of Max's enterprise."

Max then got off his chair and said "If you don't mind I need to take a few pieces of clothing off."

"What do you mean; you want to take your clothes off? But why?"

"Yes I do. Once you have a look at my body, I can start telling you the details."

The senior officer said. "Well go ahead if everyone agrees with this?"

"We want to see what he is going to show us." said all the journalists.

Max then took his shirt off followed by his pants. There were massive scars on his neck chest and legs. On the back his spin showed massive scars.

"As you are aware, the plane that crashed last year. Me and Sandy were passengers on it. Through a lot of luck we did not die in that crash. However I was left in coma for a few months and when I gained consciousness, I was told that I will never walk again. However there was a man and two women that never gave up on me. A man after my father's death became my second father. This young woman next to me cared for me during my recovery, whereby we escaped from one place to another, while people were attempting to take my life."

Someone from media screamed. "Who wanted you dead?"

"If you give me a bit of time to finish, you will find out soon enough."

"I call up on the media here to witness me handing in all the documents to prove that I am not dead and that I am still the rightful owner of Max's enterprises."

"I also have documents left for me to prove that Don's empire belonged to his four children which was forcefully taken away from them."

Max then handed the papers to the senior officer and said. "Sir, here is all the evidence that the chain and Angelo were behind all the attempts to kill me. They have over taken my company, my home and assets with false documents."

By this stage the media was unstoppable. Some ran outside and told their colleagues to be ready for what would be a bigger outcome. A second of what is to follow cannot be missed whatsoever.

The officer turned to Sandy. "Mam what do you have to say about all this?"

I am Sandy, the rightful owner of Don's empire. This will clearly states that I will be in charge of all Don's estate, to divide the assets of my father fairly between all his children once he was gone."

"But Don's empire went broke almost a year ago, and Don's children were hunted by the suppliers of his companies."

Sandy then showed the senior officer another set of paper work. "These are the suppliers that my dad's company used since the beginning of his empire. You may call all of them and you will find out that there was never any unpaid debts."

While talking Sandy, saw the little blue lights gathering in the conference room. She whispered in Max's ear that danger is close by.

Max looked around and then got off his chair. "Sorry this meeting has to be left for another day." He then looked at the officer and said "I hope these documents are enough for you to start your investigation until we meet again."

The officer quickly called Brad. "Something is going on. Take these documents. Don't let anyone know you have them. I will contact you in time to look at them."

Max and Sandy started running outside but the media had to see them once they were outside. They had run through the back door to the escape car. Following an emergency call from Jo, Brian and Jason blocked the other two sides, so no one could chase them.

When they left the, police station was placed on high alert. Everyone was asked to leave the building.

The little lights left the police station and covered Jason and Brian's cars so no one would be able to take their plate numbers.

Finally they all arrived back at Brian's house. Brook laughed and said, she had felt like a spy, and even think that she had done better job than agent 007.

They all laughed. However inside they were all worried about what the outcome was going to be.

"Here everyone." said Brian. "Drink to a job well done."

After such a morning they all needed a drink so they grabbed their glasses and cheered to their achievement.

While they were drinking the little lights started gathering around Sandy. She excused herself and went to her room. When she got there, her room was lit with beautiful blue light. As she walked in, she found herself in a massive ballroom surrounded by tables. Behind each table a massive light sat on a chair. She couldn't see any faces but for the second time she was amazed for being in that ballroom.

A voice came from the top table. "You had a hard time and kept your loyalty to your gift as the queen of Karma. Now we have come to a decision to allow you to let the people around you know who you are."

"But they won't even believe me."

"They will because now they know the presence of the little lights could mean danger or calamity. We also wanted to tell you for centuries there has not been one like you. All previous ones were so blinded by the power given to them that they tried to use it for revenge and harm, but you have been so wise and all the soldiers which are the little lights, love you and hang around you all the time. If you noticed they helped you and the others quite a few times."

Sandy said thank you then found herself back in her room.

When later she walked to where everyone else was sitting, they all looked at her strangely.

"What is the matter? Is something wrong?" She asked

"Nothing darling." replied Brian.

Sandy then sat back in her chair and carried on having her drink.

"Where did you disappear to earlier?" Josh asked

Before answering she looked at everyone's faces and said. "Promise me you won't freak out."

"Nothing is going to be freakier than your disappearance." replied Joshua

Everyone was staring at Sandy curiously, when she said. "Josh turn the lights off."

When he turned the lights off, everyone could see hundreds of little lights around the room. They started to panic but Sandy said. "Don't worry they are harmless to you."

Sandy then got up and went to the corner of the room where all the little lights followed and gathered around her. She then closed her eyes and opened her arms. All of a sudden she became a massive globe of light with her authority stick in her hand and her crown on her head.

"Oh my god." screamed Mandy.

"Sh" Jason said

Sandy then opened her eyes and asked Josh to put the lights back on. After turning the lights on, Sandy went back to being herself again.

Jason asked. "What was all that about Sandy?"

Sandy then started telling them of how she helped Charlie and how he had come back and gave her a gift that a woman asked to give to the person that he thinks is worthy of the gift.

Josh screamed. "Is it the gift, that one afternoon in mum and dad's house, Jasmine made a big deal about it?"

Jason uttered. "Oh yes. Is that what you are talking about?"

"Yes. That is what I am talking about."

"Continue" Brian uttered.

"Well the reason the gift was given to me was because I was the chosen one for this century to carry duties of the queen of Karma."

"Queen of Karma?" asked Brook

"Yes queen of Karma. I only found out about this after the plane crash. For days I was stuck in the mountains and in coma at one point, arguing my case and wanting to reject the burden that was about to be put on me."

"Arguing with who child?" asked Brian

"With the gift keepers. I was telling them that I don't have the heart to be the queen of karma. However they told me there was nothing I can do after days of arguing in the court rooms in my coma. Finally they decided to give me a second gift which was forgiveness. I was told that I had the power to give people a chance to change their ways and become better people before karma knocks on their doors. If I failed and could not stop someone from doing bad then they would pay the price according to their evil selves or bad doings."

"Is that why you begged our sisters so much?" asked Josh

"Exactly." she replied.

"What is going to happen to them?"

"I don't know. I will not know until it happens."

"But if you are the queen, you can stop everything." said Mandy.

"I cannot use my powers for personal dealings because if I do I will be abusing them."

"Just tell me something. Why was it that when Jasmin picked the gift up, black smoke came out of it. But when you took it off her, it turned in to these beautiful lights?" asked Josh

"The black smoke was the inner self of Jasmine, and when I took it back from her the little soldiers got happy and showed themselves."

Josh then asked. "Which soldiers?"

"All these little lights are. They are the ones that helped us escape so many times, and warned us when danger was close."

"I remember, Jason must have known something about the little lights that day at the coffee shop." Jo uttered.

"I didn't know. Something just told me that we were in danger." Jason responded.

Josh joined in the conversation. "And that day with that beggar in the alley."

"All of it just happens. The little lights were never allowed to do any work that they are doing now with previous queens. The head of the gift keepers told me that since I was chosen they can't control themselves and at all times they want to be around me. No queen with the gift, ever in past centuries was allowed to reveal her secret. Somehow they allowed me to tell you people that are here and those who really need the good Karma to help them out".

"That is amazing." said Brian. Since the moment I met you I knew there was something special about you and when we got up that morning to that amazing vision of the house and the cattle, confirmed to me that you are not of this world."

"Come on, Brian, of course I am from this world. It is just that some special person thought I deserved to have that special gift."

While they were talking, the news came on. Some journalist had recorded everything that went on inside the police station and outside. The news flash was "Max the owner of Max enterprises whom last year we broadcast as disappeared and then death is alive.

This morning at around elven o'clock it was confirmed that Max is alive. After he walked into the police station and handed in all the necessary documents. No one knows why they suddenly got into a panic and rushed out of the station.

The journalist continued, "Somehow unintentionally, we helped them escape. As they were running all the journalists were running after them to ask questions, but as you can see in the video we tried to ask questions but they jumped into a getaway car and took off. Only minutes after they left, while we all were making our way back to the police station we heard a big bang followed by thick black smoke which covered the whole area. While everybody was rushing around to get away, me and our camera men went back to police station and found it burning due to a massive explosion.

The police have now confirmed that the attack was meant for the police station. Something triggered the officer in charge of the shift to ask everyone to evacuate the building.

"We asked him why?

He said "I don't know as soon as Max and Sandy started running I knew something was not right, so I asked everyone to leave the building, and how thankful I am for doing that because everyone was out of the building when the explosion happened and no one got hurt."

"It seems that a super natural power is behind all this. Previously in the news we have seen how every time the police got close to arresting the fugitives, a great blinding light appeared and helped them escape."

"I was in the helicopter the last time the police surrounded the liquor shop where one of the brothers and their sister were located but this great blinding light made it impossible for any vision and all the helicopters were forced to land and wait until the light allowed them to leave. It is unfortunate that some areas of our videos have mysteriously disappeared but we hope that we can at some stage give our audience a visual of this great light."

Chapter 27

Angelo's men told him about the gathering at the police station and when they asked why? Some journalist told them they didn't know yet. But whatever it was it would be a big story.

When Max showed up, Angelo's men again called him and told him that it was a desperate situation because the fugitive that we were after, showed up at the police station with hundreds of detectives and journalists waiting for him.

"Couldn't you take a shot?" asked Angelo

"Sir that was just impossible." replied one of his men

"Was that useless Alex there?" asked Angelo

"We didn't know who was inside but his partner came out and chose a few camera men and journalist to go in and cover the story that was taking place inside."

"Oh god what kind of idiots am I dealing with." Angelo screamed. "Well go and keep an eye and try to get your hands on any evidence that might hurt us, and I will send you further help in a few minutes."

However Angelo did not send help. Instead he sent his two most powerful assassins. "Blow the place up" he told them as they were leaving.

As soon as Max and Sandy left the police station through the back of the police station. It was bombed by the assassins. They then, dressed in police clothing went into the police station to finalize the death of anyone inside. But the police station was empty and the assassins thought something was very wrong so they left and called Angelo.

"What do you mean the police station was empty?" Angelo screamed again. "How can a police station be empty at that time of morning? What about Max and his partner. Did they get arrested?"

"No sir. They got away. They had cars waiting outside on each corner and that blinding light appeared on top of their cars again and no one was able to get their registration numbers."

"That is an obvious joke. What about the cops inside?" Angelo asked

"Well from what we heard the officer in charge felt in danger and evacuated the police station. All the documents were gone with him."

"Do I have to dictate everything? Well find him and take all the necessary documents from him."

The men obviously did not know where to start. They went around asking who was in charge at the time of the conference but no one was able to give them any names, so they called Alex.

"Your partner Brad was there this morning. You need to find out who was in charge of the police station this morning."

"Why do you want to know who was in charge?"

"Because whoever it was, still has the documents that Max handed to him."

"What documents?"

The ones that prove Max was still alive. If we don't find the documents we are all dead."

"I will see what I can do."

An hour later the men called him again. "Did you find out?"

"Yes. Brad was there but then he was asked to leave."

"We didn't see him leaving."

"Apparently they had a secret escape underground. He was told to leave through there."

"Is that how all the cops disappeared?"

"By the looks of it I am not sure. " Although Alex himself was inside and could hear everything said and discussed but he would not leak any info. This was his opportunity to get rid of the chain and finally leave in peace.

Brad to whom the documents were handed was asked not to go back to his place and find a hotel and secure the documents.

The chain now has arranged for an emergency meeting. They called in all their men and put them in search of the documents. As to all these years of the practice the chain had never had any problems because they easily got rid of the people that were a threat to them but now that they had witnessed supernatural powers and the fact that their money cannot buy those powers was annoying for them.

One of them said "Grab Alex's family. That way he will definitely try to find a way to grab the documents in exchange for his family."

The chain then assigned a few men to do that.

Angelo suggested that Brad should be found and brought in as well. "We might be able to force the truth out of him." More men were assigned for that.

By that evening hundreds of the chain's men were out looking for the evidence that could destroy them. Anywhere they went they couldn't find the people they were looking for.

Alex's house was evacuated before the men got there and when they went to Brad's house the neighbours told them that he hadn't been back all day. The men then decided to sit and wait in front of his house but Brad never showed up.

The senior officer, after leaving the police station met with Brad at a hotel room. After studying the documents he realized that they had a war on their hands with master mind criminals. That was when he warned Alex and Brad to disappear until he found enough evidence to press charges. He too, moved his family away so they couldn't use them as bait.

"Michael, get the girls to come and join us." Angelo pleaded.

When the girls arrived all the giant business men went quiet. Angelo with a smile on his face said. "Don't worry they are on our side."

But the Chain wasn't satisfied and asked Jasmine. "What do you think about all those allegations that you saw on the news?"

As she was about to ask what allegation, the waiter dropped the tray of drink on her. She got off her chair and slammed the tray in his face. "You low life. Look what you did."

Although he apologized a few times that did not stop them from firing him. Jasmine then turned to her sister and Cindy. "Would you girls come with me to get some dry clothes?"

The two girls agreed and they left the room. When they got outside Jackie said "I don't think we are welcomed here."

"Why do you say that?" asked Jasmine

"Did you see how quiet they all went? And the way Angelo said, don't worry they are on our side."

"Did any of you watch the news?" asked Jasmine

"No. Why?" asked Jackie

"Didn't you hear them talking about the allegations shown on the news?" Jasmine continued. "Anyway first let's find some dry clothes for me." while walking into this boutique." Oh, my god." she said when she had a look at the clothes. "Is there any other shops close by?"

"Not for a few kilometres." replied the shop keeper.

"Oh well find me something close to what I am wearing I don't want to touch anything. "

The shop keeper then went and brought out her most expensive branded clothes, from the back of the store.

"This dress is so nice. Try it on Jasmine." said Cindy.

"I suppose this should do." replied Jasmine. She then went into the change room and changed.

When they left the boutique she said. "Ok now let's go to that coffee shop and ask him to put the TV on."

After ordering the coffee Jasmine asked, "Any channels showing the news now?"

The bar tender replied. "It depends what news you are after? Right then the news flashes keep on coming up every five minutes on all channels.

"Do you mind turning your TV on then?" Jasmine asked.

"The bar tender then went and turned the TV on and left to prepare their snacks.

The girls were not kept waiting for long when again the news flash came on "This morning Max the owner of Max enterprises showed up at the police station with all the necessary documents to prove his identity. The police believe that the daughter of Don's empire accompanied him. Minutes after Max's arrival at the police station they felt frightened and ran through the back door.

No one knows exactly what went on behind the closed doors but the documents handed to police proved to be of importance to a group of criminals because minutes later the police station was attacked but luckily there was no one inside."

"That is what made the chain panic? I thought they were more powerful than that, plus they probably don't know that my sister is a loser and there is nothing she can do to harm any of us." Jasmine said

"She is probably after her shares now. Anyway who got her shares?" Asked Jackie

"We all did. She did not have any shares." replied Jasmine.

"This is not good at all. That means that Josh is with Sandy as well" panicked Cindy. "If he gets to me he will make my life miserable, I am so scared."

"Please don't come to conclusions, I am sure Alberto will do something about it and stop them from harming you." Jasmine said.

After the girls finished their coffee they went back to the office Michael called out. "You were away for a long time. Where did you go?"

Jackie replied. "We went and got this dress for Jasmine. Then we went across the road for a cup of coffee."

"How stupid was that," screamed Michael. "Don't you know if the media locates any of us in public, they will bombard us with questions?"

"Sorry. We didn't know what was going on. We just saw the news flash now." replied Jackie.

"From now on you don't go anywhere in the public. All the food and necessary stuff will be brought to your houses. All your telephones will be disconnected and you should not communicate with anyone outside this chain."

"We have nothing to be scared of." Jackie replied.

"Do as you are told before you are made to feel sorry." screamed one of the men.

By now the girls were starting to worry, so they decided to keep quiet until they were driven home.

On the way home at least four men were assigned to drive them home, two in a car at the front and two in a different car at the back. Half the way home there was a deafening sound and everybody started screaming. For a few minutes the car kept on going but out of the blue it stopped. When the bloody driver opened the top of the limousine he put his head out but couldn't see anything apart from mud surrounding the car and the head lights of the other car from top of the hole. They had found themselves at the bottom of a huge ditch.

All they could hear was a voice saying, "If you are alright don't move. We will get help." The three girls were crying and carrying on while the driver tried to settle them down. "You heard the man. Help should be here anytime."

Minutes later help arrived they threw a rope in the hole to pull them out. The girls were the first ones to make it out. They were covered in mud and blood. When they got to top looked back and realized they had been caught in a sink hole. Minutes after everyone was pulled out they heard harsh noises. The mud finally gave in and the car went down until it disappeared from the view. Cindy started crying. "Oh my

God we were in that car a few minutes ago. We all could have been dead."

Jasmin was trying to get off the ground. She pointed her hand to a man standing by to help her up but the man looked at her and said.

"Karma got you devil woman."

She looked at the man. He looked so familiar but knowing how she hurt a lot of people in her life, Jasmine didn't know if he was one of them.

All of a sudden the little light started gathering. No one but the girls could see them, and then a voice could be heard. "You were given the opportunity to change but you chose your own evil ways."

Jackie screamed. "That is another trick. Whoever you are, you can go to hell. Can't you see we are hurt?"

Everyone looked strangely at Jackie because they didn't see or hear anything. They thought the poor woman is in a shock.

The traffic was shocking, as the cops blocked the streets. In the middle of the very busy street lay a massive hole. No one knew how deep it really was.

After being examined by the medics, the girls were released to go home. In seconds Anglo's men surrounded them.

When they arrived home they all got into their own showers. Minutes later they were back in the lunch room. No one was saying anything. Angelo, Michael and Alberto arrived shortly after to comfort them.

"You must have been horrified?" said Angelo

Jasmin looked at him. "We are so lucky to be alive. God knows where that hole goes to."

"Are any of you hurt?" They said one of you was covered in blood.

"No" replied Cindy. "I think when the driver tried to open the top cover of the car, he hurt himself. It was his blood."

"Poor guy. I should reward him for his bravery in risking his life to save yours." Angelo implied.

"Where did he go to?" asked Jasmin

"He was taken to hospital. He has lost a lot of blood and has a broken wrist." replied Angelo.

After a few drinks the girls seemed to settle. The chef had made the dinner ready. The maid walked in. "Excuse me Miss Jasmin, dinner is ready to be served."

When the food was going to be served the chef found himself in a very unusual situation. He called the maid. "Come and have a look at these."

The made screamed. "Oh my god what is that?"

"I don't know." the chef replied. You were with me in the kitchen all the time and you saw how beautiful everything looked. I don't know how all that food I made turned in to worms."

After waiting for a while at the dining table Jasmin got annoyed, and called the maid. "Why are you keeping us waiting for so long? Where the food is?"

The maid started crying. "Mam I think you should come and see with your own eyes."

"See what?" screamed Jasmine. "Can't you see I am very upset?"

The maid started crying harder. "I am sorry mam but if it was not important I wouldn't ask you to come and check."

After seeing the maid like that, Jasmin got off her chair and went to the kitchen only to find all the prepared dinner plates full of worms. She then went to all the pots on the stoves only to find that they were all full of worms as well. She turned to the chef and the Maid with anger. "What is this?" Is this a joke?"

The chef tried to explain the situation as he saw it to her. She was so angry that she did not want to listen. "If you think we are worthy of eating worms, then pack your bags and leave right now."

The Maid screamed. "But mam"

"There are no buts. Leave now or I will call the cops." Jasmin then turned around and looked at all the plates. "Clean all the mess you made first, otherwise I will make sure that no one hires you again."

Jasmine then went and apologised to the girls and their company. "Something has gone wrong in the kitchen. We need to order food from outside."

Angelo got very angry and went to the kitchen. "If there was no food why did you call us to the table?" He slapped the maid so hard across her face.

"But sir." she called out.

"No buts. I will deal with you both later." He rushes out of kitchen.

Jasmin asked him. "Did you see the mess in the kitchen?"

"What mess? There was no mess." He replied. "Just two lazy people that tried to laugh at us."

"When I went there was so much mess they couldn't have cleaned it up in this short time."

She rushed back to the kitchen and found it all tidy with all the stuff put away where it belonged. All the worms had disappeared.

"What did you do with the worms? Where did you put them?"

"They disappeared." said the chef.

"You stupid person. How can they disappear on their own? Where are they?"

She then started looking in the rubbish bins which were all empty and clean down the drains. She looked outside the kitchen in the yard but there was no sign of the worms. She then came back to the kitchen.

"What kind of games are you playing with me? Who helped you to get rid of all that mess?"

The chef and the maid had no answers. They were still in shock. The minute Jasmine walked out as they were about to start cleaning, everything started disappearing. Neither of these two hard working people had any idea what was going on around them.

Jasmin slammed the door and walked out. The maid started crying.

"Where would I go at this time of the night, I have nowhere to go from here."

The chef who had a car said. "You can stay with me at my mum's house until you find another job."

The two sneaked out of the house before Angelo or Jasmin come back to the kitchen.

Jackie ordered the food. After it had arrived Jasmine, every time she picked the food with her fork she remembered the worms and couldn't eat. She stayed at the table until everyone finished eating. When she called the maid to clear the table, they realized that both the maid and the chef have disappeared. So they all helped in clearing the table and washing the dishes.

The boys went to their own homes but Cindy stayed with Jasmine and Jackie. They had a hard day and none of them wanted to be alone.

In the middle of the night one could see that Cindy was struggling in bed. It was as if she was trying to get away from something. Jackie went to check on her and found her all sweaty. All her hands and legs were moving at the same time. "Cindy wake up I think you are having a nightmare."

Cindy woke up and looked around. "Thank you for waking me up."

"That is ok. Why were you panicking so much in your sleep?"

"I dreamed that I was locked in this room surrounded by all kinds of insects. I tried to run but the doors were locked. Then my children came and stared at me. When I called out to them to open the door they said that was the same door that you closed on us and now you can open it yourself. There were all sorts of things crawling on me and I was trying to take them off. As the boys were walking away from me I was screaming, "Please help me" but they just stared at me."

"That must have been a very scary dream. If you want to come and sleep in my bed so I can keep an eye on you."

"Thanks Jackie" replied Cindy. "I will do that."

Next morning when Jackie went to bathroom she screamed, "What are these things?" She continued to scream. When the others came they saw insects everywhere.

"How did all these get here?" asked Jasmin. She stopped and went into a deep thought. "I bet you it was those two idiots."

Jackie screamed. "Which two idiots?"

The chef and the maid. Then she told the girls how she went to kitchen and there were worms everywhere.

"But last night they were already gone plus Cindy and I used the bathroom. It was clean."

"I don't know. Let's call a pest controller." said Jasmine.

When the pest controller arrived, he was shown the way to the bathroom. After going there he came back, and said. "There was nothing there."

The girls screamed "There were millions of them and they can't have disappeared like that."

The three of them then followed the man to the bathroom. There was nothing there. Everything was back to normal. They paid the man and thanked him for coming at such short notice.

It didn't take long that morning for Angelo to call and check on the girls. "Jasmin did you start looking for another chef?"

"No, not yet. I think we will order from outside for a while to be on the safe side."

"That is up to you," replied Angelo. "If you and the girls need anything let us know. We are going to the office to deal with our other problems.

When Angelo and his two close friends got to the board, everyone else was sitting around the table waiting for their arrival.

"Good morning gentlemen." said Alberto. "Why the long faces. It is a new day."

One of the members of chain replied. "How can it be a good morning when all our lives are in danger of being exposed?"

Take it easy." replied Alberto.

Another chain member said. "May be you three should disappear for a while until this mess is sorted out."

Angelo reacted angrily. "I have been in this game for a very long time and if you think you can dig my grave you are very wrong. If it wasn't for me there would be no chain and no board of directors."

"We were doing well before you decided to rip other people off."

"Until now you were enjoying the money and asked for more businesses. Now I am at fault. How many times you yourselves mentioned Max and his business. How much the chain pushed me to hurry up and take over Max's enterprises? Angelo screamed.

The head of the board then said. "We made our decision. You three have to keep away from the board for a while."

"In that case I resign from the board and will take all my assets and whatever I personally worked on." replied Angelo.

"Unfortunately there is nothing you can do right now. Go home and think about what has occurred." replied the head of the board.

Then he turned to Michael and Alberto. "You two can go as well. We will contact you if necessary."

This didn't go down well with Angelo and his friends especially when they were told not to even bother going to their own companies because the guards won't let them in.

The fact that the chain had overtaken their businesses scared the three friends to breaking point. For the first time in his life Angelo felt the pain.

"How about if we buy lunch and go to Jasmin's place?" Angelo asked.

"We have nothing else to do so that sounds like the only option." replied Michael

Angelo then calls Jasmin to let her know they are on the way.

After having lunch everyone lazed around in the couches. All these high fly business people were now without jobs sitting at home. Angelo knew that if Max was not taken care of he would take them down.

"Jasmin presume if your sister attempts to take her shares back what will you do?" Asked Angelo

"What shares? That idiot doesn't have any brain to do such things. Do you think people will believe me or a bugger like my sister?"

Chapter 28

Days have gone by. The media and police are seeking answers of what triggered the fright in the police station that forced Max to escape.

The senior officer in charge after meeting with Brad and Alex read all the documents. He then had higher authorities to help him with what was very sensitive and dangerous case.

The authorities told the officer. "Tell your men we have four other police stations that can be used as a meeting area. However Max should not notify the media because the less the media knows, the less Angelo and his men will know. We will put cameras all around and record everything to be on the safe side. At the next meeting we will have Special Forces ready and dressed as normal police."

The officer then told the authorities, "Brad and Alex are my best men. They have to be involved in every step you take."

"That is not a problem for us. If you want you can even make them in charge of the Special Forces while this case is taking place."

Brad was asked by his superior to contact Max and arrange for him to come in and give a statement and any evidence that wasn't handed in the last time due to the attack.

The two detective partners Brad and Alex, happily departed from their superior and called Max to give him the good news.

"I am glad you called Brad. We were all worried about you." Max said.

"And we were worried about you. I am glad that we have some of the best people on our side like our superior. He sat next to me and went through everything and now he has asked me to arrange another meeting with you. This time they will tell us which police station because they are going to install cameras and have Special Forces dressed in cops' uniform to protect the place."

"So they know for sure that it is me?" asked Max.

"They sure do."

"Ok. Let me discuss this with Sandy and others. I will get back to you as soon as we come up with a decision."

Quickly, after finishing the phone call Max ran to Brian's house where everyone was sitting around for their afternoon drinks. When he walked in Sandy looked at him and smiled.

"You already know what I am going to say, Sandy."

Sandy smiled "I do but others don't."

"I just received a phone call from Brad and he told me that the authorities have asked for another meeting. I need your help on deciding when we should make our next appearance but please everyone don't leak any info to anyone. The media would not be notified they told Brad. "The more media is involved the more Angelo and his men will know."

"Wouldn't that be risky? What if that is a trap?" asked Jo

"For some reason, for the first time, I think we are dealing with genuine people." replied Max. "What do you think Sandy?"

"I think we should do it. I feel safe enough. I even think we should do it in two days."

Max then turned at the others "What do you think?"

They all replied that they were ready. "Let's do it in two days." They all giggled and cheered about next step.

Max couldn't stop the excitement, so he rang Brad straight back and told him they would meet in two days.

Sandy was a bit quite. Later on Max asked. "Are you worried?"

"Not worried, but confused. Since mum and dad died, I have never opened their phones but this morning when I was looking for something I saw the phone, I turned it on and went through some of their pictures."

"Is that why you are sad? You miss them don't you? It always worried me that one day this would hit you. You have never had a chance to mourn properly and it's all my fault because you had to take care of me." Max said with remorse.

"Oh don't be silly Max. There was a video recorded by my dad on his last days."

"What was it about?"

"I will show you. Come to my room." When they went to the room Sandy turned on the video for Max to look at.

"I Don remove all my previous wills and make this final one. I only have days to live and I thought this recording is the best way to change my will. I am now leaving Don's Empire to my daughter Sandy. She is fair unlike others and am I sure she will do the right thing by her brothers and sisters."

"The reason behind this change is that past few months, although unfortunate but clear as sunshine. My children's behaviour. I have watched everything that went on and how the chain took over my company. At the time Sandy was in coma and no money in the world would have made me leave her sight."

"I also leave this message for Angelo. When I heard what you did to my company I was not weak but had more important things to look after than bother with you or anyone. Remember this. Up to the day that you die, all of you will know that none of you held a power like mine. Sorry I will not be there to see you all go down but every grave you dodged for others will be your own."

"Sandy thank you for looking after us. After I got sick your mum told me what happened when your brothers and sisters came to hospital to visit me. I feel sorry for no one any more.

Put your money straight into helping those who are really in need because the day will come when they will return all your goodness. I am leaving you my entire empire because I know you are wise and will take care of things that I couldn't when you were in hospital."

"Oh I forgot. I never signed any documents to transfer my assets to anyone. My accountant and lawyer were both abused by Angelo's men to get the information they wanted. Both these men left their offices due to numerous break ins. Sandy you are smart and I give you the authority to take all that belongs to you back."

"This will be my last communication as I mentioned I have only few hours or days left of my life."

Max turned and looked at Sandy when the video finished. "What are you going to do with this?"

"Not sure yet but I am worried that Jason and Joshua might get upset."

"You know we have to tell everyone about this and let them see it before our appointment with the cops."

"But how?"

"I will break the news to everyone if you want."

"Thanks Max"

Minutes later Max walked down with the phone. Everyone seemed concerned and asked him if Sandy was ok. "There is something that you all should see." he said. Sandy was worried that some of you might change your feelings towards her when you watch this so I brought it down to show it to you all."

When the video played Joshua and Jason broke into tears. "Dad I wish we could go back and fix everything but it is too late and we have to live our lives with the guilt." called out Jason.

"How right you are Jason." said Joshua? "What kind of spell were we under? We deserve whatever comes our way."

"Stop the self-bashing." Max said loudly. "This is not the right time to break. We can use this video against Angelo and the chain."

"You know what that means? That means that we have betrayed Dad. We spent his money while he was in pain, waiting to see if his daughter is going to gain consciousness. Oh my god, what have we done?" cried Joshua

"I think none of you were listening to Sandy when she said. "I have to try and save them. It is like a second chance for them to move away from doing bad." Max said. "You know what that means? That means that you all have been saved and will not face the Karma because you all changed even before Sandy or Queen of Karma tried to give you that second chance. You were trying to save your families and lives. That is why you fell into the traps of those greedy people."

Brook went and sat between Jason and Joshua. "I am sure your father is very proud of you right now because you did not let evil move you away from your younger sister. Be happy. Happiness brings happiness and when this is all over you will have your lives back."

However the two of them could not stop crying at this time Sandy walked in and said. "For what it is worth you may see what no one else can see." At the wall appeared the picture of Don and Donna in a beautiful garden. "Joshua and Jason what is the matter with you? We always knew the good in both of you and now we are so proud that you found your sister and are living together happily. We can finally be at peace."

Only Jason and Joshua could see and hear Don. When the picture disappeared they both looked at each other got up and hugged Sandy. Each from one side "Thank you." they said.

"Now are you going to stop crying?" Sandy asked with a smile on her face.

Two days later Max appeared at the police station where the meeting was set. He had a video of his discussions with Don when Don gave him the money to save his company. He also showed them the video that Sandy found on her parents mobile phone. Then he put more documents on the table.

"These are the original documents that Don signed to leave everything to Sandy. As you can see, two doctors at the hospital witnessed them." Among those papers were copies that Don had gained from loyal employees.

When his assets were passed to his children on these copies he wrote. "These are forged signatures but I don't have time to fight over them. My daughter Sandy and my dear friend's son Max should use all these documents to get back what lawfully belongs to them."

There was also a twenty page document that Don had put the names of all those people whose lives were destroyed by Angelo and the chain.

On the third last page Don had written. "These are the names and address of those who were on the hit list of the chain but I was able to get to them first and help them escape."

Lunch was brought to them during the meeting. Hours later after a senior secretary read all the documents out loud, the superior officer said. "What are we dealing with?"

Sandy and the rest were waiting in their cars the whole time. Finally late in the afternoon, Max came out and everybody felt at peace.

There was an unusual silence in the car, driving back home. "What is the matter son? Did something go wrong?"

"No everything went perfectly."

"Then why are you in such deep thought?"

"I just cannot believe that Don helped me when he was alive and now that he is dead he is still helping me."

"How?" asked Brian

"I never took those documents out of the envelopes because Don made me promise to only open and use those documents if things get really bad. The videos that he had recorded and those document he provided, named every single member of the chain. Their names, their crimes and you name it. The cops will now investigate all those that Don helped and see if they will testify against the chain."

"I never believed that there was any good people left until I met Sandy. You can see that she has a lot of her dad's qualities." Brook said.

"So when you said all those who Don helped, what do you mean?" Asked Sandy

"Apparently they were all on the hit list but Don saved their lives by helping them escape."

"How and when did he do that?" asked Sandy. "My dad always amazed me. He was gentle and kind but he never opened up to anyone."

Brian who was sitting next to her hugged her and said. "He was a wonderful man who thought of every little detail to help people survive the chain."

When they got home it was almost dark. Joshua, Jo and Jason were briefly updated by Max of what went on behind those closed doors and told them it was now only a waiting game.

Looking with fear at her brothers. Sandy said. "When all this goes down Jackie and Jasmin will be in the middle of it. I truly hope nothing happens to them."

"After all they have done, you still worry about them? My god, Sandy what is wrong with you?" screamed Jason

"Jason instead of shouting. How about you be the bar tender tonight, I believe everyone needs a drink."

"Oh, yes" shouted everyone at the same time.

"Ok" said Jason. "On one condition. When I pour the drinks, no more talking about our problems. We all have to say a funny story or a joke."

"I can live on good jokes and this beautiful brandy." A voice uttered.

"Me too Josh." replied Jason, before he broke down in to tears.

"What is the matter? I thought we said jokes and laughter, not tears? asked Josh.

"I remember how many times Dad asked us to do this with him but we never had the time."

"Dad loved you all the same." Lovingly said Sandy. "Plus he and I had so much fun together that I never heard him complaining.

Sometimes when we use to have a drink he would say "Do you think your brothers and sisters know what they are missing on?"

And I use to say "Yes a good brandy."

Sandy carried on. "Sometimes in life things happen to help us wake up from the dream that we live in. We should not blame ourselves for any mistakes we made when we were younger. Or things that we could have done and never did. The fact is if we did not make those mistakes we wouldn't be here sitting like this and drinking."

"Remember Jason time sometimes is against us Dad and Mum understood this perfectly and you should not bash yourself for not having made the time to drink with them. You have used this experience and became a better person for your sister, brother kids and wife."

"Ok let's start with the jokes." Jo said impatiently

<h1 style="text-align:center">Chapter 29</h1>

Angelo's anger was now fiery. He still hadn't been able to find security guards to cover his work and now that Jasmin's maid and chef had left, they both have been advertising for new people. The word spread very quickly. The previous workers have put a bad word out there that "if you love your life you will never accept a job from these people."

Jasmine and Angelo tried so hard to find and punish the two of them. They had gone into hiding and without help from the police there was no way they would find them.

Angelo calls Alex and asked, "I thought you were going to bring me new men. What happened to that?"

"I am sorry sir, but we were all sent on an assignment and were not able to go anywhere."

"Are you telling me you won't bring me men?"

"Give me two or three days. When this assignment is finish we will visit you."

"I don't have much time. I am very short of men. I will give you another two days to show up with your men."

Being suspicious, Angelo then rang some of the crooked detectives and asked. "Do you know what kind of an assignment Alex is on?"

One of them that worked in the same area as Alex said. "Not sure it seems top secret because only certain people are aware of it. It must be something big because they work around the clock."

Angelo told the man, "Try to find out what is that top secret?" then hung up.

Jasmine and Jackie had no choice but to start cooking themselves. They were sick of ordering food from outside. This day in the kitchen Jasmine asked. "Jackie I don't know what is reflecting in here but it is really annoying."

"I was going to ask the same of you."

They both then stopped and had a proper look at what it seemed a reflection of something. It was only little balls of light black and blue mixed. The black ones seemed like a black dot but were jumping all around. When Jasmine followed one of them to where Angelo and Michael were sitting, she noticed that the two of them were surrounded by these little black dots. "What is the matter with you two? Can't you see all those mosquitos?"

The two men then look around themselves and saw the whole place covered in the black dots, thinking they were mosquitos. They tried to kill a few.

Minutes later everything went back to normal and those things disappeared.

"The food is almost ready." said Jasmine. When Cindy and Alberto arrived, Cindy went helped the girls and Alberto joined his two partners.

"I am very worried." said Alberto. "There is so much super natural activities in my house I think it is haunted."

"Is this a joke?" asked Angelo

"No," I am serious. When I woke up this morning Cindy was covered in these black dots. I tried to take them off but they disappeared from one place to another. When she woke up she screamed at me for waking her up and everything disappeared."

"The other day in the kitchen, she was getting a glass of water and I could see them all over her. When I screamed they disappeared and she asked "What is the matter with you?"

"I wonder what they are because right now, me and Angelo were surrounded by them but when we tried to kill them they disappeared."

"Come on you two, stop being superstitious." Angelo said. "Stop drinking and you won't see them anymore."

"Right now we have to concentrate on finding Max." Angelo continued. "If we don't find him he will destroy us all. You both know I haven't been able to hire new men but was wondering if you two can put more people to work so they can find him?"

Alberto puts his head down and said "I don't have any men left. They all disliked Cindy and ever since I have been trying to hire people. It's been impossible."

"I told you at the beginning don't let her get involved in your work. You didn't listen." Angelo screamed.

Alberto sank in the couch with no reply. Once more the black dots appeared. Two little blue lights kept on flying around Alberto as if they were keeping him safe from something.

"Have you seen your wife and children lately Michael?" asked Alberto

"No, why?"

"May be these dots have a meaning?"

"I told you to stop being superstitious."

"I am not I can see the facts. I truly love Cindy, but the way that she treats people is not right. You yourself-hurt a lot of people. Maybe it just might be that these lights are just a warning to change."

"I really don't have time for this shit. Believe what you want but don't waste our time like this."

"No worries Angelo. The reason I said something is because friends tell each other about things that concerns them."

"That is all right. Now tell me how many men you have?"

"Only around ten to twelve."

"That is not much. I thought you had more."

"Why would I need more men? It is hard enough to manage these ones."

"Can you spare some of them to start looking for Max?"

"I sure can, but isn't it better to forget about Max?"

"What is wrong with you Alberto?" asked Angelo. "He can destroy us all if he has proof in his hands."

"I never had any dealings with Max, but I knew his father he was a good man."

"Do you get the point?" Michael asked. "We stole his company from him."

Alberto stopped for a second. "If we did steal his company then he has every right to fight for it."

"For god's sake Alberto. Go home before I spit on you." Angelo shouted again.

"Why. All I am saying is to leave the young man alone. When his father was dying he asked me and Don, to look after his son. I walked away but Don looked after him as if he was his own son."

"Don't lecture to me now. You will understand when you are rotting in gaol."

"Well if I have done something to deserve being in prison then let it be."

Things were getting really tens between the partners. When Cindy walked in, "she said dinner is ready. Come."

Michael turned around. "We are coming. Look guys stop bashing each other with words. Let's have lunch. Maybe then you can think clearly."

"Jasmine and Jackie. Has any of you heard from your sister or brothers?" asked Angelo

"No, I don't think they will try to contact us again." replied Jackie.

"I want you to pretend that you are sorry and get close to them. Without inside help we will never be able to find them." implied Angelo.

"It's too late for that." replied Jasmin.

Angelo was getting very aggravated with girls response. He put all his effort into withholding his anger. He knew that sooner or later he was going to need their help.

"Well I can't even go near them, continued Cindy. Because if I do they will be asking about the kids and I don't want them to know where they are."

"Do you miss your kids?" asked Alberto

"Not really. Plus I am over them because I know they are in a safe place."

"What about you Jasmin?"

"Sometimes I think about them and wonder if they will ever think of me as their mother."

"Did Adam ever tried to contact you?" asked Angelo

"After what happened he never wanted to talk to me, plus he thinks I would be bad influence on his kids."

"Over time we will take care of him too. In fact if you know where he lives we can go right now." Angelo said.

"I don't think I would like to do that right now" Said Jasmin with a very serious face.

Angelo's phone rang. He talked to a person and said. "We will be there shortly."

He then turned to the boys and asked them to go with him.

"Where are we going?" Michael asked.

"We need to pay Brad a visit. Apparently he is trying to cross us. Right now he and Alex are at a coffee shop only about half an hour away from here. Apparently he has been helping Sandy. The detective that just called me said that one of his friends saw Brad meeting with Jason and Sandy. You two better call some of your men to meet us there."

When they started driving a voice filled the car. "When are you going to learn? People are not your slaves."

Angelo yelled. "Which one of you said that?"

"We never said anything." the boys said.

"Then my grandfather came from grave and said it. There is no one else in this car apart from us three."

"What were you thinking when you heard the voice?" asked Alberto.

"I was planning how to torture Brad to get info out of him."

"Maybe something is telling us to let go."

"If you want to let go, then get out of the car." said Angelo after pulling over.

"I am not giving up but from the bottom of my heart I think something is trying to warn us."

"Are you starting with that non sense again? I don't like it."

All of a sudden the black dots started appearing. By now they had arrived at the café that Alex and Brad were in. Angelo looked and said. "What a nice assignment they have. Siting having coffee."

Michael's men had already arrived and were waiting for directions when they saw Angelo arriving. They started walking towards the car but Angelo's car was covered in black light which looked like black dots and a horrifying voice again came over saying. "Call your men off and go back."

Freaking out, Alberto said. "For god's sake let's go back. This is the second warning in less than twenty minutes."

Angelo reacted angrily. "I am so close to them now, there is no way I will let them get away."

The door on the side that Alberto was sitting opened and a blue light dragged Alberto out of the car. He was so scared and started screaming. When a calming voice said. "Don't worry I am saving your life."

As soon as Alberto was dragged to a secure place, a horrible noise filled the atmosphere. Everyone in the café and outside started panicking. As the noise was getting closer everyone was running for shelter. Michael and Angelo tried to get out of the car but it appeared a giant truck, which lost control, smashed into Angelo's car. Then all the noise stopped and people started running towards the truck. When they opened the truck door they found the driver unconscious at the steering wheel they pulled him out and dragged him to safety. Those who went to help the people in Angelo's car were standing uselessly staring at what was inside the car.

By now Brad, Alex and all the other people from inside the café were running out to see what happened.

Alberto ran towards Alex. "I told him to go back but he wouldn't listen. Something was warning us in the car but Angelo just wouldn't give up and he wanted to torture Brad."

Alex looked inside the car. Both Angelo and Michael were unconscious. All the front of the car was flattened and both men were trapped in the car. He then turned around and looked at Alberto. "How did you get out?"

"I was pulled out by some sort of power."

"What was it exactly?"

"It looked like a blue light."

"Are you kidding me? Blue light! I think you just were not meant to be in the car."

Brad then looked at Alberto. "I believe you, I have seen those little lights."

"Don't tell me you believe in that shit." Alex said.

By now the emergency services had arrived. All of Michaels men took off before the cops get there, the crew was trying to cut their way into the car so they could pull the two men out. The truck drive was air lifted to hospital. It looked as if he had a heart attack."

Throughout the night and early morning, the emergency crew worked until they were able to pull out the two men from the car. They were still unconscious and also air lifted to the hospital.

It did not take long for the news to broadcast the accident, measuring it as the worse ever seen.

Alberto took a cab to Jasmin's house and told them about the accident and how they all heard the warning in the car and how Angelo refused to take the warnings seriously. "I think we all should give up on our bad doings. Maybe just maybe, we might be spared."

"Two of your friends are in hospital and you are sitting here lecturing us. Go to hell." Jasmin said.

"Cindy. Please believe me."

"How did you get out of the car?" Cindy continued. "Was that all planned to get them in the car and take them to that place?"

"What do you mean? It was Angelo that told us we needed to go after he received that phone call."

"Then why are you not squashed like them?"

"It is not fare Cindy. Me and you have been living together all this time. You know how much I care about you and I even asked you to let the kids live with us but you didn't want the responsibility. I thought you knew me better than this."

"Whatever." said Cindy while walking away. "Oh you better go home I don't think the girls want you here."

Putting his head down with unbelief Alberto started walking towards the door. This time he is all by himself. He alone has found the goodness in himself and cannot get the others to change their ways. Tears were pouring from his eyes while driving. After all he had done for Cindy. He thought that she loved and appreciated him but now at this moment he could see that his beautiful partner was a selfish human that only cared about what is good for her.

The house was all dark and quiet when Alberto got home. His shirt was wet from his tears. He poured himself a drink and sat on the couch. Oh god what is wrong with people? Is there any goodness left in humans? You yourself, oh God, know that I have never been involved in any dirty works I have earned my living by honesty and honour and the only reason I hang around with these guys was that I was scared they might target me if I didn't mix with them. He started crying and fell sleep on the couch. He then started dreaming. There was a beautiful statue made out of shiny silver.

As he was admiring its beauty, the statue smiled and said. "I have found you again."

In the morning the girls went to the hospital. Angelo's wife was there with her son Jo. She looked at Jasmin, then put her head down without saying anything.

The hospital had rung them and told them that Angelo was in critical condition and they were not sure if he would survive the operation. Jo looked at Jasmine and said. "He is going to make it. Only part of him."

"What do you mean only part of him?"

"That means he will be disabled for the rest of his life."

"Oh my god." screamed Jasmin. "If it is ok with you can we wait here?"

"Do as it pleases you, none of us care." replied Joe.

"What about Michael? Any news from him?" asked Jackie

He is still in the operating theatre."

An hour later a doctor came out and asked Jo. "Dose Michael have any family?"

"I don't know replied Jo, ask his girlfriend."

"How would I know? We never talked about our families. Doctor how is he doing?"

"Well we couldn't save his right leg and did our best with the left one. It is now only a matter of waiting to see if the operation worked."

The girls then said goodbye and left the hospital. While driving home, Jasmin said, "I will not take care of a disabled person. I didn't even look after my own children so no one should expect me to look after him. Plus he is now useless for me."

"Me too." said Jackie. "Let their families look after them. Why should we?"

Alberto got to the hospital after the girls and when he saw Jo he started crying. "Oh son I am so sorry about your dad."

"Don't be. When did you ever see him acting like a father towards me?"

"You are so right."

"How come you were not with them when this happened?"

Alberto then told Jo all the weird things that had happened in the past few days especially last night before the accident.

Getting up from his seat Jo looked at Alberto and smiled.

"Let me hug you because it seems like you are a nice and kind man."

"Thanks son. If there is anything I can do for you and your mum, let me know." Then he departed."

Days passed and the two men were till unconscious. The doctors were able to stabilise the driver of the truck. After his release from the hospital he went to check on the two men. That's when he met Jo and told him "I have no idea what happened that night. However I am very sorry to have caused such damage to your dad."

Jo replied to him, "You didn't damage him. He did it to himself because he was a very mean man."

The driver's eyes filled with tears and said. "I never thought that a son could hate his father so much."

"Go in peace." said Jo. "If you have children be a good father to them."

The driver then departed and never went back to that hospital.

Weeks went by and finally Angelo came out of coma, but when he found out that he was disabled he became very aggressive. At times he would fight with the nurses. "Did someone pay the doctors to do this to me? Do you know who I am? I will fix all of you."

Michael by now had regained consciousness as well. He is so quiet his loving girlfriend hadn't been back to visit him since the accident. The nurses asked him. "Do you have a family that we can notify?"

"I did but they are all gone." replied Michael with tears. He then asked the nurse for his phone. When she brought the phone it was still in working order. He was so pleased he grabbed it and called Jackie. "Hi Jack, how are you?"

"I am good." she replied. "How are you doing?"

"Well you know I can't complain. I will start rehab today. Hopefully in a few days I can start walking. They have ordered a bionic leg for me and hopefully I can walk with it."

"Glad for you." said Jackie. "I have to go."

"Ok bye."

Days went by for the two men. They kept each other company every now and then. Alberto would pay them a visit to see if they need anything. The rehab started helping them both. It was in one of the rehab session that Angelo moved one of his legs. The doctors were called and when they saw it moving said. "It's impossible."

Three weeks later they were ready to be released from the hospital. There was still no sign of the girls. Angelo called Jasmin. "Can you and Jackie come pick us up?"

"Why don't you call your wife or son?" she replied.

"I called you, didn't I? Hurry up don't let us wait."

An hour later there was still no sign of any of the girls. It went in to the second hour. Angelo called Jasmine again but there was no reply. Then Michael called Jackie's phone and there still was no reply.

Four hours later out of choice, Angelo rang his wife to come and pick them up. Being a very kind and generous woman she got in the car and went to pick them up.

On the way back Michael said. "You can drop me at my own house."

But Michelle Angelo's wife said. "I am not dropping you home. You still need a lot of care and there is no one at your home. You will come to our house until you are independent once more."

When they got home she called her two very loyal maids to help her get them inside. Each were taken to a massive bedroom.

The maids helped the two men into their beds and brought them some light refreshments.

Two nurses came in the morning for their routine rehab exercises. When they finished the two nurses gave them two new wheel chairs and told them that they should start riding the wheel chairs by themselves. After being confident that the two men could be more flexible on their own, they left.

Angelo brought his chair next to Michael. "Did you see that those two bitches didn't come to pick us up? I will teach them a lesson that they will never forget."

"It is heart breaking after all we did for them to treat us like this." Michael then called two of his men to come and visit him at Angelo's.

When the men got there Angelo said with Michael's permission. "Can you two go to the mansion and keep an eye on the activity of the three girls? Come back to us with reports every second day." The two men left as soon as they received their instruction.

Two days later Michael called his men and asked them to come in for a report. The men recorded almost everything that they were instructed to do.

An hour later the two men arrived Michelle gave all of them a shout of scotch. She then left the room so the men could attend to their meeting.

"Did you guys record anything exciting?" Michael asked.

"Not sure what is exciting to you but we did record everything as you instructed us."

"Put it on then." Angelo said impatiently.

The first video was an hour after they left Angelo's place. Everything around the mansion seemed so quiet there was no movement at all. The next morning the girls all dressed left the house. They were followed to a restaurant where they met with some friends. Seeing how they were dressed and how happy they looked started making Angelo aggressive. "Do you believe these bitches?"

After the restaurant the girls were followed back to the mansion. At around seven a van drove into the mansion. Two men started taking things from the van into the mansion. They looked like musical instruments. Half an hour after these two men went in people started arriving all dressed for an official dinner party. Men in tuxedos and all the women in long and beautiful dresses. Soon the sound of music was heard and laughter filled the air.

At the end of the night when all the guests left, Jackie and Jasmin walked out arm in arm with the two young men laughing, hugging and kissing.

When Michael and Angelo saw that, they were furious. "Enjoy while you can. I will reduce you to nothing."

The meeting was disturbed by Michelle come and eat something. The food is ready.

When Michelle was at Collette and Colin's anniversary with Don and Donna. She picked so much on Donna about what she was wearing. But now she is so different, yet still very beautiful, down to earth and simple. If Donna was here now, she would not believe this is the same woman. Some say that she has become like that because Angelo neglected her. Although he provided the best in life for her but he couldn't provide love in their relationship.

Before the men left Angelo said. "Next time when they go out, call me. I want appear at their lunch date."

While having their meal Michael looked at Angelo. "You are so lucky to have a kind and forgiving wife like her".

Michelle smiled. "Thank you."

Angelo had no compassion for anyone, only for himself. He did not say anything regarding the comment and pretended that he didn't hear Michael.

A week later the men called Angelo and told him the girls just met some friends at a restaurant. He quickly pushed his chair touched Michael. "Hurry lets go."

"Where to?" asked Michael.

He replied. "To the restaurant. I want to see what those bitches will do when they are face to face with us."

One of the associates drove them and dropped them at the front of the restaurant. They wheeled in their chairs. The girls were too busy with their new boyfriends. They didn't pay attention to who just drew up next to them.

"Michael do remember those poor women that we helped. I wonder what happened to them?" he said. In a loud voice that Jasmin heard and recognized the voice. In a panic she turned and looked at him. Her smile froze that grabbed the attention of those having lunch with her.

Jackie quickly, "Let's go"

"Where said their friends?"

"Anywhere but here." replied Jackie.

"What is the matter?" Angelo said. "Did something bite you?"

While they were grabbing their bags to leave. "Do you know this man?" One off the companions asked.

"This disabled man? No never seen him before." Jasmine continued. "By the looks of it he is not all there."

Angelo pushed his chair and grabbed her hand. "This disabled man will make your life miserable. I will send you to the same hole that I took you out of."

The girls then quickly threw their money on the table and left followed by their companion. "Where do you girls want to go?"

Jasmin said. "Home. We will make something to eat there. I don't feel safe right now."

On the following day Michaels men came around to pay him a visit. Angelo asked. "How well do you know the mansion?"

"Well by now very well. Remember we went inside to get those videos, and we know the in and out of the mansion."

Angelo then pulled a bag of money out of his safe and said. "Here I want you to buy cocaine and plant it inside the house. Make sure there is enough in all rooms to be found easily."

"What do you want to do?" asked Michael.

"I am sending them back to where they belong."

"What do you mean, I don't know what you are up to."

Angelo then turned to the two men and said. "Do this well and you will be well rewarded. Once you plant the cocaine then you will ring the cops and tell them that you think those women are doing drug dealing from inside the mansion. Make sure the cops can't trace the call back to you."

"Are you sure?" Michael asked. "Maybe we should let it go."

"What they did to us, was it fair? Do you think I liked it, when you happily rang Jackie and she treated you like that, or that bitch that said? "This disable. I don't know him."

"Do as you want." replied Michael

The two men then went on their way.

Days later Michelle called out "Angelo, Michael come and see."

When they went to the dining room the news was on and the camera was right on Jasmin in hand cuffs, trying to hide her face.

The journalist said that the cops surrounded the mansion in the early hours of morning after a tip off. Three women were arrested after the police found close to a million dollars in cash and drugs inside the mansion. At this stage the identity of these three women has been kept a secret until they appear in court.

A few hours later, the two sisters and their sister in law were all alone in their cells. They had no one to call to come and bail them out. The morning they were taken straight to court and all their assets were frozen. The bail was set at two million dollars each.

After the court they were moved to one of the toughest prisons in the country.

"What are we going to do? How are we going to prove that those drugs didn't belong to us." cried Cindy

"We should call someone to bail us out." said Jackie

Jasmine asked. "But who, I bet this is Angelo's doing."

"We can't call them. How about Joshua? Anyone have his number?"

"No. Remember we spat on them." replied Jackie

Angelo was very pleased and knew sooner or later the girls would call him out of desperation and his expectation came to satisfaction when Jasmine called him.

"Hi I am so sorry. Please help us get out of here."

"What did you say?"

"I said I am sorry. Please get us out of here. I will do whatever it takes to get out of this dump."

"Ok. I will come." said Angelo.

When he hung up, as he sat in his seat, he smiled. "Let them wait like we did in hospital."

Minutes later the doorbell went off followed by someone shouting open the door or we will break it open. Michelle panicked thinking something has gone wrong with her son Jo. However when she opened the door she found Special Forces at the front door. One pushed her out of the way while others rushed in. Michelle fell on the floor. Out of shock she stayed there staring not knowing what was happening. Minutes later an officer felt sorry for her. He went and offered his hand to help her up.

Tears started showering her beautiful but aged face. The rushes of tears felt like the stormy rain in autumn. "Her we have a warrant to search the house."

"But why?" she asked.

"You will soon find out mam. Let me help you to a chair." said the nice officer.

When they made it to where Angelo was he screamed. "What is the meaning of this?"

"You are under arrest for murder. Attempted murder, fraud and forging documents." The officer replied.

Before Angelo could open his mouth a second officer put on the hand cuffs on and started pushing the wheel chair out to the police car. As he went out he saw Sandy, standing far in the garden glowing like a shiny star. With her mind she spoke to him.

"You never respected the word karma, but here it is at your door to pay you back for all the wrong doings."

He started screaming. "You low life I will kill you."

However while none of the officers could see or hear Sandy. Angelo was told. "Sir stop frightening the officers. You are only making it worse for yourself."

Minutes later Michael was brought out and both were placed in two different police cars. They were taken to an unidentified place so that the chain could not try to free them.

Sitting behind the desk Angelo uttered. "Do you know who I am? What is all this about?"

The senior officer said. "We very well know who you are, and hope that for your own sake you would co-operate with the interrogations." Then the officer continued. "The days to kill and frighten people have passed there is enough evidence to put you away for the rest of your life."

Michael had nothing to say. He quietly followed the instruction in the interview room. At that point he had nothing to live for. His beautiful wife and son had lost their lives in accident months ago and then his girlfriend Jackie used him and now he had lost his leg and independence.

The officer then sat in front of Angelo and started calling names and asking Angelo, if he knows them.

"Of course." said the officer. "You won't remember their names because you thought of them as rubbish. Why you would remember their names?" The officer then gave rise to another ten names. "Do you know them?"

Angelo replied. "No I don't."

The officer said. "Oh I forgot. You ordered their murders."

"That is an accusation. replied Angelo.

"It was until we found Don's documents and found those people who he had helped to escape your death penalty."

"What documents? Don died a long time ago. All his documents and belongings were burnt in a fire."

"Do you really think he was that dumb to keep important things like this at home? Yes Don died a long time ago and that is how long it took me to find all those people and build a case against you."

"What case? I have not done anything. I am a highly regarded business man." replied Angelo.

"You mean the business that you built from sending small businesses broke so you could take them over. Tell me when you were going to stop?"

Michael was read the same names in a different room. He said. "I knew them but they left their jobs and I never saw them after that."

"Left their jobs or forced out of their jobs." The officer stated.

"As far as I know, they left. I didn't have much to do with them anyway. I have my own men and staff and they are a handful."

"Did you ever order anyone to kill someone else?"

"I would never do that."

"Do you remember Don?"

"Off course I do, and was sorry for what happened to him and his kids."

"Were you not dating one of his girls that is now under arrest for the possession of drugs?"

"Yes I did. "What was wrong with that? I was lonely and when they told me to go out with her I was happy to do so."

"Who asked you to go out with her?"

Michael did not reply to the question. He was asked over, and over but no reply was forthcoming.

"Did you ever hear Angelo ordering someone's death?"

"No. I never did. Why would he do such a thing?"

The interviews stopped there. Both men were moved to another room and shown a video that was recorded by Don. The video was of so many sensitive cases that involved the whole chain. How they ordered the death of people.

In the video, Don presented the faces of all those on death row, which he helped to escape. The torcher, the robberies.

The video stopped for a second before the second part started. Michael was frozen in his chair staring at Angelo, to see if there was any emotion forthcoming but there was none.

Before the second part started again a light appeared. No one could see the light a part from the two men.

"What are you doing here again?"

"I am here to witness every moment of your misery."

"Go to hell before I myself send you there."

The officers couldn't see who Angelo was talking to. One of them said. "Sir I am not going to warn you again. Stop frightening the officers."

Angelo screamed. "I am not talking to the officers. I am talking to that bitch."

All the officers looked at each other and thought that Angelo was mentally unstable.

The second part of the video started where was taken inside Don's office as he had hidden cameras everywhere. It showed people hired by Angelo to re-write Don's will and others who forged his signature, how everything was given to his children.

More hired people arose to pretend that they were creditors and how the company was in trouble and forced Don's family to walk away with absolutely nothing.

A further part was from Max's business. How his old loyal operations manager was bashed and frightened to show them the materials that were used in products, and what was put in them. Then the meeting of the chain and telling the staff that Max had passed away and the chain was now in control of the business. Every detail of how forged documents were prepared to prove that Max was dead.

Then the lights were turned back on and one of the officers said. "There are more video's like this that will put you away for the rest of your lives."

"You can either assist us by giving the names of all people from what you call it the chain. If you do cooperate a reduced sentence is more likely.

Angelo replied "These videos don't prove anything. They are probably made up by someone to make me look guilty."

Michael again was quite. He looked as if had gone onto denial and could not remember any of that shown to him.

The next morning the men quietly were presented to the court. When they were wheeling Angelo's eyes were focused on the judge. The judge was Sandy, she was again in her beautiful blue glowing dress with a judgment stick in her hand and a scale next to her hand.

"They told me Sandy is stupid but look she is a judge." the officer wheeling him said.

"Who are you talking about?"

"The judge." replied Angelo.

"What judge? He hasn't even come in yet?"

Then Sandy smiled and disappeared again.

After presenting all evidence to the judge he said, I am aware that this is a criminal case and needs a proper jury and from what I can see it is a lengthy one. The hearing is set for five months from now. So both prosecutor and defence can prepare their case. The jury can be decided upon.

The defence asked for bail.

"Bail is set at ten million dollars each. Also while they are on bail, they should live in their own houses and not have any outside communications." The judge read the terms of bail.

The two men agreed to the terms. Their defence was only a legal aid solicitor who just started practicing.

The defence lawyer then calls Michelle on Angelo's behalf to arrange for a twenty million dollar bail amount. The poor woman said, "How am I going to come up with twenty million?"

The lawyer then goes back to Angelo and tells him. But Angelo asked if he can call Michelle himself. The freedom of one phone call was granted.

He looked around to make sure no one was listening to him. He said to Mitchell "You know my library? There is a desk. Go and sit on the chair. Put your hands under and tap it twice, then stop and tap it three times then press the bottom under the arm of the chair. Bring the money and bail us out."

Michelle followed the instructions as she did the chair started moving down. She found herself in an underground safe full of jewellery and money. She looked around and found two brief cases. She puts ten million dollars in each before she sat back on the chair. In going back up she looked around. Although she took twenty million dollars there was still twenty times more money on the shelves. She then called the lawyer to collect the bail money.

The two men were then released in to home prison.

The two men were so lucky that there was no leakage of their arrest. They were both still safe from being killed by the chain.

Michael was dropped at his own home. As the two men were not allowed to have any contact, he called his loyal old butler and asked him if he could come to his house and help him for a while. The butler agreed.

On the other side of town, the girls were now sure that Angelo couldn't bail them out. They all had a visit from the light but none of them realized that was Sandy.

By now their hopes were down. They drained all their options. They did not leave one person out of their circle who could possibly bail them out. Their beautiful garments on the night they were arrested have been replaced by prison clothes.

One night Jasmine started screaming. When the prison officers went to her cell they asked. "What is your problem?"

"This cell is full of mosquitoes." she replied.

There is nothing here screamed, one of the officers. "If I hear your voice one more time I will transfer you to a cell, which is graded below this one."

The black little lights were surrounding Jasmine but she was the only one seeing them. At that a voice said. "How does it feel not to have a voice?"

She looked around and couldn't see anything. Soon the disruption started again trough screaming of Cindy and Jackie who were cell mates.

The whole prison inmates were wakening. The lights started going on one by one. By the time the prison officers made it to the cell, the two girls were both unconscious. The medics were called in and examined the two girls. When they came around the medics asked them. "Why were you screaming and what made you unconscious?"

Cindy and Jackie looked at each other then checked their surroundings. We were covered in black mosquitoes." Cindy said

"Is that why you were screaming too Jackie?" asked the medic.

"Yes." she stated.

"But there are no mosquito bites on any of you."

The nearby prison officer felt scared. She was the one that attended to Jasmin's cell earlier and she heard the same story from her. She then called the medics out and told them "I think these three are haunted." Then she explained what happened with Jasmine earlier on in the night.

The medics believed in super natural forces and suggested that cameras be installed in to the two cells so they could observe the movements of the three girls.

This was done straight away without the knowledge of the girls. The three of them were put in one area while the cameras were getting installed. The guards, who were watching over three girls, were told to have a camera focused on the girls the whole time.

Everything was quite in the cell, so the guards fell asleep during the night. The next morning when their superior asked to watch the tape from the night before, everyone was shocked. The recording showed an activity at around three thirty in the morning. Hundreds of little lights appeared in the cell. Then a massive figure like a queen appeared on a corner of the cell. There she was saying something. The voice was not recorded but you could see the three girls looking at it and at different times it looked like they were answering some questions.

Everyone who was watching the tape felt uncomfortable. None of them had ever experienced super natural stuff like that suddenly the light glowed right into the camera and said. "Those of you who are watching this, there is the queen of Karma. This has been revealed to you in case of any wrong done by you, can allow you to have a second chance."

All those in the room ran towards their phones apologizing to whoever they might have offended. Those who were honest enough to mean their apologies started to see little blue lights hanging around them. However those who tried to get away with lies saw the black mosquitoes coming at them, so they started screaming and apologizing for being dishonest.

Chapter 30

Jo spent most of his time trying to help his mum. With the little time that he had, he would spend it with Sandy and her brothers. Every time he was around them he felt at peace and wished that time would stay still.

Although Brad and Alex were so involved in Max's case, Jo was the first person to tell Sandy and the rest about the arrest of their sisters and Angelo. No one was pleased about this news as they still had feelings for their sisters.

It was hard for Brad to break the news of the arrest of the sisters to Jason but he was a loyal friend and he told Jason. "There is no one to bail them out"

Jason for a second felt heartbroken but remembered the day that Sandy approached those three and asked them "please change your ways and become better people" but they spat at her and later came up with the lies that they were robbed at gun point.

When Jo saw the sad look on Jason's face he said. "Jason I truly say to you that I wish I had a brother like you."

"Thanks." replied Jason.

"I am serious. You, Josh and Sandy have shown me the beautiful side of the road and god knows how many other people like you are responsible for finding the right road."

"We all did what we thought was right and if we were not. May god himself forgive us?" Jason said.

On the day of Angelo's arrest Brad again called Jason. "Jason please promise me that you will not leak this information for our sake."

"I promise. Now can you tell me?"

"Angelo and Michael were arrested and released in to home prison for now until their hearings. Both of them were given an option to co-operate with us for a lesser sentence."

"What do they have to do?"

"Well because Angelo was the front man and the cruellest of all of them. We have enough evidence to arrest him and put him away. However in none of the videos were we able to see the faces of the other corporate that run the chain. My superior has gathered all the people that are going to give evidence in court. They have all said that the orders were coming from a higher place but none of them ever saw their faces."

"So what does that mean? If they don't co-operate"

"They will be put in prison for the rest of their lives. That means the crimes will slow down but will still take place. The only way we can put a stop to everything is to find all the members of the chain."

"I see."

"Before I forget they have found the doctors that had given a death certificate for Max?"

"Off course our superiors will not press charges against the doctors because their families were kidnapped until the chain got what they needed, which in this case was Max's death certificate."

"Right now a few officials are working on gathering info and evidence so Max can go back to his normal life, and here is the shocking news. Your dad's solicitor and accountant have come forward with videos of how their offices were ruined and how they were frightened to hand in Don's journals and assets. They even brought in the original will of your father which clearly shows your sister is the rightful owner of Don's Estate."

"So what will happen now? Are we all going to get arrested for accepting the shares that we thought were passed on to us by our father?"

"No, because none of you knew about the forged signatures and change of will. Alex was telling me that the plan was once the chain got hold of your sisters assets they were going to kill them as well."

"As far as I am concerned they are already dead. I will never forget how much Sandy begged them to come back to us but instead they went and made the allegations that we held them at gun point."

"Well Jason, do you know that your sisters and sister in law are in gaol and all their assets are frozen. It's been awhile and no one has bailed them out."

"Were they arrested after your investigations?"

"No. They were charged with possession of cash and drugs."

"I know those three are inhuman but drugs, never. This must be another one of Angelo's doings."

"I know, but the amount of drugs that were planted in their home was too much to turn a blind eye to."

"Ok. Brad thank you for everything. I hope that one day I can be as good friend to you."

Jason got very depressed when he heard about his sisters, Jo asked him. "Jason why the long face all the sudden?"

"Although I don't like what my sisters did, they are still my sisters and I don't believe that they would be doing drugs."

"Probably my dad had something to do with that, because when Angelo and Michael were being released from hospital, he called Jasmine and asked her to pick them up but they never did, so my dad called my mum and we went and picked them up. Dad looked really angry."

I have a friend that works at this restaurant. He told me that this woman called him disable and he grabbed her hand and told her. "I will make your life miserable."

"But they seemed so close to each other."

"Yes, but now that my dad and Michael are disabled, the girls don't want to have anything to do with them."

"Oh my, how cruel are these women? How can they fall in love and fall out of love as soon as the other person becomes useless for them?"

Joshua who was sitting the whole time listening to their conversation said. "They deserve everything that happens to them.

"Look how they imprisoned my kids in that school."

Jo's eyes filled with tears. "That is how I feel about my dad. I don't even know why I am calling him dad. He has been a monster."

Sandy smiled and said. "But look what a beautiful son he made. It is all about choices we make. If we are generous and kind, we will get kindness and generosity back but if we are miserable, eventually the misery will come our way."

During this whole time Mandy and her children were sitting quietly listening to everyone. "I never knew what a family means until I married Jason. His parents treated me like a daughter but stupidly I fell into the trap of the other three."

Brian got off his chair. "Come on everybody, let the past disappear into thin air because nothing we say or do can change any of it. I am pleased that all of you here, found your better inner side and now we have to concentrate on all the tomorrows."

"Always wise words." said Joshua.

"Who is going to come outside for barbeque mash melon?"

Even before Brian moved they all started pushing each other to be the first one out of the door.

"I said mash melon I didn't say kill each other."

They all laughed Brian's son had already prepared the fire. It seemed that it was a tradition to do this once a week, on a certain night of the week.

Sitting around the fire Max said. "I sure will miss this place and all the happy times we have had here."

"You are not going to moon Max are you?" asked Brook. "Plus we were hoping that you all might come and live here forever. Even after you get your lives back to normal."

"Oh that would be a plus for me. Mandy said.

That night these beautiful people gathered around each other. They laughed told jokes and mucked around. Times like this are so magical that no one wanted them to finish but finally the time came when they all started getting sleepy. A part from Sandy, she had little solders showing up slowly and she knew that she was getting called for duty, so she took off before everyone else.

When she got to the bedroom a picture was playing on her wall. It was Alberto sitting on the corner of his bedroom covered in tears talking to himself in a very loud voice. "Cindy after all the bad things you did to me how dare you call and ask me to bail you out? Oh god help me. I can't just let her rot in there and if I bail them out they will laugh at me again. I am so confused; I don't know what to do? Damn you Cindy."

All of a sudden Sandy appeared in front of him fully dressed in her queen gown and crown. Alberto looked at her. "Are you the angel of death? I am ready to put an end to this misery."

Sandy then pointed to the wall. On the wall there was Alberto helping a beggar that Cindy and the two sisters pushed out of their way and fell on the floor.

"Don't you dare helping him Alberto?" yelled Cindy.

But after reaching the restaurant Alberto used the excuse of going to the bathroom and went back to the beggar. He offered his hand to the man. "I am so sorry for what my companions did to you."

The beggar said, "Go in peace. It is ok."

Alberto then reached into his pocket and pulled out an enormous amount of money. "Here please. At least take this money." Before the man could say, anything Alberto forced the money in his hand and ran off.

"And who says all the rich people are bad?" said the beggar.

Another episode followed of him going into this building. In alley way, where he carried a lot of bags with him, so many that he went backwards and forwards a few times to carry them all, he changed into working clothes and started cooking. There came two homeless people who helped him. Hours later all these homeless people started walking in and there he was, Alberto serving them warm meals that he had made with the help of the other two.

All of a sudden, he screamed, "Yes. But have seen the other part of me? You have not been shown one of the bad things I did?"

"Like what asked the queen."

"Like, like oh like going past the hungry pretending they don't exist and walking into an expensive restaurant and how these girls asked me for help but I was not helping them."

The queen laughed. "You were in love but you did not let love or money stand in your way of helping others."

"So are you ready to take me now?"

"Take you where?"

"Well you are the angel of death, and you have come to take me with you."

The queen smiled again. "I am not the angel of death, I am the ..., but she stopped."

"You are what? Why did you stop?"

She then pointed to the wall again. It's Alberto again, kneeling in front of Cindy asking her to go visit the kids and bring them home but she tells him they are her kids and she knows what the best is for them. Alberto finds the name of the school and starts sending the kids presents pretending they were from their mum.

"Who are you?" Asked Alberto

"Those who did good will be paid with goodness and those who were cruel and careless about the others they will be dealt with cruelty. We all get a second chance in life but before you get yours, you changed your ways and became a kind loving person and here I am to tell you not to worry about those who didn't use their second chance to be better people. You go on doing what you do best, helping those who are really in need."

"But those girls asked for my help. How can I deny them off that?"

"The same way they denied you. They were given more than two chances."

"What do you want me to do?"

"You spread goodness, through spending can show the right path to others and warn those who are doing wrong about Karma, because it does not forget anything."

As Alberto was preparing his next question, the queen disappeared.

Sandy arrived at the ball room and all the lights were off. Her little blue lights started flying around her to let her know she couldn't come there unannounced. Soon the lights behind all the tables turned on with a voice saying. "What is the meaning of this? No one is allowed to come here without being called to come." the irritated voice then shouted. "Arrest them all." But instead of arresting Sandy, all the little lights made a circle around her so no one could get to her.

The voice said. "Are you disobeying my orders?" One of the little lights left the bunch and went to the front. After he approached one of the lights, the voice again said. "Welcome Sandy. I didn't realise it was you. Why are you up here?"

"I am confused and need help." she replied. My sisters are in goal and I don't feel anything towards them but at the same time I don't want anything bad to happen to them."

"You are not confused queen." said the voice behind another light.

"Yes I am very confused."

"No you are not." said the voice. "The part that feels weakness is your judgment. The part that still worries you about your sisters is your kind human nature and that of course will affect your judgment and you should work on it."

"How but?"

"If a person kills a person what do you think their punishment should be?" asked one of the others.

"If we are a hundred present sure that he did it, of course he should be punished."

"Have a look." said another voice. She was shown how Cindy lied and put Josh in jail, and how she paid extra money to keep her kids' prisoners in that boarding school. Then it showed Jasmine and her argument with Adam and how as soon as he took the kids, the only thing that she was worried about was the money that he would get for having the kids.

She ganged up with Angelo to rid of Adam in the meantime. She treated her staff as rubbish most of the time. Then came a section where she has a maid kneeling in front of her and she is saying. "Say you are a dog. Come on say it." Tears could be seen falling of Sandy's eyes. However another voice said. "You have to watch it all."

Then came Jackie whom Angelo and Jasmine planned to break her up with her husband. Their plans worked perfectly because Jackie wasn't any better than Jasmine. For all those years she thought she needed her husband to look after their kids, but as soon as she was shown a way, she got rid of all of them, and then came the pictures of Joshua's children and how sad they have been since their father disappeared from their lives.

All this was followed by the moments she had the accident and how her parents stayed next to her bed day and night. What followed were then the moments that her brothers and sisters came to visit their father in hospital and how they started a fight and left, of course never to visit their dad again.

"How do you feel now queen?" asked another. "Do you still feel sorry for them? Is there a person that would give a good character report about any of these three women? "

Sandy had her head down the whole time. She felt sad may be even embarrassed but definitely disgusted.

The voice again said. "You did not answer my question. Should more people suffer at their hands?"

"Off course not." yelled Sandy

"Then go and do your job. We have bent the rules with you and given the opportunity to people with second chances and with your judgments, we also given you the power to forgive if you can. But you know when it comes to the judgments of the queen of Karma you cannot use your heart as a human. Your judgments and forgiveness should be fair."

"I am sorry to disturb you." Sandy said. "Thank you for clarifying everything to me."

The queen then disappeared again and found herself in the cells of the three woman. They were talking about her. "I wonder what that loser Sandy is doing. Now that she has no money or life, at least when we are released we would have all the money in the world." Jasmine said.

"I know. She is probably sitting in a corner crying as usual. Help me please. My dad and mum spoiled me too much." Jackie said in her relation of Sandy.

The three of them laughed as one. That was not funny from Sandy's point of view. She made herself appear before them "Here I am. Laugh on my face"

"I told you she is a freak." screamed Jasmine.

"Yes I am a freak for forgiving you so many times. In fact more than enough."

"How did you get in here loser?" laughed Jackie.

The little soldiers were getting frustrated with Sandy for putting up with all the abuse. They started making circles. Each circle created enough wind strong as a storm. Everything around them started flying in to the wind. A few others move around Sandy so many times that she turned in her queen's garments. They then attached themselves to each other. Once they were a giant light one of them said, "Behold the queen of Karma, you might hide you sickening personalities from everyone but not from karma. Here now before you stands the queen of Karma. Kneel and show your respect."

The three girls laughed their heads off. "This loser Sandy? What can she do to us? She is broke and poor."

Suddenly she turned into a glowing light. "I came here in good faith to help my sisters, but now I can see that you have lost yourselves to the devil and there is no way I can bring you back. I will now tell you, your husbands and kids will have the greatest life. They will see you but not recognize you while you are begging for a piece of bread.

This judgment will not be reconsidered and harsh because you have been given more opportunities to turn your backs from doing things and become better people but you have refused to change. Now you will all find out that there is more powers beyond the powers of money."

"Now you are frightening us?" Cindy said. "You loser. Go and beg for lunch."

"I am done begging, especially you as you imprisoned your sons. You should be imprisoned, as you denied your husbands, you will be denied of all rights towards your kids. You will beg your own kids for help but they will not help you because of the negligence you have shown towards them.

Your own staff who you treated like rubbish will become your superior. Now you can laugh as much as you want but don't come begging for forgiveness when the Karma comes for you."

Again the three women laughed but when they turned around, she was gone and all the blue lights were replaced by dark lights which looked like dots.

"I told you, she is a witch." implied Jasmine.

"I totally agree." said Jackie

In the morning when Joshua saw Sandy missing from the breakfast table, he went to her bedroom and knocked on the door. When she didn't reply, he opened the door and found her sitting in a corner. All her clothes were wet from tears. He ran towards her and hugged her. "What is the matter?" he asked.

"Oh Josh, what does it take to make people understand they can't be cruel to others. They cannot rob and expect to get away with it. What about the neglect of your children? If you bring a life into this world you are supposed to look after it."

"Sandy you know you can't save the whole world." he replied.

"Why can't I have the power to save everyone?"

"Because they chose not to be saved, and there is nothing you can do about it.

"Oh my god, I am nothing but a failure if I can't save my own sisters."

"Come on get up. You even making me sick. How many times have you tried with our sisters?" Joshua continued, "Any vision about my children?"

"You will have them back soon." Sandy did not want to tell him how miserable they felt.

Chapter 31

Cindy disappeared again to call Alberto. "Hi Doll." she said. "When are you going to come for us? I miss you."

"There is no time, replied Alberto. I don't want to be a part of your world anymore. I had a visit form the Angel of death I and am going to behave."

Cindy laughed out loudly "Are you talking about Sandy? If you are depending on her you are nothing but a loser just like her."

"Whatever." said Alberto before hanging up on her.

Weeks went by, and the judgment day for the three women arose. The defence had a tip off that Angelo was the master mind behind the planning of the drugs.

The kids of all three women have been picked up by police and brought to the court room.

Cindy was presented as a loving mother by her defence and that a loving mother like her would never engage in such illegal stuff like drug dealing. Not only would that have been inappropriate with her kids. She had no need for any extra money as she was sitting on millions that she took from her husband.

The jury felt for Cindy when they heard the defence but one of her kids stood up before the prosecutor and said. "Which loving mum? Since our dad went missing, we have been imprisoned in this boarding school. There has not been one night that we didn't think of killing ourselves."

"Who are you son?" Asked the defence

"I am the son of that loving woman that cared about her children so much."

"Oh I didn't recognized you." yelled Cindy.

"Off course you wouldn't." said the son. "You put us in a boarding school and paid extra so we would be kept as prisoners."

"I would never do such thing." said Cindy.

"Let God and the jury decide your faith, you evil woman." answered the son.

With such a sight in the court room the judge, called the prosecutor and the defence to the bench. "Which one of you arranged for these kids to be here?"

"None of us." they replied.

"How did they get here then?"

"We don't know."

"Well you better find out. Those kids seem really hurt I do not want them to be in emotional danger. I will call a two hour recess."

During those two hours, the prisoners were taken back to their cells. The defence lawyer and the prosecutor approached the kids with some court Clerks as witnesses.

"Are you Cindy's kids?

"Yes." answered the older son.

"How did you get here?"

"We don't know. Last night when we both were praying, we felt the presence of an angel that gave us comfort and we went to sleep. I opened my eyes in the middle of night and saw these beautiful blue lights flying around us as if they were protecting us. Then I went to sleep and this morning we found ourselves here but we don't know how."

"One of the Clerks said. "Poor kids. They are so traumatized that they are imagining things. Maybe we should call the children's support group?"

"Do you think that was a dream?" asked the prosecutor.

"No Sir, I saw it all just like I can see you now."

The younger one screamed. "Sir, do you know where my daddy is?"

"No, but if you give us a few minutes we will find out."

The Clerks and the two men walked out confused. The defence lawyer went to Cindy and asked. "Did the school know your court would be on today?"

"N," Why?"

"I need to call the school and find out how those two got here."

"Ok. Go on then."

When the defence called the school the principal was very happy. "Thanks god" he said. "I was worried to death."

"Do you know how they got out?"

"No Sir. The other kids told me there were some sounds coming from their room last night and when they went to investigate there was a bluish colour light visible from their room so the other kids thought they were aliens and went back to their rooms.

This morning when I saw they were missing from the breakfast table, I went to their room with my assistant only to find their beds empty and a lot of glowing powder on their floor."

"Is there any secret way that they may have found a way out of school?"

"No sir. At nights all the doors are alarmed, so if anyone goes near any doors or windows the alarms will go off. After we noticed them missing we tested all the doors and windows only to find out that the alarms were working perfectly."

The defence lawyer then went to the prosecutor and told him of his discussions with the school. The prosecutor said. "I found the files of when their father was imprisoned. Apparently during his time in goal the wife sold everything and put the kids in boarding school. Then she moved into a very high class area.

From the time the father was released from gaol no one has seen or heard from him until the news flash introduced him as a fugitive from the law. What is worse is that? There was no physical address for him."

"Like any most people when he left the prison he would have gone home, wouldn't he?"

"What home? As I said the wife had sold all his assets. The woman that bought his house said, he had come here and got such a shock when he found out that she owned his house."

"Poor man. I heard that even those recent accusations were created by the same woman that put him in goal."

"What are we going to tell the judge? He will laugh at us if we go to him with the son's story of how they got here?"

"Well it is, what it is."

The two then went to the judge's room and told him the story. He got angry and told them. "I will give you twenty four hours to take them back to their school and find out how they got here today. See if you can locate their father."

"Defence, I heard that you are representing the other two women as well. I hope what happened today won't be repeated in my court room."

"Sorry your honour. I will make sure of that."

Alex who was sneaking in around the court room, overheard the prosecutor and the defence talking about finding Joshua. He quickly rang Josh and told him what had happened and asked. "Josh do you want me to sneak your telephone number in to the prosecutor's office?"

"If you do that I will forever be in debt to you. If my kids need me I will go to them even if it means getting arrested."

Alex then wrote on a piece of paper. "I am a total stranger and I could not help overhear that you are looking for Josh. Here is a telephone number for you to contact him."

The prosecutor ran to his secretary. "Did you see who dropped this note?"

"No sir."

"How did they get past you?"

"I was here the whole time. I only left my desk once when an old lady fell on the floor and I tried to help her."

He then goes back into his office and calls Joshua. "Sir this morning was your wife's appearance in court and somehow your children showed up at court and started arguing with their mother. The judge got upset and delayed the court for twenty four hours. Your younger child asked me if I knew where you were and I promised him to find you."

"My poor babes." cried Joshua. "Sir you know that I am a fugitive until the appointed authorities do their proper investigations?"

"Since the allegations against you was made by these three women who have criminal charges against them, I personally promise you that no one will arrest you or make any attempts to do so. But please do come and take your children back to their school. I have to warn you that they might have imaginary friends because they reckon some angels brought them to court while they were asleep."

"Ok. I will be there as soon as I can."

"Can I send a police car to collect you and bring you here?"

"No thanks. I will drive myself."

The happiness in his heart was overwhelming. Joshua turned and looked at Sandy in tears. "Little angels ha. I wonder how my kids learned about little blue angels."

While asking Brian for his car keys he looked at Sandy. "Thank you. I know it was you."

Brian wouldn't hand the keys to Josh. He made it clear that he would drive him. "Josh I am not going to give you my keys then sit here worried to death until you come back. Come on I will drive. You are too excited to drive anyway."

The prosecutor and defence are waiting impatiently. The prosecutor told the oldest son. "Your dad is on his way."

"Did you really find him?" cried the eldest.

"Yes. I did."

The two young kids hugged each other and sat next to each other holding hands as if they had no one in the whole world apart from each other.

Two hours later, Josh knocked on the prosecutor's door. "Here I am sir."

Before the prosecutor said anything, the two kids recognized their father's voice and ran towards the door. When the door opened Josh kneeled in front of the two kids. The three of them hugged and cried in a very loud voice. Josh was kissing them from everywhere. "Oh god, I missed you. "

It was such a sad atmosphere. Tears filled the eyes of others that were in the room. How was such a loving father taken away from his kids?

"Dad where did you go? They told us you were dead but we knew that you would one day come back to us." Uttered the younger son.

"Guys. Dad would have never left you. But the trap they set for me was so bad, that only a miracle could save me. When we have more time I will explain it all to you."

"Are you going to put us back at that school?"

"It is up to you. Don't you like your school?"

"We don't mind it but other kids were picked up for Christmas and holidays but we spent all the summer holidays alone in that room."

Josh then turned to prosecutor. "Sir. Do I have to take them back to school now or can I please spend one night with them?"

"I will have to get a release document from the court and we need an address where these kids will stay on the night."

Josh got very confused. He asked if he could make a phone call then he called Brian in relation to his address. Brian asked him if he could go in and when he did he said. "Sir they are staying at my house as my guests but this address should not leave this office, for the security of both kids and their father."

The prosecutor went to the judge and quickly got the approval to release the two kids into their father's custody.

"Do you want them back in court tomorrow morning?" asked Josh.

"No." said the prosecutor. "If needed, we will bring them in as witnesses but right now the judge does not want them to be more traumatised than they are. I will call the school tomorrow around ten am to make sure that you have returned them."

"You have my word."

Josh walked out with each kid holding one of his hands. When they got out, he kneeled in front of them again. "I can't believe that after all this time I am hugging you again." He then looked at Brian. "This nice gentleman is Brian, your true uncle."

Brian was so pleased of the way that Josh introduced him to the kids, he said "I bet you haven't had burgers for a very long time".

The oldest son replied. "We even forgot what they look like."

"Josh, what do you say if we skip Brook's lunch today?"

The younger child said. "Are we going to have chips as well?"

They all laughed and Brian said. "The whole works, burger, chips and drinks."

Next morning Cindy fronted court again and was found guilty for the possession of illegal drugs and sentenced to six years in gaol. While crying with unbelief she looked at her defence. "Please re appeal. Call my husband and ask for his help?"

But when the defence called Josh he replied. "Let her drink from the same cup that me and my kids drank from. Let her know the grave that she dodged for the three of us is now hers and do ask her what it is like to be innocent but accused falsely?"

The defence lawyer was speechless. He went back to Cindy with Joshua's reply, she yelled. "You small time lawyer you are useless."

The defence lawyer grabbed his briefcase. While walking out he said, "My god what has that man put up with all those years."

The following day the same judge handled Jackie and Jasmin's cases. "This is the first time in my entire life that I see three accused, that no one would come and give evidence to assist their case. I felt for the defence the whole time and got my officers to do some research about this case.

Every employee that worked for them was so happy that they were in prison. A security guard was forced to go to school and pay the school extra money to keep the children quite. All these three women made an attempt on their husband's lives to gain further money."

The judge continued. "Following the findings of the prosecutor and the interviews that my personal team did with the employees and the families of these three woman, I am convinced that they will do anything to have more money. With confidence I can say I find them guilty with the possession of drugs and unlawful cash. Therefore I sentence them to six years imprisonment. Maybe then they will be rehabilitated."

From prison they started calling everyone that they knew but no one would come to their aid.

Unaware of Angelo being in home prison and being disabled he was unable to do much to assist them.

One afternoon the floors started shacking. Soon alarm bells in the prison went off. "It's earth quake one of the guards called out."

All the cells were opened and all prisoners were taken to the yard while the earth shook. Jasmine and Cindy kept on pushing everyone to get to a safe place.

A pregnant prisoner was one of those pushed. She fell on the floor and her scream covered the hall wall while she was on the floor not being able to get up, she called out. "Please help me." The two women looked at her and left her behind.

From the yard they could see the buildings was collapsing but then the earth under their feet shook and opened up while they were hanging on to the rails Jasmine and Cindy started calling for help. Seconds later everything went quiet. The earth had swollen both of those two women. From under the rubble could be heard their moaning sounds. Everyone was running around helping others.

They managed to hold on. This woman covered in blood went and had a look to see if she could help. Jasmine with a very pleading voice "Please help us."

The woman looked at them. "That is where you both belong"

"Please." said Jasmine again.

The woman then said. "Wasn't I asking for your help when you pushed me down? You left me there while the rocks were falling on me. If it wasn't for those people with little lights I would be dead. Just tell me why do you expect me to help you?"

The woman then walked away. Minutes later Jackie appeared on top of the hole and pulled her sister and Cindy out.

Weeks went by and the three girls received a subpoena to be present in court to give evidence. On the day of court they were taken in through the back door of the court room. It was full of people. All the seating was taken and hundreds of others were standing. They had no idea what was happening. The front door was opened hundreds off camera flashes could be seen. Angelo was being wheeled in by the Clerks.

The jury was watching all this closely with question marks on their faces. They were overwhelmed with what was taking place.

Finally the lawyers and the judge arrive. Everything went quite.

This was the first time the girls had seen Angelo, following the incident in the restaurant. They could not believe this major figure was no longer the powerful man they once knew.

Angelo looked around for the first time in his life fear had taken over him. He can see many familiar faces. Those who he had stolen from, those who were supposed to be dead because of him, were present at the court room.

The most shocking moment of all was when he laid eyes on Max, who was standing right next to the prosecutor, fit and alive.

Angelo cried out aloud. "All your bones were crushed. How did you manage to walk again?"

"Let's say, I am a walking miracle." Max responded.

Angelo then then leaned towards his lawyer's ear. "I don't stand a chance. All these people are against me. If they don't kill me, the chain definitely will."

"What do you want to do?" asked the lawyer.

"I am dead either way."

The judge then said. "Angelo you have been charged with robbery, murder, forgery and the list continues. How you plead?"

"Not guilty." he replied.

The mumbling of people broke the silence in the court room.

"Prosecutor, are you ready to present your case?"

"Yes your honour." As he stood up.

The prosecutor turned to jury. "This man is guilty of every charge. As you all know we work hard in our lives to gain a comfortable life for ourselves and our children but there are those, like this man presented to you today, who was not satisfied with what he had. Most of us need three life times to have what this man had. However there was one thing he didn't have, satisfaction. He wanted more he wanted other people's hard earned money as well. During the next few days I will present to you all the people that he tried to kill so he could have their money."

The defence then start their case: "This man that prosecutor, with so much confidence calls guilty, has earned every penny he owns through hard work. Throughout the course we will prove that none of the accusations made are true, but rather alleged."

The first thing that the prosecutor presented to court was the tape that Don left behind. When the tape was played the girls were shocked. The whole court room went silent. Staring at Angelo, the jury had already made their minds up, with a guilty verdict because obviously the tape was full of evidence.

After lunch the prosecutor called the three first witnesses. The three that were tortured in Don's tape and what undertook to save their lives.

The questions asked by prosecutor and the answers given from the three were:

"Why did Angelo and the chain wanted you dead?"

"They wanted us to hand our businesses to them."

"You mean to buy it?"

"No sir, by force. They tried to send us broke when we didn't hand them over we were kidnapped, beaten and ordered to be killed."

"Naturally you were not killed."

"We are so lucky and thankful to Don. He paid the guys that were going to kill us to disappear and told them he would personally take care of us. He got private doctors to treat us and when we were well enough, he paid us enough money to take our families and ran away."

"Why didn't you or Don go to the police?"

"Because there were cops, detectives and other high flyers government bodies that were connected to Angelo and the chain. We just did not know who to trust."

There was no chance after that for further questions as the earth started shaking. The judge was quickly taken through the back door and every person present started running for their lives. As everyone was struggling to make it out the building, three girls were pushed back toward their cells.

Angelo's defence team went out to see what is happening and left him behind. A massive blow from under threw the wooden court chairs in air and pushed Angelo on the floor. Being disabled, he called for help. A woman who was passing by didn't look at

Angelo's face but offered her hand to help. A young hand pulled hers back. When she turned, it was Peter Nancy's oldest son. "Mum you can't help him. He is the man that pushed me on the floor and got his guards to chase me. If it wasn't for Don and Donna, god knows what would have happened to us."

Nancy pulled her hand away from her son and said. "If you don't let me help him we could become as bad as they are. Don't ever try to avenge your enemies at their time of need. Let God and time take care of them."

During the time that Nancy was talking to her son, Angelo was frozen on the floor staring at something. He could hear voices in his ears. "Life is precious isn't it?"

"Of course it is."

"Then how did you destroy so many lives and kill many?"

"I am sorry, truly sorry but they deserved it."

"How do you think those people felt when you ordered your men to kill them? Do you think they were scared like you are now?"

"I can't go back and fix it. What do you want me to do?"

"There is nothing you can do. You used all your chances."

"Oh please." Angelo cried.

Nancy turned towards Angelo and said. "Who are you talking to?"

"I thought it was you."

"I was talking to my son."

"Please help me back in my chair."

Nancy and Peter helped Angelo back on to his seat and helped him outside. When they made it into the street, it was full of cracks and cars were hanging over large holes. People were helping each other to carry those who were unconcise or seriously injured.

The voice said to Angelo. "Look around you. Not one good person has been injured."

When he looked around he saw the detectives that helped him all those years ago crushed under the stones with only their faces showing.

They were all dead. "Lucky them. They don't have to go through the courts."

"That's because their punishment is a lot lighter than yours."

"Please take my life too."

"Not before your eyes witness the power of Karma."

"What Karma? Don't be superstitious things happen circumstances change."

Nancy again yelled. "Sir have you lost your mind? Who are you talking to?" Then she grabbed Peter's hand and started giving a hand to those who were injured.

The emergency services arrived. Shortly after the authorities located Angelo and tried to take him back to his cell.

He kept on screaming. "I have to make a statement."

There were no ears to his pleading. He was taken home and two guards were placed at his premises.

Once at home Angelo poured himself a drink and placed himself in front of a window. It was time to make peace for his, own sake. "Who is this person that keeps on talking in my ears?"

He tired himself with questions but when he tried to sleep he kept on having nightmares about everything that he did wrong in his life.

He then decides to stay awake, grabbed a pen and lots of paper and on the paper he made a confession of how he set the girls up with the drugs.

When he had completed the confession, he puts it in an envelope. On it he wrote "I am sorry."

Angelo who had never known how to say sorry, had finally broken down and was trying to make things right, unaware of how late that was.

Angelo then grabbed another note book and started writing the names of everyone involved in the chain, all the directors, all the crook cops and detectives. Then he wrote a history of all the companies he took over and the involvement of the chain and so on.

By now three days had passed. Angelo was still busy writing. He had no food or sleep during all that time. He was determined to make things right.

On the fifth day when he finished writing, he started writing a letter.

My Dear Son Jo,

I am so glad that you turned out to be a good person and never followed my dark footsteps.

You grew up with the love of your mother, a wonderful woman who for a while followed me but after being infected by me with greed and disease she finally healed herself and became a better person with so much love to share.

At this moment I am not a proud person for what I did. I feel humiliated for not being a father to you. I thought people fed on money and power but how wrong I was because only now have I found out that people, feed on love, kindness and sharing.

I am already sentenced to death and it does not matter if it is by court or the chain. The fact that all my wrong doings haunt me in my dreams and they keep me awake are enough to claim my sanity.

Using my only son to date younger girls haunts me. All those that I destroyed haunt me. All this pain I am now suffering is nothing compared to the hurt I did to others.

I should make you aware that after the chain dismissed me and due to that reason I transferred all my assets including my personal companies to you. I am definite now that you will use all this wealth wisely.

At this point. I ask you to forgive me. Do look after your mum. She lost all her friends because of me, and no money on earth can again buy back those friends for her.

For what it is worth, here for the first time, I say to you I love you and am glad that this letter will finally make peace between the two of us."

He then put the letter in another envelope and wrote, "My only Son."

After the earthquakes weeks went by, life was once again back to normal. Until this date all the news and other media were only covering the earthquake and the conditions of those who survived it. Now the footages from the court start appearing on all different programs of TV.

By now most of the people knew the quake had happened during Angelo's trial. All the channels were plagued by phone calls to try and find out the date of when the trial would start again.

When Angelo saw all the footages on TV he went to his hidden safe then called one of the guards, handing some money to him and said "I want you to take this letter to your superiors."

"I am not allowed to leave my post sir."

"You could contact your superior and tell him that you have important information to hand in."

"That is true."

The officer went and called his superior. "It is ok. I will arrange for someone to come and collect it."

After reading the letter, the officer went to the prosecutor and showed him the letter. The letter was presented as new evidence to the court on following day and that became the key to release the three women from the prison.

Knowing that the chain would have seen all the footage as well, Angelo knew it would not be long before they tried to kill him. He again called the two guards, handing an enormous amount of money to them. "Please take this when your shift is finished. Tonight I want you to take these two letters and hide them somewhere safe. If anything happens to me, please make sure that my son gets this letter and hand the thicker one to the authorities."

One of the guards asked. "Are you scared you might face the death squad?"

"No. I am just conscious you don't know the people that I was in partnership with."

The two guards were at the gate late at night changing shift with the new guards. A horrific noise filled the air. When they turned around they saw the whole house being demolished.

It did not take long for the emergency services to arrive. When they put the fire out they went looking for bodies. There he was the giant Angelo dead on the floor.

The four guards were questioned but only the two with the letters ended up going to the authorities where they handed the letters in. The authorities then called Jo and his mother to identify what was left of Angelo's body.

One of the men asked Jo. "Are you his son?"

"Yes sir."

"Here your father left this for you."

Michelle and Jo read the letter together. They could not believe that the letter was written by the same person that they knew all their lives. A small light appeared to them "He was visited before his death and that visit affected him so much that he wanted to make things better for everyone before his death."

Chapter 32

Joshua walked in downcast. Jason screamed. "Josh what is wrong? What happened?"

Josh looked up and said. "Yes something did happen."

"What happened? You are killing me."

Without saying anything Josh opened the door. Brian appeared with two little kids holding his hands.

Jason and Sandy in disbelief ran towards the kids. "Oh you brought them home." they cried out.

The two kids hugged their uncle and aunt. "We missed you so much." they said.

"Sorry Brook, I had a treat with these young men we had burgers and chips." said Brian.

Mandy was the last to appear and hugged them. When they saw their cousins they were so happy. "We have a lot of catching up to do." said the oldest to his cousins.

"I know you are all happy to see them and so am I. But the boys are only allowed to stay the night and I have to take them back to their school tomorrow morning."

"Why can't they stay longer?" asked Brook.

"The prosecutor did me a favour because he felt sorry for the boys. In fact I wasn't to see them until the court hearing. For now I am going to cherish every moment with them."

The following day Josh did as promised, took the boys back to school and handed his cell number to the principal. "Call me if the boys need anything."

The principal was so pleased. "I am glad that finally you came back for them. Your kids are very good kids. They were heart broken and unhappy all the time."

Josh smiled. "Now you boys be nice to your principal. Don't let him worry about you."

They hugged and Josh walked away.

A few weeks down the track Alex called Max one morning and said "Oh my god Max, your fight is over."

"What do you mean?"

"Angelo left a letter behind with his guards on the night of bombing."

"What does that have anything to do with me?"

"Well he named, and shamed everyone involved with the chain including all the directors, crook detectives and next to each name he wrote their crimes."

"Oh my god Alex, was your name among them?"

"No. For some strange reason he either forgot to mention my name or a miracle happened to stop him from doing that."

"What happens now?"

"It's already happening. As soon as the authorities got their hands on the list they created operation Chain. All this time they were busy collecting civilian's videos and lots of other evidence. Massive raids are about to take place."

"That is the best news I heard in the past few months."

"I personally wanted to give you the news before you saw it on news shortly."

"Thank you. I won't take much more of your time."

Max ran outside to where everyone was doing little jobs and yelled, "It will all be over soon."

"What is going on?" Asked Brian

"The raids are on their way."

"On their way to where?"

"The directors of the chain. Angelo named them all before he died."

"That is great news son." Brian said.

"Where is Sandy?" Max asked

"Oh you know. She disappeared a few hours ago."

"Where to?"

"You should know better. She has duties."

"Hurry up everyone." shouted Max. "Let's go and wash up. Soon we will have great entertainment. "

Joshua, Jason, Mandy the kids, Brian, Brook, Max, Jo and his mother they all went inside washed up and sat in the lunchroom. Brian turned the TV on while Brook went to make some finger foods.

Minutes later the news flash came on. "Hours ago one off our choppers, while checking traffic for the news noticed a lot of police activity on the ground and contacted the news room to investigate. We were able to dispatch a few of our camera men and news group to a few sites. No one has any idea of what they are doing but by the looks of it they are getting ready to raid a few mansions."

"Our journalists were able to talk to a few people to find out what was happening but no one had any idea until. We received a call from an UN identified person saying. "Finally the chain is going to be broken."

On the ground you could see many news trucks were arriving. All the camera men were put on emergency call. When the sound of the first bang was heard, Special Forces forced their way into the first mansion.

A sneaky camera man has made it all the way to the inside and is sending live video's to the news room. It did not take long before a man and his three security guards to be arrested and brought out with hand cuffs.

On the second site the same things were happening but everything was recorded from a distance. Up to ten sits got raided at different areas.

Forty men and a hundred body guards were arrested. The media kept on pressing the police commissioner for information, he was left with no choice but to face the media and make a statement.

The commissioner addressed the media "Thank you all for being here.

This operation started months ago. Our first lead came in from a very honourable source but we had to keep it quiet until we had a lead to the major people involved in the chain. Although we had videos of their activities but no faces and no names, those who were bitten by the chain were too scared to give any evidence, even Angelo the giant business man whom we all knew. Angelo who was in trial at the time saw his death coming, so he sent us the names, activities and a lot of proof which led to all these raids today. Every single director of the chain is now in custody, including their leaders and body guards."

"On what charges?" one yelled.

"Murder, money laundering, bodily harm, theft, bribing police officers and the list continues."

"Is the Giant Angelo among all those prisoners?" asked another reporter

"No. Hours after we received the information, his dwelling was bombarded and he lost his life during those explosions."

The commissioner then put his hand up and said "No further questions will be answered." and walked away.

"What does this mean for you guys?" asked Brian.

"We will find out soon." replied Max.

Josh then gets off his chair and said. "I wonder what the other three are doing in prison."

"You don't need to worry." said Jo. "Days before Dad dies he wrote all these letters. One of those letter was a confession from him of how he framed the three women. They all have been released."

"Why didn't you tell us before?"

"I am sorry, I completely forgot. I am still in a shock that my dad wrote such a letter to me."

"He must have been a changed man after the accident?"

"No he wasn't. But from what I heard, some little angels paid him a visit."

"Not Sandy's Angels." laughed Brian.

"Believe it or not, I think yes."

"I don't feel like working anymore." cried out Brian. "Does anyone want a drink?"

They all laughed. Jason got off his chair to give a hand to Brian by pouring the drinks.

Hours later Max, again said. "I am starting to worry about Sandy. Has anyone seen her?"

Josh with a smile said. "I will go and check her room."

He knocked on the door and walked in. The beauty was laying on her bed.

"You truly look like angel."

"Sure Josh, just because I am your sister."

"No I truly mean it. Any way it looks like your mission was very long today, forty of them?"

"What do you mean forty of them?"

"They arrested all forty chain directors."

"How did you find out?"

"It was all over the news. We all sat around and watched the whole raid."

"Do you know their families had no idea what kind of monsters they were living with? Their wives and children were shocked. Normally kids and the wife cry with situations like this but they all seemed relieved when the man of the house was taken away."

"Did you give them second chances?"

"Their crimes are beyond the second chances they all had to change prior to these arrests. I have been watching all their crimes. I also helped some of the victims where I could. That is why I have no mercy left for those men."

"Are you going to come down? Max has been very impatient knowing you are not here."

"Sure I will change and come down. "

"Hi Sandy" uttered Max. "How was your day? Good enough to have a drink?"

"I can always do with a drink."

Weeks went by. Brad and Alex told the brothers and sister to sit still and wait until they were contacted. By now everyone was starting to get impatient, including Max.

"We are in the worse situation."

"Why do you say that? We drink, eat, have fun and have the best family on earth." Jason responded.

"I don't mean to sound ungrateful, but this waiting game is like a silent killer, not knowing how everything will turn out, is eating me because right now I am caught in between the earth and skies."

"Nothing holds for ever. said Sandy. "Remember when all your bones were crushed and you were told that you could never walk. But you walked away from that nightmare and you are walking again.

"That is true." replied Max.

"I want you all to remember nothing will last for ever. The pain comes and goes. Hardship hits but we overcome it. We lose but then gain more through the experience of our losses. Take every day as it comes sunny or cloudy, because none of us can do anything about the sun or the clouds.

When this is all over remember these days and don't take life for granted. Be generous and dig deep in your pockets when you see people in need.

And lastly look around you. We lived with this nice family all that time and now they have become our only true family. Through the goodness we received goodness and when we share our fortunes with those in need, Karma will pay us back when in need."

"Bravo." said Brian. "Only if there were more of you, then there wouldn't be so much hurt on earth."

Weeks went by. Everyone kept themselves busy on the ranch doing whatever they could but there was still no news. Then one night while everyone was gathered in the room a little glowing soldier came in. Then another and then another until the whole room was full of them.

They all got worried and looked at Sandy. "Is this the sign of danger?"

"No. This the sign of celebration for those who committed all those crimes are finally put to justice."

"What do you mean?"

"You will find out tomorrow."

The next morning Max knocked on Sandy's door to come for breakfast. When he opened the door she was missing again. Instead there was a strong and strange light that filled the bedroom. He sat on Sandy's bed. "Sandy is that you?" He didn't get an answer so again he called "Sandy is that you?"

A voice replied. "Sandy is on a mission."

"Who are you?"

A little light came around and pointed to the light. The voice said. "Stop there and do not move. We are the elders of the gift, those who chose Sandy to be the queen."

"What are you doing here?"

"We are here waiting for the queen. She has earned another gift today. Then one of the lights turned into a slide show. "Look." said the voice to Max.

When Max looked it was Michael, alone in the wheel chair. While Sandy was looking at him he could not see her. "If I ever get out of this I will spend all my money to create a dwelling for so many homeless people. I will educate them and when they are ready to start their lives I will bring the next lot in. Oh god please take me out of this misery and help me to repay my debt to people and community." He then dragged himself to the photo of his wife and son. "I truly hope to join you soon."

The queen of Karma appeared before Michael. "Your wish has been granted." For a moment Michael got so scared but then everything disappeared. As he turned his wheel chair, he fell on the floor thinking that he was unable to move. He dragged himself to the chair but then he realized that his legs moved. He was able to move more and more. He recognised that he was walking again, while he was dancing and carrying on, the doorbell rang. When he went to the door two detectives were talking to the guards outside. "Can I help you? he uttered.

"Yes." sir replied one of the detectives. "These guards are going to be taken away. We have your release documents here ready for your signature."

Michael in a shocked voice said. "But how?"

"Your name did not appear on Angelo's list and there was never enough evidence to convict you."

When everything went back to normal, the voice said "Max, as you can see Sandy has earned another good spirit." The lights then disappear again.

Max went to the breakfast table quietly and didn't say much while they were eating Sandy appeared in the middle of breakfast.

"You do have a hard mission and judgments that you should make, but the elders of the gift told me they have something to give to you."

"How did you meet them?"

"They were in your room."

"Did you see their faces?"

"No, only voices, and lights."

The conversation was broken by a phone call. Brian picked up the home phone.

"Good morning sir." the voice said

"Good morning." replied Brian.

"I believe you brought in Joshua to pick up his kids the other day. I am wondering if his sister and brother are also living with you."

"Who wants to know?"

"Please do not panic sir I am the prosecutor. I need to send them a court date to officially deal with their father's empire."

"I will pick it up and give it to them when I see them. But I don't know where they are staying."

"You can't pick it up sir. We will courier it to your address this morning. It should arrive by lunch time. If you would be kind enough to pass it on to them, also please let them know that their other sisters will be in court on that day."

The courier arrived by lunch time and brought two subpoenas, one addressed to Max the other to the two brothers and sister to be present at court on the Thursday which was only two days away.

"What do you think is going on?" asked Jason.

"Are we framed again?" said Joshua with a very worried voice.

"Jason, why don't you call Brad and see if he knows anything about this." said Brian.

"There is no need for that." continued Jo. "I just spoke to him but he has no idea. He said not to worry show up at the court and we will be ready for anything. I personally guarantee that I will put enough men there to protect you or make you disappear if necessary."

"Oh well, he has never let us down before, so we better show up at the court." said Jason.

"I will bring a few cars and friends, so if you need to escape we will be ready for you." uttered Jo.

Finally the day arrived. All the family was dressed for the occasion. When they got to court the other three women were already, there dressed in their best garments. Again they looked at Sandy. "Where did you find that suite, in a second hand shops?" They then laughed.

Sandy looked at them. "You poor souls, there is nothing I can say to you, apart from how sorry I feel for you."

There were three rows of empty seats behind the prosecutor and that's where they were directed to sit.

The court was full of media. They were allowed by the judge, to film everything that happens in that court room during this one special case.

In minutes hundreds of people poured into the court room. With thousands more waiting outside the judge ordered a microphone to be turned on so that the people outside could hear everything.

The judge walked in with two Clerks carrying massive files in their hands. The court officially started and the judge had this to say.

"It is always a pleasure to be in court on days like this. A group of young people went through hell fighting for their lives. False fully accused of crimes they never committed, they were robbed of their home and belongings."

"Not only had these young people fought hard to stay alive. They also helped us to break the biggest criminal chain in this country. Before we resume with the case I would like to personally call Max to come forward if he is here."

Max got off his chair and started walking towards the judge. As he did, the judge grabbed a few things from the clerks and also started walking towards Max. When they reached each other the judge said. "Son I don't know any one that has walked in your shoes and is still be alive, but I am pleased to say and will announce to the country that Max of Max Enterprises is not dead but present right in front of me this moment."

The cheering from outside could be heard inside. All present started clapping and whistling. The judge puts his hand up to stop the noise followed by. "Max I hand you your identity back."

Max was in shock. Tears would not spare him even a second to speak a word."

"I also say unto you. Max Enterprises have been transferred to you a few days ago. Your house was sold on your behalf. If you want you can buy it back with the money that we got from the chain." The judge stopped talking for minute and handed all the documents to Max.

"Have a look around. All your employees are gathered here and with their help we were able to give you back what was lawfully yours."

Max kneeled on the floor and looked at his loyal staff. They were there, cheering for him. He was in such a big shock that couldn't even move his legs. Finally one of the Clerks came to his aid. He looked at the judge and said "thank you."

The media now started screaming from all directions. "How did you survive?"

With tears running down his face and a look full of sadness he replied.

"Sleeping in the arms of death every night,
And waking up with a smile in the morning wasn't easy.
We lost our faith in people and did not know who to trust.
There was no, calming words for us nor a shoulder to cry on.
It all became over whelming,
And nothing was easy.
Times and times we tried to give up
But there they came, little glowing angels singing in our ears.
Here you are a walking miracle
And that was all that mattered.

Tears filled the eyes of all those present. The judge shook his hand and walked back to his seat.

"Max, you are free to go." The judge called out.

The cheering started from all the loyal people that came to court for Max. Some of them walked up to Max and started carrying him on their arms. The crowds went crazy when they saw Max being carried. Max's clothes were all wet from his tears but he managed to put his hand up as appreciation to all those who were cheering him.

A different group of people were now rushed into the court room, while the judge announced a fifteen minute break.

The court restarted when the judge walked in. He saw people sitting on each other's laps. Hundreds and hundreds had squeezed themselves into the court room.

For the first time in the history of his court, the judge didn't force anyone out of the room; instead he sat on his chair, looked at the prosecutor and said. "Is Sandy from Don Empire here?"

"Yes your honour. Here she is."

"Please make your way to the middle of the court." called the judge.

Once she was at the front, in the middle of the empty part of the court, the judge called out. "Stop there"

"Sandy Don we found all the necessary documents to prove you are the sole beneficiary of Don's empire."

"But your honour." said Sandy. "There is nothing left of the empire."

"Let me finish then you will be surprised. This will be discussed privately in my chambers."

He then asked the Clerks and the prosecutor to approach the bench. "Use any man power you need to bring all the brothers and sisters to my chambers. None of them have any idea why they are here."

When they all went into the chamber the judge started. "As I was saying, the court heard and examined the evidence against the directors of the chain. As you all know their houses got raided and on numerous sites we found forged documents. Among them was Don's original will, making Sandy the sole beneficiary of his empire. "

"We were able to convict them through the evidence of those involved to do the forgery by force."

"The transfer of Don's empire was done illegally and those who received benefits will be dealt with to regain the moneys lost."

"After a lengthy examination we found hundreds of made up supplier invoices that were meant to be destroyed but somehow they were not. A recording by an anonymous person showed how the directors of the chain paid people to pretend they were suppliers of Don's empire so that his children would believe the empire was going into receivership."

"Millions of dollars were transferred to your brothers and sister's accounts from Don's Empire as Angelo forged legal documents to get the money in to their accounts and then slowly dried them up."

"Unfortunately your house was sold and we can't get it back, but we managed to collect the selling money from the chain."

"Your brother Jason must have smelled a rat so the money that was given to him, he put in to a trust account which has been untouched."

"The sisters went and bought mansions for themselves with that money and by the looks of it they forgot the family values and tried to get rid of their husbands to hold on to the lot. These mansions will be repossessed and auctioned in order to get your money back."

"You can't sell our mansions. Jasmin said.

"Sandy is lawfully entitled to all the assets, which includes the mansions." The judge continued. "And young lady, I don't like people interrupting, while I am officially talking."

"Your brother Joshua, he was framed by Angelo and Cindy, his wife and spent time in prison. During the prison time his wife Cindy sold the house and took all the money again used it to buy a mansion which again, was done illegally and repossession is on the way."

"There were two houses that Don asked his loyal friends Carlos and Nancy to buy for emergency use. Those were also taken and sold by the chain."

"I personally took great interest in this case, when I saw the entire chain was not a match for a young girl like Sandy. And I say unto her, I am sorry for all the suffering you went through; the accident, the coma, being chased, attempts on your life, taking care and carrying three sick people, running from place to place. Again I say sorry for having corrupt detectives and police that were able to locate you every time you moved."

"In saying all this here in front of the prosecutor, the Clerks and your family I hand you entire Don's estate apart from those mentioned that are still in process. We will keep you posted on other matters."

Joshua and Jason happily clapped but Sandy was covered in tears. "Dad you are not here to see this. You got all your money back."

Joshua and Jason hugged her and cried with her, while the others were sitting there angrily.

"All the false charges against you and your two brothers have been removed. You may all go home and celebrate."

When Sandy and her family left the chamber the judge said to prosecutor "Come back and see me tomorrow morning. I will draw up arrest warrants for those three women for fraud, misleading the law and use of illegal money."

But outside the chambers, unaware of their future Jasmine and Jackie attacked Sandy. "Now you know why we never liked you? There is no way you can get your hands on our money."

"My own sisters." said Joshua. "How could you turn against your own brother?"

"You were our brother before she poisoned you." said Jackie.

"Why would you exchange your own brother with his wife? I cannot understand, and you Cindy, why did you destroy my life.

Ok if you didn't care about me what about the kids? They never did anything to you."

"Ah shut up." said Cindy. "Even your kids will turn like you into losers."

As Jason was about to interfere Sandy gave him the eyes not to say anything.

Max was waiting for them in the hall way. When they all opened the court door to leave they were shocked. Hundreds of people were standing there waiting. The minute that the doors opened they started clapping and cheering, and the media, quietly filming all their movements.

As the crowd was cheering Sandy, Max and the other two looked into the crowd and blow kisses to them.

Sandy then screamed "Trust justice. If the law does not catch up with people Karma always does. Be good and do good. Never have your eyes on your friend's food when you are full. Greed gives rise to evil so don't be greedy. Just be happy with what god has given you."

The crowd again cheered.

Minutes later Brad and Alex arrived with quite a few of their friends all dressed in their uniforms and driving police private cars. They escorted Sandy, Joshua, Mandy and Jason to three different cars and escorted them away from the crowd. Some of those detectives stayed behind and blocked any movement in the street for fifteen minutes. This would have given them enough time to go home without being chased.

When they got to Brian's house there were cars everywhere and the sound of music filled the garden, Brad and Alex quickly went to investigate the traffic Jam.

"Hi detectives." said Brian. "Don't worry these are all Sandy and Max's friends that I met in the court room. We decided to come here and try to surprise Sandy now that it is all over."

As Sandy approaches, the closer she got tears were forthcoming, looking with disbelief. The first people to come to her were best friend Mona and her partner Steve.

"I am going to kill you." said Mona. "You didn't even trust me. I can't believe you went through all those things by yourself".

"I couldn't put anyone's life in danger but it is so good to see you."

Rebecca and Susan were the next people to hug her. They cried without any words being exchanged for quite a few seconds.

"How happy I am to see you two. "How is everything? Did you two settle in your lives?"

"Definitely, thanks to you." they replied.

"How did you find me?"

"The investigation was so thorough that they even found out about us working together. We were interviewed a few days ago. We were told if we want to see you, to show up at the court today." replied Rebecca.

Carlos and Nancy kept their distance trying not to bother Sandy but when she noticed them she went straight to them. My dad's loyal friends, don't you wish he was here today to see that doing good always pays back."

Carlos tried to hand her an envelope.

"What is this?"

"This is the money you gave us the day we got away."

"I owe you my life. Now it is not the time for settlement. We should celebrate." Sandy responded.

Minutes later Jo walked in with his mum. She went straight to Sandy. "Oh, I hope your mum forgave me before she passed for being the bitch I was to her."

"What was done in the past belongs to the past. Tomorrow we can change together." replied Sandy.

Jo was relieved when he heard Sandy's reply. "You are truly an angel." he uttered.

"Only angels can see angels." said Sandy.

"I arranged for a microphone, Brian said. "All these people want you to talk to them."

"Yes Sandy." called out someone from the crowd. "Give us a speech."

"Thanks Brian." said Sandy while grabbing the microphone from him.

The first thing Sandy did was to thank everyone for being at the court today to support them.

Someone else screamed. "How did you survive running from one place to another carrying three sick people with you?"

Every drop of rain hid the tears of my sorrows
My bed, the only witness to my agony
Was made of nothing but thorns?
The day stole the comfort from me
And the sorrows kept on replaying at nights
Having no time to rest the body tried to give up
But the mind kept on playing and there
Was no time to rest?
Those who were with me became my enemies
Even those who were my own blood and flesh turned
    against me
The broken bones from pain carried the weight of others in need
Yet there was no one to give me a break or comfort my soul
But something inside kept on going and those against me
    did not see how
Broken I was.
I held on to those whom I loved until the last minute
But the cycle of life didn't let me enjoy their return
To you all I can say it was not easy
But here I am again standing high and proud
For good friends like you made it all easier.

With every drop of tear that poured from Sandy's eyes a light turned on by the time she stopped talking the whole place was covered in beautiful blue lights.

Brian grabbed and hugged her. "Oh darling I wish I was with you then."

Now came a very familiar face, the one that gave Sandy the gift.

"Oh, how sorry I am to hand you the gift. said Charlie.

"There is nothing to be sorry about, the gift chose me and used you to deliver. replied Sandy. "Now let's celebrate our hard work, for every single one of us was brought together for a reason.

Max was staring at Sandy the whole time. Then she disappeared.

The gift keepers have come to her. "You have made a big difference. We are aware that you and Max have grown to have feelings for each other. He will soon come to you and you can make the choice, to stay the queen or become Max's queen by accepting his proposal."

"Max is my true friend, and I love him. During all these hardships I lost my heart and a lost heart cannot be given to anyone."

"What about his feelings?" asked one of the other gift keepers?

"He will find love again but I cannot be that love."

Then a sudden soft breeze blew in and filled the room with good and happy feelings.

"Is it time?" anther asked.

"Time for what?" asked the other.

"Sandy's, gift for being the only special queen in centuries."

"I don't think I can handle another gift. Please give me a break." Sandy cried out.

"Go and enjoy your celebration." said the voice "Your gift will arrive when you are not expecting it."

Worrying that another burden would be put on her, Sandy went back to the others.

When she reappeared Max, noticed coldness in her eyes.

"My friend by the looks of it you have made your choice." he cried out.

"You and I are a part of each other and nothing can change that but you my friend shall find love again. Carry on with your life.

We will never be far from each other but we were never meant to be partners."

Those who heard the conversation could not believe the sacrifice that Sandy was making. Mona burst into tears. Even Mona couldn't comprehend.

"My friend don't you want to have children and live happily ever after?"

"I have a duty and I will not walk away from it." replied Sandy. "Brian where is my drink?" she called out.

"Let's celebrate." then she looked at Jason. "You never failed me did you?" followed by a massive hug.

Joshua who was blaming himself for everything didn't say much but then Sandy said "Oh Josh if you knew how the cycle of life works, you wouldn't be so harsh on yourself. The point is you didn't need my influence to become a better person because you already were." Then she got closer to him and in his ear she whispered. "Your best years of life are yet to come."

"All that matters to me are my kids. When I again live under the same roof as them, I will be the happiest man on earth."

"And the day is not far ahead." uttered Sandy.

The celebration went right through the night. Max, Sandy and the two brothers couldn't believe that the cards finally were at last on their side.

Brian and Brook were happy and sad at the same time. "Do you think we are selfish?" asked Brook.

"No why?" questioned Brian?

"Because we don't want to see them go."

"Don't worry love. Just think we have a big family now."

Chapter 33

The next morning the prosecutor went to the chambers of the Judge and picked up the warrants to search and arrest the three women.

"Preparing these documents was the most pleasing thing I ever have done in my life." said the judge. "Take them and good luck."

The prosecutor then handed the warrants to the police. When they arrived the girls put up a fight over getting arrested. "We haven't done anything wrong. What is all these about?"

It was all useless. The fact that they were involved with Angelo and the chain had put their names in as partners because they helped getting the assets of Don's empire.

The courts auctioned the three mansions and paid Sandy all the money back but the girls were each sentenced to five years imprisonment for false accusation.

For Cindy the penalty was heavier. The judge said, "I have never met a woman so cruel. To do what you did to your children, your poor husband was imprisoned because of your misleading accusations, not only that but he was disadvantaged as a parent and then you took all he had and left him homeless on the streets. I witnessed, the day your son attacked you in this very court room and for that I give your ex-husband Joshua, the sole custody of your kids. The money from the sale of your mansion will be equally divided between Joshua your husband and the rightful owner of the estate, Sandy."

"What will I do when I am released, with no home and family?" asked Cindy

"You should have thought of it when you became really greedy." replied the Judge.

"As for you two sisters." continued the judge. "You went along with your sister-in-law and did nothing to help your brother out of jail as you promised him. Your own husbands and children did not want to see you. That is why none of them are present here today. I will read to you what the police found in one of the children's diaries."

> Mum, I thought that parents will always be there for their
>   children according to nature
> But do you know what it was like not to have a mum?
> It made us feel unwanted, shameful and judgmental.
> Yes off course our dads have been there for us
> But the warmth of a mother's arms
> The love that eased the pain was not there.
> The woman that gave us life was never in our lives
> Did we cause this coldness because we were not what
>   you wished for?
> Or was it simply that we were a burden on you.
> These men next to us who work hard tried to replace you
> But we could see the struggles they were going through.
> But again they didn't let us down even for a second.
> They wiped our tears, they feed us and they shared our
>   sorrows
> While you who gave us life, spent your nights in the arms
>   of the enemy.
> For me, I heard of you in a story and that story was told
>   and finished
> I hope one day you will find your heart because at this
>   moment it seems like it is missing from your chest.
> I will keep my arms and heart open to this man
>   that became my mother and father
> But will erase you from my mind and heart forever.

"Any person with a heart would look after what they gave life to, but you tried to take back from them what you gave them and that was life. I wish I could have some compassion for you women but after reading this letter I lost it all."

"While you are in prison we will give your husbands and kids what is rightfully theirs but there will be nothing left to give to any of you."

"Like the letter said, I hope that you will find your hearts in the prison."

Later the three women tried a re-trial but it was refused.

"Those women need to have a taste of their own doings." A judge said when refusing the re-trial.

The two sisters and their sister in law are once again in prison. So desperate they call their brothers. "Please help us. " Pleaded Jasmine.

"I was where you are now awhile ago, all thanks to my wife and you." Responded Josh.

Jason was a bit more compassionate. "By the time you close and open your eyes, the sentence will be over and we will be here for you then."

Adam was the next person Jasmine rang. "Oh I miss my kids so much. Can you please bring them for a visit?"

Jackie made the exact same phone call to Anthony a few days later Anthony and Adam took the kids to see their mothers.

"Oh darlings, I missed you so much." Jasmine said.

The oldest son said. "And who are you?"

"I am your mum."

"Are you sure? If you are my mum then why don't I know you?"

"Because your dad took you away and I couldn't do anything."

"Why did he take us away? Can you please tell us?"

"I don't know. Maybe he had a girlfriend or something. It doesn't matter now. I am happy to see you." Then she looked at Adam. "Can I please have some time alone with them?"

Adam approves and walks away

Jasmine grabs her younger son. "Oh darling, hug mummy" then she whispered. "Daddy did this to mummy so he can have all the money to himself. You remember how rich granddad was. He left me all these money but now they are taking it away from me because your dad and others are lying."

"What do you want us to do?" asked one of them.

"Find out how much of my money he got then try to get some of it to me."

Jackie played the same trick with her two kids, and almost got what she wanted but then they said. "Dad recons you need help and now we can see why he said that."

"I don't need help. I just need my money back to get out of here."

"Sure mum but dad has no money left?"

"Then what happened to all my money?"

"The courts gave it back to aunty Sandi."

"I am your mother. You should help me."

"Why?" said the oldest. "So you can hire more people to kill Dad?"

"Off course not."

"You did it before, and you didn't even think that if Dad dies we become homeless."

"I will look after you."

"The same way you looked after us when you went after Michael?"

Jasmine and Jackie then started crying. "They have poisoned our kids against us." uttered Jasmine.

All of a sudden the ground under their feet started crumbling. All the windows and cell doors started opening and a shouting mix of light blue lights and dark black ones started gathering around Cindy and Jasmine and then appeared the queen of Karma to them. "When will you admit to your mistakes? How long are your poisons hearts and minds going to torture those around you? I told you before, what you planted and what you cooked you will eat." By this time the black dots had separated from the blue ones so the queen turned to the black ones and said "Two women with no hearts or compassion. I am done with them. You can have them." Then she disappeared.

Adam and Anthony ran toward the meeting rooms to make sure their children were alright. The kids ran to their fathers and asked to leave while the black dots took over the two women.

"What happened in there?" asked Anthony.

"Nothing." said the oldest son. "Mum was telling us you put her there because of her money and she tried to convince us to steal from you to give to her."

Adam's older son looked at his cousin. "That is exactly what happened with our mum."

"What did you say?" asked Anthony

"We didn't have to. A bright light came in the cell and when it left she couldn't talk anymore."

"What do you mean a bright light?"

"Well it was so bright but somehow I feel it had the figure of a queen."

Anthony then asked "Should I start worrying about you seeing things?"

But the younger one screamed. "Dad that is exactly what happened."

Adam then looked at his kids with a question mark?

His oldest was fast enough to say. "Dad and uncle we saw the exact same thing."

Later that day Adam rang the prison to say to Jasmine how she dare try to use the children. The prison officer told him "Sir those two women have been like statues since the visiting time this afternoon. The doctors came and checked them but they seem to be in some sort of coma. They can walk but they can't hear or talk."

Adam and Anthony then got together and decided to contact Sandy and her brothers so as the kids would have some sort of contact with their aunt, uncles and cousins.

Jackie and Jasmine stayed with no speaking ability for over two years. Their eyes were always locked in one spot as if they were staring at something.

During the five years Cindy became closely aligned with a prison gang. Her mission to use her newly made friends to eliminate Josh. However the gang only used her for what she was worth and never complied with her personal quest.

Chapter 34

Sandy is anxiously waiting outside as Adam and Anthony told her they were bringing the kids over. She has dressed Jason and Joshua's kids for the occasion. They too are next to her, waiting for their cousins.

When Adams car showed up from a far Sandy started running towards it and finally short of breath she caught up with the car. Adam stops the car the kids run towards Sandy and land on her chest. "Oh my darlings, how I missed you." few minutes later Anthony's car arrives and they all hug and kiss. The cousins were very pleased when they saw Joshua's kids and Jason's kids there waiting for them. All the cousins gathered and went to a different room from where the adults were sitting.

As usual when Brook heard they were having visitors she started preparing extra food.

"How is everything going?" asked Adam.

"Good." Sandy replied. "You might be aware that the three mansions were sold and the money total of thirty five million was given to me."

"Well deserved." said Anthony.

"Now this is our plan, you need to tell me how much of this money you need to live comfortably and to have enough for your kids educations."

Adam looked at Anthony then said "I think we are both in a very comfortable situation and do not need any more money. What is your plan?"

"Brian, can you please explain." Sandy pleaded.

"Well there is another ranch next to us for sale and since Sandy likes helping people we all decided that we should buy this ranch and build a big house in it. Those who we find homeless on the streets, we will bring to this ranch and help them by teaching them gardening, how to deal with animals and how to grow fresh produce. We will also have classes for them with proper teachers so that those who do not go to school can be prepared and re-introduce to higher education. Those who are older we will have technical courses for them such as computers, electrical, management and so on."

"If the first batch successfully completes their journey here and become ready to go back to start a new life we will help them financially to start then we will go on to the next batch of homeless people."

"Who will be paying for all these expenses?" asked Adam

"They will be taught to sell whatever they make. Say they grow tomatoes. They will try to sell them. If they can fix computers then they will offer services to those who need it and so on."

"That sounds really good." said Anthony.

"Can we help in any way?" asked Adam

"Yes off course if you want. Brian continues. "We want to keep this in the family so the more family members that are involved in the running this place the better for all of us."

"What about the Don's empire Sandy?" asked Adam.

"I have already nominated the two loyal staff of my father to take on the running of the empire. Nancy and long-time operations manager Carlos."

"You know since me and Adam, are playing the roles of both mother and father, we always tried to have more free time for our children. If the ranch is going to be run by the family, we are both in. That way our children can not only help with daily chores but they will be around their cousins all the time."

"I agree a hundred percent. The other benefit I see in this is that they will learn to be compassionate around those less fortunate."

"What about you Joshua and Jason? Are you in it as well?" asked Anthony.

"There is nothing to stop us." replied Joshua. "We all had miracles happening to us in the past few months and now we are all ready to share that blessing."

The cousins then came around and asked Brian if they could go and have a look at the animals. "I can escort you if you like." Then he put all of them into this train and drove around the farm to show them the animals.

A month later the ranch next to Brian was purchased. They built two massive buildings each with thirty bedrooms and a house further up from the buildings for Don's family, who were going to run the place.

The next step was all those involved. Jo, Joshua, Adam, Anthony, Brian, Brook, Mandy, Michelle Jo's mum, Jason and Sandy were all out in different cars driving through different suburbs.

Whoever they located as homeless they approached them and told them about the ranch and then asked them if they wanted to use this opportunity.

On the first night out they gathered more than forty five people and the night after they, again went out and brought enough people to fill all the rooms.

Everything started smoothly. All the cousins would go to school during the day and at night they all helped their families with small chores. All involved were so happy with the results. During this time Sandy found Charlie and offered him and his family work at the ranch and they accepted it with no hesitations.

Max was still heartbroken about not having Sandy as his wife. She was the woman that he loved.

Soon the elders appeared to him and presented him with a secret vision and whatever that vision was, made Max want to go back to the ranch and help the others.

Two years later the first batch of homeless, were ready to go back into society. They were all educated in management, agriculture, and computer software. Any of them who found work were helped by the ranch to rent a place and given enough money to start fresh.

Although everything was going as planned, Sandy at times could feel lonely and scared. She would stay alone for the rest of her life but when Max came back to the ranch she was so pleased to see him. However the empty space of her parents was always playing upon her.

"What was your other gift that the elders were going to give you?" asked Max.

"I don't think I ever received it. However having all my family around like this is a gift. To help all these people is a gift."

One night when they were all sitting outside for their traditional BBQ marshmallows, a little light approached Sandy. She looked but couldn't see anything else. It was as if her power had been taken away from her. But then came. Another and another until the whole area was filled with them.

Everyone was looking amused and no one knew why the little soldiers were there.

Suddenly Sandy was in her queen's garment looking so beautiful. Everyone quietly stared at her.

"What is going on?" asked Sandy

But before anyone can answer the elders appeared on all the corners of the ranch. They were gigantic and could be seen from miles away. "Your gift as promised." said one of the elders.

All the little soldiers started moving towards the driveway. They formed a beautiful arch of lights from the beginning of the driveway to where everyone was standing.

They all thought the art work of the soldiers was the gift but all of a sudden the lights of a car appeared.

"Who can it be at this time of night in the middle of nowhere?" Asked Brian

"May be it is one of those who graduated from ranch coming back to see us." replied Sandy.

But then came another car with its head lights on.

"Should we worry?" asked Mandy

The cars were driving under the beautiful arch of lights and then the cars arrived at the end of the driveway. The door of the first car opened and an elderly man walked and came towards Sandy. He asked "Do you remember me?"

"No sir, I don't."

"The man then came close to Sandy. "Look in to my eyes and see if you can remember me."

"Oh my god, of course I remember you. Look at you now."

Josh screamed. "Sandy do you want to introduce your friend to us?"

But the man turned to Josh. "You were with her that day, when your sisters pushed me on the floor but Sandy came and gave me all that money."

With disbelief Jason said, "Oh my god. From that to this, I am so proud of you sir."

"For what you gave me that day, here today I give you this." He then points to the second car. All of a sudden the door opens and Don walked out.

Sandy screamed "If this is a joke it is not funny at all." She broke down in tears.

Then a woman walked out behind Don. "Oh my god Mum." yelled Joshua.

"It is impossible. I buried both of them. They were dead." cried Sandy, Josh and Jason.

"What is the matter with you all? Are you happy to see us or should we leave?" said Don.

But no one had any energy in their legs to move. They were shocked and speechless.

Brian ran toward Don, they hugged. "My old friend welcome."He then greeted Donna.

All the kids screamed "Grandpa, grandma." while running towards them. Don and Donna kneeled on the floor and hugged every single one of them.

Don then looked at Sandy. "My beautiful child, look at you more beautiful than ever."

Both Donna and Don then rushed to hug their children. Sandy was still in shock. "Is it because we are dead, that is why we are seeing you?"

The man from the first car then turned into a massive light and moved away. "No you are not dead. This is your very special gift from the elders." he said while disappearing.

Seconds' later fireworks started and when they were finished one of the elders addressed Sandy "Be happy for what is given to you as a gift and never question the work of elders."

"Thank you for giving our parents back to us. "called out Sandy. Thousands of little soldiers then came and stood in front of Sandy before disappearing into thin air. After the last light, Sandy appeared in her normal clothes again.

Joshua and Jason wouldn't let go of their fathers creaming. "Please forgive us"

"We are happy to see the three of you back together, this means the world to me and Donna." said Don.

Donna grabbed Sandy. "Oh how I missed you."

"And who said miracles don't happen." Mandy called out.

"Your drinking partner is back, Sandy." said Brian with a smile on his face.

"Brian you know you will always be my special drinking partner." Sandy quoted.

"We haven't had a drink for so long and right now both me and your mum can do with one."

Time went. Now it was the sixth year since the opening of the ranch. Three lots have been educated and released back into community with new starts. The team as usual went back onto the streets for the next batch. Among the next batch picked, were three women all broken and covered in grey hair.

When they first made it to the ranch the speaker said. Welcome you are the fourth batch. Those before you learnt and accepted their second chance in life and now are working and have a good life. I truly hope that you will all follow their footsteps and may this first night be the beginning of a new life for all of you."

All of a sudden someone from the crowd called out. "Sandy"

She recognised the voice. Turned around and saw her two sisters in conditions that she never hoped to see them in. She then quickly ran outside and found Josh. "Jasmine and Jackie are among this new batch."

"What are you going to do?"

"I don't know Josh. I can't just ignore them. They are still our sisters."

"Let's call an urgent meeting with the others and see what they think."

"That sounds great, you gather everyone at the private house."

Fifteen minutes later everyone is at the meeting "Now was not a good time to call for a meeting. These poor people just arrived here," said Brian.

"That is why we called an urgent meeting. Jackie and Jasmine are among them." said Sandy.

Adam and Anthony got worried. "You know we don't want them around our kids." said Anthony.

"May be six years in jail has changed them. Should we give them a chance to get back into the family?" asked Sandy

"Brian what do you think?" asked Max.

"Maybe they have changed may be not. I think they have been punished enough. Give them another chance."

Jason, Joshua and Sandy then go in and approach their sisters. By this time Cindy who was in the bathroom has join the sisters. Josh started talking. "We are giving everybody a chance to get back on their feet. We hope that you three can participate in all the classes and gain some skills."

The girls didn't say anything.

Months went by and the three girls were settled in but Brian noticed that every day one of the people was going missing. He approached the family and shared his concerns. "Maybe we are doing something wrong. All those who were doing really good are disappearing without saying good bye."

"What if we install some cameras? That way if there is anything that we miss, it can be recorded on cameras." suggested Jo.

"That sounds good." Everyone agreed.

"I can ask Brad and Alex to help me do this but we will have to get everyone out of the building."

"I will arrange for an outdoor activity if you tell me when. "replied Josh.

"This is an urgent matter. The sooner they are installed the better." said Brian.

It was arranged and cameras were installed two days later, and then they were tested to make sure everything was working properly.

At the end of that week, another person went missing and when Brian checked the cameras he saw how the three forgiven women were pushing the others to do their chores by telling them, "Our family owns this place you scum bags." On a few occasions people were even pushed on the floor then walked over.

When the tape was shown to the rest of family they were really disappointed and had to come up with decision of what to do. Eventually a decision was made. Jason and Joshua went to their sisters and asked them to pack their stuff that was recently bought for them by family.

"What for?" Asked Jackie

"You three have been given more than enough chances. You have to leave and never to contact any of us."

"We wouldn't be in this situation if you and the rest of the family didn't take all our assets." Jackie said while screaming.

"But was it ok when you took all Sandy's shares. Remember how you said "who cares about that loser." Now I am telling you talk to someone that cares. Pack or I will call the cops and get you removed."

Scared that they might end up in jail again Jasmine said. "But where would we go with no home or money?"

"You should have thought about it when you were abusing your housemates that were here just like you for a new start. Thanks to the kind heart of that scumbag she asked us to find you a place and to give you enough money to restart your lives."

The girls just wouldn't move but Jason went to their rooms and grabbed their stuff and forced each one of them into the car and drove them to a motel inside the city. Then he threw a bag at them. "There I hope you use this money wisely." Then he drove off.

During this whole ordeal Dona and Don would not show their faces to the girls, and those girls had absolutely no idea that their parents were alive.

"Don, how do you feel about this?" Brian asked

"About what?" replied Don

"That your girls are getting thrown out?"

"I really don't know those monsters. I watched everything they did to their sister. I watched my son crying in jail for something that he didn't do and if that wasn't enough I watched him being homeless. If they had any relationship with me they would not be so evil."

Don's speech was interrupted by Donna's loud cry "Oh my god what about all those times when she had to carry me and Max running from one place to another. I watched her every day running around looking after others and at nights I saw her crying from pain and desperation."

"When I laid my eyes on her I knew she was very special and I am forever grateful to her." Brian said, in a very sad voice.

On the way back Jason said. "Josh do you think people like them will ever learn?"

"Those who have sold their souls for evil will never change but the time will come when even the Devil will not want anything to do with them." replied Josh.

Josh and Jason didn't go back home. They first looked in the streets for those who ran away from the help house and when they found them they begged them to come back and when they agreed Josh said. "Promise me from now on you are not going to disappear if something goes wrong. Come and see any of us and we will take care of it. This is a new start for you and we want you to be happy at all times so you can concentrate on your future goals."

After all the drama, things went back to normal again. The family would have three meals together. All the kids were going to the same school and would spend most of their time after school together. Nothing could be better.

Those who came and left the ranch for new beginnings would come and help from time to time and by telling their stories to the new batches. They encouraged them to follow their footsteps.

Brad and Alex wouldn't take any money for all their help during the desperate times. The family bought each one of them a brand new two story house as a gift. The family that meant tough love and kind hearts had grown so big now.

One night just after the family said goodbye to the last batch of people they helped, they heard a big bang just like fire crackers. Everyone left their seats in the lunch room and ran outside to find beautiful lights gathering in colours the rainbow glowing and making the sounds and displays of fire crackers.

Max said. "Sandy what is this all about?"

"I have no idea what the little soldiers are doing."

The lights then gathered and started making words. They did not stop until the word happy anniversary queen appeared under the blue sky.

"What anniversary?" Everyone started asking Sandy was there something you hadn't told us?

"I have no idea." replied Sandy, with a smile on her face.

All of a sudden the picture of the moment, when Charlie handed her the gift appeared in the middle of the lights.

"Oh my god on this very day, I was chosen by a gift to serve." then she turned into a giant light.

"Here I am the queen of Karma. Here and now I tell you to be good and never bad. Everything you do comes back to haunt you." Sandy continued. "I am no god nor a queen but a messenger to teach good and bad. Let those who are cruel and are doing wrong turn from their evil ways and become better people."

Suddenly Sandy and the lights started disappearing but the very last one said "Ops duty calls."

"Beware of Karma"

The End